THE Phoenix AND THE Sword

J C SNOW

CONTENTS

CHAPTER 1
MEETING

BECAUSE THE BAR was small, smoky, crowded, and hot, with far too many people talking too loudly, and because she was tired from the day's training, Aili sat in a dark corner next to the counter and quietly watched other people have a good time. This was not a new experience for her. The bartender had long gotten used to ignoring her; she never spent much money, and he was much more interested in the men.

A woman with dark hair cut just to her chin, slicked back for the evening to look shorter, leaned in next to her. "You're not doing me proud here, Aili," Nora said, breathing deeply. She nodded toward a woman in a gauzy blue skirt entwined with a taller woman wearing pants. "How far did you even get? Did you kiss?"

"I did talk to her," Aili said defensively. She hated to disappoint Nora after she'd gone through such efforts to set Aili up with someone. "We didn't...Well, we weren't really interested in each other."

"You mean you stared at her and let her talk, right?" Nora rolled her eyes. "Did you even offer her a cigarette?"

"You know I don't smoke."

"Not the point, Aili. She does. It's your job to show your interest, right?" Nora patted her head. Aili was much taller, so Nora always took advantage while she was sitting down. "I'm tempted to give up, but never let it be said that I let my

1

best friend go out to a war zone without ever having any action in her life. Just get a kiss in before we leave, at least. Maybe there will even be someone who will write you letters when we're somewhere rescuing naval aviators in the Western Sea. Time's running out before we go. Is there anyone you do like? How about that one?" She tipped her chin toward a woman sitting in a corner booth, talking animatedly with two others, all giggling and hiding their mouths. "I know for a fact she came alone tonight. This is her first time; her friends brought her."

"And how do you know that?"

"Because I know her friends." Nora smiled at the girl, who smiled back. Nora smoothed her hair back, and the girl smiled more widely. "If you're not interested, mind if I give it a shot?"

Aili nodded. "We have to get back to base, though, ok? No more than another half hour here. You're going to need to fix your hair before we go back." *And put the regulation skirt on, and change out of what would almost certainly be a lipstick-stained shirt*, she thought but didn't say as Nora swaggered toward the corner booth. Aili sipped a little more beer.

The bar was mostly full of sailors ready to head out on the next carriers for the island war in the Great Western Sea taking their last opportunities to mingle with men they could secretly enjoy before months trapped on a ship. The women were much fewer, mostly locals. She and Nora had agreed not to tell anyone new they met that they were in training, but truthfully, since they both lived in Easterly anyway, Nora had already met just about every girl in the bar and Aili, who had been tagging along behind her for three years, wasn't very hopeful that there would be any surprises showing up in the next few weeks. Although, it would have been nice to have kissed someone, to have that memory before shipping out.

There was one interesting person, small and delicately-made, with dark eyes and shoulder-length, straight black hair. Not Anglish like almost everyone else in the room — most likely Daxian, or perhaps Kunorese. She thought Daxian was more likely. The bar wasn't far from Little Daxian, and surely any Kunorese people would not be out in public now for their own safety after the attack on the Western Islands. Some of the sailors had nonetheless decided that this person was a Kuno in their bar, and a group of the drunker ones was starting to make unfriendly noises while looking in his direction.

The young man himself, however, seemed unaware of all this. He looked through the bar carefully — eagerly examining faces, pushing through the crowd so he wouldn't miss any of the furthest corners — as though there was someone he expected to meet, and he was late for their appointment. He came close enough to the bar to sweep his eyes over hers along with all the others sitting there.

Even though Aili had never been interested in men, she felt that there was something very intriguing about this man's expressions and the intensity of his gaze. He looked delighted at seeing someone, and then suddenly startled and confused. The man pushed his way out toward the door, unfortunately bumping right into some of the more drunk sailors, who, of course, followed him.

Aili sighed and got up. On her way out, she tapped Nora on the shoulder. "Come on," she said, "let's head back."

"In a minute," Nora said, "in a minute."

Aili went outside to wait for her. A few men and women were scattered outside, talking and smoking, but not many, not loud. No one wanted to draw attention to this place.

Since no one was speaking loudly, no matter how drunk they were, it was easy to hear the sound of several threatening voices and one lighter one from around the corner, as Aili had half-expected, and she walked quickly toward the alley between the bar and the tottering wooden boarding house next door. There were four of the sailors with the Kunorese guy in the middle; they hadn't progressed from threats to fists yet, but it was only a matter of time. Aili was tall enough and experienced enough and just drunk enough that she thought she could handle at least two of the men, but four was a little too much, so she'd talk first.

She walked down the alley and sidled between them; "Hey fellas, you know this isn't—"

To her shock, one of the sailors suddenly slashed down with a knife, and even more shockingly, the Kunorese guy pushed her aside to take it in his forearm.

Except it wasn't a guy. It was very clearly a girl, and her arm was sliced down to the bone.

Aili yelled and pushed the bleeding girl behind her while kicking at the least protected parts of the sailor, who groaned and fell backward. "Get the hell away!" she shouted, but the other three started pressing in closer.

The voices around her sounded eerie in the darkness when she couldn't see their faces; the men circled around, their blood up. She had done enough fighting to know when things were getting dangerous, and this felt very much like one of those times. Aili tried to keep the girl behind her for her own safety, backing them both into the wooden wall of the alley. Very unhelpfully, the girl seemed to want to keep touching her, which was distracting, and kept trying to duck in front as though she thought that she could defend Aili even though she was much smaller.

Suddenly there was the familiar, oh-so-welcome sound of a gun cocking from the bright entrance of the alleyway. Nora said, "Aili, we're late. Boys, I know what ship you're from and who your officer is, get the hell out of here before someone makes a report."

The sailors shuffled out of the alley, their shore leave uniforms wrinkled and sweaty, giving Nora looks of deepest contempt. She smiled happily at them, the barrel of the gun never wavering.

"I love you, Nora," said Aili weakly, leaning back against the wall to get her breath.

The girl stood beside her, silently. Aili couldn't see her face, only the silhouette of her body against the light of the street. Definitely a girl.

"Where did you get the gun?"

Nora shrugged and carefully holstered it. Although she had drunk much more than Aili, she was far less affected. It was something Aili had always envied about her; she could keep a clear head through anything.

"It's mine. Obviously I don't bring the Navy one out with me. I stopped at our place in Easterly earlier to pick up some things. I usually have it with me when we're out late for just such occasions as this. How did you end up in an alley with four drunk sailors?" She craned her neck to see better. "Is there someone there with you?"

Aili pushed herself upright away from the wall, and, remembering Nora's advice to always be chivalrous, tried to determine how to hold the girl's arm and walk her out to the street. Which arm had been injured? When Aili put her hand on the girl's arm, though, she shivered and made a little gasping noise, so Aili immediately let go. "Sorry," she said awkwardly.

When they reached the street, Aili saw that the girl's face was shining — as though the most exciting thing in the world had just happened to her instead of nearly being killed by drunk Federation sailors.

"Hello there," said Nora, looking uncomfortable.

Aili realized belatedly that Nora, who was definitely the more patriotic of the two of them, probably thought the girl was Kunorese, and certainly, she would have been shocked to find Aili with pretty much anyone, given her total failure in that line to date. And it was as though the girl didn't see Nora at all. Even though it was really Nora who had rescued her, and all Aili had done was get her slashed by a knife, she stared only at Aili's face, with a huge, delighted smile.

The girl suddenly stepped closer, far closer than felt comfortable for Aili, and looked up into her eyes. She was very small, her head coming up barely to Aili's collarbones, and when she tilted her face upwards, her eyes dark but brilliant and her hair falling back from her forehead in a shining black wave, Aili felt as though she might faint, that there was something making her dizzy. She couldn't look away from her eyes.

The girl said something in another language. Aili looked helplessly at Nora, who clearly was not feeling helpful anymore and was staring pointedly at her watch.

"I don't speak Kunorese," Aili said.

The girl looked surprised for one flash of an eyebrow, but then smiled, and said, "It was Daxian, but of course we should speak Anglish, sorry. I forgot."

Aili tried to think about why the girl would think they would know Daxian either, and gave it up as a problem that would require her to not have drunk several beers recently. At least the Daxian Republic was an ally, so Nora shouldn't be upset.

"You got hurt," said Aili, trying to be professional. This was going to be her job, after all — fixing up people who got slashed and shot on battlefields. She reached out for the girl's bloodstained sleeve, carefully pushing it back from the wound to see how bad it was. Aili always kept a few necessities on hand just in case; she had the small kit with her in her jacket pocket.

But there was no wound.

The girl smiled, and took her arm back, smoothing down the bloody sleeve. "Healing and not dying, that's pretty much all I've got," she said, as though it were an accepted thing between them, something she had said many times before. Her voice was low and clear and vibrant. She was still too close, and suddenly she laughed out loud and said, "You're so tall! And your hair!"

Reaching up, she actually touched Aili's hair, golden-brown and bound up in a braid and pins. She left her hand on the nape of Aili's neck for just one moment too long. "I like it," she said, nodding decisively.

If Nora's eyes could have fallen out of her face, they would have. Aili could feel her own skin starting to heat up, but the girl seemed completely unbothered. She stroked Aili's ear gently with two fingers, smiling.

"I don't...know you?" Aili finally managed to stammer, though she didn't have enough self-control to grab the girl's wrist, or to do any of the things that Nora would have recommended had this been another girl who was not so strange and forward.

"What's your name?" the girl asked.

"Aili Fallon," she said. "And yours?" Chivalrous, chivalrous; Nora should approve.

"Tairei," she said, laughing, "you should call me Tairei. Aili," she added. "That's a nice name."

Nora cleared her throat. "Aili, we have to get back. Really."

Tairei looked distinctly unpleased by this news, but nodded politely. "I'll see you again," she said, and smiled one last time at Aili before walking off down the street, her white blouse catching the streetlights.

Nora looked disapprovingly after her. "Femmes shouldn't wear men's pants," was all she said. "At least she's not Kunorese. Come on, we need to get back on base. We're going to miss the ferry now if we don't run."

The Sand Island naval base was a collection of recently-built wooden dormitories and giant airplane hangars, with a seaplane lagoon and a set of docks for the carriers and transports that came and went for the war against Kunoru and the Twin Empires in the Western Sea. Aili always woke up early because the window in her room faced southeast, and the morning sun hit her face as soon as it peeked over the horizon. Even without that, though, she would probably wake up early after spending the first sixteen years of her life on the farm, rising before dawn to do chores and help her mother.

Most of the people living on or visiting the base were men, and presumably men eager to have access to women, so the flight nurses in training slept in a dormitory somewhat apart from the others under the supervision of their chaperone who checked them in every night. She had marked both Aili and Nora down for demerits for their lateness and sloppy dress when they'd returned the night before. Nora grumbled; they had gotten in before the curfew after all, and had changed back into regulation dresses instead of the pants, button-downs, and vests they had worn at the bar. As they worked through that morning's physical exercises and then sat in class, listening to the teaching nurse's lecture on the importance of proper sanitation in field wound dressing, Aili found herself drifting off to the events of the night before. Nothing like that had ever happened to her — no woman had come close to her like that. Her pulse raced whenever she thought of it.

She liked to think of it.

Nora hissed, "Aili, pay attention!"

The training nurse said, "Trainee Fallon, please tell me the steps you would take to field dress a bayonet stab before moving the patient."

Aili took a deep breath and recited: triage, cleaning, sulfa, packing the wound. The trainer nodded, and Aili breathed out slowly, and immediately started thinking about that girl's face again. Tairei.

At the lunch break in the canteen, Aili brought her tray to sit with Nora, who looked quite proper and feminine in a tailored blouse and skirt, her hair curled nicely around her face, just as regulations would have it.

Nora looked over at Aili and rolled her eyes. "Hello, lovebird," she said dryly. "I'm guessing that wound care wasn't really on your mind this morning."

Aili smiled and shrugged. "How do you think I could find that girl again?" she heard herself say.

"You want to?" Nora asked, surprised. "After all this time that I've tried to get you together with someone, suddenly it's this weird Kunorese person you meet in an alley with a bunch of sailors?"

Aili shrugged, blushing. "She's Daxian," she said weakly.

"Not the point," Nora said, looking at her closely. "Are you actually blushing?"

"I want to see her again," Aili said, stubbornly.

Nora shook her head and began to eat. "I don't know why. She was really odd, the way she smiled at you that whole time. But if you did, you should hurry, because we're shipping out in a month. Assuming that someone has actually done her homework and will pass the final exam."

Aili's fork stopped partway to her mouth. "A month? It's posted?"

"There's still the exam, but yeah, all of us have been assigned in our cohort. They announced it today while you were in dreamland. We'll ship out in four weeks. So, if you meet your little friend again, remember not to tell her. Loose lips sink ships and all that."

A woman put her tray down on the other side of the table, facing them and smiling in a friendly way. To her surprise, Aili saw that this woman was also Daxian, though she didn't have much in common with Tairei otherwise; her hair was styled in curls instead of straight and loose, she was almost as tall as Aili, and she was wearing what looked like a pilot's uniform.

Aili inwardly burned with envy. She had wanted to enlist for pilot training, but they required a high school education. For various reasons that she didn't care to explain to the enlistment officer, she didn't have one. They had only accepted her for the nurse's training because she had been able to demonstrate practical skills. Again for various reasons, she had had a good amount of experience in setting broken bones and cleaning up flesh wounds.

Nora said, "Aili, this is Edna Lee, she's one of the Lady Aviators. I don't think you were here last time she was on base."

Edna smiled and reached over to shake hands. "Pleasure, Aili," she said. Aili noted her wedding ring and decided that she would not be able to tell her about Tairei, but Nora beat her to it.

"Edna, we met a Daxian girl at the bar in Easterly last night," Nora said bluntly, and Aili mentally put her face in her hands.

"Don't worry, Aili," Nora added. "Edna and I went to school together. She's from Easterly, she knows everybody and everything, no secrets, hey? So, we met this really strange Daxian girl, Edna — looked about our age, but I'd never seen her at the bar before. I was wondering, do you know her?"

Aili physically put her face in her hands.

Edna laughed. "It's all right, Aili, Nora's right, I'm safe to talk to about this. Anyway, I've got to fly back tomorrow. I'm ferrying bombers...logistics are a nightmare." She sipped her tea and nodded toward Nora. "But Nora, some discretion, please. You're on base, you could get in trouble if you're not careful."

Nora said, "Sorry, Edna, it's just so good to see you. I forgot it's not like we're back at school again. Are you and David moving back here?"

"Mmm," she said, "my parents are here, and now I'm flying in here a lot. We decided we might as well head back here. He's in Easterly next week looking for a place for us, and an office for him." She turned back to Aili. "So, I don't know everyone, but I do know most of the Daxian girls near our age from Little Daxian, anyway. What was her name?"

"Tairei?" Aili said, uncertainly.

Edna choked on her tea. "She said that's her name?" She shook her head. "You were right, Nora, this sounds weird."

Nora nodded. "I told you. This girl was strange. I'm worried about my farm-girl here, she's so innocent."

Aili looked back and forth between them, confused. "What's wrong with Tairei?"

"She knows you don't speak Daxian, right? The thing is, tairei isn't a name at all, it's...well, it's hard to explain in Anglish. We don't have Anglish words for these kinds of things, but it's more of a title of respect, it shows your relationship."

"Which is...?"

"Younger sister."

It was now Aili's turn to choke on her tea. Nora snickered.

"Don't worry," Edna said quickly, "it's not like a biological sister. More like you're in training together, it's a special relationship that's like a family, right?"

Nora and Aili looked at her blankly.

Edna rolled her eyes. "Nora, come on, I've explained this kind of thing to you before. The ones who are training you are an older generation, and there's special words for them too, but the ones who are training with you are in your generation, and you'd use tairei for anyone who's training with you in your generation but also who came in after you did. It's really weird to introduce yourself to someone that way when you've never met. She didn't explain why you were sisters, right? It's like she's claiming a relationship that doesn't exist."

"Would you come tonight and see if we can find her again?" Nora asked. "Because it's just…" Nora nodded toward Aili, who was staring at her plate in a stupor.

"Why not?" Edna smiled. "It's been a while since I've been able to visit Little Daxian."

Nora said, "We can get some food too? Take us to a good restaurant. I haven't been to a Daxian restaurant since you moved away. Have you ever had Daxian food, Aili?"

Aili started from her daze at being addressed directly. "Oh, no, yes, no, that would be good," she blurted out, and looked back down at her plate.

Less than ten minutes after Edna, Aili, and Nora settled into a round table at a tiny, packed restaurant in Little Daxian, full of smoke and loud voices, Aili looked up to meet Tairei's fierce, dark eyes. Tairei's eyes flicked over Nora, frowned briefly at Edna, and returned to meet Aili's. They hadn't even gotten a chance to discuss how they would find Tairei if she didn't appear at the bar again — in fact, they hadn't even ordered food — but here she stood, now wearing neatly-tailored pants and a blouse that Nora would consider femme-appropriate attire, Aili thought. Aili's throat closed up when she looked at her.

Tairei put a hand on her shoulder, and said, "Aili, it's good to see you, may I join you? Who are your friends?" as though they were the closest of companions already, instead of strangers.

Aili jumped up and pulled out a chair for her, again belatedly remembering Nora's frequent instructions for proper attentive date behavior. The effect was somewhat spoiled by her bumping into the man seated behind her — the place was just so small, and she was just so big and awkward — who broke out into a torrent of Daxian that sounded vaguely abusive. Both Tairei and Edna started talking back to him in the same moment and looked at each other, startled.

Tairei recovered first, smiled, and said something to Edna in Daxian, who responded and apparently started asking rapid-fire questions. Tairei smiled and answered all of them, but Aili noticed a little bead of sweat starting to run down from under her hair. This was, in itself, so fascinating that Aili just stared at Tairei's face and listened, entranced, to the language she didn't understand, completely ignoring Nora's expressions. At last, Tairei nodded her head politely toward Edna, who looked somewhat dissatisfied, and turned to Aili.

"Aili," Tairei said, "I think there's something here you'll really like. I'll order for you," and proceeded to yell something in Daxian at the waiter.

Edna looked surprised again, and Nora looked scandalized. In fact, every man and woman in the place stopped to look at her for a moment.

Tairei blushed a little bit. "Sorry," she said, "I forget sometimes that I'm not supposed to raise my voice in this...restaurant."

When their food came, it was placed in large dishes in the center of the table, with small bowls of rice for each of them, and Edna and Tairei took turns pointing Aili and Nora toward the things to put in their bowls. Tairei was especially insistent that Aili try something she called tofu. Aili gamely put it in her mouth and chewed and swallowed, but the texture was so very odd that she politely refused any more.

Tairei seemed, for a moment, quite startled by this. She looked seriously at Aili's face. "Really? You don't like it?"

"It's fine," Aili said diplomatically, drinking as much tea as she quickly could. "I like some of these other things better, though."

"Like this, right?" said Nora, waving a piece of roast duck on a fork. "This is delicious. And these are the noodles, right, from before, Edna? I remember these! I wish you were still around. This food is so great."

Edna said, "You can come here without me, silly goose. Just remember, that's chow mein. Just say that and you can get it on your own."

Aili watched Tairei out of the corner of her eye, a little worried. Quietly, she ate the tofu, and had some vegetables and rice as well, but avoided the duck; her smile had dimmed, and she looked preoccupied. When they had finished as much of the food as they could put away, she asked tentatively, "Tairei, do you want to go for a walk with me?"

Tairei's smile came back with the force of the sun rising, and Aili stared at her, then wondered if her mouth had fallen open.

"Yes," Tairei said. "Yes, let's walk. I'll– I'll– Yes, let's go." She grabbed Aili's hand, and Aili felt herself tugged to her feet — the girl was much stronger than she looked — as she waved helplessly at Nora and Edna.

It was fully dark now, Tairei's hand warmly entangled with hers.

"Do you know your way around here?" Tairei asked. "I haven't been here long. I just came from the Daxian Republic recently."

"I've lived in Easterly for a few years, but I don't spend much time in Little Daxian. When did you arrive?"

"Just last week."

Aili wondered how she had come; surely civilian ships weren't coming from the Daxian Republic now through the war blockade, but Tairei continued, "Is this your hometown?"

Aili shook her head. "I'm from a very small town. Nobody's ever heard of it, just farms."

"What's it called?"

"Fallon," she said. "Truthfully, it's not a very nice place; I was glad to leave."

"It's your surname, though, isn't it?" Tairei asked doubtfully. "Is it your clan home?"

"I guess so...My great-grandfather was one of the town's founders." Aili found herself not wanting to say any more about Fallon or her family, neither of which were pleasant topics for a romantic walk. "But what about you? Edna told me Tairei– It's not your name, right? Would you tell me your name?" She immediately thought that this was unforgivably awkward and wanted to slap her own face.

Tairei was quiet for a minute. "Why are you talking to Edna about me?"

"I don't really know Edna," Aili said quickly. "She's Nora's friend."

After a pause, Tairei said, "My name is Liu Chenguang."

Aili thought she sounded rather sad, and said, "I can call you Tairei if you want, though. It's already how I think of you."

Tairei smiled, but withdrew her hand; Aili's hand groped in the air for a moment before she found her pocket and tried to pretend that this was in no way complicated to manage. They were quiet for a while, walking from light to light pooling on the dark streets. There was a rich scent in the air, and then something medicinal and bitter.

Tairei raised her head and pointed with her chin. "That's the apothecary. I'm going to start working there tomorrow. I've been trained as a physician, but I can't really practice here. They'll just have me put the prescriptions together."

Aili said, "Is it like a pharmacy? I'm training to be a nurse now," and then remembered she wasn't supposed to tell anyone this. Well, Nora and her strictures were somewhere in a Daxian restaurant several blocks away, and Tairei was here now, pointing to a row of Daxian characters running up and down on a signboard.

"Come on," said Tairei, "it's still open. I can take you in and show you."

Aili looked around with interest at the wall full of tiny drawers, the counter showing roots and pills and oils, the scales and charts. "I wish I could read Daxian," she said, "I can't understand anything."

"I can tell you about things," Tairei said, and drew her finger along a chart showing a human body covered with mysterious figures. "These are the meridians that carry energy, and these are the acupuncture points, each point in combination with others addresses various disorders and imbalances in the body's energy..." After a while, she ran out of words, and smiled. "It's a very complicated system; it takes a long time to learn."

"It's fascinating," said Aili, mostly finding Tairei fascinating. She had soon gotten lost in the complicated lecture about elements and something called yin and yang, and wondered what kind of prodigy Tairei must be; she looked barely twenty. "It's very different from what I've been learning. It's mostly field dressings — not for chronic illness, just for wounds."

Tairei turned. "For wounds? What wounds? Field dressings?"

"Well, in the war."

"The war," Tairei said blankly. "Oh, yes."

"Didn't you just come from the Daxian Republic? Edna was saying that the Kunorese are occupying–"

"Yes, of course," Tairei said quickly. "I noticed that, of course. It's impossible not to notice."

It would definitely be difficult not to notice your country being invaded and occupied — and from what Edna had described, occupied with extreme brutality — yet Tairei sounded as though she had forgotten all about it, as though it wasn't anything particularly notable. Was she so traumatized that she was unable to think? Or perhaps she wasn't really Daxian at all? But she clearly spoke Daxian...Edna had spoken to her...and she suddenly remembered how the wound in Tairei's arm had simply disappeared. Why had she not even thought of that until now, as though a knife slash in an arm healing itself in a moment was a normal thing that didn't even deserve notice? Confused, Aili stared silently into Tairei's eyes.

"There's enough pain everywhere," Tairei said eventually. "After a while, it all blends together."

"I don't understand." Aili cleared her throat. "Was it because of the war, that you had to leave Daxian?"

"No, not because of that. I just had to come here."

"Why?"

"For you," Tairei said, simply, as though this was the most obvious thing in the world, something that both of them already knew. "For you, to find you, of course for you."

"What?" Aili said. She took a step backward. Tairei's eyes became anxious. "What, why for me?"

Tairei opened her mouth, and then closed it again. Finally, she said, "Don't you know why?" Her voice shook slightly. "You don't...know me?"

Aili stared, but nothing more was forthcoming. Tairei's eyes were very beautiful — that was all she could think of — but something wasn't right.

Tairei said, "You don't remember?"

Aili shook her head, which was starting to ache. It must be the alcohol at that restaurant; she knew she didn't have a good tolerance. She raised her hand to her forehead, and felt Tairei's hand cover it. Tairei was standing very close, too close, Aili could feel the nearness of her body, the pressure of her fingertips. Aili focused her eyes on a wall painting, partly illuminated by the streetlamps. In the dim light, the mural seemed alive to her.

"Are you all right?" Tairei asked. "Aili?"

"The painting," Aili said. "That painting – what is that picture?" Her head ached fiercely.

Tairei turned to look at the wall mural, painted in vivid colors. "It's just for a restaurant," she said, her voice thin. "It's a picture of a phoenix and a dragon."

She reached out for Aili's hand and Aili stepped back again, trying to get her balance, trying to stop her head from spinning. Tairei's fingers, warm and firm, were suddenly against the inside of Aili's wrist, pressing gently. "Aili, something's wrong?"

"I should get back to them," Aili said. "Too much to drink. It's late."

"I'll walk you back," Tairei said quickly. "You might get lost otherwise–"

"No, that's all right, I have a good sense of direction." This was not a lie; Aili had a very good head for knowing where she was and how she had gotten there, and the streets that had taken her and Tairei almost an hour of wandering and chatting through took less than ten minutes to bring her back to the restaurant. She almost ran back, away from this sense of unreality and dizziness and Tairei's hand over hers.

Reality was there, waiting for her, Edna and Nora outside the restaurant where she'd left them — Nora smoking a cigarette with her dark hair already losing its fashionable curl, and Edna looking worried. The pain in her head faded as though it had never been.

"I'm glad you're back," Edna said when she saw Aili. "There's something very strange about that girl. She's not telling the truth about who she is or where she came from. I think you should avoid her."

Aili said, "Yes, I agree."

"You do?" asked Nora.

Edna's mouth hung open, ready to argue more.

"I do," said Aili. "Let's go home."

Nora put her arm around Aili's shoulder. "Don't worry, little sister, big sister will help you find a better one before we ship out."

Edna and Aili said together, "Don't say that. It's weird," and started laughing.

As they got on the boat to cross the estuary to Sand Island, Aili looked back from the railings. Sure enough, a slight, dark-haired figure stood by the pier, watching the lighted ferry push through the dark waters. It only occurred to her, then, that she had left Tairei standing there in the street without even saying goodbye, and for some reason thinking this made her heart hurt. She put her head down against the wooden railing, took a deep breath, and looked up again. The figure had disappeared.

CHAPTER 2
TRAINING

THERE WERE LESS than four weeks left until embarkation, less than four weeks until the final tests. The days didn't leave much energy to visit bars at night anymore, and even Nora's amorous energy flopped asleep on the bed at lights out. The flight nurses would be evacuating maimed and bleeding soldiers from active battlefields on remote islands for long flights across the Great Western Sea to safe bases, and in addition to the medical training they needed to train in swimming, running, strength, orienteering, and using their issued guns.

Nora struggled swimming in the cold water of the bay, and Aili swam with her whenever they had a free moment, encouraging her to get her strength up and letting Nora use her as a test weight to prepare for the final watermanship test. They would need to be able to swim a mile — which truthfully seemed fairly inadequate if they crashed mid-Western, but Aili didn't mention it — and tow an unconscious person a quarter mile in ten minutes. Aili made Nora swim for at least an hour at a time, but still secretly worried that Nora wouldn't pass.

Aili had grown up swimming in the cold Helena River and in the rough, dangerous surf of the ocean at the river's mouth on the northern coast, so she anticipated no problems in that area. Truthfully, the medical training was also fairly routine — only systematizing what she had learned about treating wounds as a child through trial and error and providing her with better tools than she had had back home. Thus, she had ample mental space during class time and practical demonstrations to think about Tairei: when she went to sleep; when she woke up; when she was bored; sometimes when she should definitely not have been bored. It was infuriating, the way Tairei's eyes and smile were always waiting for her in her mind, and the way in which sometimes she would remember the figure waiting on the shore, quietly watching.

Nora's years-long crusade to set her up with interested girls had always begun well — with a good number of women quite interested in Aili's tall, blonde figure and something they interpreted as an air of quiet mystery — and had always flopped due to Aili's whatever it was: shyness or reserve or dislike of being touched. She had never felt drawn to anyone before. And now, there was this person, this strange and completely unsuitable person, occupying her mind only weeks before they left. Aili's fascination was only matched by Nora's growing concern about it.

"Aili," Nora said one day in the dormitory after Aili had missed three questions in a row in the classroom, "what's going on with you?"

Aili shook her head. "I don't know," she said.

"Still thinking about that person? Tairei?"

She nodded.

"Is it because she keeps showing up outside the gates and staring through the bars to see you?"

Aili blushed. "You noticed?"

"Of course I noticed, I've also noticed that you have to walk past the gates on errands you make up three times a day. I'm amazed they haven't just kicked you out of the program."

"I only saw her once or twice," she protested.

"You want to see her again, though." Nora sighed. "You know who else has noticed? The sentries. The chaperone. Half of our training cohort. Aili, we are on a military base in training, she looks Kunorese–"

"She's Daxian–"

"We all signed those papers about our romantic preferences. You know you'd get kicked out if anyone suspected." Nora put her arm around Aili's shoulders where they sat on Aili's bunk. Quietly, she continued, "Aili, I know it must be exciting to finally have these feelings, after all this time–"

Aili flinched a little bit, under Nora's arm, but knew more was coming.

As expected, Nora continued, doggedly, "This person isn't trustworthy. She gave you a false name. She pursued you and said that you should know her, and there's no possible way you know her. Edna says she is definitely not telling the truth about herself and where she came from. She said she changed dialects in the middle of their conversation, whatever that means, and now she's basically stalking you. You finally have a career — something to do that you can be proud of doing, right? You've come so far and you're ready to live a good life now. And that all goes down the drain if you trust the wrong person about this kind of thing. There will be other people, better people for you."

Aili didn't respond, looking down at her hands. *Nora is my best friend, my only friend,* she thought. *Nora knows me better than anyone else in the world.*

But she's wrong about this.

"You're ignoring me," Nora said, brown eyes narrowed. "I know you, Aili Fallon. You're so stubborn even though you never argue. You just do what you're going to do."

Aili smiled, knowing Nora wouldn't let it go until she did.

"That's better," Nora said. "In just a few days, it'll be the final exam, and then we'll leave. Are you going to visit your mother before we go?"

Aili sat up and said, "You really are getting all the hard conversations done at once, aren't you?"

"Might as well. It's not as though I get a lot of time with you where we can really talk. There's always other people around. If you don't want to contact your mother that's fine, you can stay here with me. But this might be the last chance. You might regret it if you don't."

"I've been thinking about it, I really have. I think...I think I should...but I'm..."

Squeezing her shoulders, Nora said, "We've talked about it. You don't have to go if your father's there, right? You can ask that friend of yours to just bring your mother to the restaurant to see you. He'll never know."

"He'll know," Aili said, absolutely certain.

"Well, he probably won't know before you're on a troop carrier in the Western Sea," Nora replied practically. After a pause, she added, "I know you've always missed your mother. You may not have another chance."

Aili nodded, and then said, "I should say goodbye to Tairei, too. The same reason. I might not have another chance."

Nora slapped her own forehead in exasperation. "Just let it go, Aili. I won't say any more. It's too late anyway. We'll be leaving soon, and you need to focus." She got up. "It's time for dinner. Are you coming?"

There was no possible way they would meet each other again; civilians weren't allowed onto the base, so Tairei couldn't come looking for her, and she... she couldn't go looking for Tairei.

Unless she did.

Aili stood up and said, "I'm signing off base for dinner tonight."

She didn't see Tairei in the restaurant, and it was too early for the bar, so she wandered toward the apothecary, as Tairei called it. The astringent, medicinal smell was stronger now, and through the windows she saw Tairei standing behind the counter, pulling roots and leaves and mushrooms and what looked like tree bark out of different little drawers and weighing them. Aili watched as she smiled at a customer and spoke something Aili couldn't hear, using a knife to cut the mixture up into thin pieces and wrapping it with white paper before handing it over.

Aili stood, unmoving. A rush of warmth and joy seemed to come from somewhere else but was most definitely inside her body, a tingling yearning to go closer that almost made her hair rise on her scalp. Tairei's hair was still loose and shining, swinging back and forth to cover her face, and once she put her hand up to brush it back behind her ear, Aili found her eyes following her hand... She took a few deep breaths before going inside.

When their eyes met, Tairei's brightened and glowed. "Aili," she said, "it's so good to see you."

Aili swallowed. "Do you want to get dinner with me?"

About twenty minutes later — after Aili had enjoyed watching Tairei get more roots and bark for prescriptions and listened to her explaining things in low-voiced Daxian to the customers, who looked oddly at the big, blonde person awkwardly wedged into a corner of the counter — the two of them walked down the darkening street toward an even smaller, but less crowded restaurant.

"I thought you might like this one," Tairei said. "It's more of a northern style. I thought that maybe that last restaurant's food was too unfamiliar to you."

"It was my first one. I've never had Daxian food before."

"Ah, yes," Tairei said, "I keep forgetting."

After dinner and drinks, Tairei laid some money down and asked, "Aili, would you like to walk with me?"

Aili stood up, hot all over as she imagined what it was she might like to do with Tairei, and stumbled after Tairei out into the dark street. She really had no ability to handle whatever liquor they served in those little bowls.

There was a curfew in place, so there were few people out now, most headed home for safety. The windows of the buildings were dark or covered, and the streetlights almost all shaded to avoid giving a target to a possible air raid. The

18

Kunorese hadn't raided the mainland yet, but everyone knew there were subma-rines off the coast. There might be carriers, too, and then the entire San Toma Bay would be a military target with all the bases and munitions factories here.

The darkness and hushed voices on the street felt strange — such a crowded place where it seemed that everyone was hiding. Aili shook her head, trying to clear it. Tairei took her hand and led her forward; she seemed to have extremely good night vision.

"We missed the sunset," Tairei said, unnecessarily. "But we can still go look at the stars? Down by the estuary, there's a good place. I found it the other day."

Aili's sense of direction told her that Tairei was leading her toward a part of town that most people would consider unsafe. She was personally quite familiar with it.

"How do you know your way around in the dark so well?" Aili asked. "I thought you'd only been here a few weeks."

Tairei said, "Careful, the sidewalk's broken there. I go out at night. To help people that I find in alleys, things like that. I don't sleep much."

"What do you mean, helping people?"

Tairei said, "I'm a healer. People need healing all the time, not only when they come looking."

Aili put her arm tentatively around Tairei's shoulders, and in the dimness could see the flash of Tairei's smile and her eyes shining up at her.

"You come here, alone, at night?" Aili asked. "Are you safe?"

"People do try things, sometimes," Tairei said offhandedly, "but I'm very fast. It's not a problem."

Aili frowned from the depths of her alcohol-fueled boldness. "Tairei," she said sternly, "you need to be safe. Who takes care of you if something happens? Isn't there anyone to protect you when you go out? I can. Do you want me to go with you?"

Then she realized that this wasn't much of a solution, as she'd soon be on a ship to an undisclosed island base, and added, "A gun, maybe? Do you know how to use one? I can ask Nora–"

"Why on earth would I want a gun?" Tairei asked. "I'm out there to heal people. Why would I want to put more holes in them? And in any case, I can't use a gun. The killing intent in those things is so high it would probably explode in my hand even if I just pointed it at a brick wall."

"Killing intent?"

"Never mind...well...you know...some things, they are weapons, but they can be other things too, right? They're not just for killing people. Like a scalpel, for instance. So a gun– Watch out!" Tairei pulled her to one side to avoid the carcass of some kind of rodent in the middle of the sidewalk. "A gun, it doesn't have any other purpose than killing. So, that means it has a high killing intent. It's infected by its purpose, and I can't use it. I've never even tried to touch one."

"I don't understand."

Tairei laughed. "You're drunk. It doesn't matter, it's not important. It's you I'm more worried about."

"About what?"

"The war you're training for. You said you'll be in combat areas. You were telling me." Tairei became serious. "When you're out there trying to help patients, what would you do if someone came at you with a weapon? Would you run?"

"Of course not, I'd try to protect the patient."

"With what? Polite arguments? Your body? What good does that do, in your situation?"

"What do you mean, in my situation?" Aili tried to clear her mind; Tairei sounded so worried. "Tairei, do you think that everything here is safe? It's not. There's nowhere totally safe…" Aili didn't know exactly how to say this. A war zone would be different than the streets of Easterly — of course it would, but home had never been a safe place either.

"Aili, truly, do you care so much about this war that you'll go lose your life for it?"

They had come to the edge of the seawalk now, but Tairei was looking at her, not at the stars.

"I don't want you to go. I want you to stay here, safe with me. Does it make a difference if I say it out loud?" Her eyes were dark and serious, pleading.

Aili said, "You're nervous." She could feel it in the sudden tension in Tairei's body. "Do you…I'm sorry," she said, and let go of her as she stepped back.

"No," Tairei said immediately, "it's not that." She looked around her. "There's something there. Someone watching us."

The stars over the bay were bright and clear in the absence of the city lights, but there was no moon, and around them everything was dark. Despite that, Aili could see Tairei's eyes shining, moving from one corner to another. Aili didn't sense any person nearby, though she was normally very sensitive to this kind of thing. Perhaps the liquor had made her fuzzy. Everything was silent — only occasional rustles of rats running through the dry leaves.

The rustling became louder, heavier, sounding almost like the beating of wings.

Softly, Tairei said, "Aili, get behind me."

Aili was slightly insulted. She was, after all, significantly taller and stronger, even if Tairei was one of those women who didn't like to be protected, which wouldn't at all be surprising. She put her hands on Tairei's shoulders again, and despite her protests, gently pushed her against the railing of the seawall so nothing could surprise her from behind. Then she stood in front of her, waiting.

Tairei was so sure that something was wrong, and for whatever unknown reason, she trusted Tairei. She did wish she at least had a knife. She was always better equipped than this before she started military training, but ironically, now she couldn't carry unauthorized weapons. "Do you have anything to protect yourself?" she asked.

Tairei shook her head. "You know I can't. I can't use weapons."

Something hissed from behind Tairei, where there shouldn't have been anything at all — in midair, above the water of the bay. Aili felt a shock through her body and moved before she was aware, pushing Tairei out of the way and jumping for the thing reaching for Tairei's back, bearing it down into the water underneath her before she even saw fully what it was. Luckily, it was high tide, so she didn't fall fifteen feet straight down onto sharp rocks. She heard Tairei scream as she fought the thing down into the cold, dirty, oily estuary water.

It was not a normal person; she was certain of that. It seemed to be half smoke and half slime, but somewhere in all the slipperiness and sludge, there were sharp teeth and bright yellow eyes, and something that wrapped around her forearm like a rope with glass shards, tearing at her skin as it pulled her beneath the surface. When the silt cleared slightly, she saw that it was a long tongue. Though a small voice in her mind protested that this thing couldn't be real, any shock was completely overwhelmed by her determination to kill it. She felt preternaturally calm, focused on the task at hand: to rip apart this thing that dared attack Tairei.

They had struggled down about five feet below the surface, black and dark, tangled in additional slime and sludge from the bottom, stirred up so there was barely a difference between the water and the earth as they fought. The only light came from the thing's yellow eyes glaring at her in the silty gloom. The shape of its body was hidden in the dark murk, but it was powerful and large — larger than she was. It seemed to have no problems breathing underwater, and to know that she herself couldn't. Its eyes gleefully blinked at her, and its tongue tightened around her arm, pulling her closer to what she now saw was a great mouth of irregular, needle-sharp teeth. Wherever the tongue touched her, it ripped and burned her skin.

She was a good swimmer, and she was strong, but that wasn't enough when she was held still and forced face-first into the mud. Aili groped helplessly in the sludge where the thing was slowly burying her alive, drowning and suffocating her with the filth of the estuary's bottom. Her free hand touched rocks, and bits of rubber, and trash, and then something sharp and hard. At last. A piece of metal. A weapon.

Aili brought it up slowly, knowing that the water's pressure would keep her from making any sudden moves, and stopped resisting the tongue dragging her into the needle-rimmed mouth. Just as she felt the first teeth pierce the skin of her entrapped arm, the thing's eyes glowing with delight, she carefully brought up the shard of steel from a long-destroyed ship and slammed it into the yellow disk.

The thing convulsed and released her, shuddering back into the black waters surrounding them. Aili shot to the surface, gasping for air.

"Tairei!" she rasped out when she had enough breath to do it.

"Aili!" Tairei's voice came, but nothing else; Aili couldn't see her.

The thing had dragged her several yards away from the shore. She swam over to the seawall and scrambled enough to grab the lowest bar of the railing, then pulled herself up, arms shaking. The arm that had been wrapped in the thing's tongue was a mass of blood and blisters, with yellow matter already pouring from pustules. It made her sick to look at, so she stopped looking. Of course, it hurt too, but that she could ignore.

She had left her precious metal shard in the thing's eye beneath the water, so when she staggered upright and squinted to see Tairei surrounded by four or five shifting, uncertain shadows, she had very few options. She simply ran straight in and used her momentum to bowl away two of them, catching the third around its middle, falling on top of it, and reaching out to grab its head with both hands and smash it against the pavement.

Tairei screamed again, and Aili felt Tairei's weight land on her back.

"What?" She startled, and then felt a sharp thump through Tairei's body that meant something had hit Tairei, hard.

"God*damn* it!" Aili yelled. "Tairei!"

The thing underneath her was not a person. Its face was covered in what seemed to be black feathers and its eyes were misshapen, one far larger than the other. The other half of its face was a short, sharp beak full of short, sharp teeth. Her effort to grab it by the cheekbones and smash it into unconsciousness was destined to fail.

Aili rolled to one side, doing her best to catch Tairei and protect her beneath

22

her own body, but Tairei struggled frantically.

Tairei screamed, "No, no!" and pushed her back off violently, stumbling up. "Aili, just run!"

There were still four of the creatures surrounding them — all some uneasy blend of human shape and animal characteristics — giggling and hissing and clacking. Aili tried her best to get Tairei to back up against a wall so at least they would only have enemies in one direction, but it was too late. The most they could do was stand back to back.

Aili tried and tried to think, but nothing came to her. They had no weapons and there was no one nearby to call for help. The police would be unlikely to interfere in a fight in this part of town. Her arm hurt now, badly, her whole body shook, and she was having difficulty focusing her eyes. Pain shot up into her chest and throat from the damaged wrist and forearm, and her heart hurt with every uneven beat.

"Aili," Tairei cried urgently, but Aili couldn't really hear well now.

She fell to her knees, then to her hands, then down to the ground. Something laughed. She felt Tairei touching her, smoothing something warm and soothing over her arm, touching her lips for some reason. She tried to focus her eyes again. Was Tairei giving her medicine? Was Tairei crying?

Someone walked confidently out of the darkness. A man, by the shape, though it was too dim to see his face. He said something in a ringing, edged voice, in a language she didn't understand. The beings surrounding them growled and snapped, but one by one they disappeared — not walking away, but simply winking out.

Looking up at the stars, Aili could hear the soft susurrus of the water striking against the slimy stone of the wall. For some reason she hadn't been able to hear it, all this time. It was refreshing to hear. The pain in her arm was fading.

"Chenguang?" she called out.

Tairei's hand tightened on hers, but she didn't respond.

"Liu Chenguang," said the man, "you're taking risks out here, night after night."

"Get away," Tairei's voice came, hard and cold. "How dare you come near me."

"You're not even going to say thank you?" the man asked in mock-hurt tones. "I made the vermin leave. What was your plan to deal with them?" Coming closer, he said, "And what is–"

"*GO AWAY!*"

Aili felt Tairei jump to her feet.

"You don't come near! Get away from her!" Tairei's voice sounded raw, high-pitched, almost hysterical.

The man stopped as though surprised. Aili, moving her eyes though she couldn't move her head yet, watched him hold his hands up, protesting. "I'm leaving, I'm leaving," he said, placatingly. "We'll talk another time. When you're not so...overemotional."

Tairei responded with something that sounded very much like a curse word, even though the language was a mystery.

The man disappeared, as the others had.

She heard the beating of wings.

Aili tried to sit up, and she did feel much better, but sitting up was all she could do. She looked at her arm. She must have imagined those terrible, pus-filled wounds; there wasn't a mark on her.

"Tairei, where did they hurt you?"

Tairei was kneeling next to her, rocking slightly back and forth, head down almost to her knees, her arms wrapped around herself, not looking up.

"Tairei," Aili said, concerned. She reached out, pulling her into an awkward embrace, "Show me where you're hurt–"

"I'm not hurt," Tairei said through her muffled sniffling. "I'm not hurt. It's you that got hurt." She started sobbing — big, ugly, gasping cries, as though she could barely breathe.

Alarmed, Aili pulled her closer and tried to get her to calm down, calling her name over and over, but she couldn't stop. Moment after moment, it increased until Tairei was nearly screaming wordlessly, her body shuddering with each sob.

"Tairei!" Aili finally yelled, not wanting to hit her though they'd been trained that this kind of thing was best dealt with through a sharp slap. She shook Tairei gently, by the shoulders, trying to break the rhythm of sobbing cries and bring her back to reality. Tairei's shining eyes were red-rimmed and unfocused in the starlight, looking past her into the dark, as though she was seeing things that weren't really there.

"Tairei!"

Tairei put her arms around Aili in return and laid her head against Aili's shoulder, gasping, her muscles rigid with the effort of trying to control herself.

"No, not like that. It's all right, it's all right." Aili stroked her back gently, like she was a little cat.

Eventually, Tairei looked up at her; she was so very close, her eyelashes glittering with tears and her lips slightly parted as she breathed heavily.

Aili took a deep breath and closed her own eyes; she had never felt anything like this before, never touched or held anyone this way. Especially not someone that was looking at her with eyes like Tairei's. Aili swallowed and tried to think of petting the cat again.

"Aili," said Tairei at last, her voice soft and a little hoarse. "Aili, please don't go. Don't go, don't go." Her arms tightened around Aili's neck and shoulders. "I will do anything, anything, anything. Don't go to this war. Stay with me. Please stay with me, be safe with me. I can't even keep you safe here. You can't– you can't go."

Tairei's hands softly traced along Aili's neck, making her shiver, and then she said, "Your hairpins are all crooked. They're sticking you."

She pulled them out, one by one, while Aili sat there as though she were frozen. Aili stared past her as she concentrated on unbraiding Aili's hair, running her fingers through it, and Aili started shivering, and then Tairei's fingers stroked the edge of her ear, and she closed her eyes, and then. Then. Tairei's breath, Tairei's lips against her ear, so gently.

Aili gasped and blindly turned her head, finding Tairei's mouth, kissing her uncertainly, shyly, until she felt Tairei press forward against her. Aili held Tairei's face between her hands, then kissed down along her throat to feel the heartbeat beneath her lips, breath quick and uneven.

Body softening against her, Tairei called, yearning, eager, "Deming, Deming, please…"

Whatever had been happening inside her crashed and stuttered into coldness.

Aili broke off the kiss and opened her eyes. Tairei's eyes met hers, panicked.

For a moment the two of them sat there, frozen, staring at one another, sitting on the cold, bloodstained pavement in the dark, with no sound but the soft, slapping waves. Aili shivered all over with the shock of what had happened — what had stopped happening.

"Who is Deming?" Aili asked, at last. A sharp stab of pain lanced through her temple, and she held her hand to her forehead.

"Deming isn't anything. It's just a Daxian word for– for kissing," Tairei said quickly.

"Tairei," Aili sighed, "that's not even a good lie."

Tairei looked down at the ground between them. They were still entangled with each other.

"Deming is a name," Aili said. She didn't know how she knew this with the utmost certainty, but she did. "Deming is a person's name. I'm not that person."

Tairei shook her head, shivering.

Aili stood, shaking a little bit.

"Aili," Tairei said, pleading. She stood up too. "Aili, I…"

Aili wanted to say *We're done now, there's no possible explanation for you call-ing me some stranger's name while you kiss me*, but she looked at Tairei, so small and miserable after they had just been touching one another so tenderly, and she couldn't do it. She couldn't even keep her own dignity and walk away as Nora would certainly have advised. Instead, seeing the tears trickling down Tairei's cheeks where she stood with her head bowed, she carefully put her arms around her again and kissed her on the top of her head.

To her own surprise, Aili flushed again at the sensation of Tairei's hair be-neath her lips. Aili took a deep breath, another one, the scent of bitter medicine and incense overwhelming her, and then carefully set space between them.

"Tairei, you're so upset. This isn't– this isn't– Look where we are," she said, trying to be a decent person.

Tairei's eyes settled back into consciousness from whatever frenzied world she had gone to and she took a deep breath. "Aili, I'm sorry. You don't– you don't– you don't want to…"

Of course she wanted to, but they were lying in the cold muck in the worst part of Easterly and they had just been attacked by god knows what, and Tairei seemed to be near some kind of nervous breakdown, and…She almost couldn't bring her mind to remember it, Tairei's voice calling someone else's name. Aili compromised by holding her protectively.

"What happened here, tonight?" Aili asked. "What were those things?"

The attackers, the dousing in the filthy estuary, the thing under the water, the man that had come. It all seemed unclear in her mind now. She had been drunk, after all; no doubt it was all just a fight. Nothing new. She had fought so many times just like this, at night, on the street. It wasn't anything unusual — and no harm done, she didn't even have any wounds — but something was not right. Not right at all. Her mind was as entangled and confused as her body, and that piercing pain kept coming and going behind her eyes.

Tairei swallowed. "I can explain," she said, at last. "But it's…very complicat-ed. Can you let me think about how to explain it, please? Just…give me a little time."

Her hair still had that scent to it. Aili didn't dare come closer; something about that scent stirred her in every possible way.

"I need to get back to the base," she said, resolving to avoid everything in favor of simple reality. "I can't see you for a few days. We're in our final testing."

"I'm sorry," Tairei said, her voice still raspy. "You'll be tired tomorrow after...all this."

"I'm fine," Aili said, and physically she did feel fine aside from that headache and, sometimes, a shooting, stabbing pain in her chest. "If I pass, they'll give us two days of leave before we go. I'll see you then."

Tairei nodded, and though she didn't seem to want to let go, eventually she did and walked with her to the ferry. "I'll be waiting," she said. "I'll meet you in Little Daxian."

CHAPTER 3
DEPARTURE

ON THE DAY of the final watermanship test, rain poured down. Aili felt that this was really quite helpful, as they were already soaked and freezing cold before they jumped in. The water of the bay felt warm by comparison to the cold wind, though in reality, their body heat was being leached away rapidly. The wind whipped up huge waves as well. The final mile-long swim to shore left every one of the cohort — except those who had to be rescued themselves — literally dragging themselves on hands and knees onto the ramp and then lying there like dead things. Eighteen hours from crash simulation to final crawl to the deck, but it was done.

Aili and Nora both made it in. They lay there on the dock together staring at the dark afternoon sky, letting the rain crash down on them, and trying to breathe again until they were met by towels and the final evaluations from the trainers.

"I passed," said Nora, finally. "I did it."

"You did," said Aili. "Congratulations. Me too, by the way."

Giggling weakly, they collapsed onto their bunks. "What are you going to do during last leave?" asked Nora. "I'm going to spend it in Easterly."

Aili shrugged. "I'm going to Easterly tonight, want to come?"

"Absolutely not. I'm sleeping. I'll go nice and early tomorrow. Why are you going out again?"

"I just like Daxian food now."

Nora groaned. "No, not her. Haven't you learned your lesson?" she asked, and almost immediately passed out, still shivering slightly.

Aili piled another blanket on her, put on a sweater, and went to sign out. They had two and a half full days of leave. At noon on the third day, they would be given their uniforms with appropriate ranks and would embark on the ship.

It wasn't quite dinnertime, so Aili loitered around the places she had seen Tairei before: the restaurant, the bar, the apothecary, the ferry stop. It was just as well that she hadn't told Nora what had happened that strange night with Tairei, she thought. Nora would have tied her to the bunk before letting her go again. It was an uncomfortable feeling. She had never lied to Nora before, never even come close to lying. The only time she had ever concealed the whole truth from Nora…well, it had only been about bad things, shameful things. Did that mean that looking for Tairei — dreaming about Tairei — was a bad and shameful thing?

She stood still in the rain and stared at the painting on the wall again. The phoenix was a red bird with golden eyes, surrounded by elaborate flames. As the rain ran down it, the flames looked as though they were flickering in the last dim light.

With all the effort she'd put forth today already, and with the cold rain still coming down, her low body temperature kept cramping up her leg muscles. Just as the shops were beginning to close up for the evening, she had to sit down to catch her breath and massage her legs. She found a little bench up against a wall, probably used for someone to display their wares during the day, and leaned back against the bricks with her eyes closed, rubbing her calves rhythmically.

"Are your legs sore?"

"Tairei!"

Tairei was kneeling next to her, looking up, concerned. She reached out to continue to massage Aili's knee; Aili jerked in surprise and nearly kicked her in the face. Luckily, Tairei had excellent balance. She laughed and sat on the bench next to her, protecting them both with the umbrella she was carrying.

"I'm so glad to see you," Aili said, weakly.

Tairei looked like herself again — smiling, her eyes shining as usual, as though that night had never happened. Aili wasn't quite sure what to make of it. For days now, she had been remembering Tairei's tear-filled eyes and her sobbing gasps for air even more vividly than the impossible things that had attacked them or the strange man who had driven them away, both of which comparatively seemed unimportant.

Tairei seemed to know what she was thinking. "I'm all right," she said. "It was just...a lot to happen in one evening."

Aili nodded. Somehow, she didn't want to talk about it either. Let Tairei explain in her own time and way. This was the last day they would spend together for years at best — perhaps forever, if her luck was bad — she didn't want to ruin it with demands.

"What about your legs?" Tairei asked. "Do you want me to heal–"

"Ah no," she said quickly, "no need. I'm not injured, just tired. We had our final test today, to see how long and far we could swim. I'm just exhausted and my muscles are complaining."

Tairei smiled and pulled her upright toward a restaurant. "Aren't you hungry?"

After they had begun eating the rice and braised fish, Aili took a deep breath and said, "Tairei."

"Mmm?"

"Tairei, you know I'm leaving soon. The day after tomorrow."

Tairei's chopsticks stopped in midair, then continued toward the fish. "So soon," she said. Her eyes and face became very quiet, the shine in them at its lowest ebb.

"Can you choose not to go? Please?" she asked, at last.

Aili shook her head. "I'm committed. It would be desertion. And I wouldn't want to back out...this is...this is..."

She tried to find some words for it — to explain the ways in which she felt so unable to protect and help the people she loved in the past, how she wanted so much to be able to do it in the future. "I've never really accomplished anything good before," she said at last. "I'm able to do something meaningful, something important now, something that can...help people who are hurt. I don't mind taking risks to do that."

Tairei nodded quietly.

"Could you choose...not to go out at night while I'm gone?" Aili asked, even knowing what the answer would be.

Tairei just smiled quietly at her.

"Never mind," Tairei said. "Never mind it. Let's trust that we will see each other again when you come back. Let's...let's send you off with happy thoughts and memories. So you'll want to come back."

I do, Aili thought, looking at her. *I want to come back to this person.* She turned that over in her mind a few times. There had never been a person that she had wanted to return to.

"How long till you need to go?"

"The day after tomorrow."

"Then that's two days we'll have together, no matter what," Tairei said firmly. "And two nights."

Aili stared at her, chopsticks midair, mouth suddenly dry.

Tairei looked as though she was caught between laughter and tears, then put her own chopsticks to Aili's lips with the piece of fish she had just dipped in sauce. "Eat," she said gently. "There's something special I want to do with you. Before you go."

Aili choked on the fish and grabbed for the liquor again.

"Aili," Tairei sighed as she handed it over, "please get your mind out of the gutter, it's not that."

Aili spat liquor all over the table.

"Although," Tairei continued, now openly laughing at her and reaching over to wipe Aili's lips with a napkin, "I'm also open to that option?"

Her head down on the table, Aili prayed that Nora would never learn about this conversation. When she felt like she could look Tairei in the face again, she raised her head and coughed. "It's– it's just that I need to make a trip to see my mother. My mother lives in my hometown. It's not close," she said. "That's why I can't spend this time all with you…"

Then, she thought that sounded very presumptuous, and felt the blush that always showed in her skin. She reached over and gulped more of the liquor, which did not help.

"I mean," she said, after the burning went away, "I mean. If it were up to me…I would like…you're the only person I would want to– to spend the time with…?"

Tairei's face fell, then she said, determined, "I'll come with you. I can see your hometown and meet your family."

"No," Aili said loudly. "Absolutely not." She sat up straight, her whole body tense with the idea of Tairei in her family's house.

Tairei stared. "You– you don't want me to come?"

"It's not that," she said, tumbling down from her sudden clarity back into liquor-fueled confusion. "My home isn't a good place. That's why I've never been back. I won't go all the way home myself, even. I'll ask a friend to bring my mother out. She needs to know–" she stopped short, not wanting to say, *She needs to know I might die,* because she was fairly sure that Tairei would get upset and she didn't want to ruin their last evening together.

Tairei said, "I could come with you anyway. There's this thing I want to do

31

with you, but I can't do it yet. The time's not right."

"Ah," said Aili as though she understood this completely, and ate more fish.

Tairei said, "Please, Aili. I have to come with you." Her eyes were fixed on Aili's, dark and sad. She added, "I'll follow you if you don't let me come with you."

Aili wavered. She truly didn't want to leave Tairei. Not so quickly, not without…it would be safe enough, surely. "You could come and just see the town. Not my hometown — another one, where my friend lives," she said. "And maybe I'll take you to see the ocean. Not Fallon. But the bus leaves tonight. Do you mind sleeping on the bus?" She found herself looking forward to that bus ride, to Tairei falling asleep on her shoulder.

Tairei beamed, relieved. "That's fine, as long as we're together." She added, "Do you think that we can find a quiet place, away from people, just us? Outdoors somewhere. After you see your mother."

"Oh, that would be no problem at all," Aili said, relieved. "The one thing I can tell you about my hometown is it's…very quiet."

The main street boasted twenty or so buildings, and other roads ran back with houses on them, but not many. Tairei looked around at the tininess of the place, amid the vast golden hills spotted with single oak trees and standing rocks.

"You can practically see the whole town from here. Is there anything you want to explore in particular?" Aili asked, smiling.

"Is this your home?"

"Just the closest town," she said. "It's a few miles walk from here to where I grew up, or maybe I can borrow a car. I thought I could settle you in here while I visit my…my mother."

She found that she didn't want to say home in the same sentence as Fallon or her family. This place wasn't home; in any real meaning of the word, it had never been home. She was already regretting trying to do this — spoiling her last moments with Tairei with this — but they were already here, and her mother… She should at least check on her, at least let her know that she was alive before she got on a ship with the possibility of dying in a distant country. They had never been able to say goodbye properly. No matter what, in the end, if she died her mother would get the telegram. She deserved to know that this was happening.

Tairei was watching her, concerned, but all she said was, "I'd like lunch. Is there a restaurant?"

"In the hotel. It's kind of strange there's a hotel, I guess, but in the old days people used to visit more...Anyway, most of their business is really the bar and selling food to folks. Not Daxian food though," she added quickly. "There's no Daxian people here."

"At all?"

"None. There are some Kunorese families with farms around, further north..."

They entered the darkness of the bar in the little hotel. The whole building had only two rooms on the first floor, and maybe four on the second. As their eyes adjusted, Aili saw the person she had been hoping to see: Old Mrs. Mitchell — looking feisty as ever with her graying blonde hair up in a bun — leaning against the bar to talk to Mr. Bullock, nursing a drink, and eating what looked like potatoes and ham.

Mrs. Mitchell looked over, and her voice stopped. Mr. Bullock looked up too.

"Aili Fallon," said Mrs. Mitchell. "Aili Fallon, I never! You've gone and grown up! It's been how long? Six years? And never a postcard or a note!" She hurried out from behind the bar to give Aili a hug.

Mr. Bullock kept staring from behind his moustache.

"Where are you coming from, are you staying? Have you seen your mama yet?"

"No," Aili said when she got her breath back, "not staying, and haven't seen Mama yet. Haven't been home. We just wanted to get some lunch. What've you got today?"

"Ham and potatoes, chicken pot pie, and some chicken soup, too, if you want that... Whatever you want, you let me know!"

When they had settled at a table with ham and potatoes — Tairei carefully poking it with a fork to separate all the meat from the vegetables — Mrs. Mitchell sat down with them. "Who's your friend, Aili?" she asked, peering to try to see Tairei's face better.

Aili didn't introduce Tairei, just letting Mrs. Mitchell run on as she knew she would.

Lowering her voice, she continued, "Aili, you know your mama's not in a good way. Your dad is still your dad. You should go see her as soon as you're done eating, all right? Your dad's not at home. I know for a fact that he went out of town yesterday with his drinking buddies. They'll be out for the weekend, no doubt, that's their usual way. You can take my car if you want to. Just don't go back to wherever without seeing her."

Aili swallowed. Well, this couldn't be any better; it was the best she could hope for, really. Her mother wouldn't need to risk leaving the house in Mrs. Mitchell's car and having that reported to her father later. Aili would be in control. She'd have a car. She'd be able to leave quickly.

"Ok," she said. "I'll go see her."

It would be quick.

"She'll be glad to know you're well and healthy, Aili. Will your friend go with you?"

"Is it ok if she stays here and waits for me?" she asked.

"Sure, sure, I'll give her a lemonade," Mrs. Mitchell said, and went back up to the bar.

"I want to go with you," Tairei said immediately.

"No."

"This is part of our time together," Tairei said stubbornly. "Don't leave me in a strange place with strangers and lemonade. I don't know how soon you'll come back."

Aili stared at her. She hadn't realized Tairei could be so argumentative. "It's better, Tairei, really…The place I grew up, it isn't a good place."

"I'm coming, Aili," Tairei said, as though it wasn't up for conversation. "I need to be with you."

"Why?"

Tairei looked back down at the potatoes, and said, at last, "Time is short."

"But…"

It was true, time was short; they only had a few hours left together. Her father wouldn't be there. It should be safe, and they would be quick. There was also a part of her that wanted her mother to meet Tairei — to have her mother know that she wasn't alone and friendless after everything.

"All right," she said, and Tairei raised her head and smiled.

The car bounced down the back road between the town and Fallon, crossing the little river and tracing along it into the valley that lay behind the looming rocks on the other side. The hills rolled golden around them, surrounding them and the green flat near the creek. Cows grazed around it, the standing rocks breaking through the soil in a pattern that no one could ever quite grasp. The fog came down, silencing everything, bringing an eerie stillness. The river seemed to come from nowhere and go nowhere, yet there was a path of water through the hills somewhere that they couldn't easily see. It was as though the hills were hiding all the ways one could go in order to leave that valley.

Tairei looked through the windows in silence, and at last said, "This is a strange place. Beautiful but strange."

When they pulled up to the white house on the steep hillside over the water, Tairei looked up. "There are a lot of crows," she said. "Are there always?"

"Yes," said Aili, getting out of the car and taking a deep breath. The sight of that house had been like a punch to her gut. It looked no more welcoming than it ever had, and more dilapidated than she remembered. The lace curtains stirred at the windows behind the porch.

"There've always been lots of crows here. They probably like being near the house because of that windbreak there. There aren't a lot of tall trees around except those. Someone planted them when the house was built."

Tairei looked some more, then turned to gaze back over the valley. There was a little frown between her eyes again. "There's something strange here. This should be excellent qi orientation, but it feels…" She shook her head.

Aili stared at the silent house. She could hear cattle lowing, far away. The crows calling. The wind whispering in the tall trees. Nothing else but the silence she remembered from her childhood, as though it were waiting for something.

This was Fallon: a group of six or so houses strung along the road, the hill at their back, the water in front, the rocks sharing a message no one could read.

"There used to be a flower garden," Aili said suddenly. "Maybe it got too much trouble to water, after I left." She looked at Tairei. "I should have told you…my mother doesn't talk much. I don't know how she is now. I haven't seen her since I left — I was sixteen then…"

Tairei took her hand. "It's all right. I'm with you."

Aili nodded and walked hand in hand with Tairei up the stairs to the porch. The front door was slightly open, no need to knock.

"Mama?" she called, tentatively. "Mama, it's me. I'm here to visit…I'm coming in, ok? I have a friend with me."

The scent of old wood, wax, mildew, meals eaten long ago, dust…Aili walked quickly through the sitting room. There was a radio now — she didn't remember that being there when she left — mumbling something to itself.

It's good Mama has a radio so she's not so lonely, Aili thought.

Down the corridor, past the stairs; it was too narrow now for Tairei to walk next to her. Through the door to the kitchen at the back of the house.

The kitchen had always been the best place — the place that felt more alive than the rest of the house — and it was where Aili's mother spent most of her time. There was something simmering on the stove, something with the scents of Aili's childhood. A tall, broad-shouldered woman, silver-gilt hair braided and pinned around her head, stood in front of it, apron tied neatly, carefully stirring. She turned around, and her blue eyes filled with tears.

"Aili," she said, and crossed the room in three wide steps, grabbed her, and held her in a hug. "Aili." There seemed to be no other words her mother could get out for a while, until finally, "I am glad."

Aili held her mother, a few tears on her cheek.

Aili's mother struggled again to find words. "Good to see you," she said at last. "Good that you left, good that you come back."

"Are you well? Are you ok?"

Her mother wiped her eyes. "I am ok," she said. "Just glad to see you, and know you are safe."

Aili pulled Tairei toward her. "Mama, this is my friend, Liu Chenguang."

"You have a friend," her mother said. "I'm glad. Welcome to our house, Miss Liu."

Tairei tilted her head to one side, as though considering something, then spoke in another language. To Aili's shock, her mother's face lit up and she began to talk rapidly, grabbing for Tairei's hand as she continued to hold Aili's and nodding energetically, pulling them both toward the table.

"You speak Sammish?" Aili said, dazed. "I barely even speak Sammish. There's no one else here who does…She's never had anyone to talk to, since my dad used to yell at her whenever she didn't speak Anglish."

"She wants you to know…" Tairei concentrated, then began translating almost simultaneously as Aili's mother continued. "I told her that you will be leaving soon, but didn't tell her why. She said she is so happy you are safe, and all this time she has been praying for your safety, and she doesn't blame you for leaving. She's glad you left, glad you got away, you should leave before he comes back–"

Aili was too stunned to explain to Tairei that she could understand Sammish, just not speak it well. "Please, tell her to come with us."

"Who is this that she's glad you got away from, Aili? She says that she can't leave, she doesn't have anywhere to go."

Aili found herself clenching her nails into her hands again. It was true. Her mother had nowhere to go; there was nowhere Aili could bring her, she had no way to support herself without Aili's father, and Aili was about to leave for the war. Who could possibly take care of her? Her Anglish was limited, she'd been isolated here all these years with a husband whose language was limited to slaps and curses, and she was — like Aili had been until she was sixteen years old —

36

too afraid of the consequences to run.

Tairei said something back to Aili's mother, but her mother shook her head, more firmly.

"She refuses, Aili. She says she doesn't want to be a burden to you, and she wants you to take some cookies she has made. You should take them all, and you should go. She says you have been the best daughter she could ever wish for, all her life. She wants you to know how much she is happy for you to live well."

Aili's mother's hands — long-fingered, large-knuckled hands identical to Aili's — were rapidly wrapping some cookies and treats into wax paper bundles.

Aili found her eyes so full of tears she could barely see.

"She says she wishes she knew you were coming so she could have made more, and there's also a shawl and a prayerbook she wants you to have. She'll go upstairs to get it," Tairei said as Aili's mother shoved the package into her hands and rushed off.

Tairei sat down in a chair, breathless, looking at her. Aili stood still in the middle of the kitchen, holding the cookies, her eyes squeezed tight to keep the tears in. At last, she took a deep breath and opened her eyes. She could hear her mother rummaging around upstairs, probably in that old cedar chest she had; that's where all her most special things were.

"Thank you," she said to Tairei. "I'm sad that I can't even talk to her. Not like that, so it's easy for her. I can understand, but we were never allowed to speak it. How do you know Sammish?"

Tairei looked at her, silently, her eyes very quiet and dark with the shine off of them. "Your name is Sammish, so I knew that someone in your family must be. It's not a common name. Usually, someone would have to talk to me so I know what language they speak. I just guessed this time."

When Aili didn't respond, Tairei asked, "This seems like a big house, do you have brothers or sisters?"

Aili shook her head, and finally said, "I had two younger brothers, but they died a long time ago."

"I'm sorry," said Tairei. She was very pale, as though all the blood had drained from her face. "I'm...I'm sorry, Aili."

"It's not your fault," she said, wondering why Tairei seemed so upset. She rubbed her eyes. Her mother looked just the same as she had when she had run away. It was so good to know that she was still safe and that she didn't blame Aili for leaving.

"When my mother comes back down, can you help me explain about... about the military stuff?" She had never written to her mother, in all these years.

A letter would have been too risky for both of them. "She won't understand it as well in Anglish. If you help, she can ask questions."

As they heard Aili's mother's footsteps coming down the stairs, the sound of a car engine came into the yard.

"Damn," said Aili under her breath.

Her mother's footsteps quickened desperately. She ran at full speed into the kitchen, shoving some fabric into Aili's arms, hugging her fiercely and quickly and kissing her hair, then said, "Go, go, go now, quick."

There was no point in running out the back door. He would already have seen the car.

Aili squared her shoulders and walked down the corridor. "Tairei," she said, a little too late, "you should go out the back, ok?

Tairei ignored her, following close behind.

The man who opened the front door was slightly drunk, but still very handsome — black hair with not a streak of gray, bright blue eyes, and a chiseled face that looked attractively flushed, rather than florid.

"Aili," he said, leaning against the doorjamb to get his balance. "Look who's back, huh? I knew you couldn't make it out there…Need to come back…I knew you would. I knew it." He fingered something in his pocket. "Get upstairs."

"Shut up and get out of the way," Aili said, her heart beating painfully with terror. "I'm not here for you and I'm not staying."

She was proud that her voice didn't shake. When she left, she had been so frightened of him that she ran away in the night, while he was passed out cold.

Tairei silently moved to stand in front of her, quicker than Aili could push her back.

Her father's eyes lit up. "You bring this for me? I got room." He reached out and grabbed for Tairei's arm.

Tairei twisted her hand and blocked him, grabbing his wrist, but that seemed to be all she could do. Once she let go, he would grab her again.

"Don't you touch her!" Aili got between them and pushed him away forcefully, furious.

He really was drunk, or maybe she was stronger than she'd been as a teenager.

At her touch, he lost his balance and flew back to slam against the wall, as though she had thrown him. A mirror fell off the wall and crashed next to him, covering him in shards of glass. He looked at her, open-mouthed and dazed, with blood on his forehead, but that wouldn't last long.

Aili grabbed Tairei's hand and pulled her out, practically pushing her in the car, then jumping in herself and cranking the engine.

One of the things she remembered about her childhood was that no one ever heard anything. Even though the silence over the valley was so complete that you could hear your neighbor cough at night, no one ever came to investigate the screaming and yelling at their house. No one ever saw anything either. No one ever came to check. No one helped them.

Once Tairei grabbed the wheel to keep them out of the ditch, Aili realized that she was driving blindly by instinct toward one of her safe places from her childhood. She stopped and put her face in her hands, trying to get her breath.

"This wasn't a good idea," Aili said, sitting up. "I'm sorry, Tairei. I shouldn't have brought you. My mother…I wish…"

Her hair had come unpinned and was falling around her face. Tairei reached up and put some strands back behind her ears, carefully, as though touching something very fragile.

"There's so much pain in your home," Tairei said. "I'm sorry for all that pain, for you."

"It's not my home," Aili said. "Nora is my home, if I have any home at all."

Tairei was silent, still stroking the hair behind her ears. "I wish," she said, carefully, "I wish. I wish I could save you from that."

Aili shook her head and picked up Tairei's hand to hold when she stopped touching her hair, hating herself for her uselessness and fear. "This is a bad place. I shouldn't have brought you here."

Even now she was too afraid to go back to that house, to see that man's eager eyes and share breath in a room where he also breathed.

"I'm glad you brought me. I'm glad you weren't alone." Tairei said, a little fierce. After a while, she looked out the window. "It's getting toward dinnertime now…Tomorrow you need to be back, don't you?"

Aili nodded. "We'll have to leave this evening, Mrs. Mitchell will drive us to the station, she said."

"There's still something I need to do," Tairei said, almost shyly. "Can you bring me to a place away from roads, and houses, and people? A place with a tree would be best."

"Of course," Aili said, shaking herself back into mental order. "There's a lot of places like that here. We can just leave the car here, just walk…A little less than a mile, there's a good place like that."

"Good," said Tairei, sounding determined. "That's good. Let's go now, Aili, please?"

Aili laughed a bit, getting out of the car and opening Tairei's door for her.

"Are you in a hurry?"

"A little," Tairei said, looking toward the angle of the sun moving toward the horizon. "A little bit of a hurry."

There was only one enormous tree, nestled between the steep hills. The coast oak was always green, even in the hottest summer, even surrounded by the grass turned to dry gold on all sides.

"I used to come here when I was young," Aili said, ducking under the spreading branches and touching the oak's thick, rough trunk. The branches spread out low and long from the trunk, wider than high — an easy tree for a child to climb, hiding from adults and the world outside. Aili found the rough bark comforting against her forehead, and looked up at the sky through the branches of the tree. The sunlight was thick and golden-red. "Well, we're here."

There was a nook between two high roots where Aili had liked to hide when she was young, which could fit her and Tairei if they were close to one another. "It's not that tall," Aili said. "Further north, there's enormous trees. You wouldn't believe them."

"Will you take me someday?" Tairei asked. "When you come back."

Aili nodded. "Yes." When she came back. They could start over then. "I would like to do that with you. When I come back."

Then, she thought of that name. *Deming*. A spasm of pain wrung inside her.

Tairei must have seen it in her face. She said, seriously, "Aili, I want to explain to you– I promised to explain. It's just…it's very hard. I don't know where to start. So I wanted to start with this." She lay her hands on either side of Aili's face and kissed her, not passionately, but yearning, hopeful.

Aili closed her eyes and felt Tairei's lips on hers again — like that time on the dark, wet street that night in Easterly — and pulled her closer, wanting to hold her. For some reason, she felt not joy and excitement, but a deep sadness welling up from somewhere she couldn't name. "Tairei," she said, at last, "Tairei, I'm not…that person. Is this even for me? Is it me that you want to be kissing?"

Tairei's face was so close that her lashes brushed against Aili's cheek. "It's for you, Aili," she said, "I promise, it's you that I want, I know who you are." She drew back a little bit. "Do you want me?"

"Yes," Aili said. This was too deep in her heart to deny or equivocate or protect her own dignity.

Tairei took a deep breath, and exhaled, slowly. "There's something…because

I want you to be safe–"

A voice came from outside the sheltering tree branches. "Aili, get your ass out here now."

Aili froze. He must have seen the car, parked where she had left it by the roadside.

Tairei stood up.

"Get out here!"

A gunshot rattled through the leaves over their heads.

"Did he just shoot at you?!" Tairei clenched her fists.

Aili stood, trembling in automatic obedience, but Tairei grabbed her arm as she passed.

"Don't bother," she said, her eyes glowing. Her hand felt hot on Aili's arm, as though she were suddenly running a high fever.

"Tairei?" she asked, turning toward her, frowning. "Are you all right?"

A second gunshot rang out. This one clipped Aili on the shoulder — just a graze, enough to make her cry out and bleed a little bit.

Aili's father laughed and his footsteps came closer, crunching on the grass.

Tairei held onto Aili's wrist with a grip like hot iron, and the blood running down from Aili's shoulder combined with that heat was making her dizzy.

"Dad?" Aili called, confused. Her will was in fragments, wounded by so much in so little time. If she was obedient, he wouldn't hurt anyone. If she was a good girl…

"Dad, just wait, I'll come out, just give me a minute."

Tairei bit her own lip until it bled, and leaned over to kiss the wound in Aili's shoulder.

Aili shook her head violently at the touch of her lips. "Tairei, what–"

"You!" shouted Tairei suddenly, turning her head to look out through the branches. "You nearly killed your own daughter!"

"She's mine to do whatever with," said the man. "You shut up, girlie, I have plenty here for you too."

Tairei laughed.

The laugh had such a strange edge to it — not of hysteria but of something else.

Tairei shouted, "You have thirty seconds to live."

"What!?" Aili tried to pull her hand out of Tairei's grip, harder, but she couldn't get away. She needed to do what her father said, then Tairei wouldn't be hurt–

The sharp-edged, strange laughter stopped almost as quickly as it had start-

41

ed.

Tairei turned back to Aili and met her eyes. "I'll explain later. Aili, we've run out of time, please trust me."

Then, suddenly, Tairei raised her other arm to her mouth and ripped her own wrist open with her teeth.

Aili screamed, "*Tairei!*"

The blood poured out, spurted out, leapt out, decorating the leaves and the grass and Aili's body. The tear in Tairei's arm didn't close.

Tairei didn't look at her or let go of her hand, though Aili desperately fought to put pressure on the dreadful, ragged wound. Her face was not like Tairei's face anymore; the gentleness and playfulness that Aili had always seen there was gone, and in its place was something hard and furious and empty.

She could hear her father running beneath the tree branches, stomping over the golden grass that was dappled with blood. But something was happening to the blood — where it had fallen on the grass, it began to smolder. Where it was pouring from Tairei's arm, it fell like a waterfall of sparks, surrounding them in a whirlwind of tiny fires.

Tairei turned back to Aili, raised Aili's arm to her bloody lips, and bit down, not gently, but strong enough to tear Aili's skin and rip the veins beneath. Aili screamed again and struggled, but even with one hand, the smaller woman was stronger.

"Aili," Tairei said, her eyes narrowed and fierce, "I will keep you safe, you understand? That's all I want. For you to live a good life. You'll be safe. I'm sorry. I'm sorry for everything."

Tairei held Aili's bleeding wrist against hers. The sparks quickened, increased, mixing with Aili's blood and making it burn in her body. All she could see was the river of fire surrounding them.

"*Tairei!*" Aili screamed again. "Chenguang, what are you doing? Stop it, stop it right now! Get away from me! Let go! I–"

And then, Liu Chenguang, still holding Aili's hand, erupted into a pillar of fire.

CHAPTER 4
HEALING

THE LEAVES OF the tree were green and rustled in the wind.

Everything else was black.

Aili was lying on the charred ground, staring up through the leaves of the tree. It seemed untouched by anything, as though it hadn't noticed the explosion, or whatever it had been.

Tairei—

She sat up, the blackened grass crackling beneath her, and leaned with her hand on the tree trunk for balance until she was on her feet. Was it still the same day? Had a night passed? Was it still morning, would they get back in time? Mrs. Mitchell would drive them back to the station. She couldn't miss the embarkation.

"Tairei!" she shouted. Aili coughed a little, but not as though she'd just been through a conflagration, breathing the smoke of the valley's incineration around her. "Tairei!"

There was no answer.

She grabbed at her wrist. There was no pain. There was no mark at all. Her shoulder, where the bullet had grazed it, was unscarred, unhurt.

Had she lost her mind completely? What had happened?

She turned around and around in the bowl of the little valley. The black burning covered everything to the rim of the hilltops and then stopped, evenly, as though it were an ebony bowl with golden decorations. As though the fire had expanded out and then simply disappeared, down to its last sparks and embers.

The charred grass wasn't hot; the ground felt cool, even damp. Had it rained? Had the fog come through?

She walked out across the crackling blackened grass. The crows were gone. All life was gone. There was no answer to her calls.

Perhaps Tairei had woken up first. Perhaps she had left.

But Aili knew this couldn't be. She knew Tairei would not have left her here. Tairei would not leave her alone.

The blood, and the fire.

Aili laughed a little bit because she had to do something or she would scream, or cry. Then, she decided that she should, indeed, scream and cry.

"TAIREI!" she screamed until her throat was raw. "CHENGUANG!"

Eventually, there was nothing else to do but trudge out of the ebony bowl, across its golden rim, and back out into the world. The tree rustled, green, behind her as she climbed. Just before the rim of the bowl, in the golden grass that hadn't burned, she found a fallen figure, but it wasn't Tairei.

It was her father.

She squatted down next to him and observed, clinically.

He had not died painlessly. There must have been a wave of heated air and smoke that had overcome him as he ran; he had clawed at his throat as tears ran down his sooty face. He had not been burned, except perhaps inside, where the lung tissues had been unable to take in air. He had suffocated, he had known he was dying. He must have been frightened. It must have hurt.

She found that this didn't bother her at all.

Aili tried to think of something that would make her feel sorry, or at least that would make her feel some pity for this person who had died in pain, but there was nothing. Her heart was cold.

"You were right about me, Dad," she said finally. "I'm very glad you're dead, and I hope you rot in hell."

She still didn't feel anything.

As she drove Mrs. Mitchell's car back to town, she realized for the first time that her clothes were half burned off her, hanging in torn rags. There were no burns at all on her skin beneath. She managed to sneak into the hotel and change quickly in the bathroom; she held the burned remnants in her hands for a few moments, then looked more closely. What was left of her right sleeve was bloody. Tairei had cut her after all. That part hadn't been a dream. Not cut her — bit her until she bled. But the cut was gone now.

Tairei was gone.

She just had to move one step at a time. One step. Nothing here was solvable. Tairei was gone, and her father was dead on the hillside. She couldn't leave these burned clothes here. People might connect her with what had happened, even though she had no idea what had happened. She stuffed them into her duffel bag and took them with her, along with the bag Tairei had brought.

"Where's your friend, Aili?" Mrs. Mitchell asked, firing up the car for the trip to the station.

"She ran into someone she knew when we were out. She's going to go visit them for a few days. We'll meet back in Easterly sometime," Aili said.

It seemed as though she was watching all of this from somewhere else, through a glass that made everything seem distant and quiet. She vaguely remembered this feeling from her childhood, when things were bad at home. She was in her body, but not; her body was doing things that it needed to do, and her mind was doing whatever needed to be done to protect her, including, apparently, lying as though it felt nothing at all about the person who had been so special to her just a few hours ago.

She suddenly, vividly remembered kissing Tairei that strange night in Easterly — Tairei's mouth and skin and hands, and the pulse in her throat under her lips, and Tairei's voice calling her someone else's name. Deming. That felt real, as though there was a hot spike in her heart; she actually groaned a little bit and hunched over. But then, it was gone. The glass was back over everything, keeping it far away from her.

She threw the burned clothes away in Easterly before she went back to the base. Nora wasn't there yet, though other women were. Talking, chatting excitedly, putting on the new uniforms that had been laid out for them, and packing the few personal belongings they would be allowed to bring.

This was all happening through the glass.

Aili smiled in greeting, but that was already as much as she could do. She put on the uniform and unpacked her duffel and trunk, which held almost nothing anyway, then picked up Tairei's bag because she couldn't bear to throw it away with the burned clothes. Tairei's bag held a change of clothes — a shirt and pants that smelled like her, that scent of bitter medicine and incense. Aili looked at them for a long time before carefully folding them and putting them into the bag she would bring onto the ship, along with her own clothes. There was a book, too, in Daxian characters, and a pendant made of jade on a string of braided red silk. The pendant was a little smaller than the palm of her hand — a flat circle containing a bird with outstretched wings. She put the pendant on and hid it

45

under her uniform. The book went in the bag, too.

Then, there was nothing left to do but lie on the bed and wait, so she did that, staring unblinkingly at the ceiling.

"Aili," said Nora's voice. She sounded concerned. Nora sat next to her on the bed. "Aili, what's wrong?"

Aili looked at her very slowly. She couldn't seem to make words come out of her mouth. Nora wasn't Mrs. Mitchell. Lies didn't want to be told to Nora. At last, she said, "Tairei left."

"Is that all?" Nora put her hand on Aili's forehead. Her dark eyes were worried. "Aili, did something happen? You look..." Like you did when I found you, Aili knew she was going to say, but didn't.

"Ok. I'm ok." With an effort, she sat up. "I visited home. With Tairei."

Nora gently slapped her arm. "Aili, what the hell were you thinking? Was it bad?"

"It was bad." She thought for a moment. "I don't know what I was thinking. I shouldn't have brought her there."

She remembered kissing Tairei, and the fire, and pulled the glass back over everything. "My mother gave me a shawl, though. It's in my bag."

"Aili."

"Also cookies. My mother made cookies. You can have some."

"Aili, stop it."

She laid down again and stared at the ceiling some more.

Nora kept her hand on Aili's arm, refusing to let her go. "Aili, snap out of it. You can't be like this when it's time to board. They'll take you out and put you into a mental ward for observation. I'm not joking."

"I know."

"Is this just because Tairei left? Was it because of your dad? Did he try something?"

"Yes," she said. "I can't talk about it. Just let me be for a little while. I'll be ok, I promise. When they call us."

The ship loomed, enormous, over the tiny figures queuing to board in regimental order. There were twelve flight nurses going, all from their cohort, and they were placed in their tiny, shared quarters before the men boarded. Aili managed to look alive as they were given their rank pins and ushered into the bunks to await departure, pretending to be excited and nervous like the others. She couldn't play it too convincingly, but she had always been quiet so no one really noticed much difference. Their quarters had nothing like a window — this was a ship of war, not a cruise — but they could hear the roar of the engines starting and feel the lurch as they left the dock at last.

Their officer came to tell them they could take a turn on the deck as they passed the Sunset Gate, flags flying proudly. Ship discipline would provide times for deck, times for training and shifts in the sick bay, times in the mess hall, and times for other duties as assigned. But for now, they were able to stand together and watch the bridge pass over their heads, unbelievably high, and squint their eyes toward the sunset pouring its red-gold light onto them.

Aili took a deep breath.

Nora squeezed her arm. "It's really happening, Aili. We're really going. We did it."

"Yes," Aili said, and she smiled a real smile. She would not think of Tairei anymore. That was all there was to it. It was all behind her, as her home had been left behind when she ran away those years ago. There was a way of shutting a door in her heart so that she could live again. Nora had helped her do it before, but she knew the way of it now. This was a familiar territory. She took a deep breath again, pretending that the sunlight was liquid and she could drink it, bathe in it, be healed by it.

"You'll be ok," said Nora. "Just think about the future."

"Are you scared at all?"

Nora snorted. "Hell no I'm not scared, why would I be scared? This is a real adventure, Aili. This is the best thing we've done in our lives so far."

Nora was shorter than Aili by almost a head, but sturdy and strong; the cold wind blew her thick dark hair all over, tangling the curls. The official nurse's uniform when not wearing the flight suits was wide-legged pants and a matching jacket, with a cap that was unlikely to stay on in this wind. It suited Nora's style well. She stood with her legs spread and arms akimbo, looking into the Western Sea as though daring some yahoo on the streets of Easterly to come say that to her face. That was just Nora, as always.

Their main duties were taking shifts in the sick bay to deal with the array of accidents and illnesses that happened on board over the weeks it took to reach their destination: cuts and burns, broken limbs, waves of cold and flu and anything else contagious. Often, they just sat there and played cards; the other nurses — aside from Nora — flirted with the doctors who were also doing busywork and counting supplies. The orderlies were darker-skinned men from the rural provinces, mostly soft-spoken and trying not to draw attention to themselves. Aili recognized this strategy since it was more or less how she had survived her childhood. They had names on their tags like everyone else, but no one in sick-bay called them by name; the doctors called all the orderlies *boy*, talked down to them, and told them to run errands that shouldn't have been asked, which they did unquestioningly. Aili recognized this, too. It made her feel a sense of kinship, though like the other nurses, she didn't talk to them.

One of the orderlies was extremely good-looking — tall with very deep brown skin, high cheekbones, and expressive, intelligent eyes — and once, one of the nurses decided that, despite everything, he was a worthy recipient of some flirting glances and conversation. The doctor on duty immediately sent the orderly to go swab out the latrine. Aili's eyes met his as he left, and he raised his eyebrow at her in an expression she couldn't interpret. She shook her head, not wanting the doctor to pay any more attention to the man, but after that, she saw him regularly, and it seemed as though he was watching her as well.

Nora also noticed it. "Why's that orderly always looking at you?" she asked quietly after one shift. "It's making me uncomfortable. Should we report it or something?"

"No," she said at once, "he's not doing anything. He's probably watching everyone. It's his job to keep an eye on things, isn't it? He's not bothering me at all."

"Has he gotten friendly with you?"

"Are you joking, Nora? Of course not, he's never even spoken to me."

"It's just weird…"

"You're reading too much into it."

Nora sighed. "You know what's weird, really? Being in a place full of desperate men when I'm only interested in Nurse Sarah."

"Nurse Sarah is only interested in Dr. Jones."

"Yeah, I know." Nora sighed again. "I knew it would be hard, but not this hard! There's even guys hitting on me, so you know the bar is low. And they're definitely looking at you, tall, blonde, and intimidating as you are. So just be careful, ok? Things happen on ships."

Aili nodded. "I'm always careful."

One night shift, very late, there was an accident in the boiler room. Three men were brought to the sick bay badly scalded, all in shock, one already near death. Aili started soaking bandages while Nora went with the doctor to prepare the surgery for grafts. There was only that strange orderly on duty, the one who always watched her. Since he was alone, Aili helped him carefully lift the burned men one by one into warm saline baths to give them some relief.

The one that was worst off had taken the steam blast directly in the face; he had breathed it in, burning his throat, and the airways were swelling.

"He'll suffocate soon," Aili said. "We should trache him. I'll confirm with the doctor. I'll be right back."

The orderly nodded, silently holding the man up to keep as much of his body from touching any other surface as possible.

When she came back, however, the man was breathing easily, and the burns were beginning to look better.

"The saline bath is very helpful," said the orderly blandly.

Aili didn't know when she had gotten so suspicious of everything in the world, but there it was. She looked at the orderly, meeting his eyes.

He raised his eyebrows at her again. This time he spoke directly to her: "That's a nice necklace you have there, Lieutenant Fallon."

Aili realized that Tairei's jade pendant had somehow fallen out of her uniform blouse, probably when she twisted to help pick up the men without hurting them. "It belongs to a friend," she said.

"Oh," he said. "Yes, I thought so. Where's your friend now?"

"She– she disappeared. In a fire."

"Ah," the man said, as though this was completely unremarkable. "Well, I suppose it was the time."

Aili's heart nearly stopped in shock. "What?"

The man ignored her question. "Come over here," he said, leading her to the second burned person; he had passed out from shock as well. "Let me show you a little trick I learned to help with burns. Not everyone can do it. Your friend with the pendant could do it."

"What? What are you talking about?"

He bit his finger until blood came out, dripping softly down toward the palm of his hand as he moved toward the injured man on the bed. The orderly smiled reassuringly and said, "It's all right. It doesn't hurt me, or him."

Tairei. Tairei ripping open her arm, the blood everywhere on the golden grass.

"Don't," whispered Aili frantically. "Don't do it. I don't need to see– You can't, the fire–"

49

"Why should I not do it?" He gently spread blood on the burned skin. "There's no fire involved."

Blood speckled the burned lips of the man as the orderly put his fingers inside his mouth, deft and quick.

Aili took a step backward, then another one and another. "What are you doing? Who are you?"

"How long have you spoken Niforu?" asked the orderly casually.

"I don't speak Niforu. I don't even know what that is. I only speak Anglish." Aili was still whispering. She couldn't take her eyes off his bloody finger, which immediately healed itself. The cut was gone as though it had never been. The blistered skin was already healing on the burned man.

Like Tairei. Like Tairei's knife cut that disappeared. Like the wounds on her own arm that night in Easterly, gone without a mark, Tairei smoothing something warm on her skin, putting something between her lips...

"It's an East Shanyu language," the orderly said. "You've been speaking it with me for the past few minutes now, very fluently. No accent at all." Suddenly, he grabbed her hand. "Your turn."

"No–" she said, "I'm not–" Her heart's door was shut, and her mind's door was closing rapidly now too. The glass over reality was getting thicker, more opaque. "You can't make me."

He laughed gently. "You're quite right, I can't make you. Don't you want to try?"

"No," she whispered. "I don't want to try." To her shock, she realized that they were now speaking Daxian.

"Stop hyperventilating, you're going to faint," said Nora's voice. "I know the burns are awful to look at, but it seems like they're going to be ok. The doctor's prepped for grafts now, but look at them now, the saline baths must have done the trick, right?"

Nora walked over to the worst patient, the first, and added, "Even this one, breathing easily now." She ignored the orderly as though he didn't exist, and he stood back as though he were actually invisible, looking calmly over her head. "Only this one, he might still need grafts."

While the other two patients were now sleeping comfortably in their baths, their skin turning a gentle pink, this man was writhing even while unconscious. Every time he moved, the burned and blistered skin tore. The water was full of red streams from the cracks in his legs and feet.

The orderly looked down from the contemplation of space and met her gaze, his eyes compassionate and encouraging. The man in the bath made a little wheezing moaning noise.

Nora winced. "Let me set up a morphine drip," she said, and turned to the back counter.

Faster than she thought she could move, Aili suddenly found herself next to the man in the bath; she had a scalpel in her hand and slashed it quickly across her palm. With one shaking finger, she traced her own blood over the man's face, dripped it onto his lips.

His breathing eased immediately, but Nora was already there, inserting the drip into his hand, and already, the skin on the arm was healed enough for her to easily find a vein.

"See," she said, "he's feeling better. They'll all be fine, Aili, don't worry so much."

"Yes, you're right," she said. She washed her hands in the sink, the blood draining down off of her hands. Her unblemished, unmarked hands.

The doctor came back and expressed pleasure at the improvement; obviously, the nurses must have miscalculated the degree of burning, these men would all be fine. "Write it up, nurse," he said to the air, and went back to his office.

For the remainder of that shift, the orderly ignored Aili completely and she did her best to ignore him. She and Nora went back to their quarters soon after, and Nora immediately fell asleep. The other nurses were either sleeping or headed to sickbay for their own shifts. Aili couldn't do anything except stare into space and scream in her mind for Tairei.

Experimentally, she reached out with her hand and found the sharp edge of a screw that had come loose from the bulkhead. It had torn her sheets a few days ago; she'd reported it so it could be repaired, but it was still there. She drew her hand back and drove it down, hard, at an angle. She could feel the slash through her skin — a tiny cut, but deep enough that she could feel the blood dripping. Aili wiped her hand against the sheet, and in the dim safety light that stayed on all night, she could see the stain.

But when she lifted her hand in front of her eyes and touched the spot with her fingers, there was nothing. The cut was gone.

She slammed her head against the pillow a couple of times and then stopped. There was no point, people might hear.

She needed fresh air; she needed to be alone, to think; she needed to talk to that goddamn orderly. He had done that on purpose — had made sure she saw. He had recognized Tairei's pendant. He knew something. He knew. He might know where Tairei had gone, what had happened...how could she find him?

She staggered up and hit her head on the top bunk, seeing stars, but the pain was gone even before she could yell in surprise. "Well, that's a plus, I guess," she said out loud.

"What?" Nora asked, sleepily.

"Nothing." She left the bunkroom, taking the steep, laddered stairs up toward the deck. She might not find the orderly, but she could at least get to the point where she could breathe fresh air and see the stars.

No one was supposed to wander the ship at night, but there were lots of excuses that people used to be able to get out of the crowded, smelly bunk areas, and she wasn't alone standing in an out-of-the-way spot and breathing deeply. In the darkness, the great Bridge of Souls blazed across the whole sky, and the beginnings of black turning to deep blue in the east teased that dawn would make it all invisible soon. But the stars would still be there. Even if they couldn't be seen, the stars were there. Their paths continued.

Aili looked down at her hand again in wonder. "Tairei," she whispered softly. "Liu Chenguang."

She had failed in her life in so many ways — failed to protect the people she loved — but Liu Chenguang had not. Tairei had protected her at a cost Aili couldn't comprehend, but she would pay it. She would find Tairei again and protect her in turn. The door in her heart had broken, and with her mind quiet and her heart full, she looked at the stars.

CHAPTER 5
DESTROYING

AILI'S EFFORTS TO find the orderly again petered out. There were over two thousand men on the ship and the flight combat nurses were supposed to avoid all of them. She didn't want to ask directly about him because it would lead to trouble of one sort or another — certainly for him, if not for her. She was able to discover that the orderlies really were just recruited from the mess hall staff, which was where almost all the provincial enlisted men had been assigned. The orderly must have been sent back to the mess hall because he wasn't showing up in sick bay anymore; she never saw him in the kitchen, either, but the ship had more than one galley and perhaps he had been assigned to a different one.

A few days later, Nora saw her holding a book in Daxian characters on the bunk while the other women were on duty and sat down next to her. "Can you read that?" she asked, surprised.

"No, guess not. Guess that's something you have to learn," Aili replied.

"Well, of course it is," Nora replied. "No one just magically learns Daxian."

Aili laughed.

"What is it, did Tairei give it to you? Or Edna?"

"It was Tairei's," Aili said. "I don't know what it is. Tairei left some things behind...anyway, I took them to keep them safe. There's this, too." She pulled the pendant over her head and held it in her hand. It felt warm from her body, smooth to her touch.

53

Nora examined it. "It's pretty," she said, finally. "Do you want to talk about what happened with Tairei, Aili?"

Aili considered for a moment, then put the pendant back over her head. "I don't really understand what happened at the end, to be honest. But we kissed and she called me someone else's name."

"Oh my god." Nora shook her head. "That woman…I knew it. So, that was the end of it?"

"I don't know if it's the end of it. We separated and then I had to leave, so I don't know…I'd like to find her again."

Nora looked at her, surprised. "You– Well, fine then. Can you write to her?"

"No, I don't know how to get in touch. I don't know where she went. When we get back home, I'll look for her in Little Daxian. That's all I know how to do." She wondered if Tairei would try to find her again, too, wherever she was.

"Hmph." Nora shook her head. "Well, Aili, all I can say is you're a forgiving person. Or else that woman must be a really good kisser."

Aili snorted. "As though I have any basis for comparison."

"My point exactly." Nora looked at her carefully. "You look…better."

"You mean not catatonic?" Aili smiled.

"Yes, exactly. I was really worried about you when you came back, and when we boarded. So, I'm guessing, she's a good kisser? I have to watch out for you; you're my little sister." Nora reached out and ruffled her hair, making the braids get messy. "My little girl, all grown up."

"Shut up," said Aili, pushing her off the bed.

Two of their other bunkmates came in and began taking their bags out of the storage lockers.

"You girls ready to go?" asked one. "We're going to be making port late today, the word just came down to get ready. They want us to go straight to the airstrip in flight gear — they're going to take us right off the ship. I don't know where we're going from there, but there's an airstrip ready somewhere and I guess some evacuations to get to."

Nora looked over. "Aili? Why are you staring at your hand?"

Aili smiled. "Ready, Nora."

The first evacuation was smooth, just like they had practiced back in Sand Island. They didn't have to go onto the battlefield, and they weren't under fire. Field medics had already brought the wounded to the airstrip, triaged for evacuation; all they had to do was keep them alive through the multi-hour flight back to the base and settle them into the infirmaries.

After that, they were always on alert. It didn't always go so well. On one island, they landed under fire, while the marines were still coming up onto the beach and being shot in the surf. It was complete madness, finding men floating in the water who were still alive and dragging them up onto the beach beneath covering fire. Aili found that this was an ideal situation for blood healing, however; no one could see what she was doing through the seafoam and bullets, not even the men she was healing, and the blood washed away immediately after doing its work. She wasn't stealthy enough to manage it in the close quarters of the plane, where the men, orderlies, and other nurses were always close by.

By the time they boarded — bringing only the men she hadn't been able to heal, since the others were miraculously able to walk and grab their weapons as soon as they hit the sand — she was dizzy and lightheaded and had to lie down in a bunk herself.

"What happened to your hand?" Nora asked, sitting next to her. "Lucky we have a spare bunk for you. What happened? Did you slash it on coral or something? Remember they told us you could get coral poisoning?" She picked up Aili's hand and looked at it. "Those are deep. You might need stitches."

"Really?" she asked, dizzy. She held her own hand in front of her face and tried to focus on it. Sure enough, there were slashes in it, like a raw chicken that someone was planning to stuff garlic into. The saltwater had cleaned it out and it wasn't bleeding much, but she realized that it throbbed painfully.

"How weird." It was unusual now, to feel pain that didn't go away. Why wasn't it healing? She frowned at it. "I feel kind of…drunk, maybe?"

Nora shook her head. "Stay here till I can get back to you. I need to check IVs. No getting up till I say, got it?"

"Got it!" she giggled. "What the hell is happening…"

The man in the bunk across from her looked over. "Same question, little lady, same question!" He wiggled his bandaged foot at her. "I saw you drag my buddy out. Looks like he was ok?"

"I dragged a lot of people out," she said honestly, focusing on making her words make sense in Anglish. "And everyone I dragged out was ok, so yes."

"Wish you dragged me." He winked at her. "Looks like maybe you'll have a few days recuperation. Want to get a drink with me when we're off duty?"

Aili looked at him, trying to imagine it. Instead, she imagined Tairei's facial expression if she knew Aili was getting asked out by random marines and naval aviators several times a day, not counting the ones who just copped a feel when she walked by.

"No," she said at last. Belatedly, she added, "Thank you." Then she looked at her hand again. Maybe it was starting to close up a little bit? But why was it still there at all?

Nora decided to go ahead and put stitches in Aili's palm on the flight back, and then she did indeed have a few days of recuperation before she was sent out on an evacuation again. She spent them relaxing near the mess hall, trying to politely fend off men and lurking around in the hopes of seeing the mysterious orderly, but he never appeared. The wound in her hand healed very quickly — much more quickly than normal — but not immediately.

Was whatever Tairei had given her limited? Was it wearing off, somehow?

But the next evacuation, the healing still worked. She saved it this time for the most heavily wounded, just in case she really was running out, and felt fine for the whole flight.

A few weeks later, the nurses were told in the preflight briefing that they would be landing in a secured airstrip, but this time they would be going with the combat units into an active battlefield, so they had the choice to carry weapons or not. Nora would, she knew. They would be responsible for bringing the wounded back through the jungle along with the extra orderlies assigned to their units to help with transport.

Aili looked up and saw the orderly sitting there, looking very serious, along with several other men she remembered from the sick bay on the ship. His deep brown eyes met hers, but he made no movement to indicate that he knew her. The evacuation planes were lined inside with bunks three high; once in the air, it was expected that the nurses would be moving around, not sitting down, so there wasn't much in terms of comfort from the bumps and noise of the plane's roaring engines. She would have had to get pretty close to the orderly to talk to him, and she couldn't figure out how to do it unobtrusively. He didn't approach her, instead staring calmly down at the floor of the plane, his arms folded over his chest.

An hour into the flight, there was a huge crash, and the plane banked suddenly sideways. One of the pilots yelled and the plane dove hard. Aili screamed in shock despite herself, grabbing onto one of the bunks for balance. One of the nurses who had been walking down the aisle was thrown headfirst, her forehead striking the metal skin of the plane with a sickening cracking noise. She lay crumpled against the wall, her head bleeding, but before anyone could get to her the plane keeled heavily to the side.

"Mayday, mayday, mayday!" she could hear the pilot yelling.

Aili pulled herself toward the cockpit and looked out through the windshield at a sky full of explosions like flowers. A small plane dived toward them, its guns blazing. She ducked as the gunfire came through the windshield. One of the pilots sank down, covered in blood, held by the harness to his seat.

The other pulled back on the controller, yelling, "Prepare to evacuate! Water landing! Water landing!"

Aili let go of the handle and let herself half fall, half tumble back toward where the parachutes, life jackets, and life rafts were held ready. "Water landing!" she yelled at the people waiting there.

The orderly was holding the arm of the woman with the bleeding head wound, but she was standing on her own now.

The pilot seemed confident they would land, not need to parachute, but just in case, they all watched silently through the small window of heavy glass, trying to gauge how high they were. Not high, and dropping quickly — they were already close enough to see not only waves, but the individual ripples of bullets and debris falling into the water like evil rain from an unimaginable sky. A part of a human torso fell silently to one side as they glided in toward the water.

"Brace!" yelled someone; they all grabbed whatever stanchion or handle was nearest. The entire plane screamed and shuddered and banked and crashed and jolted violently, and at last, they were still, except for a gentle tilt and a sloshing noise.

Aili took a deep breath; her arm had been a little strained as they were thrown around inside the plane, but no real injuries.

"Out," yelled the pilot, running down the aisle toward them. "Open up, get out the rafts."

There were plenty of rafts — enough to evacuate a fully loaded plane with sixty patients — and they launched them all to provide more options in case some were sunk. There were people in the water from other planes and ships, many already dead but some waving hands to be fished out. Aili and Nora were in the same raft, but in the evacuation, she had lost sight of the orderly and couldn't locate him as the rafts diverged and spread out in the water.

The broken plane behind them slowly sank.

Once they set up the distress beacon and began rowing, there wasn't much else to do. Nora and Aili both took turns despite the protests of the men on board, but it was exhausting work in the hot sun. The rafts were all equipped with water and emergency rations, which by common consent they tried not to use; there was no knowing if the land they found would have fresh water or food available. There was also no knowing if the land would be held by Federatives or by the Kunorese.

"What happened?" Nora asked eventually. "We couldn't have been anywhere near the battlefield yet. It was only an hour plus in the air."

The surviving pilot wasn't in the raft with them, but there were a few marines who had come aboard from the ocean. "Convoy of ships was attacked," said one of the men. "You all were just collateral damage. Wrong place, wrong time."

A small, red bird suddenly landed on the hull of the raft. It tilted its head to one side, observing them with golden eyes, then flew away again.

"We must be close," said the rowing man. "That's a land bird for sure. Follow it. That's the best way to find an island."

The little red bird fluttered ahead of them, vivid against the turquoise ocean, never quite out of sight until a green triangle heaved over the horizon.

"Land," said Nora, unnecessarily. She looked rather seasick and had sat out the last bout of rowing.

Aili's hands were blistered, but since they healed almost as soon as she stopped rowing, she kept offering to take a turn, feeling a little guilty that it wasn't as painful for her as for the others. She looked back over her shoulder at the red bird, who seemed to be as excited by the sight of land as they were. It suddenly shot ahead and disappeared into the green wall that bordered the shining white beach.

"What do you think?" whispered one marine to another. "Don't see any flags or any sign…"

"You wouldn't," said the other, grimly. "Anyone got weapons, get 'em ready to fire. Girlies, get ready to duck."

Nora shot him an evil look and took out her gun. Aili just kept rowing. The two marines knelt at the front of the raft, guns pointed toward the beach, carefully sweeping this way and that.

"What happened to all the other rafts?" someone asked. "Are we the only ones that made it?"

"There's one over there," said someone else. "On the beach by that crooked tree. But…"

"Damn," muttered one of the marines. He aimed at something in the trees and pulled the trigger. At almost the same moment, he fell into the water with a splash. The water, which was so clear that you could see the white sand at the bottom, immediately turned red. The man sank and didn't come up again.

Nora moved up to the front to take his place, crouching behind the low edge to try to get some cover.

"Sitting ducks," muttered the surviving marine.

"Should we swim?" Aili asked uncertainly. She didn't see how they could beach without all being shot in the water at the convenience of whoever was hiding in the trees.

"They didn't shoot till we did. They may want prisoners." The marine shuddered. "Let's take some down with us."

It wasn't at all clear who he was talking to, but he slipped into the water and huddled behind the boat, using it as cover and as a balance for his weapon. Whoever was in the raft now immediately became part of the cover, so one by one, everyone else got into the water as well.

Aili stayed where she was, rowing.

"Get in the water!" hissed Nora.

"If no one's rowing we're just going to float back out to sea," she hissed back. "We're not close enough to shore yet. I'll get out when the waves will carry us." She wasn't sure whether the protection Tairei had given her would really heal her from something as serious as a bullet and kept flinching in the middle of her back as she rowed, but nothing happened. When she could feel the tug of the waves bringing them in, she slipped quietly into the water as well. They turned the boat sideways to provide more room for them to hide behind it and let the current bring them into the surf. It wasn't a violent beach like the ones she knew from home, where the waves crashed and threw the cold foam dozens of feet in the air, with sharp rocks underneath. There was nowhere to hide on a beach of small, gentle waves coming into soft white sand.

At last, they couldn't hide anymore; the gradual slope had brought them to the shallows, and they had to stand. A voice came over the sand toward them, shouting for them to surrender and drop their weapons. No one but Aili understood what the voice said.

The marine went first, running ahead onto the beach to meet the ragged, dark-haired figures that converged out of the trees, shooting carefully. One of the figures fell onto the white sand and didn't move again. The marine also fell, bleeding heavily and moaning. Someone from the land side came and looked down at him, nudged him with his foot, and then took out a long, sharp knife and cut his throat.

Aili looked at the blood pouring onto the sand and listened to the voices of the Kunorese, who were trying to decide whether to shoot the remaining people or take them prisoner.

"Don't shoot," she said to the others in the raft, then yelled out, "Don't shoot us! We're medical personnel." She was only half-aware that she was speaking Kunorese.

Nora stared at her as though she were a stranger.

Aili saw it out of the corner of her eye, and her heart sank, but she continued, in Anglish, "Everyone, if you have a weapon, throw it on the ground."

Nora very slowly threw down her gun, as did two others; either no one else had a gun, or no one else was going to disarm.

The man standing across from them shouted in Kunorese, "If you are really medical personnel we will accept your unconditional surrender! Do you surrender?"

Aili looked around helplessly. "They are asking for unconditional surrender. Do we agree?" She was shocked to realize that she and Nora were actually the highest-ranking people left. The marines were dead, and the remaining men were lower-ranked pharmacists, medical assistants, or orderlies.

No one spoke.

"Nora?"

"I agree," said Nora. She didn't say anything else, like *since when do you speak Kunorese?* or *who are you?*

There was no other noise for a moment except the waves whispering into the sand. The two bodies lay on the beach in spreading red pools.

Aili suddenly remembered and called out, "Before we surrender, we need to know what happened to the other people on that raft." She pointed to the one that had been beached before they came, empty and crooked on the sand.

The man replied, "You do not need to know that, and you do not have a choice. You can surrender or be killed. If you surrender, kneel."

Nora squeezed her hand, standing next to her. Without looking at her, she whispered, "If you get back and I don't, promise me you will visit my mama and tell her what happened, ok? Nothing really bad — just that I was brave, or whatever. And that I love her."

Aili squeezed her hand in return as they knelt together, along with the other men from the raft. The Kunorese soldiers came closer, and suddenly, from somewhere behind her, Aili heard a gun cocking.

"No," she whispered, but it was too late.

Not everyone had disarmed after all.

One shot was enough to bring a barrage of return bullets from the Kunorese. The sound was simultaneously overwhelming and tiny, guns roaring, bullets whining past, and men screaming and dying everywhere, all falling into the greater silence of the endless waves.

Nora and Aili tried to stay together and take cover, but there was no cover. No safe place. Bullets flew in every direction, and in any direction they ran, they were likely to be shot before they were recognized.

"White flag," hissed Nora, but there was nothing white nearby.

Aili grabbed the first aid kit and hoisted it over her head as some kind of *don't kill us* symbol. The men who had been in the raft with them fell to the sand, one by one, and both Aili and Nora ran back toward them instinctively after all their training. Simultaneously, they crashed to their knees in the sand next to the closest groaning body. All of this felt familiar, now. Both she and Nora moved with confidence, as though it didn't make a difference whether they would be shot or not, their hands moving in sync to check pulses and look for wounds.

"Dead," said Aili, moving on to the next one. "This one's alive. Nora, do you have anything for a tourniquet?"

"Grab the dead one's belt," Nora said, and then someone yelled in Kunorese behind them.

"Here it is," said Aili, passing it over.

"Tie that tighter. I'll hold him down. You're doing ok, buddy!" Nora said encouragingly to the man gasping on the ground; his leg had been shot through the bone, just above the knee. "You're gonna be just fine."

"Do you have a scalpel? Anything sharp?" Aili asked, wanting to do something more effective, in fact literally itching to do so; in a minute she would just start biting her finger, the way she had seen the orderly do.

"Surgical kit, in the raft," Nora said. "I've got this guy. Go grab it. We'll need it."

She was back at the raft, her hand on the surgical kit, when she heard the order to execute the prisoners.

Everything seemed to happen quite slowly, then — so she could remember it well later, perhaps. She turned around and ran through the heavy sand, holding the scalpel in her hand so she could stab someone with it, or cut their throat, as she heard the first bullets.

The men on the ground were shot in the head one by one. The fourth bullet was for Nora, who was standing up now, her hands in the air to show that she was unarmed. It went through her forehead cleanly, and she fell over very, very slowly.

The soldier doing the shooting kept on working, methodically. One by one.

Aili felt something come out of her throat that was like a scream, but sound-less, because after she heard those bullets, nothing made any sounds anymore.

She slashed her hand while she ran toward Nora, who could not possibly be dead. She would heal her.

The Kunorese soldier was suddenly in her way, a gun pointed at her face. There was a loud noise and a terrible, sharp pain. For a moment, her eyes were filled with blood, and she felt herself falling, but as soon as she was on the sand, the pain was gone.

She wiped the blood out of her eyes and started crawling toward Nora. The soldier had already turned away and was looking back toward the trees, shouting in Kunorese.

But Nora — Nora was still alive. She would save Nora.

But Nora was dead.

Nora lay quietly looking up at the bright sun with blind eyes and an obscene hole in her forehead.

Shaking, Aili sprinkled some blood on the wound, on Nora's eyes and lips, but nothing happened. She looked around, dazed.

Nora was dead on the ground, but wasn't that also Nora, standing at the edge of the trees, waving at her? She was mouthing something, perhaps she was saying *goodbye*, but Aili couldn't hear it because the silence all around her was so deafening.

Nora turned around to leave.

Aili stood up, stumbled over a body on the ground. Wasn't that Nora's body?

But Nora was there, through the trees. Aili could see her leaving — she had to follow her, she couldn't let Nora go.

She felt sharp pains in her shoulder, in her leg, through her hand, but nothing that would stop her. Everything healed.

The Kunorese soldier was in her way again, eyes wild, yelling that there was a ghost, a demon. He raised his gun again; he would stop her from following Nora.

She screamed and raised her left hand — the hand covered in her own blood — and brought it down hard in the air.

A whip of fire burst out and ensnared the Kunorese soldier, who started begging for mercy, for his mother, for the pain to stop, but the fire didn't stop there. As though it had a life of its own, it scattered and sought out all the living beings it could find, Federative and Kunorese alike, and wherever it fell, they burned. Their voices clamored, a cacophony in her mind, their skin breaking, and then falling silent, one by one. She watched all of them turn and leave the beach; behind them were bundles of burned flesh.

She knelt by one of them, her hands shaking, and slashed her hand again and again, deeper and deeper, blood spurting all over the body on the sand. Her hand continued to heal, but the blackened corpse in front of her would not move.

A red bird fluttered to the ground in front of her.

She heard the orderly's voice: "Stop. They're dead. There's nothing you can do for them now. You'll only weaken yourself if you keep trying."

Aili screamed, not knowing whether it was with her body or her mind. The red bird hopped closer. The orderly's voice was very slow, very calm. The golden eyes looked into hers steadily.

"You need to get away from here. Follow me."

Like a sleepwalker, she followed the red bird as it flew inland toward the mountain at the island's core. The undergrowth was thick, and there were still bullets flying. The red bird flew ahead of her but had to keep returning as she was hit and stumbled, or had to push through vines and undergrowth. When the slope became steeper, she simply knelt down and stopped moving.

The red bird landed in front of her, shimmered, and became the orderly. Aili watched this happen dully and without interest. The orderly looked at her, frowning, and reached out to touch her wrist with two fingers. She flinched back.

"Ok, let's rest. You need to recover. You've used a lot of power." He sat down with his legs crossed, feet on his thighs. "Can you cultivate?"

"What do you mean?" she asked.

The orderly said, "Cultivate. It means to gather spiritual power. You'll recover more quickly if you know how."

"I don't understand."

"Ok, ok then," he said. "Just be quiet for now and rest."

She hadn't been resting for more than fifteen minutes when she said, "I have a lot of questions."

"I'm sure you do." He unfolded his legs and sighed. "I also have a lot of questions, so I may not have answers for you, but go ahead."

"Where's Tairei?"

He choked. "Tairei?"

"She...she..." Aili swallowed. "Liu Chenguang?"

"I can't believe..." The orderly shook his head, smiling a little bit. "That person. Tairei. All right, if she's Tairei you should call me Tainu."

"Elder martial brother," Aili said automatically, and then stopped. They had been speaking Daxian; she hadn't even noticed.

Tainu cleared his throat. "Tairei is most likely in the spirit realm. That's where we go when we are reborn."

"Start that over and explain to me what it means."

"Got it." Tainu smiled gently, encouraging. "You know, in ten thousand years, I've never actually needed to explain this to anyone?"

Aili stared at him.

"Tairei and I, we are spiritual creatures," he said. "Our natural home is in the spirit realm, and when we go through rebirth we return there, but it's a very dangerous place, since we can't defend ourselves–"

"What do you mean, rebirth? You can't defend yourself? What about the fire?"

He shook his head. "That fire...we can't control it. It only comes at our time of rebirth, and all we can do is try to contain it — time it so it comes when we're in a good place, away from mortal beings that can be hurt. Normally, we enter rebirth fire every thousand years or so."

Aili looked at him, stunned. She decided to let go of the thousand years and focus on what she had done. "But I...I used that fire to..."

"I know," he replied. "I saw it. But that's nothing that we can do. What you did, using the fire to attack...we can't do that."

He watched her and waited for her response, but there was none. "You're not quite like us, but I don't know what all the differences are yet. You seem to have the gift of languages, like us, and you can heal yourself and others, like us. You can use weapons, unlike us, you can produce the rebirth fire as a weapon. That's completely strange. We can't use weapons at all. I couldn't even slap someone if I tried– Well, watch." He leaned over toward her, very quickly, and swung his fist toward her face.

It was as though a strong breeze had picked him up and spun him around, away from her. She felt the wind of his hand passing her cheek. He laughed; his laughter, like his voice, was warm and kind, and she felt herself soothed in spite of everything.

"So, our self-defense abilities are very limited. We can block, but we can't make any aggressive moves toward any living being. Basically, we can run, and when we transform, we can fly." Tainu transformed again into the red bird, then back. "Those are my two forms here in the mortal realm. The mortal body, we call it. In the spirit realm, my transformation is a bit different. That's my true body. So my next question for you is, can you transform?" He looked at her expectantly.

She stared back. "How?"

"You just...do it." He did it — man to bird and back again. "Just, you know, think about it, and it will happen?"

64

She stared at him some more. "That's it?"

"Just your intention should do it...?"

She gave it some intention. Nothing happened.

"Well, maybe there's something I'm missing, but let's assume that you can't transform for now. That may make it difficult for you to enter the gate I'm thinking of. We'll have to just see."

"What's the gate?"

"Phoenix gates are gates of pure fire. Fire without mortal intention. There's sky fire, lightning or wildfires started by lightning; earth fire, volcanoes; and spirit fire. That's our rebirth fire. Entering the pure fire allows us to enter the spirit realm."

Aili looked up the slope. She couldn't see the top of the mountain from where they were. "Are you saying you're taking me into a volcano?"

"That's all I can think of," he said, spreading his hands. "I'm a few centuries away from rebirth fire right now and this place seems too damp for wildfires, even if some lightning were to hit. But there's a volcano here. Very handy."

She nodded. She still felt dazed and sick, and when she remembered Nora's dead face, the fire burning and the screams in her mind, and the sharp pain of the gunshots that should have killed her, she had to flinch away inwardly and not think about it anymore. Nothing made sense, and so going into a volcano with an orderly who turned into a red bird seemed perfectly fine and sensible.

But Tairei...Tairei would make sense of everything, if she could find Tairei then all this would be fixed somehow. "And then we'll see Tairei?"

"Well, it depends on where the gate brings us in the spirit realm, but once we're there, I'll be able to take you to her. Of course, it will take longer if you can't transform. We'll have to walk." He added, "Keep in mind she may look different when we find her. After rebirth, we spend some time as children in the spirit realm, we need that time to culti– to gather power for our adulthood. It's a very dangerous time for us, so hopefully she's already gotten to a refuge. Normally, we'd also change our mortal body after rebirth, but knowing her," he rolled his eyes, "she'll have kept the one she met you in."

"Why?"

Tainu asked, surprised, "You don't know?"

"No," Aili said, suddenly angry. "I don't know. I don't understand what's happening." She felt her eyes tear up. "Why did Tairei– why– this is the part you have to explain most."

"This is the part I can't explain most," Tainu said. "I can't, Aili. Tairei needs to explain things to you."

65

His voice was so final that she reluctantly nodded.

"All right," he said. "Now, you. You obviously were not born a phoenix—"

"A phoenix?"

"That's what we're called," he said patiently. "What happened to make you... like this?"

She tried to explain and Tainu listened, quietly, his eyes growing larger and larger.

Finally, he held up his hand. "Go back," he said. "So she met you only a few weeks ago?"

"Yes."

"And you told her that you were about to leave and go into a war zone without weapons or combat training?"

"Yes, I told her that because that's what was happening," she said.

Tainu swore quietly and put his hand over his eyes.

"What is it?" she asked. "What's wrong?"

"All right," he said, breathing out. "I don't think that she was likely able to make good decisions. Let's put it that way." He shook his head and stood up. "You seem to have gotten some energy back. Let's keep going. Just...when you see her, be kind. That's the most important thing."

"Why would I not be kind?" she said, getting to her feet as well.

"I don't know." He turned to walk up the pathless mountainside. "I just know she can very easily be hurt by you. That's all. Everything she did, no matter whether it was good or bad, just remember that she's very...vulnerable. To you in particular."

Tainu muttered to himself every time they got stuck in vines or mudholes, which happened fairly frequently, and they were both scratched and bitten by insects and snakes, which was annoying but, for them, not dangerous. They didn't have to go all the way to the top of the crater. Tainu led her into a deep crack in the side of the mountain, which rapidly grew hotter and hotter. It opened up deep in the volcano's core. Up above, Aili could crane her neck and see a misshapen circle of blue sky, deepening now toward sunset. Below, very far below, she could see a trace of red light. Both of them could feel the heat and smell the sulfur and acid. Aili coughed once; Tainu just looked down.

"This is where it would be helpful for you to transform," he said, after a little bit of staring into the abyss and thinking. "Try again?"

She tried. Nothing.

"Ok, well, we'll have to work with what we have, then." He looked at her closely, as though weighing her. "Are you afraid of heights?"

She shrugged. "Doesn't seem like it."

"All right. This is as close as I've been able to find to get us to the actual pure fire. I can fly down. I'll do that and hover above the fire. You just jump, and when you get down there I'll fly in front to take you through the gate."

"Jump," Aili said flatly. She couldn't even see the bottom of the hole.

"It won't kill you," he said helpfully. "Even if you can't get through the gate and just hit the magma, I'll be there to heal you."

"How exactly are you going to drag me out of the magma? You're the size of a large sparrow."

Tainu didn't seem to be insulted. "Well, I'll figure something out. I can get bigger if I need to. Just don't bother, usually...The transformations do take quite a bit of spiritual power."

Aili looked at the bottomless hole. "'It won't kill you' isn't all that reassuring. And are you sure it won't?"

"Well, no," he said. "I don't know how much power you have, if you have the same kind of healing ability we do, or if you're still mortal really. I'm not even sure you can get through the gate. It's all trial and error. There's no manual, you know."

She hesitated at the edge. "No manual?"

"It's not like somebody gave us an instruction booklet. We just figure things out as we go."

"All right then." She took a few steps back, ran, and threw herself over the side.

Tainu yelled, "Idiot! Wait, we have to time it!" He ran for the edge and jumped, transforming as he fell.

CHAPTER 6
SPIRIT REALM

THERE WAS A valley of gold, and in the valley was a tree. The gold was like ocean waves, and when the wind blew it made a sound like distant music.

The tree was enormous, towering up to the sky, with leaves of deep golden-red. At its foot was a small woman with lightly tanned skin, shoulder-length black hair and black eyes, and great feathered wings the color of the tree's leaves. She sat still at the foot of the tree in a lotus position, her eyes downcast and her body unmoving, but the wings seemed to be awkward for her, not obeying; fluttering around, stretching, as though they were uncomfortable.

A man flickered into being at the top of one of the golden hills, blue-eyed and brown-haired, and walked down steadily toward her, his handsome face decorated with a broad smile. When he passed through the golden grass, something seemed to be moving underneath it, as though the land was like water and he was not walking on it, but wading through it. At the foot of the tree, however, as the grass grew short, his feet were moving quite normally. He, too, dropped into a lotus position, but he held his face in his hands and grinned at the woman cheerfully.

Finally, she opened her eyes and looked at him.

"Hello!" he said, delighted.

She closed her eyes again.

"It's lovely to see you, Liu Chenguang," he said. "You remember me, don't you?"

She ignored him.

"How about this?" he said. His body seemed to waver and shift as though seen through a heat mirage, and instead of a tall blue-eyed man, there was a smaller man, pale features extraordinarily perfect, with sharp black eyes and long black hair partly bound up with a jade pin. This man wore long robes with wide sleeves made of deep green silk, layered with inner robes of contrasting colors, and closed with a wide, embroidered sash.

He fell back into the lotus position again. "That's much more comfortable, I have to say. I've been wearing an illusion enchantment for a while now. It gets old."

She still ignored him.

"Do you still hold it against me?"

She kept her eyes closed. "Zhu Guiren, whatever you did to me is long done. It's not as though I'm a mortal, you couldn't actually kill me."

"So, no hard feelings then?"

She got up, flicked her wings, and started walking away from him.

In amazement, he asked, "Are those things really just to look at?"

"Shut up."

"Was this really your plan? Reunite with that person, and then this? You're here in this bizarre form…doing what? Sulking? Meditating? Waiting to meet me?"

"Get away from me."

"Or you'll do what, exactly, phoenix? Bleed on me?" He snorted.

She stopped at the edge of the grass, where it started to grow long, and fluttered the wings again, but nothing happened. Then, the wings disappeared.

She turned around, came back to the foot of the tree, and started climbing.

Zhu Guiren put his chin back in his hand, his eyes following her. "You're kidding."

Liu Chenguang found a sturdy branch about twenty feet above the ground and resumed her lotus position. He leapt up after her, light as a feather, and sat opposite her.

Her eyes snapped open. "What do you want, demon?"

He held his hand up. "Just to talk," he said, seriously. "That's all. I'm curious. Or I'm bored. However you want to think about it, really. Done is done, right? That's what you phoenixes say."

"Done is done," she recited, "and pain is pain." She closed her eyes again, and the demon fell silent.

After a while, she said, "You're right, my plan was pathetic to start with and it didn't go very well. So if you need to know, demon, I am actually in quite a lot of pain right now and would like you to go away and leave me in it, because you are definitely not helping. Capture me if you want to capture me. Otherwise, leave me be."

Zhu Guiren looked at her body carefully. "I don't see any wounds."

She snorted. "It's not that kind of pain."

The demon put his head to one side. "I know, I'm just messing with you. Demons feel pain too, you know. But it's only physical, for us. Did you know that?"

"I can honestly say I have never given any thought to the feelings of demons."

Zhu Guiren laughed. "That's a little unfair, isn't it? You know that unlike you, I can actually die. Surely my pain should be of interest to you? At least as much as a mortal's?"

Below them, an invisible sun was setting. The sky changed from azure to emerald, then to a deep green, nearly black. The golden grass started waving on its own; the music it made now sounded rather sinister.

The demon stood up, lightly balancing on the tree branch. "What's your plan, phoenix? Shouldn't you have gone to a refuge by now?"

"I can't," she admitted reluctantly. "I can't transform, and I can't fly, and I can't sense where the refuges and gates are."

"Wow," he said flatly. "This plan of yours is of truly legendary proportions. Just because I'm bored, I'll keep you alive overnight."

He leapt down to the ground and took up a guarding position at the foot of the tree. As the night became complete, the woman in the tree could hear a hissing sound coming closer, weaving through the grass toward him.

He was unconcerned. "Liu Chenguang," he called, "while I'm taking care of this little vermin problem we have, why don't you make a better plan?"

But the woman in the tree did not answer. She leaned back against the bark, perfectly balanced, her eyes closed. In the light that flashed through the leaves from something that was like a star, but not quite, her face shone with tears.

As she fell, Aili felt a strange sense of exhilaration. It was only a few seconds, but there was nothing to worry about now; everything that could be done had been done. Her brothers were gone, Nora was gone, her father was gone. Falling was as though she was leaving it all behind. All her life, done and undone. It was behind her now.

The heat started to crisp her clothes and hair. Next to her a red bird dove with folded wings like a falcon, its head stretched toward the fire below them. The bird flicked its wings and suddenly was directly ahead of her, below her, falling at a constant speed that matched hers; she could have reached out and grabbed the scarlet tail feathers.

"Don't," said Tainu's voice. He sounded strained, as though he couldn't manage anymore. The wings of the bird stretched very carefully against the blistering wind, very slightly outspread, bit by bit; they started to catch fire, first a flow of individual sparks, then a rush of golden-white flame that surrounded her with a comfortable warmth, as though she were enclosed in the tail of a comet.

The molten rock beneath them rushed closer and closer, the heat incredible, and then suddenly, everything around them was black.

Aili spilled out onto something hot and spiky in bright sunlight, a red bird zipping up into the air above her as she rolled and tried to catch her breath. Behind her, she saw a glowing ring in the air — an outline of white-hot fire that immediately faded away.

"Get up, get up, get up!" The bird swooped back down, trying to grab her by the hair, but she managed to stand on her own and wave her hand in the air.

"What's going on?"

"Run! Follow me!"

Running. That, she could do. She pounded behind the red bird at top speed, breathing evenly to keep herself focused. "Where– are– we– going?"

"There."

The only thing she could see that was "there" was a line of hills in the distance.

They were not close.

She kept her breath measured for running and turned around only once.

Behind them was a line of shadow like a wave on the ocean, and like foam on the ocean, there were bits that were flying and reaching out ahead. Some of these bits, in the split second she had to see, seemed to have faces, but the faces were all alike, and all monstrous. Whatever this thing was, it was one being, not many. The faces had eyes and noses, but no mouths; the mouth was the wave itself, growing higher and higher behind them.

Never turn your back on the ocean, she thought, panicked.

Aili dug her toes into the earth, which felt like deep sand dragging her down even though it looked like ordinary golden grass. The grass ahead of her got longer, and she realized it wasn't quite ordinary. It was as sharp as razors. As the grass blades slashed through her uniform pants and the skin of her legs, her blood spattered all over them. They made a gleeful, high-pitched laughing noise. Her skin healed immediately, but the slashing continued, and she started to feel a tingling in her muscles.

She couldn't tell if the wave was catching up. Instead of looking, she put her head down and ran for her life.

Before they reached the distant hills, they started to pass boulders — first, small ones, then larger and larger, some as large as houses. They reminded her of the standing stones near her home, set into the gentle hills without rhyme or reason, but these were a crystalline blue, not the rough, gray rock she was familiar with. The red bird swooped off to the left, and she followed it, but now they were running parallel to the wave and it immediately took advantage. The smallest bits of shadow were splashing near her feet when she saw the red bird perch on a single blue rock straight ahead.

"Get in, get in! Just keep running without stopping!"

The crystal face loomed up in front of her and she ran full-tilt into it, not even taking time to wonder what it would feel like to smash her skull on a rock. Suddenly she was surrounded by a dim, filtered light. The red bird landed beside her, transforming into Tainu's tall form. He still wore the uniform of an orderly, torn and dirty, gray and ragged against his warm, brown skin. He looked down at himself in distaste, picking at his collar with two fingers.

"Ugh," he said. He took a deep breath. "Well, we made it."

Aili bent over, gasping, to catch her breath before looking around. "Why– why were you worried?" she asked at last. "I thought we can't die?"

"I don't know about you, to be honest. You're a special case." Tainu stretched, and then went toward the back of the room where there was a standing wardrobe; he reached into it and started rummaging around. "Thank goodness, there's some stuff to change into here…"

He came out with a dark blue tunic and trousers and casually started unbuttoning his shirt.

"Do you want some privacy?" Aili asked. "To change?"

"Eh, it's ok, you're not my type," he said. "You should change too. Here." He tossed her another tunic and leggings. "It'll be loose on you and tight on me, but at least it doesn't stink."

Aili realized that her clothes were not only ripped, but also stiff with blood — her own and others' — and she couldn't get them off fast enough. She found that with the opportunity to get something clean on, she didn't particularly care about privacy either. With clean clothes, even in such a bizarre situation, came some ability to think.

"Who put this stuff here?" she asked. "Is it for…phoenixes? Do people stock this like a rest station?"

"I have no idea," Tainu said. "Probably not phoenixes. We don't do long-term planning, and we're not here that often. This is someone's house. We shouldn't stay that long."

"This is what now?" Aili looked around, instantly uncomfortable.

"Some spirit being's home. There are a lot of beings that belong here. Plenty of them never enter the mortal realm at all. It's not interesting or needful for them."

"Don't they…lock their doors?"

"Not well enough to keep me out, luckily," he said. "I know a few ways to break a ward. It's not my first time with this, believe me."

"Ok," she said, "fine. But before we leave, what was that thing?"

"There are a lot of dangers here. And to answer your previous question, I don't know what your situation is, and I guess we won't know unless sometime in the future, you can't be healed from an injury. But for phoenixes, in the mortal realm, we can't truly be killed. If we have an injury we can't heal from, we'll be reborn. That's how it is for us. In the spirit realm, though, death is death for us. This is our home, and our bodies here are versions of our true bodies, no matter what we might look like. There are beings here that hunt phoenixes. That's why—"

"Hunt you? Why?"

"For power." He shrugged. "It's not like they tell me their reasons. Anyway, that's why the period of childhood is very dangerous for us, because we have to spend it in the spirit realm. And *that*," he added, linking his hands and cracking his knuckles, "is why there are refuges with strong wards to protect phoenixes after rebirth. I'm hoping that Tairei is in one of them by now."

He closed his eyes and whispered something under his breath.

"What?"

"Quiet," he said, and whispered again. He turned his head from side to side, as though listening carefully, and then nodded. "She's here. In that direction, over those hills."

"Aren't we going to be chased again when we get out?" she asked.

"This is why we normally fly," he admitted. "I don't have a lot of solutions, aside from flying. On the other hand, though, I don't think you're as defenseless as I am. Let's experiment."

He rummaged through another wardrobe, then a chest in a back corner.

"Aha!" Tainu took out a long, thin piece of metal. It took Aili a moment to realize that it was a sword.

"There you go!"

"You are…you're serious? I can't use a sword."

"Sure you can. I believe in you!" He grinned widely.

Gamely, she hefted the sword, which was surprisingly heavy, and gave it an awkward swoosh through the air. It clanged sadly down on the stone floor.

Tainu laughed and patted her gently on the shoulder. "There you go. Remember, the end of this is that you get to see Tairei again, right? Just give it your best shot. Anything that comes near us, attack them."

She lifted the sword awkwardly in her right hand; her wrist ached briefly. "Can't I just hit them with fire again?"

"No idea. Feel free to give that a try too. I'll ride on your shoulder and fly away if anything comes."

Aili had to laugh. "Are you and Tairei really the same kind of thing?"

"We're siblings," he said, slightly insulted.

He took her hand, muttered something under his breath, and pulled her through the wall of the crystal boulder again. On the other side, he briefly turned and bowed toward the stone and murmured something again. He held his hands together with his fingers bent in odd positions, then clapped them together.

"What's that?" she asked. "I didn't understand it."

"Really?" he said. "That's interesting. It's our native language. We only use it for spells and blessings. Anyway, that was just my giving payment for what we took. I put a spell of safety on the house and its inhabitants. It will warn them of danger for the next quarter cycle."

Tainu turned back and held his hand over his eyes, squinting at the hills, golden against a brilliant green sky. "We're lucky, the sun just rose when we arrived. We have a whole day to make progress. I think we'll find her in less than a week. Doesn't feel like she's that far…although I've never walked before, so I guess I'm not a good judge of distance…" He shrugged. "Well, off we go." He transformed and flew up to her shoulder.

They trudged up the hills, the crystalline blue rocks poking up from the golden grass around them, and then, were surrounded by only rocks as though they had passed some kind of tree line. It wasn't cold — in fact, it was quite hot, the sun's reflection off the crystalline faces enough to burn — but Aili couldn't shake the idea that she *should* be cold, surrounded by these lumps of what looked like glaciers.

When she turned back near the top of the first peak, she could see the golden plain spreading out beneath them, shot through with rivers. At least, she assumed they were rivers, although they were colors she had never previously associated with water; one seemed to be just a ribbon of fog, and another one to be made of sparkling lights. She blinked and rubbed her eyes.

She turned back to the path to see Tainu looking closely at her, now in a human form. "I've never seen a mortal here before," he said abruptly. "I don't know how it will affect you. Are you all right?"

"No," she said. "But I don't think that's really about the spirit world."

Tainu walked next to her for a while. "We're unlikely to meet much here. The high peaks aren't home to any malicious beings. It's only if we were very unlucky and a demon flies right over us."

She nodded and kept walking.

"Your friend died," Tainu said. "Wasn't that your friend? The one on the beach that you were trying to heal the others with?"

"Yes," she said. "Nora."

"I'm sorry," he said, "about her death. You should know that there's probably nothing you could have done. Even if you were ready to heal immediately, with a wound of that kind, she was probably dead before…before you could have done anything. Even before I could have done anything, if that makes you feel any better."

"Why did you lead us there?" she asked.

"I didn't know that there were people on the island that would attack you," he replied sadly. "I should have thought of it, but I'm not omniscient. I just wanted to guide you to land, and there wasn't any other land."

She didn't answer for a while. Then, she said, "I was shot in the forehead too, but I'm still alive."

"Tairei somehow gave you that protection, I think," Tainu said, "for just such a reason. In case she wasn't there to heal you in time. It seems as though you have the same self-healing ability as a phoenix. So, at least in the mortal realm you probably can't die."

"Is that something that happens a lot? Are there other people like me?"

"No," he replied. "I don't know how Tairei did it. There's no one like you."

That phrase seemed to echo in her mind a bit; she shook her head to clear it.

"I wish I had something to carry this in," she said, irritated at the awkward weight of the sword. She had to carry it slightly away from her body so she didn't slice herself by accident, which was annoying and had already happened several times.

They had started to descend from the peak now, and it seemed as though the mountain range was really only one ridge deep. Below spread another golden plain, this one dotted with more forests. The leaves of the trees were dark purple and black, sometimes shimmering with iridescent blue.

"Why did Tairei come to me?" she asked at last.

Tainu answered with a question: "Were you happy to see her?"

She thought about it — the very first time, when she saw her in the bar, and then in the alley afterward. It had been so fast. Mostly, she remembered Tairei's eyes: such beautiful eyes, smiling at her, shining.

"Not happy, exactly," she said. "More that I couldn't turn away from her. I only felt...I needed to be near her."

"Well, you can assume it was similar for her," Tainu said, after a long pause. They had come down into a copse of trees, threaded by a brook that threw off bits of lightning. Some of the trees were scorched. "Can you run and jump that? There won't be a bridge."

She nodded, backed up, and started running, while Tainu transformed and flew to the other side. Just as she leapt, something landed on her from above, screeching.

Aili rolled to one side to avoid falling into the lightning stream. The thing was not feathered; it was more like a snake, about ten feet long, but with multiple tails and heads. It must have been waiting in the tree branches over them. One head buried its fangs in her shoulder, while several of the tails wrapped around her legs so that she was immobilized except for one arm.

Luckily, this was her sword arm.

Her body seemed to know what to do. Aili reversed the sword and stabbed down toward her own body, impaling the thing beneath her bitten shoulder where its belly lay against her back. It shrieked and sent another head to bite her sword hand, but she tore and ripped at its torso until it let go and fell to the ground. She jumped up and slashed out at a head.

"No!" shouted Tainu, who was sitting on a branch.

It was too late. The head was gone, and the thing grew two heads in its place.

"Are you kidding me?" she yelled.

"Throw it in the stream!" he shouted back.

"How am I supposed to pick it up?" The heads were all coming for her now, and the thing was obviously annoyed. Where she had torn at its belly, something thick and bright was coming out; wherever it dripped, there was a hissing noise and the ground turned black.

"Don't let the blood touch you!"

This also came a little late, but after all, she would heal. She spun in the air, came down, and slashed again, this time at the main trunk of the body. She had a sense that there was something else she should be doing — something more effective than a sword, but what else could there be? She certainly didn't have a gun.

"This sword is terrible! Tainu, I need a different sword–"

Immediately, Aili wondered where that had come from. She froze. "I don't know how to use a sword," she said, bewildered, looking at her hand holding the sword as though it knew what it was doing. "Why– what–"

The creature slithered forward to bite her again; Tainu came down to beat his wings in the thing's face, distracting it, but it seemed that was all he could do. He baited it to follow him, coming dangerously close to the fanged mouths and darting back, tempting it closer to the stream.

When she saw what he was doing, she understood. Aili waited for the right moment to rush forward, then gave it a powerful kick, leaping to twist in the air and strike with both feet.

Of course, it was far too big to be affected, far too heavy, but somehow it seemed as though her body had more power than it logically should. The thing *flew* from her strike and landed in the lightning, shrieking and burning.

Tainu fluttered to her shoulder. "Run," he said, and she did.

"How did I do that?" she asked, fitting the words into the rhythm of her running. "Fight like that?"

Tainu flew slightly ahead of her. He didn't answer until she slowed down, in an open area again. "This isn't really safer," he said. "We need to keep going. I need to get us both in a refuge or under a strong ward by nightfall."

Aili stood stock still. "Tell me. Tell me why I can use a sword. That's not from Tairei. She can't use weapons, she told me."

"I promise you, you'll understand everything soon, Aili," Tainu said urgently, "but the sun is setting. We don't have time. The night is more dangerous. We can find Tairei as long as we're able to stay safe. She's not far. She'll explain it to you. I can't. I really can't do it."

Aili stood there, watching the sun near the horizon, paralyzed. "For a minute," she said slowly, "while I was fighting, I felt like I was someone else. Not like someone was taking over my body, but like I didn't know who I was. That I'm a stranger. To myself."

He didn't answer.

She looked at him, and asked, "What is it? Why is this happening to me?"

"Don't think about it now," he said. "You need to survive now. To get to Tairei. Just think about that."

He transformed back into a person, and cautiously put his hand on her shoulder. "Aili, I'm doing my very best to help you. I don't think it will help you to think about this much now. Can you help me help you? Can you just focus on getting through these next few days, and don't let those questions occupy your mind?"

She didn't answer. Of course she could. She was very good at drawing glass over the truth. She took a deep breath and said, "All right," and they continued walking toward the forest.

When the sun rose, Tairei was still alive. Day after day after day.

Each morning, Tairei woke up and started walking aimlessly through the world. She had found clothes right after coming through the phoenix gate at rebirth, a loose shirt that her wings ripped holes in the first time she tried to transform, and loose trousers that came halfway up her calves. Since she wasn't that tall for a mortal, clearly they had belonged to something rather small before she invaded their home and found them. She couldn't find a refuge, she couldn't fly, she couldn't rest or feel safe. She couldn't even cultivate, because she needed to sit still to cultivate, and every day, she had to keep walking.

Unfortunately, she didn't have the privilege of walking alone.

"What are you looking for?" the demon asked one day, following behind her as he always did.

Tairei shrugged. "A way back to the mortal world." *I need to find Aili*, she added inwardly, but didn't share this with the demon. She was much more worried about Aili than herself, even though she was so unexpectedly crippled after rebirth. What had happened to Aili? Had she been able to protect Aili, was she still alive? Had anything she had done borne fruit at all?

"I can help you with that," Zhu Guiren offered unexpectedly. "We have our own gates, and I can take you through."

"I don't want your help," she said, and walked faster. She said this even though she knew in her heart she would already be dead or captured without his protection. The dangers of the spirit realm for phoenixes were insurmountable without the protection of a refuge. Nonetheless, having him near her and hearing that smirk in his voice made her want to scream in disgust and fury. It was exhausting to hate someone so much.

When it came right down to it, she didn't understand his motivation to protect her. She didn't know what his plan was this time, and she absolutely didn't trust him anywhere near Aili. Taking him back to the mortal realm with her would be even more of a mistake than doing...what she'd already done.

The demon caught up to walk next to her. She walked further away.

"Listen," he said, "there's a demonic gate not far from here. It's not one I control personally, but I can get you through, no problem."

She shrugged. "Stop talking. I don't want to hear your voice or see your face, Zhu Guiren." She tried to transform again, and the wings came back. That was it. She stood still and beat them heavily; they made an impressive wind, and that was all. No flying.

"They do look pretty, though," Zhu Guiren said in a faux-complimentary voice.

"Shut up," she said automatically. She transformed back again. The wings were heavy despite their total uselessness. It was easier to walk without them.

"You know," he said, trailing behind her again, "someone with less self-confidence than myself might be put off by your unfriendliness."

"Zhu Guiren, what were your last words to me?" She whirled around, enraged.

He didn't have the grace to look ashamed. "I believe I said something along the lines of 'don't be so trusting next time.'"

She clenched her fists at her side and turned around again so she wouldn't have to look at his smirking face. "Please just kill me. It would be better than having you follow me and talk to me. I can't wait to find a refuge and get inside it and keep you out."

"Well, live in hope, then. If I don't kill you something certainly will unless you find one of your precious refuges."

"Being a demon must be really boring, you really have nothing better to do than this. How shocking that you have no friends."

"Who needs friends? I just need entertainment, and here you are providing."

She kept walking, determined not to answer him anymore. Every few hours, though, he managed to get a rise out of her.

I hate the spirit world. I never really realized it before.

She hadn't had an uncomplicated rebirth for the last three cycles. Before the current disaster, the last time was...Her mind quickly shied away from remembering. In any case, she had left as soon as she attained spiritual adulthood, which she'd done as quickly as possible by cultivating nonstop. She hadn't wanted to risk missing that person's return. The time before that, she'd been driven out by demons chasing her before she found a refuge. She'd still been in child-hood when she fled into the mortal realm. And then…

There were too many memories. Yet, after eight thousand years, the memories that mattered were only Hong Deming.

That night, she managed to find another world-tree and climb high enough to avoid any grounded predators. Zhu Guiren spent his evenings guarding from climbers. So far they hadn't met anything winged. So far, she'd been lucky.

She settled into the lotus position and began to cultivate, but her mind was distracted: Aili's face the last moment she had seen it, as she dissolved into the fire of rebirth, her blood mingling with Aili's. Aili looked so terrified. Even Hong Deming had never known what she was, and Deming had known her for years. She had forced Aili into knowing so much, so fast, but she had seemed able to handle it. Aili never seemed surprised or shocked, even when they were attacked, even when she healed her. Surely that meant that, at some level, she remembered? Surely it wasn't all gone? Surely that person still…cared? Would still want to see her, whenever they were reunited again?

Zhu Guiren called up from the base of the tree, "Do you not ever need to eat? I'm hungry."

"I don't need to eat yet. I'm cultivating," she said. "There's some fruit up on the higher branches."

The demon leapt up. "For the record," he said, as he touched his feet to her branch and flew past her to a higher one, "I do not particularly care for fruit."

"Hurray." She had no idea what demons normally ate when they weren't pretending to be human. Phoenixes weren't food for demons; demons captured phoenixes for other reasons. She assumed, however, that typical demon fare was disgusting because demons were so generally awful.

"Tairei?" called a familiar voice.

Her head jerked up, and she leapt down from the tree in one bound. *"Aili?"* she half-whispered.

Aili was there, wearing something she must have found in the spirit realm. Her dark gold hair was down in one thick braid, lying over her shoulder, and she was carrying a sword, of all things. There was blood on her clothing. She looked…nervous?

"Aili," she whispered again, and threw herself forward, wrapping her arms around Aili's body and nestling her head against her shoulder. She felt Aili's arms come around her uncertainly, and gently pat her back, as though she wasn't quite sure she wanted to do this.

But it was enough. Aili was here, she was alive, she could feel her heart beating. Tairei closed her eyes and pressed harder.

"What happened to you?" came another familiar voice.

She looked up to see her sibling frowning at her and smiled, overjoyed.

"You can call me Tainu, by the way," he said.

She couldn't help snorting with laughter before she buried her head in Aili's shoulder again. She hugged her harder to be sure she was real. Her sibling had brought Aili through the gate somehow. He had known; he had helped as he always did. Aili wasn't responding to her touch, but that was all right. As long as she was here, as long as she was safe, it was all the best it could be.

"You can thank yourself for that," Tainu continued. "Tairei? Really?"

"It– it seemed...funny?" she said at last.

He shook his head. "Why aren't you in a refuge? How are you surviving–"

Zhu Guiren leapt down from his high branch, a red fruit in his hand and another in his mouth. He smiled. "That would be me."

He moved to Tainu's side, almost too fast to see, and held a knife against his cheek. The knife looked as though it were made of ice, and he carefully drew it down against Tainu's throat. "Shall we play, little phoenix?"

Tainu turned quickly, grabbed his wrist, and stabbed the knife at Zhu Guiren's throat in return. It shattered into a glittering, powdered dust before it grazed his skin.

"Well played!" said Zhu Guiren. "Phoenixes certainly are evolving these days."

Tainu looked him up and down, his expression furious. "Leave my sibling alone. How dare you even come near after what you did?"

The demon raised an eyebrow. "Have we met? I don't see why it's your business, phoenix."

"Do you have no shame at all?"

"Not really," he said, and bit his red fruit so the juice ran down his chin. "Why do you ask?"

"Get away from my sibling," said Tainu flatly.

Zhu Guiren smiled and began eating his second fruit. "Make me."

Tainu turned away from him and began walking. "Tairei? Let's go."

Aili had frozen, staring at Zhu Guiren, and begun to shake uncontrollably.

Tairei tried to hold her still and keep her from collapsing. "Get him away from her," she said through clenched teeth.

Zhu Guiren strolled over and placed himself directly in front of Aili's gaze, still eating his fruit. Tainu leapt in front of him to try to block Aili's view, but Zhu Guiren just kept circling, looking her up and down.

He bit the red fruit again. "What did you do to this one? Apparently, you're the only one who really appreciates me, Hong Deming."

Aili's eyes rolled back in her head, and she fell to the ground.

CHAPTER 7
RED BIRD

AILI FELT TAIREI's arms around her back, Tairei's head pressed just beneath her shoulder so hard Aili had trouble getting her breath. Maybe there were other reasons she wasn't getting her breath. Tairei looked just the same — not different at all, only tired and sad — and it seemed as though all Tairei wanted was to hold her and say her name.

Aili didn't know what she wanted.

She cautiously put her hands around Tairei in return, awkwardly patting her back as though to comfort her. Tairei held tighter. Aili gathered herself to try to say something, anything, as she carefully lay her hands flat along Tairei's shoulder blades, touching her with her fingertips and then the palms of her hands, feeling her warmth and the contours of her body underneath a shirt that seemed very thin — and had shockingly huge holes in it, she realized just as her fingers reached inside and brushed against Tairei's smooth skin. Both of them jumped a little bit, and Aili snatched her hand back immediately and looked up.

There was someone else there now. Someone looking at them.

This person walked toward her, talking, but she couldn't hear the words. There was a rush in her ears like the ocean waves crashing on the rocky shore that drowned everything else out, a violent and unstoppable current. The person was a Daxian man in old-fashioned, storybook clothing — handsome, with perfect, jewel-like features and dark eyes, his black hair falling smoothly down toward the small of his back. He was smiling in a friendly way as he talked soundlessly, but her heart contracted around that hot, stabbing spike, and pain ripped through the space behind her eyes.

Tairei was trying to talk to her too; she could see Tairei's expression growing more and more frightened, her own body shaking uncontrollably even though Tairei's hands were now on her shoulders, trying to hold her still, hard enough to bruise. The ocean waves grew louder and louder. Tainu moved in front of her, but she could still see the man's face.

Through the sound of the waves beating on the continental shelf, endless and imperative, she heard two words.

Hong Deming, the man said.

Everything became silent.

"Hong Deming!"

He looked up from where he was counting his arrows. "I've got four left," he said obediently.

His older martial brother, Shen Lu, shook his head. "We've got to get more than this. Taiqian will scold us."

The two of them were out in the snow, supposedly practicing their archery skills, but they also needed to bring back some food to the camp. It wasn't enough that they were both able to hit a target while leaping from one treetop to another, or leaning off the back of the horses if they had been in the plains. They were in winter camp in the mountains, among warriors now, and far from their home where food was easy to come by. The emperor's army seemed in no way eager to provide provisions. Hunting was imperative.

"What are we doing here, anyway?" Hong Deming asked. "When do you think we'll go home?"

They walked on top of the snow, not breaking its crust, practicing their lightness skills as they went. Shen Lu was the eldest of the disciples, and at twenty-five was highly skilled. Hong Deming was not quite sixteen, and still learning, but quite good for his age. He walked without much care or attention — his lightness skills already well enough developed to leave no tracks ordinary people would be able to see — leaping up occasionally onto a higher tree branch for a better view. His bow was in his hand, arrow on the string.

"I don't know," said Shen Lu grouchily. "Taiqian was called to consult with the emperor about the war. When they've made whatever plans they need to make, we'll return. There are other sects here, and he'll meet with their sect leaders as well. So, lots of meetings. There's a rabbit, taine."

Hong Deming had already shot; the arrow landed in its eye, spreading a pool of blood across the white snow. He leapt down from his tree branch to add it to the game bag. "Do you think we'll see anything bigger? Deer or elk? Boar?"

"You wish," Shen Lu replied, still grouchy; he had only shot one rabbit so far, out of the five in the game bag. "There's too many men camped all around these mountains."

"Why aren't we having these meetings in Zhashan?"

"Why are you always asking questions about things that aren't your business?"

Hong Deming flushed and bowed an apology. "Sorry, tainu."

Shen Lu waved his hand. "Never mind. You're really too easy to bully, taine."

Hong Deming, meanwhile, walked toward another red spot in the snow. "Did we miss one of the kills?" he asked, confused. "Where did that blood come from?"

But when they reached it, it wasn't a blood mark at all; it was a small, red bird, shivering in the snow.

Hong Deming reached out carefully and cupped it in its hands, lifting it out of its snow nest. "Look. It must have fallen out of a tree. It doesn't have all its feathers. I don't think it can fly yet."

He looked around the bare trees and bushes. "Do you see any other birds? Or a nest?"

"No," Shen Lu said without much interest. "Are you going to skewer it? It's a little small to bring back for dinner."

Hong Deming laughed. "Of course not! Look at it. It wouldn't even make a mouthful. And anyway, it's so…cute."

"Cute," said Shen Lu flatly. "Well, it's fluffy."

Actually the little creature wasn't fluffy at all; the snow had dampened and bedraggled all its red feathers, and it was shivering constantly. It looked up at Hong Deming, its golden eyes almost slits. He looked back down at it, curling his hands around it more tightly to give it warmth. He bent down and blew on it a little bit too.

"Elder brother?" He looked up and saw that Shen Lu was already walking on, bow at the ready.

"We need two more rabbits if everyone's going to eat tonight," Shen Lu said. "Come on, leave it."

"But it'll die! Look how small it is. I don't see any nests at all. And it's injured, too, I think. Look at its little wing. Probably something caught it and brought it here. It doesn't have any way to get home."

"Leave it to whatever caught it, then. Maybe we should use it for bait?"

"What, for a fox? Elder brother, that's disgusting. Who eats foxes?"

"Well, it's just going to burden you if you're going to hold it in your hands all the way home. You need two hands to shoot. We're here to catch animals for our dinner. Not save them from being dinner."

"Well, this one won't be dinner," Hong Deming said. Carefully, he opened his outer robe slightly and made a little pocket just above his sash, loose enough to keep the little bird from being crushed when he moved, but enclosed enough to keep it warm and safe. "There."

He quickly twisted, and shot again immediately. "And now we only need one more rabbit."

Shen Lu had to laugh at him. "Hong Deming, does it make any sense that you just killed an animal while also saving one? How are you going to pick which one you save? Are you going to save all the animals now?"

"Just this one," he said. "This is the one that was in front of me for saving."

The next day, the little red bird was still there when Hong Deming woke up. He had scrounged a little clay pot — the kind to cook rice in — and put some soft bits of cloth and straw into it so it would be like a nest. The little creature looked much better, all fluffed out, brilliant red and bright-gold eyed, looking up at him from inside the pot.

He had to laugh. "Look at it, elder brother. Isn't it cute?"

Shen Lu rolled his eyes. "What are you going to feed it?"

"I don't know. What do little birds eat?" He scratched his head. "Rice?"

Shen Lu settled his sash and grabbed his sword. "Get yourself ready, taine. Taiqian is waiting. One of the emperor's counselors is coming for a visit. Wear the formal robes, and make your hair look decent."

Hong Deming nodded and dove into his baggage for the heavy formal robes of the Crane Moon sect, with several layers graduating from white at the inmost to deep blue in the outer robe. Their usual uniform was lightweight and strong, suited for exertion and lightness practice with only two layers and a simple sash, the sleeves caught tight for archery. The only mark they normally wore was the flying crane in a circle, embroidered over one breast. The formal one was of much heavier silk, with embroidery all down the front and around the hems of the long, open sleeves — suitable mostly for standing around in and sweating while honoring important occasions. After struggling to get it on, Hong Deming tried to stroke down his hair as well. The pincrown that held hair back from his face was probably crooked, but his tainu had already left, so there wasn't anyone to help him fix it and he was already late, so...hopefully it would look all right? He picked up his sword. It was an ordinary one — he hadn't yet achieved a spiritual sword.

"Be good, little bird," he said, carefully petting it on the head with one finger. "I'll be back soon, and I'll try to get you some rice."

He went as quickly as he could over to the tent where he could see his sect father seated behind a small banquet table, awaiting the visitors. Tainu was standing behind him at attention, and he quickly went to stand at Taiqian's other shoulder, ready to serve or run errands as necessary.

Taiqian nodded at him and remarked, "Shen Lu, help your taine. It looks as though he knocked his head crooked on the way here."

Shen Lu leaned over to fix the pincrown, and quietly smacked Hong Deming on the back of his head while he was at it. Hong Deming grinned at him.

Taiqian continued to speak, looking forward. "Today, we will receive the emperor's envoy. It appears that he is trusted for his counsel and cleverness. He does not come bearing a formal message, and so we do not need to receive him as the speaking voice of the Son of Heaven. His request to visit us was deliberately made in such a way as to make clear that this conversation is to feel us out rather than making clear demands of us. I want you two here to be silent and to observe."

"Yes, Taiqian," they said in unison.

Hong Deming looked at Shen Lu under his lashes, wondering, as he had often since they left the Crane Moon sect home, why it was that only he and Shen Lu had come on this journey — the oldest and the youngest disciples. He had never asked because, as Shen Lu told him often, he asked too many questions about things that were not for him to understand or decide.

The servants put out the articles for tea, and then were dismissed for privacy. They stood still for what seemed like quite a while, waiting for the envoy to appear. When he did, Hong Deming struggled to keep his mouth closed. This person was by far the most beautiful man he had ever seen. Hong Deming observed in awe and wondered what it felt like to be as beautiful as an ascended immortal.

The envoy's shining eyes took in each of them. "Sect leader, thank you for your kind welcome." He saluted formally. "I have heard much of the intelligence, strength, and wisdom of the Crane Moon sect."

"Zhu Guiren, you are too kind. These disciples are sloppy and poorly trained, the fault is mine." Taiqian acknowledged his salute and gestured to the table.

Hong Deming went over to pour his tea, but Zhu Guiren's eyes were only for Taiqian now.

Their conversation touched on the situation of the emperor, who had ascended the throne under mysterious circumstances that neither of them seemed to want to say outright. Hong Deming, paying attention as Taiqian had told them, noticed that Zhu Guiren seemed to be insinuating that something had happened that Taiqian must know about, but was refusing to say it out loud. Taiqian's face grew stern at various points of this jousting conversation, and Zhu Guiren would always skillfully back up until the peace was renewed. The envoy spoke of the need to defend the people from the warlords that surrounded the borders, and the requirement of personal trust between the emperor and those who would support the coming of peace and tranquility. The generals of the army, he hinted, were not to be trusted completely, and so the emperor looked to the cultivational sect leaders, who were pure of heart and didn't desire power in the secular world, to provide advice and guidance in these troubled times.

Taiqian stroked his beard thoughtfully. Hong Deming, observing carefully, knew that he was completely unconvinced. Anyone familiar with the affairs of the cultivation world knew that the sect leaders were just as self-interested as court officials and were constantly competing for dominance with one another, but it was at least true that none of them wanted to be emperor or start a new dynasty.

However, Taiqian said to Zhu Guiren, "My poor advice could be of no use to the Son of Heaven, even if he were to ask for it. Even the servant of the Son of Heaven surely is more familiar than I with the important affairs of the dynasty. The Crane Moon sect is a righteous sect, and our desire is only to pursue the Pathless Way and to serve the righteous Son of Heaven."

Zhu Guiren must have noticed Taiqian's deliberate refusal of alliance and implication that the Son of Heaven wasn't righteous, but nonetheless kept his face pleasant. "You are too modest, sect leader. I will share your modesty with the Son of Heaven." He sipped his tea and added, "You are far from your temple, here. We are grateful that you came at the summons. Will you be here much longer?"

Taiqian replied calmly, "We are not certain how long we will remain. The skills of the cultivation sects are not to fight alongside the warriors in pitched battles, as you know. We cannot advise on military strategy except from studies of the ancient battles, which surely we are not as expert in as the generals of the

88

Son of Heaven. Our insignificant value must lie in our care for the common people, and in providing spiritual protection from evil beings."

"Ah, the common people!" Zhu Guiren smiled. "There is certainly a way in which you can be helpful to the emperor immediately. Might the Crane Moon sect consider visiting some villages down the mountain? Several have been attacked by bandits taking advantage of the unrest here. Because the generals must use their forces to patrol the border, bandits within the nation are able to move about unchecked."

Hong Deming's eyes lit up, but Taiqian's face was expressionless.

"I will take my disciples there to test their training," he said. "Unfortunately, our weak skills may be inadequate. May I have an opportunity to report back to the honored sir when we return?"

Zhu Guiren stood and bowed. "I will not keep you longer. Many thanks for your welcome." He saluted formally and withdrew.

When he was sure that the envoy had left, Taiqian stood. "Well, little ones, we have something to do now, at any rate. Shen Lu, it's still early in the day. Let's go now and see what there is to see."

As they went to change into their regular uniforms and gather their weapons, Shen Lu said, "Taine, what was wrong with you? You were gaping at the envoy like a half-wit the whole time. He couldn't help but notice it."

"Wasn't he handsome?" Hong Deming carefully turned away while unknotting his sash.

Shen Lu replied, "Hong Deming, get a grip on yourself. Is that all you notice in a person?"

Hong Deming blushed slightly.

"Well, you're at the age," Shen Lu laughed.

"What age?"

"The age at which you can't think about anything else," Shen Lu said dryly. "Lucky for you, the Crane Moon cultivation path doesn't require bodily purity. I think you would have a failing career in front of you. Don't worry," he added, "everyone goes through it — nothing to be embarrassed about."

Hong Deming tried to fix his hair again in order to hide his face behind his arms.

"Just tie it up, you're really too young for a pincrown anyway, that was just to go with the formal robes," Shen Lu said, already dressed and tapping his fingers against his sword.

"Oh, my bird!" Hong Deming said, running over to see as he tied up his hair. "Little bird, we have to go, but I brought some of a bun for you." He crumbled it up for the bird in its little clay pot. "We'll be back...when do you think, tainu?"

"Not that your pet bird needs to know," Shen Lu said, "but a few days, most likely. The first village down the mountain is just a couple of hours' walk at most. Taiqian had me look at maps when we arrived here. Just put the pot near the door so the creature can get out when it wants to. I'm sure it doesn't want to spend its life in a tent."

Hong Deming nodded and straightened up, quiver over one shoulder, bow over the other, and sword in hand. "I'm ready."

As they walked out, Taiqian caught their eyes and nodded, but all he said was, "Be prepared for an ambush. I am sure there was a reason we were sent in this direction."

Two hours of walking later, however, all they had found was a village that was unharmed and had no news to give.

The next day they came to a second village, full of corpses.

They had seen many such sights in their travels, but it hit Hong Deming hard regardless. This had happened very recently, and it didn't seem to be bandits; bandits would have taken the women and older children, but here they lay dead in the dirt or in their burned houses. This was simply war gone where war would always go. Hong Deming didn't have many memories of his childhood before Taiqian brought him to the sect, but the clearest was of a village like this one where he had sat down on a burned piece of wood next to a corpse and waited to die.

Taiqian put his hand on his shoulder, silently.

Suddenly, Shen Lu said, "Taiqian, there's–"

There was a boy, perhaps twelve years old, sitting up dazedly in one of the burned houses. He looked over at them, his eyes serious. "I couldn't help them," he said in a very grave voice.

Hong Deming ran over to him. "Are you all right?" he asked, kneeling down. "Are you hurt?"

The boy shook his head. "I'm fine," he said. "Nothing hurt me."

"Who did this?" asked Taiqian.

The boy replied, "I don't know who they were. Men with swords and fire."

It was about as much sense as they could expect from a little peasant boy wearing torn, dirty clothing. His hair was pulled back from his face with a ragged cloth and his face was filthy, as would be expected, but even though his shirt was ripped and bloodstained, he did seem uninjured and surprisingly calm.

Hong Deming looked inquiringly up at Taiqian.

"Little boy, are your parents here?" Taiqian asked carefully.

He shook his head, eyes downcast.

"Do you have family somewhere?"

He shook his head again.

Taiqian looked serious. "What is your name?"

He looked up, his eyes bright even through all the dirt and soot, and wiped his face with his fingers, making stripes on it and looking very fierce. "Liu Chen-guang."

There was no one else alive in the village; they would have to find someone to leave him with. The boy walked silently behind Hong Deming as they re-traced their steps.

Hong Deming listened as Taiqian and tainu discussed the situation in low voices. Apparently, it was unclear whether the emperor actually was the emperor or not; he had not waited for the nine bestowments to signal his plan for usur-pation, and there had been no signs from heaven on the beginning of his reign. Instead, things like this kept happening — incursions, invasions, bandits, assas-sinations. The world was not at peace.

Shen Lu lowered his voice further. "Taiqian, do we need to take any kind of action?"

Taiqian was silent, and then said even more quietly, "Before the emperor ascended, he brought the child emperor of the old dynasty under his supposed protection and moved the capital. At that time, he asked for the help of the cul-tivation sects. No one was willing to step forward. Without the clear mandate of heaven, how can we know where justice lies? The last two emperors of the previous dynasty were weak, and the realm was disintegrating. That is the truth. There was no safety anywhere. If there had been, then people like Hong Deming would be growing up safe, in their own families. That is why if the new emperor had tried even a little bit to support a righteous order — even after killing the child emperor he was supposed to protect — many of the people would be sat-isfied. But his power is insecure, and thus, he continues to become more violent and less trusting even of his own people. And he is always under attack by those trying to establish rival dynasties. The best we can do is to try to keep our own people safe."

"Taiqian, is that enough?" Hong Deming asked. "Shouldn't we try to protect the common people?"

Shen Lu hissed, "Taine, it's not your place."

"It's a good question," replied Taiqian. "But we are not an army. How many disciples are there in the Crane Moon sect?"

"Twenty-three," answered Shen Lu immediately.

"We are not a large sect. Many are larger, with greater numbers — even some with a few hundred disciples and ranked teachers and grandmasters. And each disciple who cultivates enough spiritual power to attain some qinggong is able to fight with greater strength and skill than any ordinary man. For some disciples, they can best ten or twenty ordinary men. For the highest ranked, even more. A cultivator who has achieved a spiritual weapon might defeat a hundred or more ordinary men. But an army is thousands on thousands strong. The arrows are like a cloud in the sky. The swords are like the stars. The ants will move the mountain in the end." He shook his head. "To protect the common people... only the emperor can do that. Only the Mandate of Heaven can provide safety and stability for people like those today, who died under bandits' swords, or the swords of the barbarians, or the Prince of Fei from the north."

Hong Deming said, "That's why we came? To see if the emperor has the Mandate of Heaven?"

"Yes," said Taiqian. "If he does, despite all he has done, I will support him against those establishing rival dynasties. In the past, at least, he has shown himself to be a great general."

They walked silently for a while. Then, the boy in the back piped up; he must have excellent hearing, Hong Deming thought. "How do you know if he has the Mandate of Heaven?"

Shen Lu said, "Address Taiqian respectfully."

"Taiqian?" the boy asked, questioning.

"No, you're not a disciple. Don't call him father. You can call him sect leader."

"Sect leader," the boy repeated obediently, "what does the Mandate of Heaven look like?" He was small and had to clamber over a deadfall while he was speaking, but he sounded very serious. "How does it help the people?"

Hong Deming reached out to help the boy balance, but he jumped lightly down on his own.

Taiqian said, "The Mandate of Heaven can look like many things. One is clear and glorious victory in battle. The new emperor had many victories, but none associated with his taking the throne. Another is miracles and heavenly movements. That, we also have not seen. Another would be good weather, prosperity, peace and stability among the common people, which clearly is not the case. Without this clear mandate, the emperor is vulnerable to many enemies, and there is continuing disorder. If there is a mandate, then all flows as it should."

The boy nodded seriously, as if he understood what Taiqian meant. Hong Deming did; there was no mandate, no victory, no miracles, no sign from heaven. And, even in simple, human terms, the new emperor was uneasy in his power, undermining his own foundations with his persecution of his most powerful followers, whom he feared might become threats.

Taiqian said, "That's enough talk on that topic, children. We're nearly back to camp. This is not something to be discussed where others can hear."

"Yes, Taiqian," chorused Hong Deming and Shen Lu.

"Yes, sect leader" said the boy.

"Come with me," Hong Deming said to the boy when they arrived back at the camp late that evening. He went directly to their sleeping tent. "There's something to show you."

The little red bird was gone. Hong Deming was very disappointed. "It was so cute," he said, holding his hands curved to show how small it had been. "Bright red, with golden eyes. I hope it's all right. I hope an animal didn't come eat it…"

"I'm sorry it's gone," said the boy.

As he came in, Shen Lu said, "Taine, don't be so silly about that bird, probably it just got better and flew away. As it should be. Liu Chenguang, go over to the servants' tent. Taiqian wants you to be bathed and to put on clean clothes."

"Yes, master," said the boy obediently.

That evening, Taiqian spoke with Liu Chenguang during dinner. Since they were traveling, meals were informal, and Taiqian ate with them at a shared table in his own tent. Liu Chenguang's hair had been taken out of its rag wrap and washed, now falling in a long ponytail from the top of his head. Clean and in overly large servant clothing, he was a good-looking boy with an air of intelligence, rather than a peasant urchin. Hong Deming reflected on the difference that good presentation made in the world and sighed.

"How old are you, child?" Taiqian asked.

The boy was shoveling rice and vegetables in his mouth at a terrifying rate, but carefully avoided the rabbit meat that Hong Deming had provided. Hong Deming watched, impressed.

Liu Chenguang swallowed and said, "Sect leader, I don't really know. Maybe fourteen?" He looked very small for fourteen, but if he had been malnourished as a child, that would explain it.

"Where is your family from?"

Liu Chenguang had already put another mouthful in, and nearly choked trying to answer before Hong Deming passed him some tea. "Sect leader, please forgive me, but I don't really know. That's why I also don't know exactly how old I am. My earliest memories, I was already alone. And I wandered. Sometimes I was chased, or came to bad places, like today. So, I can't tell you where I'm from, or my family. My name...probably someone gave me when I was a baby, and I learned it, but am I really from the Liu clan? I don't even know that."

He spoke like a well-educated adult, not like a peasant child at all; it was remarkable when combined with his extremely bad table manners. Clearly, he was an intelligent child. Taiqian looked at him appraisingly. "If you have nowhere else to go, you would be welcome to join our sect as a servant. We have many people who are part of our community, aside from the disciples."

Liu Chenguang bowed his head. "Would I call you martial father, then? And Hong Deming and Shen Lu would be my elder martial brothers?"

Taiqian shook his head. "I couldn't consider you as a disciple," he said bluntly. "Cultivation needs to begin much earlier than fourteen in order to form a well of qi. At your age, it is unlikely you would be able to do it."

The boy looked at him, almost smiling. "Could I try?"

"No one can stop you from trying," said Taiqian, frowning a bit. "But becoming a disciple is another thing entirely."

Hong Deming and Shen Lu had been silent throughout all of this. Hong Deming was disappointed that the boy wouldn't be joining them as a disciple; he didn't have any younger martial brothers, as he was the youngest himself. It would have been good to have a taine — someone to play with. But, as Taiqian had said, fourteen was too old. Hong Deming himself had been taken in at four or five. He tried to imagine how it must have been for Liu Chenguang to live on his own all this time, without any family or sect or clan to care for him, and looked at him with sympathy.

"Have some more of the mushrooms, since you like them so much," he said, and put some more in Liu Chenguang's bowl.

Liu Chenguang looked up at him and smiled.

Hong Deming thought that he wasn't as beautiful as Zhu Guiren, of course, but he did have truly remarkable eyes — shining and full of clarity, lashes long and dark.

"Thank you, Hong Deming," he said.

CHAPTER 8
ARCINIANG

TAIREI CRIED OUT, "She's not waking up, she's not waking up!"

Tainu laid his fingers on the inside of Aili's wrist. "Her qi is chaotic. Can you direct it, Tairei?"

Tairei put her trembling hands on Aili's shoulders, then slid her fingers down her arms to check the meridians. Aili was unresponsive — her heart beating, her lungs breathing, but nothing else. Tairei sent qi into the meridians, concentrating, but it was as though Aili had fallen into the ocean, deep and full of currents and waves, pushing her from place to place. How could you calm the ocean?

Tainu knelt next to her. "Just throw her a lifeline, keep a smooth flow..."

"I know what to do," she gritted. She knew, but she was so weak now, recently reborn, without an adult's cultivation.

"Let me," said Zhu Guiren, walking closer. "You know I'm good at this, Liu Chenguang–"

"Don't you dare touch her, you filth." She flung herself across Aili's body and spread the wings that had suddenly appeared, unbidden.

"What the hell are those?" yelled Tainu in shock. "You have– What?"

"I don't know either." Tairei arranged herself so her wings covered Aili almost head to foot — so Zhu Guiren couldn't see her — and put her fingers on the proper acupoints again. She breathed deeply. "It's better now, it's calmer."

"Let her sleep then," said Tainu, rising to his feet. "She's been through a lot

95

with no real rest. When you're sure she's stable, go cultivate. You, demon."

"I have a name," Zhu Guiren said.

"Whatever. Demon, I'm setting the wards now."

"You can set wards? Why hasn't she been setting wards?" Zhu Guiren asked peevishly. "Every night I just stay awake waving my sword around and killing things. She hasn't been very helpful at all."

"Again, whatever. Demon, I'm setting the wards. You'll want to back up."

Zhu Guiren tilted his head and grinned. "Make me."

Tainu took a step toward him, then another. He looked down calmly at the demon's face.

"You're in my personal space," said Zhu Guiren.

"How nice." Tainu took another step, so they were standing nearly chest to chest; Tainu was slightly taller. He stepped forward again, and the demon stepped back.

"Wait a minute," Zhu Guiren said. "What–"

"One more step please."

"No, I–"

Tainu reached out and tousled his hair. "You're really very cute."

Zhu Guiren rapidly took three steps backward, nearly stumbling in haste.

"Lovely." Tainu quickly shifted through a set of hand seals, then reached down and slapped the ground. A circle of light with the tree at its center spread out to surround Tairei, Aili, and Tainu in a glittering dome, then faded. The demon remained outside. He reached one finger out, then jerked it back as though it had been burned.

"You think that's strong enough to last the night? Even with everything you've done to it, that's still a mortal soul and it smells like fresh meat. Worse things than me will be coming."

"Well, if you can't handle them, I'll bring you in the ward, demon."

"That's not what I– ugh, forget it." Zhu Guiren turned his back on them and stomped a few steps further away. He stretched out both his hands, a sword of ice and smoke in each one. "Fine."

Tainu curled himself into a lotus position, his hands set in their seals, concentrating to maintain the ward.

Tairei's wings trembled as she held Aili's acupoints; the qi surged dangerously, then settled. Aili's body became still, her breathing deep, and Tairei relaxed slightly. "I think she's asleep," she said.

Tainu nodded from his warding posture. Quietly, he asked, "Why is that demon with you?"

"Do you think I can get him to leave? It's not as though I can fight him," she said bitterly. "He showed up immediately after my rebirth and he's just been following me."

"Just following you? Nothing else?"

Reluctantly, she admitted, "He's been protecting me at night. And sometimes during the daytime. Whenever anything attacks."

"Why?" Tainu frowned.

"I have no idea." She looked down at Aili and said, "I refuse to be grateful to him."

Tainu looked out through the wards toward where Zhu Guiren stood with his back to them, a sword ready in each hand. "Every night? Has he slept?"

"Who knows. Every night, I hope he'll be dead in the morning."

Tainu withdrew his gaze and nodded toward Tairei's wings. "Tell me about the...whatever those are."

Tairei settled into a lotus position and carefully placed Aili's head in her lap, ready to send her qi if necessary. "I was like this when I woke up. I didn't have a child body at all. Just this, the same as my previous one. And if I transform, this is all that happens — these wings. I can't fly with them, and I can't sense the refuges. I've just been walking around aimlessly, trying to run into something that would get me back to the mortal realm since I don't have enough cultivation to produce a phoenix gate yet."

"You can't transform at all?"

"This is me transformed into my true body," she said, flicking a wing. The wing disappeared. "Then this is me in the mortal body. No other difference."

Tainu shook his head. "Can you do anything to that body? Change the gender?"

"Nothing. The body is stable and immovable, unchangeable by my will. Transformed or not, this is it."

After a moment, Tainu snickered. "You're going to get tired of that equipment in a few centuries."

"Shut up," she said, but the corner of her mouth quirked up a little nonetheless. "Seriously, what's wrong with you? That's all you think about in this situation?"

"Well, we could use a little humor," he said. "How about Aili? Has her mortal body changed at all from going through the rebirth fire? She can't transform at all, as far as I've been able to see."

"I don't think so," she said uncertainly.

"You don't think so? Are you familiar with her body or not?"

Tairei said, "No."

Tainu looked at her with great, sad eyes.

Blushing, Tairei waved one hand in the air. "Tainu, I don't want to make light of it. She didn't remember me or her previous life, but I could tell that there was something underneath. And this life– there has been so much pain for her before I even found her. Whenever we got close to talking about...things...she'd start to say she was in pain. I was worried about a qi deviation if I pushed it too quickly. I didn't know what to do...what would help her remember...what would harm her, and I didn't have time." She looked down. "I'm not used to not having time."

Tainu nodded. "I don't want to make light of it either. When she told me the circumstances...I've been very worried about you, to be honest."

Tairei shook her head fiercely. "I don't want to cry right now. Let's not talk about it too much. I'm glad to see you. I've never been so glad to see you as I was tonight."

"All right then. You should cultivate. I think we should get back into the mortal realm as soon as we can manage it."

From outside, the demon called, "Does anyone want my opinion?"

"No. Go away," said Tairei.

She held Aili's head in her lap, unable to cultivate or focus on anything, her mind wandering over the past. Long ago, she had healed people as Hong Deming had healed a red bird — whatever was in front of her to save. It flew from her and was gone, and she was not changed, it did not remain in her heart. When she healed now, she saw all the loss and inevitable end, the burden of the years and the terrible swiftness of the days. They had thought there would be time, and then there was not.

She regretted it.

Aili coughed a little bit, and Tairei carefully lifted her to lie more upright, supported against her shoulder to breathe more easily. Her dark blonde braid was itchy against Tairei's skin, little curls escaping from their confinement like flames from coals, so she pushed it to the other side carefully, not wanting to accidentally pull her hair. Tairei kissed her forehead gently; Aili's sleeping hand squeezed hers very slightly, then relaxed again.

"Tairei," Tainu said quietly. "You need to cultivate. She'll be safe."

Tairei nodded and sat upright, carefully laying Aili back down, her wings still furled around them.

Tainu asked, "How long do you think you will need to cultivate to reach your adult level of power?"

"I don't know if I will. I don't know if my power will be what it was before this. I estimate two months, perhaps twice that. Everything feels different with my power now."

Tainu nodded, considering. "I can't hold a ward that long. We'll have to find a refuge."

"That's what I was going to say," called the demon from beyond the ward. "There are more attackers every night, and the mortal soul will draw different beings than just a phoenix. I can handle demons, but there are some things that will be more...challenging. Tonight will be bad. I know your pet can't fly, but walking is also an option."

"Shut. Up," gritted Tairei. "Can you not speak without being insulting?"

"No," he said bluntly. There was a sound of a hissing scream from beyond the wards. "Please excuse me. Fun's beginning."

"The purpose of the ward is that you shouldn't have to do that," called Tainu.

"I'm not allowed in the ward, remember? Oh, no you don't."

Another hiss. Another scream.

"Also, that ward can't hold off everything that's on its way. It'll be overwhelmed if you just sit behind it all night. I'll at least take the edge off. Then maybe you'll be nice to me."

"I'm being nice to you now," said Tainu. "I'm talking to you like you are a sentient being with whom conversation can be had."

"Ha, good one!" A strange noise of wings and howling arose outside, battering the ward. Tainu stood and abruptly changed his hand seal formation.

"Ugh, disgusting. I hate those things."

Something was beating against the ward's boundary near the ground, making it waver and shiver back and forth.

Tainu eyed it closely. "There's a cthonic being trying to get in," he called.

"That's not good," called the demon, gasping slightly.

"Are you all right?" Tainu came closer to the edge.

"Just too many at once. I'll switch to arrows–" Suddenly, he screamed, visceral and short.

Tainu shouted, "Demon?!"

There was a sudden thud as Zhu Guiren's body was thrown against the ward by something both large and powerful. He slumped down to the ground, unmoving, leaving streaks of blood bright in midair, unable to fall to earth through the boundary that repelled demons.

"Tairei," Tainu ordered, "strengthen the ward. Just do whatever you can, I need to bring him in–"

"No," she said.

Tainu narrowed his eyes at her. "Tairei, either you can strengthen the ward so I can get him, or I'm going to drop the ward to get him and then we're all going to die."

"Fine," she said, furious. "Fine." Tairei put her back to the boundary and spread her wings, carefully mirroring the curve of the ward, her hands held in the strongest seal she could manage. Sweat broke out on her face. "Get him."

Tainu crawled out through the shimmering light and dragged the demon in under her wings. Zhu Guiren was covered with blood, his face and arms and legs a myriad of small, deep cuts, as though he had been put into a whirling tunnel of swords or teeth. He was also missing his left hand, cleanly removed just above the wrist. Blood poured from the wound to the rhythm of his heartbeat.

"Ah!" Zhu Guiren opened his eyes, unseeing. "It hurts."

"It's all right, I'm here," said Tainu.

"That's good." The demon tried to focus his eyes. He looked up and reached toward Tainu's face with his remaining hand as though to touch him.

Tainu flinched back.

"Of course," the demon said, a little bitterly. He sighed. "Come closer, I need to tell you something."

Tainu leaned over, carefully, although not to listen. "Hold your sword still," he said. "Hold it tight in your hand."

"Closer."

Tainu leaned closer.

Zhu Guiren whispered, "My true name is Arciniang."

"Arciniang," said Tainu, very softly, and nodded. "Arciniang, hold your sword tightly."

The demon clenched his remaining fist around the sword. Tainu reached over and slashed his own hand against it, deeply, and began to anoint the demon's wounds with his blood.

Looking at his face, Zhu Guiren asked, "Will you tell me your name?"

"Hell no," said Tainu, touching the demon's lips with his blood, his eyes darting from one wound to the next. "Why did you tell me yours?"

"I don't want to die with no one knowing my name."

"So much drama," Tainu said. "You're not going to die. You have two phoenixes next to you."

"I'm completely fine with him dying," said Tairei from where she was guarding the ward.

"Ok, you have one phoenix." Tainu continued to carefully paint his blood on the demon's body. "You are quite ripped up. What was it?"

"A soul-devourer. Here for the mortal soul." Beneath the bloody smears, the demon's face was blushing with embarrassment. "I didn't realize that phoenixes could heal this kind of thing. That you could heal a demon."

"Of course we *can*. The opportunity rarely arises, given what demons are normally trying to do when near a phoenix."

"Can you forget I told you my name?"

"Ha, never. It's buried in my heart for all time." Tainu held up the stump of Zhu Guiren's left wrist. "This, though, I can't fix. Since we are in the spirit realm, whatever part of your true body this is, it's gone forever."

"Damn." The demon lay still. "That's…unfortunate. Inconvenient."

"I'm sorry."

"No, it's all right. What you did really feels amazing. My body feels great otherwise."

"Well, I'm done doing it." Tainu sat back on his heels. "Normally, I'd advise you to get some rest after injuries like this, but I'm guessing that's not happening."

"Nope. Fully cured, satisfied customer." The demon stood and shook out his ripped, bloodstained sleeves. "I am now officially angry. Who the hell do they think they are?" He reached out his remaining hand with a sharp gesture and grasped a seven-foot halberd made of ice and smoke. "Excuse me."

He vaulted through the ward, one hand on the halberd, and swung it viciously against the darkness that had crowded up at the edge. Tainu watched him as he threw his head back and shouted something in a language the phoenix couldn't understand and then smashed the pole of the halberd against the ground. Ripples of blue-black light shivered up the ward, along the earth, into the sky; suddenly things that seemed like stars were falling all around him — stars with flames of black and red and purple, resolving into beings with wings and horns and tails. All of them knelt with their various ill-assorted bodies and bowed what passed for their heads toward Zhu Guiren before he shouted again. Then, they attacked the shadows.

Through the cacophony of screams and howls and hisses and the sounds of flesh being parted, Tairei looked at Tainu. "Did you know he could command other demons?" she asked.

"How would I know?" Tainu watched the demon as he settled back into supporting the ward. "Did you know?"

"No. Zhu Guiren has never told me the truth about anything in my life."

Thoughtfully, Tainu said, "He's certainly arrogant enough."

101

"I heard that," the demon yelled over his shoulder, swinging the halberd. "Can I get a little more respect from you two now?"

Tairei was silent, settling back down to cultivate next to Aili.

Tainu considered. "No," he called back. "I think we're good."

CHAPTER 9
WELL OF QI

THE NEXT DAY Taiqian, Shen Lu, and Hong Deming made another foray out to the lower villages, leaving Liu Chenguang behind with the servants. The first two villages they visited were grateful for the visitors but had escaped attack; the third had been attacked twice and had driven the attackers off. Taiqian decided that they would wait in this village to see if the bandits would try again.

Hong Deming was eager to head home and leave this cold, snowy, brutal place behind. He supposed this was what it was like to walk beyond the bounds, homeless and defending the common people with the sword. It was much less heroic than he had anticipated, and there was a lot of boredom waiting for something to happen. Every day, he faithfully practiced his cultivation — moving through the sword forms, settling into his cultivation pose — but other than that, there was nothing to do. There was no inn, so they stayed in an old woodshed, and the villagers didn't have much in the way of food, either. They brought out their best, and Taiqian reminded his disciples to show proper gratitude, but still it was going to be a hungry waiting.

A few days later, two of the sect servants came down, bringing some additional food supplies in case their wait lasted longer. Liu Chenguang came as well, to run errands and do small tasks for them as he learned how to be a proper sect servant. He was bright-eyed, and already looking healthier than he had when they found him. Hong Deming was delighted.

Once Liu Chenguang had finished cleaning up their morning meal each day, there wasn't much for him to do until lunch time, so he tagged after Hong Deming into the woods above the village, climbing trees with him and finding things buried underneath the snow. Hong Deming found that Liu Chenguang really knew quite a lot about how to find food in the forest. Usually he could bring back a basketful of leaves, or a cache of nuts, or edible bark, or mushrooms — enough to make the glowering senior servant nod and approve, and enough to make their dinners of stored grain and hunted meat much more interesting. In return, Hong Deming tried to show Liu Chenguang how to use the sword, since that was the Crane Moon sect's cultivation path.

Liu Chenguang was surprised to learn about this. He watched Hong Deming moving through a basic sword form, frowning a little. "Isn't the sword for killing?" he asked bluntly. "How do you use it to cultivate spiritual power?"

"Well, of course it's for killing, but you can use it for cultivation too," Hong Deming replied, sweating a bit as he moved into a more advanced form in an unacknowledged effort to show off. "And then when you fight you'll also be a better fighter. You move the qi inside your meridians using the sword as a focus point and tracing a pattern that connects with the spiritual qi of the universe."

He leapt up and twirled, sending out a brief, contained energetic pattern around him. "If I was doing that full strength," he boasted, "it would have taken down all of those trees."

"How interesting," Liu Chenguang said politely. "I thought cultivation was about sitting still and meditating to gather spiritual power."

"Well, there's that too," he admitted. "If we were at home in the sect, we'd spend all morning doing that. New disciples have to do a lot of it till we've formed our inner wells. That's what stores qi when you cultivate."

"When we reach the sect, can I try to do that too?"

"I don't know, Taiqian said you're too old. And there are some other things too, about how he chooses disciples. Not everyone can do it even if they're young. But since you have free time here, why don't you try it while you don't have any work to do? And I'll teach you the first sword form. Here, take it." He grabbed Liu Chenguang's hand and wrapped it around the sword hilt.

Liu Chenguang jerked back as though he had been burned.

"What's wrong?" Hong Deming asked, concerned. "Did I hurt your hand?"

"No, no, it just gave me a little shock…I've never held a sword before. It feels…" Liu Chenguang tilted his head to one side thoughtfully. "…strange. Has this sword ever killed anyone?"

What a bizarre question. Hong Deming frowned. "Well, probably. Not by me. It's a sword that has belonged to the sect for a long time. It was given to me when I reached a certain point in cultivation. It doesn't have a strong spirit, though. I'm not yet able to control a spiritual sword. So, even if it did kill someone, it shouldn't remember."

"You've never killed anyone?" Liu Chenguang asked. "I thought that was what you people did all the time."

"I'm young," he defended. "And what do you mean, 'you people'? You mean cultivator people?"

"People with swords. That's all I've ever seen people with swords do. That's what weapons are for, aren't they?"

Hong Deming held his sword close to his eyes. It was true; it was a beautiful thing designed to kill efficiently and well. Probably, it had killed people before, and one day soon, he would also kill people.

"But we don't kill people for no reason," he said out loud. "At least, our sect doesn't. We're a righteous sect."

"Hmm," said Liu Chenguang. "Well, dead is just as dead, whether you did it for a reason or not."

Hong Deming shook his head. "How do you think we'll protect the villagers here if they're attacked? I'll certainly be killing people. Or doing my best, anyway."

Liu Chenguang reached out cautiously and touched the sword hilt again. Hong Deming wrapped his fingers carefully around it, then curled his own hand around Liu Chenguang's fist; the boy's fingers were fine and long, and felt very warm inside his own. Hong Deming found himself blushing a little bit when Liu Chenguang looked inquiringly up over his shoulder to where Hong Deming stood slightly behind him, helping to hold the sword parallel with the ground.

"It's very heavy," Liu Chenguang said, with a little surprise. "I wouldn't have guessed how heavy it is."

Hong Deming unwrapped his fingers from Liu Chenguang's fist and the sword point dropped to the ground. "When you've cultivated more, it won't feel so heavy. Cultivation gives you additional strength through gathering the qi. And your muscles become stronger too, from drills and exercise. It takes time to develop, and also the flexibility for lightness skills, that's why we have to start young."

"And the...well of qi?"

"That's the core that holds your spiritual power," he explained, feeling quite accomplished. "You have to develop it when you're very young. Once you're older, it's impossible. I don't know why."

"How do you know?" Liu Chenguang experimentally tried to lift the sword and swung it in a heavy, clumsy arc.

Hong Deming easily caught the blade between his fingers to stop it, although with that little strength behind it, the edge would have barely scratched him. "How do you know what?"

"If you have a well of qi?"

"Taiqian tests you," he said.

Liu Chenguang nodded and tried to lift the sword again. "Probably I haven't got one," he admitted. He handed the sword back to Hong Deming. The hilt felt a little sweaty.

"Don't worry," Hong Deming said, "you can still stay with us at the sect, if that's what you're worried about."

Liu Chenguang smiled. "I'm not worried," he said. "Come with me, on the way here I saw–"

Something flashed past his face and he jumped back, startled.

Hong Deming stared shocked as a line of red spread across Liu Chenguang's cheekbone. Liu Chenguang touched the blood coming down and frowned, opening his mouth to speak again.

Hong Deming yelled "Down!" and pushed him to the ground, simultaneously grabbing for his bow and shooting several arrows in succession in the direction that had sent the arrow at Liu Chenguang. More arrows came their way. He dropped his bow and started blocking with the sword, cutting the arrows out of the air.

"Liu Chenguang," he said, not sparing time to look behind him. "Jump up, grab my shoulders. I'll carry you!"

"What?!"

"Just do it!"

He felt Liu Chenguang's weight against his back, negligible, and he put his mind toward lightness. "Arms around my neck, legs around my waist — I can't spare hands to hold you," he said quickly, sheathing the sword and grabbing the bow again, three arrows ready. He leapt up for a branch ten feet over his head, easily landed on it, and then pushed off toward the next tree, running through the branches as though on a road.

To his surprise, he heard Liu Chenguang's voice in his ear — laughing, of all things. "This is wonderful!" he said. "Like flying without wings!"

Hong Deming had to laugh back at him, even as he stopped, turned, and sent the three arrows toward the pursuers. He could see them now, coming out of the undergrowth to follow them. They seemed like ordinary people, not cultivators — no real threat to him. Three arrows found three throats, and down they went. If it hadn't been for needing to get Liu Chenguang out of the way and warn the village, he could have just stayed and probably taken care of them all, he thought.

Liu Chenguang's laughter stopped, suddenly. Hong Deming kept moving through the trees, far more quickly than their pursuers could, but he felt Liu Chenguang's body twisting back away from his shoulders as though he was looking behind them.

"They're dead," Liu Chenguang said coolly. "But we're going so fast anyway, did you really have to kill them?"

"It slowed them down. And they shot at us first, and they were still shooting at us. It's not just that we needed to get away," he tried to explain. "They're certainly on the way to attack the village…"

Why did he feel vaguely ashamed of killing those three bandits? It was a fine bit of archery, actually — three on one string — he would have thought the boy would be impressed. Liu Chenguang's hands carefully grasped his shoulders, his legs wrapped tight around his waist; he was really very light.

Liu Chenguang's voice came thoughtfully. "I see."

They were at the outskirts of the village now, and the tall trees drew back. Hong Deming jumped down lightly and continued running, still with Liu Chenguang on his back.

"Taiqian!" he yelled as they came into the village's single street. "Get down," he said to Liu Chenguang. He disentangled himself and went to stand near a courtyard wall. "Taiqian, tainu, they're coming!"

Taiqian and Shen Lu ran out to join him. None of them wore any kind of armor; if your quickness and sword couldn't protect you, then you might just as well give up cultivation and go home.

"They caught us in the woods. I shot three, but I think they'll still come," Hong Deming said quickly.

"They may come from more than one direction," said Taiqian. "We'll wait here."

They didn't have to wait long. There were about fifty of them — all men in military armor, but without military discipline or officers. Deserters from various armies, likely, or else they had attacked an isolated outpost somewhere and fitted themselves out. Hong Deming quickly used up all his arrows, then moved to the sword. He thought, as his sword cut through the first man's upraised arm — armor or no armor, a cultivational sword with qi behind it wasn't easily blocked — that he would be able to tell Liu Chenguang his sword had killed someone later, when it was over.

"Try to keep some alive, remember," called Taiqian, observing their work and occasionally blocking an over-ambitious bandit one-handed.

Shen Lu quickly reversed his sword and smashed someone in the face with the hilt. "Sorry, I think that killed him anyway."

Hong Deming laughed, but he saw that Liu Chenguang stood at the corner of the wall, watching with a rather sad expression on his face.

Hmmph, he thought to himself, *he should be worried about us, not crying about these stupid murderers.*

Nonetheless, he knelt low and grabbed the next comer's leg, twisted so his knee was out of joint, and then kicked him sharply in the head. "Got one," he said, and got his sword ready again.

He heard screaming from inside the village walls and saw Liu Chenguang suddenly turn around and run.

"Go," called Taiqian, and he nodded and went.

Liu Chenguang was ahead of him, ducking into a house with its door broken down. Inside, there were three or four bandits and a woman desperately trying to shield her children, a dead man on the floor in front of them. The attackers were particularly interested in the daughter — a girl of about twelve. Liu Chenguang, completely unarmed, was trying to block them with some ineffective grabs; his forearm and shoulder were already covered in blood.

"Get out of the way!" Hong Deming yelled. "You're going to get killed!"

The men turned to see someone who was ready, willing, and able to cut them into twitching pieces of meat and let go of the girl's arm. Hong Deming cut one of them nearly in half, then took the second one in the throat on the backslash. The third tried to push past him, but Hong Deming took him with a palm strike to the chest; the man coughed blood and fell over.

"That's two alive," he said to himself, then turned. "You idiot, Liu Chenguang! Just stay here. Stay out of the way!"

"All right," came a calm voice from the dim corner of the house.

"And get a bandage on your arm!" he yelled before running back outside.

He found Taiqian and Shen Lu well in control of the situation. Each of them had accounted for at least ten bodies and there were Hong Deming's two survivors, plus Taiqian had gotten one alive as well. The remainder had fled.

Shen Lu sent a last cast of arrows toward them; no good would come of keeping them alive, since they would have no other way of survival than continuing to attack villages and travelers. "Are there any more in the village, taine?"

"I didn't see any," Hong Deming said, flicking his sword sharply to clean the remaining blood drops. "I think I have another survivor, too. Liu Chenguang is with him."

"Why are you bringing a servant along with you all the time?" Shen Lu asked.

"It was just an accident. We were in the woods together–"

"Really?" Shen Lu raised his eyebrows. "What were you doing in the woods?"

"Just playing. He's interesting to talk to."

Shen Lu shook his head. "Well, let's get some information from these people."

He and Hong Deming dragged their captives back to lie against the courtyard wall, away from the corpses.

Taiqian stood there, waiting. "Go get your other one, taine."

When he returned to the house, the woman and her children were mourning over the dead man inside. Liu Chenguang had already dragged one corpse out into the street, which must have been something of a challenge — the man certainly outweighed him by half and again — and brought out not one, but two prisoners, tied with ropes he had found somewhere. Shockingly, the one Hong Deming had gotten across the throat had survived, looking dazed from blood loss. In the dim light, he must have miscalculated the distance, though Hong Deming could have sworn that he had felt the pressure of the skin giving way to the sword edge at the time. He shook his head.

"Liu Chenguang, let me see your arm," he called.

Liu Chenguang came over obediently. "I'm fine, nothing got me."

"But I saw your arm all bloody?"

"It just spurted out from when the husband was killed. I'm fine."

Hong Deming looked at it just to be sure, then at his face. The line from the arrow was healed already; it wouldn't scar. "You were very lucky. My elder sect brother reminded me I shouldn't be bringing you into dangerous places. I'm glad you're safe. You look very pale, though." He wished he could check Liu Chenguang's pulse the way sect father or a more advanced practitioner could, but he didn't know how to do that yet. "I think your qi isn't good now. Come with me, let sect father check you."

Liu Chenguang nodded wearily and reached out to lean on his arm. He was really weak after all; it seemed like he might fall down.

"Does the sight of blood upset you?" Hong Deming asked. He'd never met anyone like that, but he knew that some people fainted when they saw blood.

The boy smiled, looking at the ground. "No, I'm fine with blood. I just... don't feel well. I think maybe I'm not very strong yet..."

Hong Deming deposited his prisoners along with the others along the wall. Taiqian had begun interrogating the men. They had little to lose at this point, given that they had been caught in the act of slaughter and pillage of unarmed people, and were part of a group that was responsible for rape and murder as well, although all of them insisted that they themselves hadn't done such things. The men against the wall knew that their only choice now was between an easy death and a hard one, and were not particularly brave, so it wasn't difficult to get the location of the bandit camp and the history of where they'd gotten their armor.

When they were done, Taiqian stroked his chin. "Send Liu Chenguang back with a message while we continue to the next village," he said. "We're not executioners, and I wouldn't hand any honorable brother over to the magistrate, but there's no sense setting these ones free. Have Zhu Guiren send people to come pick them up."

Hong Deming said, "I don't think he can travel on his own, Taiqian, he seems unwell." He pulled on Liu Chenguang's arm to bring him closer. "Anyway, we can all travel faster than he could. It doesn't seem fair to send him with the message to Zhu Guiren."

Taiqian frowned. "Boy, are you sick?"

Liu Chenguang seemed unable to open his eyes, swaying on his feet. Hong Deming held tightly to his arm, and then put an arm around his shoulders to try to keep him upright, alarmed. "He's getting worse. Taiqian, can you check?"

Suddenly, Liu Chenguang coughed up blood.

Taiqian grabbed for his wrist with two fingers, pressing gently, then opened his eyes wide. "I don't understand this," he said. "Have him sit down." He placed his fingers on Liu Chenguang's heart meridian and began transferring spiritual energy.

Shen Lu and Hong Deming watched, confused.

Taiqian transferred qi until the color came back into Liu Chenguang's face and he began to breathe normally, then removed his fingers and spoke. "He has a fully-formed well of qi, but it's empty. He's used all his qi and nearly fell into a coma. I've never seen such a thing. Even if he can form the well, he shouldn't be able to access all his qi without training to overcome the body's safeguards. How could he, at his age...and empty? Hong Deming, did you notice anything unusual with him today?"

"I...I let him hold my sword...he said it was very heavy..."

"Did he use qi to try to guide the sword?" asked Taiqian, without a word of the blame Hong Deming felt he deserved.

Shen Lu glared from the side.

110

"Not that I noticed. He said he probably didn't have a spirit well because it was so heavy. And he seemed all right afterward...He just became like this after the fight..." He looked guiltily at Liu Chenguang's closed eyes.

"Did he fight? Was he wounded?"

"Just the scratch on his face from an arrow, but that was when we were in the woods. Was it– Is it poisoned?"

Taiqian shook his head again and stood up. "Carry him. Old Ling will bring the rest of our belongings back to our camp. I need to consult on this."

Hong Deming gently pulled Liu Chenguang's limp form onto his back, holding him carefully, and followed Shen Lu and Taiqian swiftly into the woods.

Two days later, Liu Chenguang still hadn't woken up. Hong Deming was terrified. This was his fault; letting an untrained person without cultivation hold the sword must have injured him in some way internally. He hovered around the servants' tent constantly, asking irritating questions of the senior servant, except when Taiqian, exasperated by his obsessive guilt, sent him out to find more meat. He came back with six rabbits, threw them at the senior servant to preserve, and sat down outside the tent again.

"You need to go cultivate," Shen Lu said. "Get off your rump and get to work."

Hong Deming obstinately folded himself into a lotus position, holding his sword parallel to the ground in both hands. "I'll do it here. It's not as though we have a temple or cultivation ground anyway."

Shen Lu rolled his eyes. "Taiqian's doing everything that can be done. You shouldn't have let him hold the sword. That's true, and you'll need to face the wall and reflect for a while when we get back home, but Taiqian is sure that's not what caused the problem. It's none of your business. And it's unseemly for you to pay so much attention to a servant." Shen Lu looked at him carefully. "Taine, is there...something you want to tell me? About you and Liu Chenguang?"

Hong Deming looked back at him, completely clueless. "About what?"

"Taiqian's consulting the other sect leaders this afternoon before we leave for home tomorrow," Shen Lu said as he walked away. "He'll find someone with some ideas for the boy. Don't worry."

When Taiqian returned, it was not with a fellow sect leader but with Zhu Guiren. Zhu Guiren, it transpired, had been paying a visit to the leader of the Peaceful River sect when Taiqian arrived, and after a bit of dancing around discussing political issues and attempting to get Zhu Guiren to leave the room in a very polite way, Taiqian had mentioned the strange case of Liu Chenguang. Zhu Guiren immediately explained that he was not only trained as a physician, but had a particular scholarly specialty in issues regarding qi deviation and rare cultivation problems. Taiqian had, somewhat unwillingly, brought him back to examine Liu Chenguang directly.

Hong Deming bowed to Zhu Guiren when he arrived, speechless again at how beautiful the man was, but Zhu Guiren swept past him without a second glance, ducking into the servants' tent with Taiqian. Without any sense of shame whatsoever, Hong Deming quickly went around to the back, where he knew Liu Chenguang's cot was against the canvas, so he could hear better.

For a while, there was nothing — just "hmmmm" and "interesting..." in Zhu Guiren's cool voice. At last, he explained, "Sect leader, this boy has a very unusual pattern to his well of qi and meridians. I have only read of this in old books. I haven't ever seen it before. He was born with his well already formed, but he has not yet cultivated enough to fill the well for his own safety. Because he didn't need to cultivate to create and fill the well, it is drawing directly from his own vital qi. The only way he will survive is to cultivate intensively for several years. If you continue to give him spiritual energy, enough to awaken, and then bring him back to your sect as a disciple for training, that would solve this problem."

There was silence.

"I am not sure that would be convenient," said Taiqian eventually.

Hong Deming covered his mouth in shock.

"It's not clear to me what caused his sudden crisis," continued Taiqian. "There's something odd about him, even before this happened. He is a presentable, intelligent boy, yet his origins are very mysterious, and his behavior and conversation are strange. I had intended to bring him back to Crane Moon as a servant since he had nowhere else to go, but I was already thinking that that might be the wrong decision. One of my disciples seemed almost bewitched by him."

"Really?" It sounded as though Zhu Guiren was laughing. "Both of your disciples are young enough that they must get bewitched fairly easily."

Taiqian didn't laugh in return. "I don't know if this person should be brought back to our sect even as a servant, and now you are telling me that I should take him as a disciple. Given the strangeness of his meridians, is there anything else I should know about his cultivation path?"

"Well, it's likely that he will heal very easily and quickly from wounds," Zhu

Guiren said. "This is an effect of being born with the well already formed, but again, it is drawing from his own life force to do so. In addition, it is possible that he may not be able to cultivate with the sword at all. In the scrolls I've examined describing this condition, it often seems that those who suffer from it… For most of them, they die young, but those who do cultivate seem unable to use weapons well. However, it is very likely that he would be able to cultivate the healing path."

"Crane Moon is a sword path, so we'd be useless to him in any case. Peaceful River is a music path, but I don't know any sect that focuses on healing."

"No," Zhu Guiren replied, in his cold, rather haughty voice, "it's not a path that sects have really developed. The ability to follow it fully is too rare. A true healing path is something he couldn't find within any sect today. However, if you could support him in developing his cultivational foundation, I would be willing to take him as my apprentice later on, when he's stabilized his qi."

Hong Deming's eyes grew wide.

Taiqian didn't respond.

Zhu Guiren continued, persuasively, "To have such a disciple attached to your sect would be a great advantage to you. You don't know yet what a true healing path can accomplish. He will be able to heal any wound, any illness — a true divine physician. There are other powers associated with this path that may develop further for him later in life, but there has been no such person in the cultivation world for centuries, according to the scrolls. Such a disciple, in these uncertain times, would be worth having."

Hong Deming wondered why Zhu Guiren was arguing so hard in favor of the boy staying with the Crane Moon, but desperately hoped he would succeed. It would be wonderful to have Liu Chenguang around all the time; much more fun than Shen Lu or the other older disciples. He only wondered why Taiqian was so reluctant. Did he not like Liu Chenguang? And if Taiqian thought he was bewitched, well, that was ridiculous. He'd just made a bad decision in offering Liu Chenguang the sword. It was completely his own idea and his own fault — he would have to make that clear.

At last, Taiqian said, still without a commitment, "Why can't you take him now?"

"I'm not a cultivator myself," Zhu Guiren said, "only a physician of mediocre ability. I could not guide him into developing the spiritual foundation as you could. I could not teach him to cultivate as he needs to. My service to him would be in learning the classical texts and prescriptions, learning to read pulses and diagnose — the things any adequate physician can do. I can also introduce him

113

to my studies in the ancient manuals of qi deviation and cultivational health, though for me these are only theoretical as I am without any spiritual power. Nonetheless, to him, with the cultivation he will have as an adult, they'll be very useful."

Hong Deming pressed his ear even closer to the canvas wall; he thought he could hear Liu Chenguang's even breathing, very close to the cloth, closer than the voices. He closed his eyes and reached out gently to where his shoulder was pressed right up against the side of the tent. He touched it gently and thought, *don't worry, Taiqian is kind and wise. He'll give you another chance. I'm sorry I got you in trouble like this.*

Just as he let go, Taiqian said, "Very well. I will provide spiritual energy to wake him. We will return to our sect, and if he is willing to follow the path you have outlined, I will accept him as a disciple of the Crane Moon. I will need to continue to trouble you for guidance on his path."

Zhu Guiren said, "Of course, of course. If it is convenient, I will come to visit in a half year to check on him."

Hong Deming scrambled away as Zhu Guiren and Taiqian moved toward the entrance. He came around the front and was able to stand, looking innocent, next to the horse shelter by the time they exited.

Taiqian looked over at him without smiling. "Hong Deming, see Master Zhu to the gate," he said.

Hong Deming went up to Zhu Guiren and bowed. "Sir, I'll lead you out," he said, hoping his voice conveyed some gratitude for his care for Liu Chenguang.

Zhu Guiren's distant eyes brushed over him with a brief, inattentive nod, but his beautiful face, usually so cold, looked extremely pleased.

CHAPTER 10
CRANE MOON

SEVERAL HOURS LATER, Liu Chenguang sat up in the cot, drinking some broth and making a face. He smiled when he saw Hong Deming duck in through the tent entrance. "Can I call you tainu now?" he asked.

Hong Deming settled next to him. "Not yet. You haven't completed the ceremony. When we get back to the sect, you'll bow to Taiqian formally and then he will be your sect father and we'll be sect brothers, and you can call him Taiqian, and I can call you taine, too, but not till then. What's wrong with the broth?"

"Nothing, I guess. I don't usually eat meat." Liu Chenguang sipped some more. "It just feels strange for my body. But Taiqian— I mean, the sect leader insisted we're traveling tomorrow, and I have to have enough strength to ride a horse."

Hong Deming said, very formally, "I'm sorry that I had you hold the sword."

"Why? That's not what made me fall down," he said, smiling. "Sect leader said a physician came to see me. Apparently, it's something about my well, which it turns out I do have. I'll cultivate and get better. And then I'll learn to be a healer. Everything is perfect."

Hong Deming wrapped his arms around his bent knees, feeling very much the same. "The physician who came for you is Zhu Guiren. He's an envoy from the Son of Heaven. You'll study with him when you're ready. I wonder if he'll bring you to the court?"

115

"What's he like?"

"He's very cultured and refined and elegant, and he knows a lot about the empire. I didn't know he was a physician until he came to see you. And he's very handsome."

Liu Chenguang made a face. "Why does that matter?"

"It doesn't, I guess. But wait till you see him. I've never seen anyone even close to his looks — like one of those characters in tales of deities and spirits."

Liu Chenguang shook his head, smiling, and sipped the broth again. "What an imagination you have. Have you ever seen an immortal?"

"Have you?" Hong Deming was very curious.

Liu Chenguang laughed a little bit. "No deities. Only people."

The Crane Moon's sect home was located in a remote, mountainous area, south and west of the old capital. Built high up on ledges and backed by a cliff, it centered around the temple and cultivation ground, with buildings and grounds on several different levels overlooking a narrow river gorge. Crane Moon wasn't a particularly large or important sect; it was known in the cultivation world for its age — Hong Deming was a disciple of the twenty-eighth generation — and the power of its sword cultivation. Among newer, larger, or more powerful sects competing for prominence and power in the cultivation world, the Crane Moon was far from the center of things. Nonetheless, there was a certain romance to it. Whenever they visited other sects, Hong Deming always felt a sense of pride that he had been chosen to follow the Crane Moon path.

Hong Deming stretched with relief as they completed the climb up the warded stairs and returned at last into the main courtyard, leaving the horses at the stable below the mountaintop. They followed Taiqian in good order: Shen Lu, Hong Deming, Liu Chenguang, still in his servants' clothes, and finally, the servants themselves, who instantly dispersed to their own quarters. The other members of the sect — martial uncles and aunts of Taiqian's generation, and the martial brothers and sisters of Hong Deming's — all greeted Taiqian formally as sect leader and followed him into the great hall of ceremony to feast and to see Liu Chenguang's acceptance as a disciple.

Liu Chenguang bowed three times formally to the ground, quite gracefully — he had been practicing all along the way to demonstrate good manners — and Taiqian formally accepted him, receiving his service as symbolized by a cup of tea. Liu Chenguang was now bound to obey Taiqian in all things, as a father and teacher, for the rest of his life. He would belong to the Crane Moon sect forever and Taiqian, in return, would care for him as a child and teach him, while the whole sect would protect him. When Liu Chenguang rose from the final bow, his face was very solemn, and his eyes were dark. Hong Deming remembered his own acceptance ceremony; he felt that there had been more joyousness about the whole thing. This time, all the older disciples were looking at one another, though no one dared to speak, and Taiqian's acceptance of Liu Chenguang as his final disciple was spoken without warmth or a smile. Hong Deming tried to catch Liu Chenguang's eye and look encouraging without success.

At last, the banquet became more relaxed, and the disciples were able to move around and chat with one another.

Hong Deming turned to Liu Chenguang, who was seated at the lowest table near him, and smiled. "Taine," he said, teasing, trying to get him to smile back.

Quietly, Liu Chenguang said, "Tainu." He looked very small in Hong Deming's outgrown sect uniform; there hadn't been any new ones ready, since no one had expected Taiqian to take a disciple again. His eyes still looked very serious. For the first time ever, Hong Deming thought he looked a little frightened.

Hong Deming reached over to his bowl and put in a few more mushrooms. "Here, taine, you'll need to build up your strength. You can have all the mushrooms you want now. Isn't the sauce good? We couldn't have this on the road, but the food will be much better now that we're home."

Liu Chenguang looked down and poked at the mushrooms unenthusiastically, then brought some to his mouth.

"Tomorrow you'll start cultivating and training with us—"

"Taiqian told me this afternoon that I'll go into seclusion tomorrow," Liu Chenguang interrupted quietly. "What's that like?"

"Seclusion?" Hong Deming frowned. "That's normally for very advanced disciples. It's silent meditation, alone in one of the spiritual caverns..."

He himself had never cultivated in seclusion, and wouldn't until he was ready to cultivate a spiritual weapon; it was the last test before spiritual adulthood. He was inwardly shocked that Taiqian would send Liu Chenguang into the caverns so quickly. People sometimes went into qi deviation during seclusion, but for those with the strength to bear it, seclusion was the best way to focus and advance quickly in cultivation — more than cultivating as part of one's regular life and interactions with the world.

"I suppose he thinks that's the best way for you to catch up, it's for your own good. Did he say for how long?"

"Two months, to begin."

Hong Deming choked. "Two months? Starting tomorrow? You won't be training with us at all?" He had been looking forward to trying to teach Liu Chenguang the sword again.

Liu Chenguang nodded and ate some more mushrooms. "I'm used to being alone," he said, finally. "It's not that difficult for me to be in seclusion, probably, it's not different from what I'm used to." He looked up and smiled bravely. "I'll be fine. When I come out, can I look for you?"

"Of course. Who else would you look for? I'm your tainu. Come with me. I'll show you all around the place before you have to go to the caverns tomorrow." He pulled Liu Chenguang up by the wrist and smiled at him, trying to get Liu Chenguang's eyes to shine again. "Come on."

He brought Liu Chenguang to see the dormitories, where each of the disciples had their own small room; the kitchens; the cultivation ground where they practiced meditation every morning and the sword path in the afternoons; the library full of scrolls and books; the music rooms where they learned qin; the archery grounds and the meditation gardens; the armory full of ancient weapons, though of course, they couldn't go in; the hot springs inside the mountain at the lowest level; the staircases and bridges that connected the pieces of the sect together, usable for defense as well as beauty.

"Look," he said, "this is my favorite place. I come here to just…imagine the world, sometimes."

It was a wall at the second highest level of the sect, which was built back against the mountain beneath the houses of the sect leader and head disciples. The wall around that level made a second curve here and leapt back out to enclose a tiny garden, capturing a trickling waterfall from the highest level in a shallow pool. From the pool, the water ran out again through a little channel and cut through the wall at the cliff's edge; the stream continued as a fall into the air, turning into mist a thousand feet above the ground below.

The little garden had only one small tree and a few green plants. Aside from the basin and the channel for the water, there was no sign of deliberate human planning. The tree had grown wild, as had the grass. There were no benches, or anywhere to sit except the wall itself.

"Look," Hong Deming said, "this is the best time."

He brought Liu Chenguang to stand near the cliff wall, where the water came down from above, and turned him to look toward the sheer drop beyond the outer wall, where the mist of the fall that never reached the ground was blown upward by the wind from below. As the sun neared its setting, red beams came through the gorge and diffused in the mist — not like a rainbow, but with every droplet sparking like a jewel, moving and changing like stars in unpredict-able patterns that seemed to always be on the verge of making sense.

Liu Chenguang sighed. "Thank you." He didn't smile, but his eyes shone again, as bright as the drops of mist. He looked out at it until the light faded, then turned to Hong Deming.

Now, the smile was there, and Hong Deming breathed, relieved in his heart.

"Tainu, you...I'll see you in two months." Liu Chenguang bowed and turned away.

There was plenty to keep Hong Deming busy after Liu Chenguang entered the caverns for seclusion. He was still effectively the youngest disciple, and at sixteen was nearing the completion of his foundation training. He had been ne-glecting his music and calligraphy in favor of archery, sword, and horsemanship while he had been gone — a journey of nearly six months total — but all of these were cultivational skills through which he could develop, express, and use qi, and his teachers insisted he work constantly to make up the lost time. He rarely had the opportunity to think that he finally had a taine, even if his taine was kept in seclusion all the time. It was only when he had a few moments of quiet, in the walled garden, or while playing qin, that Hong Deming would remember that his taine was here, but alone and silent in the dark.

Taiqian gave Liu Chenguang only short breaks before sending him back to the caverns, again and again, for longer and longer sessions. Whenever Liu Chenguang came out, though, it was true that he seemed stronger, and he was always cheerful and happy. In those months when he wasn't in secluded medita-tion, Liu Chenguang read the works that Zhu Guiren had assigned to him on his visits, studying in the sect library. After a couple more efforts to teach him basic sword forms that failed miserably — holding the sword seemed to make him extremely uncomfortable and set him back in cultivation, according to Shen Lu — Taiqian consulted with Zhu Guiren and decided to teach him only lightness skill and to play the qin for cultivation.

Every few months, Hong Deming would look up from whatever he was do-ing, whether sword or study or archery or music, and see Liu Chenguang stand-ing nearby, his eyes shining, smiling and waiting for him to notice. When his taine was not in seclusion, he and Liu Chenguang spent all their spare moments together. He would visit Liu Chenguang in the library to hear him explain the-ories of medicine and quiz him on acupoints and meridian paths, or they would wander in the mountain woods above the temple, looking for herbs and flowers with particular medicinal virtues and talking. Liu Chenguang had very strange views of the world, and Hong Deming always enjoyed hearing him make his unpredictable statements. They would be walking by a stream, and Liu Chenguang would suddenly kneel down and point to a rock that he thought was particularly interesting or exclaim at the tiny fish swimming nearby. He had an immense capacity for stillness and could lie on his stomach examining a flower for an hour at a time, yet at the same time, was full of energy held in check, just ready to be unleashed to run or jump or climb trees.

Once, they found a rabbit in the woods, injured by a predator. Liu Chenguang practiced his healing skills on it, showing Hong Deming how the wound would be washed and poulticed with boiled, crushed herbs.

"Now, you bandage it," he said, his voice cracking a little; it was mostly settled now into a light tenor, but occasionally would return to his boy's register. His long, fine fingers dexterously wrapped the injured leg with a strip of cloth. "I'll do it loosely so he can get it off by himself later. Just to keep the poultice on for a while...I've been practicing this, but it's my first time trying with a living creature. It does feel different! Stay still, little thing. If it was a person, we'd have him stay quiet in bed for a few days, but since it's a rabbit, he'd probably be so terrified that it wouldn't be helpful for him. So I think it's best to put him back in a safe place, we'll cut some grass and put it in there with him, and in a few days he'll be well."

He looked up, smiling. "Do you think it's silly for me to save a rabbit? After all, you shoot and eat them all the time."

Crouched next to him, Hong Deming smiled back. "It's different when it's hurt in front of you. I'm not hunting now, anyway. We have plenty to eat. Look, it's so soft." He reached out and stroked the rabbit's ears, but the little thing shivered, its eyes glazed.

"It's too frightened," Liu Chenguang said. "Just let it be. Rabbits can't tell a friend from an enemy."

"Hah, if you're a rabbit the whole world is your enemy. Of course it's frightened."

"Where do you think its burrow is?"

Hong Deming looked around. "There's a hole at the bottom of that tree," he said, and looked in it. "I can see rabbit fur caught in the edge here. This is probably safe, unless it belongs to some other rabbit."

Carefully, he lifted the creature up and put it gently into the hole. "If this isn't your home, brother rabbit, forgive us. This is the best we can do."

Liu Chenguang knelt down and put handfuls of grass in. "Here you go! Be well, my first patient." He grinned up at Hong Deming. "It would be nice for you to remember this one next time you're out hunting and try not to shoot it."

"I'll do my best, but if it's not wearing that bandage, it will look like all other rabbits. At least I'm a better shot than whatever tried to get him. Little rabbit, if I come for you, it'll quick and painless."

Liu Chenguang pushed him gently. "Stop that, you're scaring my patient." He stood up and brushed the grass off his robes. "Come on, let's go wash off. My hands are all covered in blood."

As they walked together toward the lake, Hong Deming asked, "You don't eat meat — is that because of your cultivation path?"

"Partly...It's not good for me to hurt any beings, or to benefit from hurting any beings," he said, tripping slightly over a root.

Hong Deming grabbed his elbow. "Are you all right? Why are you tripping? You didn't use any qi for that, did you? Master Zhu said you're not to use qi for healing until your cultivation is complete."

"No, no, I was just thinking about things, not looking where I was going." Liu Chenguang continued, "It's really good for me to be learning from him, from all these books, so I can do other things besides use qi...I can save it for really important things that way. For things that can't be healed by any other method."

"Will you really be able to heal anything like Master Zhu said?"

"Yes," he said, bluntly and confidently, no room for doubt. "There's nothing I can't heal. Even now, I could. It's just that I don't have enough qi stored to do it safely yet for serious things."

Hong Deming walked quietly next to him, hands behind his back, considering Liu Chenguang's profile. "Will you tell me something, honestly?"

Liu Chenguang looked at him, surprised. "Of course. I've never lied to you. I never will," he said seriously.

"Did you heal that man in the house? The one I got in the throat, that time we were fighting the bandits. The time you collapsed."

"Yes."

"Why would you do that? He had just tried to rape that girl. He had killed that man. He was a murderer many times over." Hong Deming frowned. "I'm not angry, but what was the point? What if he'd killed you? What if he'd killed me? And his life was going to end either way..."

"I don't know. It was just an instinct when I was younger. Just something I did whenever I saw people hurt. That village you found me in — do you remember?"

"Of course I remember."

"I'd been trying to heal people, but the bandits came back and they hurt me too, so I was unconscious for a while as I was healing. I'd probably just woken up when you came...and I still healed that person in the house, even though I knew exactly who and what he was. I don't know. I know it doesn't make sense. I understand now why it doesn't make sense to you. I can't really justify it. Of course I know he was a criminal and he would be executed if he wasn't killed by you directly...it's just...you know. Like the rabbit. The one in front of me."

Liu Chenguang walked a little further, frowning thoughtfully. "There's something I heard once: done is done, and pain is pain. What that man had done in the past...That couldn't be undone, whatever pain he'd caused. But if he's in pain in front of me, I can do something about that. Maybe I'm the only one who can. Who knows what he will do if he lives? Perhaps good things. I can only choose to heal, or not."

Hong Deming shook his head. "Think about the consequences, though. Should you really heal everyone you see? Some people will just cause more pain in the world. Some people probably shouldn't be saved."

"Some people probably shouldn't," Liu Chenguang agreed. "But I have to save them anyway."

They reached the stream and knelt down next to each other to wash their hands; Hong Deming looked over at him, thinking how easy it would have been for that bandit to kill him that day. What would it have been if he had come just a minute later, with the three men hacking at the unarmed boy trying to block them with his body? His heart hurt a little bit.

Liu Chenguang smiled at him. "You're so serious," he said, and splashed water at Hong Deming's face.

"You are going to pay for that." Hong Deming narrowed his eyes at him and reached out to pull him into the water by his sleeve.

Several years after Liu Chenguang's arrival, Hong Deming accompanied him quite high on the mountain, helping him look for a tiny flower that only grew between rocks up above the tree line. By the time they found the lichen and Liu Chenguang had carefully collected the little flowers into a small linen bag, night was already starting to fall.

"Come on." Hong Deming looked up at the sky. "We're going to have to be fast going back down. This is a good time to practice your lightness skills."

Liu Chenguang made a face. "I'm tired," he said. Then, smiling, "Do you think you can still carry me on your back?"

Hong Deming looked him up and down seriously. "Well, if I had to, probably. But I'm too lazy today, so move your own feet."

Liu Chenguang laughed and leapt forward, moving from rock to rock down the cliff quicker than a mountain sheep, touching each stone with just the tips of his feet before moving forward.

Hong Deming jumped after him, trying to get ahead. "Ha!" he yelled. "Shameless, you went first without waiting—"

Liu Chenguang turned in midair to say something back to him, but missed the next landing point and tumbled a little way down the cliff.

"Taine!" Hong Deming shouted. He put more qi into his movements, nearly flying down to meet him.

Liu Chenguang had righted himself after bouncing off a couple of rocks and continued to leap down to more level ground, but Hong Deming could see that his movements were uncoordinated. In a moment, he would lose lightness completely and fall to the ground, still from a great height. He managed to catch up, put an arm around Liu Chenguang's ribs, and complete the movements to the bottom of the cliff.

He lay Liu Chenguang down carefully and reached for his lower leg, which was at a strange angle below the knee.

But Liu Chenguang, very pale, pushed his hand away. "It's all right. Don't worry. It'll be fine by tomorrow."

"What are you talking about?" Hong Deming asked, a little angry. "The bone is broken. I can see from how it's lying. And there's blood, too…it must have punched through the skin. How will it be all right tomorrow if we don't clean and splint it?"

To his shock, he saw Liu Chenguang reach down, his hands around his own leg, and wrench it into position.

"Ah," he said briefly, turning even paler.

"Don't pass out," Hong Deming said, alarmed.

"No, no, it's good now." Liu Chenguang panted a little bit, and color came back into his face. "Remember, I have that healing path. This is part of it. My body heals itself quickly. When I have my full cultivation, this kind of thing would heal in just a few moments, but as things are now…probably I'll need to stay here overnight." He looked around at the darkening sky.

"You can't stay here by yourself, taine," Hong Deming said firmly.

Liu Chenguang looked at him strangely. "Are you worried about me? You don't need to be. You can go back down. It's all right."

"You're not thinking well. How can you defend yourself if anything comes? You can't use weapons and you can't move. Should I carry you?"

Liu Chenguang shook his head. "I'm sorry, tainu. The leg shouldn't be moved or jostled. I wouldn't be able to hold on to you."

Hong Deming stood. "I'll get firewood."

"Is my qinggong really that bad, tainu?"

"Sloppy," he called back over his shoulder. "Can you eat meat if I shoot something?"

"Better not right now. Don't worry about me," Liu Chenguang said.

When he returned, he had brought not only a rabbit for himself but some nuts, berries, and mushrooms for Liu Chenguang. He took out a piece of cloth and laid it all next to him; Liu Chenguang looked at him, eyes wide.

"Well, make sure none of it will kill you," Hong Deming said, "but that's all I could find." He had already cleaned the rabbit and put bits of it on skewers around the fire. "It's too bad you can't eat this. Isn't it good for wounds to eat meat?"

"Not for me, tainu. It's really very different for me, but thank you. There's plenty here that I can eat. You've gotten better at avoiding poisonous mushrooms." He picked up some nuts and ate them slowly. After a while, he said, "Tainu, you take really good care of me. I'm grateful."

"It's just what I should do," Hong Deming said. "But it would be better if you had good skills. Then I wouldn't need to worry about you so much."

"You worry about me?"

"A little...just knowing that you can't use a sword or anything."

"Most people can't."

"But I don't know most people, so I don't worry about them," Hong Deming said, smiling. He reached over to poke Liu Chenguang in the shoulder. "Only my taine."

After a while, Liu Chenguang asked, "When I'm in seclusion, what do you do?"

"Pretty much the same thing I do when you're out of it. Practice the sword. Practice calligraphy and qin and archery. Only, I don't spend as much time studying in the library."

Liu Chenguang hesitated a moment. "Do you spend time with other people the way you do with me when I'm not in seclusion?"

"Well, of course. All the other disciples. But when you're not in seclusion I want to spend time with you, since it's not often..." He trailed off, realizing that when Liu Chenguang was in seclusion, life really was pretty boring. "Anyway, there's no one else who likes to go in the woods or do different things like you do. Don't you want to get to know some of the other disciples better, too?" he asked. "We're all a family."

"I haven't even met any of the female disciples," Liu Chenguang said. "But all my tainu…none of them pay much attention to me, except for you."

"We're the youngest of this generation, that's all," Hong Deming said. "They'll choose some more young disciples soon. More of the seniors are ready to teach, I think."

He took a stick out of the fire and began to blow on its bits of rabbit meat. "Did you know that Shen Lu is going to get married soon? He met a disciple from the Peaceful River sect a year ago, and it's all set. She'll come here to live, since Shen Lu will be the next sect leader."

Liu Chenguang was quiet for a while. "Look at the stars," he said, looking up and carefully lying down to see better. "It's so clear tonight."

Hong Deming finished eating his rabbit and lay down next to him. "Yes, look there — a falling star…"

"Master Zhu assigned me some astronomy readings this time, but they didn't talk much about falling stars. At least, not that I've read yet."

As the fire died down, the cold began to increase; they were still very high up. Hong Deming began to draw on qi to keep himself warm and looked, concerned, over at Liu Chenguang. "Taine, are you cold?"

"A little bit," he said, teeth chattering.

Since they didn't have any blankets, he put more wood on the fire, but the cold became more intense. He moved over closer to Liu Chenguang and said, "I'll help you keep warm, taine, all right?"

"All right," he said.

When Hong Deming put his arms around him carefully, trying to avoid touching his hurt leg or jostling him, he could feel Liu Chenguang's entire body shaking uncontrollably. "Shhhh, be still. I still don't know how to share qi."

"Hah," said Liu Chenguang, "I do know how. I just am using all my qi to heal my leg."

"I know. Don't feel bad about it." He leaned back against a rock and drew Liu Chenguang further under his arm, draping his own robe around him. He'd have to use qi to stay warm himself and to generate warmth for Liu Chenguang as well. "Go to sleep, taine."

Liu Chenguang said, "Thank you for worrying about me."

"Mm," he said, feeling sleepy and comfortable. "So silly. Don't show off skills you don't have next time. I know you're good at other things."

Liu Chenguang's hair smelled pleasant — a blend of medicinal herbs and incense. He yawned; producing so much warmth was tiring. "We can...we can work on the qinggong another time..."

After a while, Liu Chenguang asked, "How old are you now, tainu?"

Hong Deming had set his concentration on using his qi to create enough warmth for both of them and had planned to fall asleep that way, but Liu Chenguang's questions kept distracting him. When he lost his focus, he realized that somehow their bodies had become closely intertwined, and he felt a little awkward. Liu Chenguang was still small, but the weight and shape of his body half-lying on his own was no longer that of a child. He coughed and tried to straighten up a little bit, refocusing on warmth. "I'm almost twenty, I'll have my adulthood ceremony soon."

"Oh. You told me before that when you've had your ceremony you'll go to the Peaceful River sect too, won't you?"

"That's what Taiqian wants for me. He wants me to spend a few years focused on qin cultivation under their sect leader. I'm already advanced enough here."

"And you'll have a spiritual sword?"

"Yes, certainly that will be soon. I'll have to go into seclusion for that myself."

Liu Chenguang looked up at him. "I'm eighteen. Zhu Guiren will come soon to make the decision, but Taiqian thinks I probably only need one more period of seclusion before my cultivation foundation is set. Then, I'll leave with him to study. I don't know when I'll be back."

"You'll come back someday," he said, confidently. "We both will. This is our home." He looked down at Liu Chenguang, at his eyes, shining in the starlight beneath his lashes.

Liu Chenguang's eyes were always bright and interested in the world, but now they looked rather soft and sad.

Impulsively, Hong Deming said, "Don't worry, taine. We'll always see each other again. Eventually, you'll be done with all this time of seclusion and your life will get easier. I know it's been hard for you." He carefully pressed on his shoulder, comforting. "With Zhu Guiren, you'll see so much of the world. Maybe even the emperor and the court. You'll learn so many things and meet many new people. You won't need to worry about whether you can do the same things we ordinary disciples can because you'll be able to do so much more. There are thousands of people that can use swords, but you will be a divine physician.

There's no one like you, taine."

Liu Chenguang smiled. "There's no one like you either, tainu."

He felt absurdly warmed and checked to see if he'd been overdoing it with the qi generation. He patted Liu Chenguang's shoulder again. "Shh. Time to sleep."

CHAPTER 11
SECLUSION

LIU CHENGUANG HAD been in his final time of seclusion for a month already when Taiqian directed Hong Deming to enter.

As a very young disciple, Hong Deming had entered the spiritual caverns soon after he first formed his well of qi for a brief ceremony, but never since then. Secluded cultivation was reserved for particularly important steps in a cultivator's life, and highly-advanced practitioners that had reached a plateau in their cultivation would sometimes enter seclusion for years at a time in order to reach a breakthrough. Aside from this, a young cultivator in the Crane Moon sect would normally enter only when they had reached the point of developing a spiritual weapon.

Hong Deming knew that it would be dark and quiet and that there was a risk, as for everyone, of qi deviation during the intensity of this cultivation period. Beyond that, he had no idea what to expect.

Taiqian led him through the winding corridors inside the mountain, concentrating on finding an area that would be most appropriate for Hong Deming's cultivation. He ended up choosing a cavern with a small, clear stream running over a bed of silvery pebbles. The sound was peaceful, enticing — Hong Deming liked it immediately. He saluted Taiqian silently; Taiqian departed in equal silence.

Until he had a spiritual sword, he would not speak, or eat, or drink, or leave the cavern.

The darkness was complete. The only sounds were the quiet trickle of water, his own breathing, his own heartbeat. In a lotus position, he slowed both and practiced quieting his mind. There were many scriptures appropriate to seclusion, but he found that none of them suited his inner direction. Instead, he opened his mind completely to silence — only the sound of the stream, only the pebbles being slowly worn away into their new forms.

At first, he saw lights and images in his mind, and he let them go and come as they would. None left a mark and eventually, they, too, disappeared. Repeated words, phrases, obsessive thoughts, came and fell down into silence. His emotions — sorrow, loss, fear, anxiety, joy, memories of the past, imaginations of the future — all observed and released. He felt his stomach contract, longing for food, sometimes even making noises demanding it; eventually, that also wore away, like all the senses of his body. Like the pebbles beneath the stream. Like the water in the veins of the earth, he directed the qi of his body through his meridians, gradually sensing its increase in strength and purity.

There was now no boundary between his body and the darkness, and no difference between darkness and light. The qi within his body was no different than the qi of the living world around him. Like the water of the stream, it came from one place and went to another, but was all of one being in the end.

His awareness touched on other living beings, and he felt something.

Out of the darkness, beyond time, he felt something new — something in his heart that had no name, a longing for which he could place no object. Unlike all that had come before, this longing disturbed his equanimity. It called his heart out from his body, and his body out from life into the dark to seek what he so desperately needed, what he could not put a name to. Would he even know it when he found it? He flailed in the darkness, seeking in all directions for the thing without which he could not live. His heart called out in desperation, crying for something undiscovered and unknown.

His breathing broke its rhythm.

With the shift came the need to control his breathing again, and with the need for control came the loss of connection to the qi rushing through him.

Hong Deming was consciously aware that he was spiraling into qi deviation; the qi in his meridians surged beyond his body's capacity to contain it. As though from a great distance, he knew that his body was in pain. There was a small, glowing figure doubled over, convulsing, blood coming from the seven orifices. This body did not have a connection with his ability to control it, no matter how much he desired to do so. The borders had been blurred and broken. He could

129

no longer set the boundaries of the qi flooding in and overwhelming him.

Suddenly, there was a second body rushing in, a body with intention and awareness and control. This body knelt down and touched his face with fingers that shone blood red. He could feel it touching him — his eyes, his nostrils, his ears, his lips — anointing him.

With a rush, he was back inside his body, gasping for air. He could feel hands on him, hear breathing that was not his own, though he couldn't see anything at all. But in the complete darkness, touch and scent and hearing were increased beyond any normal sensitivity. From the breath, from the shape of the fingers lightly touching his lips, from the faint scent of herbs and incense, he said, without thinking, breaking the silence of seclusion for both of them, "Liu Chenguang." His voice was hoarse with disuse.

The fingers on his lips were removed, then placed firmly on his heart meridian, still in silence. He could feel Liu Chenguang's long hair brushing his wrist; he must be leaning over closely. Hong Deming shivered all over with the increased sensitivity to touch. He could feel, now, the warmth of qi entering from Liu Chenguang's fingers — a stream that went throughout his meridians, calming and healing everything that was there, all the chaos smoothed out.

"Don't. Not good for you," Hong Deming said, and tried to move his arm, but Liu Chenguang firmly grasped it, and he was too weak to move away.

When the fingers were removed, Hong Deming was able to bring himself back into a lotus position without pain. His mind felt clear and peaceful again. He regretted that he had broken Liu Chenguang's seclusion and had even required him to use qi for healing, but he had truly needed it. He didn't think that there was anything he could have done to save himself. Cultivators risked death in qi deviation from seclusion. He had known this going in. Only because Liu Chenguang had been there, had taken the risk of injuring his own cultivation to save him, was Hong Deming still alive. There was nothing he could do about this now except determine how to repay Liu Chenguang in the future.

As he felt Liu Chenguang move next to him, he reached out and took his wrist, smoothing out his closed fingers and palm. Carefully, he wrote the character for gratitude, en, in the palm of Liu Chenguang's hand. The hand remained in his own for another moment, warm and quiet, peaceful, then was softly withdrawn.

He heard the steps, felt the warmth of the living person withdraw from his cavern, still in silence, leaving him alone.

There was no way to know time's passing in the cavern, but there came a moment when he reached his hand into the darkness and felt it close around the hilt of a sword; he named it En. *Gratitude.*

He then stood up and walked out into the world again with the sword in his hand.

He had been in seclusion for six months.

Hong Deming formally presented the sword to Taiqian and told him its name and what had happened in seclusion without hiding either his qi deviation or the fact that he owed his life to Liu Chenguang.

Taiqian looked serious about this. "Liu Chenguang did not mention this when he left seclusion, and has already departed with Zhu Guiren for his further training," he said slowly. "I will write to Zhu Guiren and tell him. It may be important for him to know in case it has serious effects for him later."

Hong Deming felt as clear and calm as a still pond, but the realization that Liu Chenguang was no longer at Crane Moon was a stone that caused ripples in his mind.

Taiqian must have noticed this in his face. "Are you distressed that your taine has gone?"

"I wanted to thank him properly."

"You'll have a chance in the future. You owe him a debt, certainly. Zhu Guiren told the truth that day when he said that someone on the healing path would be an asset to our sect. Your life is already repayment for having offered him a home here." He added, "When Shen Lu becomes the sect leader, I will enter seclusion myself for a while, but he knows about Liu Chenguang's special status. I'll be sure that he knows as well that he has shown himself to be a devoted and loyal taine to you in this way."

In his post-seclusion clarity, Hong Deming realized what lay beneath these words: Taiqian had doubts about Liu Chenguang, and these doubts were shared by Shen Lu. Why would this be, when Liu Chenguang was so obviously a good person? But,he also felt clearly that this was not the time to ask, even if he had the status to question Taiqian about such a thing. He only said, "I'll always be grateful that he is my taine."

"You named your sword En for this reason. For your gratitude for him."

"Yes, that's why."

Taiqian nodded slowly. "In regard to your qi deviation, it seems that it was caused by an unrestrained longing. Did the desire have an object?"

"No. I couldn't tell what it was that I wanted or needed, yet it seemed that if I didn't have it…" He tried to put it into words. "It seemed that if I didn't have… whatever it was…that everything would fall apart, somehow. Nothing as simple as death, but that everything would…" He trailed off, helplessly. "The fear of not finding what I was seeking — it made me so terrified that I lost control of everything."

"Unrestrained desire without an object…this is what you will need to work on during your next phase of cultivation," Taiqian responded. "It may be that you need to discover what it is that you truly desire, or it may be that you need to let go of desire entirely. Both of these are possible cultivation paths, and desire can take many forms and have many objects, not all of which are acceptable or attainable. But, to desire so deeply and not know what it is that you desire…that path is clearly not one that you can continue to walk indefinitely. This is what your sword seclusion has shown you. For this self-knowledge, be grateful to your sword as well."

He bent his head. "Yes, Taiqian."

"In two weeks, it will be time for your crowning as an adult. Spend time between now and then on getting to know the ways of your new sword, and on qin. Nothing more than those two things. After your adulthood ceremony, you will travel to the Peaceful River sect for training with qin cultivation." He added, "Peaceful River sect is less strict than the Crane Moon in some ways. While you are there, make wise decisions, but don't judge harshly or be too quick to refuse their invitations. Crane Moon's path is strong, but narrow, like a sword blade. Sometimes, it's good for the spirit to experience the world differently before one comes back home."

Hong Deming looked at him, confused.

Taiqian shook his head, smiling a little. "You know that your sect mother came from the Peaceful River sect. So does Shen Lu's wife. It often happens that leaving Crane Moon to visit another sect or to wander beyond the bounds is a time to explore human relationships, and that is appropriate at your time of life. You are an adult. Your decisions are your own. Only marriage needs to be approved by the Crane Moon. That's all I want you to know, speaking as your Taiqian — that it's not forbidden, even if it's not the way we live here within our own sect home."

"I don't think…" he said, stumbling. "I just have never…I don't think I'm ready to consider marriage yet."

"No need until you are ready." Taiqian stood up, handing him back the sword. "Liu Chenguang will never achieve a spiritual sword. Though he is my youngest disciple in name, you are my youngest in the Crane Moon sword path. The name of your sword is appropriate. I, too, am grateful that you have completed your cultivation and can now go out into the world."

Hong Deming placed the sword by his side, knelt, and bowed his head to the ground, palms flat. The words he spoke were formal, but they were truly in his heart as well: "This humble person is grateful to Taiqian for his life and teaching. This insignificant person will strive not to dishonor the Crane Moon sect."

The crowning ceremony was accompanied by a feast of departure not only for Hong Deming leaving for Peaceful River, but for Taiqian entering secluded cultivation; Shen Lu, Hong Deming's tainu, would now be sect leader and Taiqian to a new generation of disciples. The feast was thus a double celebration.

No one seemed to remember that Liu Chenguang was really the youngest disciple, not Hong Deming. He felt this a little painfully — that no one but him seemed to remember Liu Chenguang at all, or care that he wasn't present. Nonetheless, Liu Chenguang would always be his taine. Nothing on earth could change that. There would be years and years ahead for them to be together at the sect. The others would realize what a wonderful person he was, and that even if his cultivation was different from everyone else's, he was valuable for that very reason.

Hong Deming left the next morning, riding toward Zhashan, first down the gorge path, then down progressively larger and busier roads and highways to the great capital — or, the capital that had once been, before the new Son of Heaven moved it to Gunan.

Zhashan was a city almost in ruins after its repeated sackings, lootings, rebellions, and forced removals. Hong Deming sat outside of the walls that remained, watching the few inhabitants trying to reconstruct their lives, the scavengers trying to find whatever they could to fill tonight's cookpot. This had been a city of almost a million people, he had read in the library of the Crane Moon. Monasteries and abbeys, palaces and ponds, marketplaces, brothels, foreigners and flowers and fruit trees — all were now gone.

Zhashan was where Taiqian had found him as an abandoned child. He thought he might be able to find the place, or the people that cared for him, but this was clearly impossible. Out of those million people, he would never know who had given birth to him or given him his name. He watched a small child eat spoiled vegetables from the ground and his heart ached, but when he offered dried fruit from his supplies the child ran in terror.

After wandering the rubble-strewn streets, he continued his journey toward Gunan. The highway was growing more crowded, and bandits preyed on wealthier travelers. Since he was a cultivator from a righteous sect, he was called upon to protect various groups, and didn't mind doing so in return for food and conversation. One such group was conveying a young woman and her dowry to her new husband in Gunan, and although they had initially had many guards, it was so obviously an excellent target that they had already been attacked multiple times since setting out. Hong Deming wasn't naturally given to solitude; after his seclusion, the lonely journey, and the depression of seeing the ruins of Zhashan, he was eager to spend time with human beings again, hearing them laugh and tell stories and share food together.

"Handsome one," called one of the lady's maids to him as he rode along their column, "come visit with us!" She stuck her head out of the carriage, smiling at him admiringly.

He smiled back and slowed his horse so he could ride alongside her.

"Handsome one, what's your name?"

"Hong Deming," he said. "And you?"

"Oh, they call me Peony," she said. She had pale skin and black hair caught back from her face with very tiny brass pins, and clearly wasn't a woman completely without worldly experience; she was well made-up, wearing a heavily embroidered dress and shawl. "I'm the maid of the Lady Su, who is the first concubine of the house. The girl being married is her daughter. Lady Su sent me along to ensure that all is well with the marriage and that the girl is happy. I suppose you can say I'm her maid now, though I'm older than she is."

Hong Deming found her very funny. It was just like the stories he'd heard from his elder martial brothers about the men and women of the world outside the sect; he hadn't believed that people would actually talk like this and be this obvious, but it appeared that this woman was bored enough to attempt to seduce an unknown cultivator hired to guard the convoy. He tried to decide whether he was interested, and discerned that he was not in the least. But at least it was not boring to hear her talk and attempt to invite him to come into the carriage without saying so, getting more and more brazen about her intentions as time went on.

Eventually, since he did actually have a job to do for these people, he excused himself and rode up and down the column slowly, keeping an eye on the woods to one side and the road to the other. He wondered if his presence alone would be enough to deter bandits, but he didn't look that impressive in simple traveling robes with an unremarkable sword, bow, and quiver. It was unlikely that the embroidered symbol of the Crane Moon on his robe meant much to anyone at this point.

When the bandits did attack, it was something of a surprise for them; about twenty came rushing out of the woods to one side as the convoy entered a narrow stretch of road, blocking off the road in front with another twenty and far outnumbering the guards of the convoy. Arrows were already coming out of the trees. He sent a few back in answer and blocked the rest with his sword, leaving only a few to strike the carriages or in the dirt.

The difficulty, as Hong Deming saw it, was protecting two sides at once; which should be first?

Woods, he decided. The arrows were annoying, and endangering his charges. He rode through the attackers, slashing from one side to the other, using as little qi as was necessary to control the sword. These appeared to be ordinary people; there was no need to use the full power he would bring to a battle with a true cultivation opponent. For something like this, he hardly needed to exert himself. Several bandits fell easily, blood spurting wherever the sword went, and those that survived retreated into the woods. By that point, he was at the front of the convoy and cut through those attempting to block the road with similar ease. He then shooed the carriages through at top speed and fell in behind them.

This all took only a few moments; he had not even needed to dismount. He flicked the blood from En's blade and settled in as rearguard just to see if any of the bandits had any further ideas. Then he thought of something himself.

"I'll be right back," he called, and cantered back, looking for a survivor. He knelt down next to a man cradling his arm in shock. En had carved a piece out of the bandit's upper arm, though truly it was only a flesh wound.

"You'll survive." He realized that the bandit, staring at him pale and terrified, was younger than he was — perhaps only a skinny seventeen. His weapon, he saw now, was only a rusted blade, such as a farmer might use to cut wood. Are all the others as prepared as you?" Hong Deming blurted out.

"We're starving," the boy said. "That's all. Why would we do this if we had any other choice?" He rocked in pain, closing his eyes.

For a moment, disconcertingly, Hong Deming thought of Liu Chenguang, who would have been able to heal him, for good or for ill.

"Just kill me. There's nothing I can do about any of it."

Trying to put authority into his voice, Hong Deming said, "Tell the others to stop attacking travelers. This is the only end they'll come to if they're not captured and executed for brigandage first."

"Execution, no execution…we're all dying anyway," the boy said, his eyes glinting up from beneath his lids. "So lucky for you — you have food, you're so smart, so powerful, you can kill us, whatever. Every day we live through an attack, we eat. Every day we eat, we live to attack again. There's nothing else to do. So just kill me or stop talking." He grunted, rose to his feet, and staggered away.

Hong Deming watched him go.

He thought of the beauty of the Crane Moon sect: the quiet library, the jeweled mist in the sunset, the cavern with the clear stream, Liu Chenguang's hand in his in the dark. Hong Deming looked at the sword in his hand, which was now clean of blood, a bond with the deepest realities of existence that allowed him to kill starving boys without even breaking a sweat.

Was there anything else he could have done?

Why had his elder martial brothers never talked about this, when they talked about the world?

He found that he really wanted to talk to Liu Chenguang.

Like Crane Moon, the Peaceful River sect was dedicated to the Pathless Way. It had long been located in an ancient abbey in Zhashan. Like all the other residents of Zhashan, the sect had been forced to move to Gunan a few years ago. Though Gunan, too, was ancient, as a result of the relocation of the imperial court, the whole city had a sense of raw, unsettled frenzy about it. Hong Deming asked through the streets until he found where the Peaceful River had set up its new sect location — an abbey built outside of the city walls on a hill set back from the river, planted with peonies. The track wound up steeply between the flowers, giving the sense of rising up above the world into the heavens. As he passed under the gate, he turned to look back at the sun across the river, the valley full of shadows as the sun neared setting.

"Why do I feel so melancholy?" he asked no one in particular.

"I have no idea," a voice answered. A young man stuck his face out from behind the gate pillar, where he had apparently been sleeping in the shade. "But it's nothing that some good liquor and conversation shouldn't cure, I'm betting." He smiled, hopped up to his feet, and bowed without the slightest bit of embarrassment at having been caught sleeping on guard.

"I'm Mo Xiang, fourth disciple of the seventh generation of the Peaceful River sect," he said. His hair was up in a pincrown, but his manner was so playful that it was hard to believe he was an adult. After the images of corpses and starving children and ruined cities that had kept intruding into his mind throughout the journey, day after day, Hong Deming found him almost dreamlike.

Mo Xiang reached down and picked up a qin. "Please forgive me for seeming overtired, but it's a hot day, and I can only play the qin for so long among the flowers and sunshine before feeling as though staying awake to guard against enemies is really pointless." He winked. "And after all, we are not expecting an enemy; I've been here the past several days to greet a friend. Who I think, judging by that embroidery on your robe, is you. Would the gentleman honor me with his name?"

Hong Deming had to laugh. "I'm Hong Deming. I've been sent–"

"From the Crane Moon, yes. Your sect leader sent a letter to expect you weeks ago. Were the roads bad? Oh, come up. You must be tired and hungry." He gestured toward the path, which continued to climb and twist between peonies and rocks. "There's a ward here. It's not all dependent on my meager skills to defend the sect. You'll have to follow me closely so I can bring you in. Just leave the horse...see, there's a place there to tether the reins? The servants will come bring it to the stables later."

He set the qin on a convenient boulder and began to play a haunting melody. Hong Deming felt a shifting of the energy of the air — something was being opened in front of them, although until it was open he hadn't realized it was closed.

"Maze ward," Mo Xiang casually called while playing. "Outsiders just get lost and then dumped outside the boundary. It's not harmful to anyone, but why make you go through that? All right, that's enough, come on."

Hong Deming followed him up the winding path, impressed with Mo Xiang's skill. Behind him, the river valley was filled with shadows, but the hilltop was bright and filled with the sound of music.

Mo Xiang brought him to a small cell with a window looking out toward the mountains of Crane Moon, which he could no longer see behind the great gates of the Sorrowful River. He bathed and changed into clean clothes, then sat near the window, his chin in his hand and the world laid out before him — cities and rivers and mountains, shadowed and bright, without any boundaries visible on it — and imagined that Liu Chenguang was there to look at it with him.

CHAPTER 12
DISTRACTION

DESPITE HIS BRAVADO, Zhu Guiren eventually had to return to Tainu's ward in exhaustion. No more soul-devourers had come, but the attacks from demons and yaoguai had been unrelenting, and he had, after all, just lost a hand, although he acted as though this was no more than a minor irritation. Despite hating him, Tairei said nothing when Tainu dragged him back inside and told him to go to sleep before further strengthening the ward.

Tairei settled herself again, closing her eyes, one hand on Aili's hair. She wasn't even trying to cultivate now — just wallowing in memories that hit her harder than they had in centuries with Aili in front of her, next to her, touched by her. When she leapt down from the world tree and saw Aili walking in from the darkness next to Tainu, sword in hand, the expression on Aili's face, the way she held her body, all of it had literally knocked the wind out of her. She had had to gasp for breath as she ran forward, almost hysterical, to touch her and make sure she was real.

Her mind had seen Hong Deming in that very posture, weary and confused and lost, covered in blood after that first battle outside Gunan. He had run toward Hong Deming then, tripping over the corpses. Hong Deming had flicked the blood from his sword, looked out over the corpses, and said none of the blood was his, but he had been hurt inside. All the certainty of his world had gone. Back then, she had seen it in his eyes; she could see it now in Aili's.

138

Hong Deming hadn't let him touch him then. He had been so cautious about touching one another at that time, she remembered. But Aili was here now. She could touch Aili. She was real, she was alive. She sighed, and stroked Aili's hair, gently. She wanted to say *I'm here. It's me; it's Liu Chenguang, your little martial sibling. I am real. You can count on me…*

But after all, in the end…

She wanted to kiss her, but Zhu Guiren was awake again. The demon was humming softly to himself, eyes closed, as though very pleased with the way all the world was going. Tairei looked at him with disgust.

"Why did you make up all that?" she asked suddenly. "All that stupidity about me being born with a cultivator's well of qi, the healing path– all of it?"

"Don't you admire my creativity?" Zhu Guiren opened his eyes. "Use your brain. Why do you think I did it? Obviously because it benefited me."

"In what way?"

"Why are you so stupid? Didn't I teach you to figure things out?" He yawned. "Think about it. What was the result of all that? What happened?"

"Taiqian accepted me as a disciple. I stayed with the sect…"

"Exactly. It was perfect. Even you didn't know I'd made it up. You thought I was a human doctor believing in myths. Mistaken, but you went along with it because it benefited you too. I knew you couldn't resist the chance of having a place to cultivate to adulthood that would be safe and warded from demonic attack. And then, when you had your full power, you'd trust me. I'd know where to find you. It saved me all the time and effort of capturing you."

He nodded. "It was a spur-of-the-moment thing…I hadn't planned to have a phoenix. I wasn't the one that had been chasing you in the spirit realm. I wasn't the one who had driven you into the mortal realm before you had completed your regeneration, but as soon as I saw you, as soon as I knew what you were, I knew how I could use it. No demon has ever had an adult phoenix to use before. And you did it willingly. Stayed near me, obeyed my orders…"

Tairei was quiet, trying to bite down on her rage. Tainu was watching them. Tainu would be upset; for some reason her sibling wanted her to be polite to this creature. *He protected us, he's lost his hand,* she chanted inwardly to calm herself. Then she said, "I didn't stay because I wanted to cultivate. I didn't stay for you. And I never fully trusted you."

"Who cares?" He shrugged his shoulders. "It still all worked out the way I planned. Why tell me now?"

"Because you should know you're not as smart as you think you are. You think you are controlling people, controlling events, but things are really happening for other reasons."

Zhu Guiren said, "Whatever. As long as I win, I win."

"You didn't win, you stupid, self-satisfied piece of garbage. You didn't win."

The demon looked at her, eyes wide. For the first time, his face showed something other than his usual expression of pleased arrogance.

Tainu's voice came calmly: "Demon, stop provoking her, or you can leave. Can't you even understand what you've done?"

Zhu Guiren's face fell for a moment, and then he said, "I made it as painless for her as I could."

Tairei said, "I wish so much that I was able to kill you for saying that."

Zhu Guiren turned toward her in what seemed to be genuine surprise. "I kept you unconscious for almost all of it—"

"Shut up," she hissed. "Shut up, shut up, shut up."

"Shut up," Tainu said firmly. "Get out."

The demon stood up and pushed through the ward.

"Do you think he'll come back?" Tairei asked after a while.

"Do you care?"

"I want him to leave. His face makes me want to vomit," Tairei said fiercely. "And don't you dare tell me done is done. There's no possible pain he could be feeling that I could care about."

"I'll be honest, Tairei, I think we are going to need his help."

"No."

"For Aili's sake."

Tairei fell silent.

Tainu continued, "Whether he helps us or not, we need to move today. He can't defend us for another nightfall regardless, it'll just get worse. We need to get to a refuge. My wards are under attack, and I can't hold much longer."

They both looked outside the wards, which under Tainu's increased strengthening now kept out even sounds, like a very thick pane of flexible glass. In the brightening sunlight, Zhu Guiren fought, one-handed, with a snake demon. It was as though someone had painted a moving picture for them. He finally managed to decapitate the thing and stood there, breathing heavily, head down. Then, something shaped like an enormous scorpion leapt on his back; he threw it to the ground and speared it with his sword, switched to the halberd, and swung it at waist level at a misshapen shadow they couldn't see clearly.

Tairei remarked, "I quite like watching him be attacked by other demons, actually. Let's stay here."

Tainu snorted. "Those are the little ones. At nightfall, the chthonic beings will come for Aili again, and he can't do much against those. There haven't been any really powerful demons yet, either, and even so, he's exhausted. Even for a demon losing a part of the true body must hit hard. He won't really recover until he gets some rest, and I can't hold this ward another night."

He stood up, walked through the ward, and dragged Zhu Guiren back inside. Tairei quickly shifted to take the burden of the ward from him, but she couldn't hold it long either, she had never been as strong as Tainu.

"Come in, come out, make up your mind," the demon said. His face was pale and sweaty, and he had a few wounds on his back from the scorpion thing.

"Turn around," Tainu said, biting his finger. He brushed some of his blood on the wounds. "Demon, we need to get to a refuge."

"How fast can you run?" Zhu Guiren asked. "Because the minute you step outside, there's a welcoming committee eager to take you for a ride elsewhere."

"I'll distract them. They'll follow me. Your job is to get these two to a refuge," Tainu said.

Tairei was as surprised as Zhu Guiren looked. "I don't want to go with him," she said immediately.

"I am the distraction," Tainu said patiently. "He's the protection. You can't fight, you can't fly, and you'll need to carry her. *Can* you carry her?" He looked Tairei up and down, clearly just realizing that she was far too small to carry Aili.

"I can carry her," said the demon.

"You will not," said Tairei, furious.

Tainu ignored her. "Can you carry her and fight?" he asked Zhu Guiren.

"Of course. I've got a useless arm anyway." He waved his handless arm in the air. "Perfect for carrying unconscious mortal-phoenix hybrids."

Tairei turned away; she couldn't stand the sight of him. After a moment, she said, "I also can't find the refuge."

"I know," Tainu said. He put his hands on Zhu Guiren's shoulders and turned him around to stare at him, considering, for several moments.

Zhu Guiren seemed uncomfortable, but he didn't look away.

Eventually, Tainu asked, "Can you protect them?"

"Of course," he said immediately. "These little things aren't a match for—"

"Will you protect them?"

"Yes," Zhu Guiren said seriously, still looking at Tainu as though fascinated by his eyes. "I promise I will."

Tainu nodded and placed two fingers on Zhu Guiren's forehead, just above and between his brows. "Can you see it? The path?"

"Yes. I see the way."

"Hold Tairei's hand when you get there, otherwise the wards won't let you in," Tainu said. "The wards of the refuge are much stronger than the one I made here. They're completely different. It will kill you if you try to force your way in. Don't mess with it."

Zhu Guiren nodded, still looking at Tainu.

Tainu turned away and said, "Tairei."

Tairei sat next to Aili and stared out through the ward, refusing to look at them.

"Tairei," Tainu said, "take him in the refuge with you. You promise?"

"I don't trust him."

"Then trust me. Take him in the refuge with you. He won't be able to fight the soul devourers that will come for Aili. He'll need protection too."

"Then he can just leave. He doesn't need to stay near us. I don't want–"

"Take him inside the refuge," Tainu said, his voice both gentle and implacable.

She closed her eyes. "Tainu, don't."

"Tairei," he said quietly. "Promise. We need his help to save Aili."

"All right," she replied at last, though the words choked her.

Tainu nodded. "All right then. I don't know if the wards of the refuge will keep out the soul-devourers that will come for Aili, but they're much stronger than these, and they'll repel anything demonic. That'll give us something of a rest, anyway. Tairei, you'll probably get there before I do. Start cultivating right away."

She nodded.

"I'll meet you there. As soon as I'm gone and they've followed me, start running. The ward will dissolve."

Without waiting any further, he walked out past the wards. Immediately he began running, followed by an assortment of demons and shadow figures that rose out of the grass.

Zhu Guiren immediately stepped forward, his sword in his hand.

"Wait," said Tairei.

Tainu began running faster, his long legs taking him into the razor grass.

"He's bleeding," said Zhu Guiren sharply.

But before he could follow, between one step and the next, Tainu's form shimmered into an enormous, winged being, its feathers the color of blood and sunlight. As it shook out its wings and took flight, golden light trailed it like a shadow. The demons touched by the light shrieked and withdrew for a moment.

The invisible ward dissolved; they could hear the beating of the wings like

slow thunder, the wind from them rushing through the grass and trees and nearly knocking them over. The golden shadow spun above them as the phoenix
called out, a music that shook the world to the horizon, stirring the bones and
the blood of all living beings into awareness.

Like a comet in daylight, the phoenix's wings struck fire and it sped away.

All the demons followed it — running, hopping, flying, slithering. Around
the tree where they waited was only clean silence.

Zhu Guiren kept watching until the last light had faded. "He's…he's very
powerful," he said at last.

Tairei smiled, feeling affectionate. "Well, he's a little bit of a show-off, but I
suppose that was necessary. It will certainly cover our tiny existence for a while."

"That would be why we never capture adults…" he said slowly.

"He's the oldest of us. Or at least the one of us who can remember the far-
thest back."

"How old is he?"

"You should ask him." Gently, she raised Aili's limp form into a sitting position. "Come take her," she said, reluctantly. She kissed her forehead quickly —
hoping Zhu Guiren didn't notice, hoping it was all right.

"Keep her safe," she said, as he stooped and picked Aili up over his left
shoulder.

"Let's go," he said, turning in the opposite direction from where Tainu had
flown. "It's this way." Sword in his single hand, he led the way into the tall grass.

Tairei followed.

CHAPTER 13
PEACEFUL RIVER

HONG DEMING WAS welcomed by the sect leader of Peaceful River and given a qin to work with. The disciples of Peaceful River were dedicated to their own cultivation path, but compared to the austere world of the Crane Moon, it seemed to be a path of joy and pleasure. The days were filled with music, and the nights, quite often, with wine and poetry as well. It was all a balm to his heart after the darkness of the past year.

The cultivation of the qin required a deep silence of mind and focus of the body, the movements subtle and small compared to the large, active movements and risky cultivation of the sword path. It was almost as though the younger disciples needed to balance this with active celebration and play.

Unlike at Crane Moon, the female disciples joined the males in their studies, and often for the nightly celebrations, with no elders forbidding it. Hong Deming found this bizarre at first, but got used to it quickly. The women were intelligent, skilled, and strong in their way. Some were even studying the sword or archery along with qin, though not at the cultivation level of Crane Moon, and he was happy to help them practice. This became more comfortable after a few of the women disciples had tried to interest him in more intimate activities and he refused clearly; apparently, they spread the word, and after that, the female disciples treated him just as the men did — with friendliness and humor — which set him at ease.

The only places the women disciples didn't accompany the men were to the pavilions and houses of pleasure in Gunan. Since the Peaceful River sect was close to a great city with all a city's attractions, and since their cultivation path didn't require bodily purity, a good number of the younger disciples regularly visited the pleasure quarters. They always went to the most respectable ones, known for their music as well as other entertainments — never to the cruder or more vulgar places. Hong Deming felt uncomfortable with this practice for reasons he couldn't fully understand himself, but he didn't want to offend his friends or stay at home alone, so often he would go as well, though he always stayed in the main room listening to the music and drinking.

"Why don't you ever go upstairs?" yawned a rumpled Mo Xiang one night, back down after a session. "They've got all kinds here. Whatever you like."

Hong Deming shrugged.

"Are you really that stoic? How can you be surrounded by such beauty and remain unmoved, week after week? I'll bet you a jar of wine that I can find the one you'll like most." Mo Xiang looked around; he waved over one of the musicians — a pretty girl with her hair pinned in complex coils and dressed in lightweight silks who had been playing a stringed instrument on a low dais at the center of the room. "This is Jade Blossom. She's talented in many areas!"

Jade Blossom raised her lashes briefly in a shy smile. "I've noticed the gentleman listening several times," she said in a cultured voice. "Might the gentleman be interested in music? Or perhaps in poetry?"

"Thank you, I'm honored to hear you play and sing." Hong Deming didn't smile back. "But I wouldn't want to deprive the room of the pleasure of hearing you to while away the hours."

Jade Blossom smiled again, offered a curtsy, and returned to the stage to begin another song.

"Hmmmm…" Mo Xiang looked around the room again. "No…no…probably not…I've got it!"

At Mo Xiang's drunken wave, a slim young man came over to them carrying a jar of wine. His hair fell smoothly down his back, accentuating his gentle features and shining eyes. He gracefully reached out and poured wine for both Mo Xiang and Hong Deming. As he offered the cup to Hong Deming, he smiled, and one of his fingers gently brushed Hong Deming's hand as though by accident.

"What is the gentleman's pleasure tonight?" he asked. His lips curved very slightly as he looked at Hong Deming, who blushed.

Mo Xiang, watching carefully, said, "Oh, my friend is looking for someone he can chat with while he waits for the others. Perhaps you could offer him a game of chess?"

"Do you enjoy chess?" the young man asked Hong Deming. "I can play many other games as well."

Hong Deming blushed even more.

The young man smiled. "My name is Wu Fan. May I have the honor of knowing the gentleman's name?"

"I'm Hong Deming," he replied, but it was difficult to get it out past the constriction in his throat. This person's physical closeness — his quiet, intimate voice, his dark eyes — combined with the entire air of the place and the sounds Hong Deming could sometimes hear from upstairs was making him feel heated and awkward. He gulped. "It's– it's all right. I'm happy just listening to the music while I wait."

Mo Xiang smirked and went over to a distant part of the room to drink with another beauty, leaving Hong Deming with Wu Fan alone in their corner. Wu Fan moved closer on the bench, close enough that Hong Deming could feel the warmth of Wu Fan's body through the thin robes he wore.

Wu Fan listened quietly to the music for a while along with him, then leaned over and whispered: "This song is very tragic, isn't it? Lovers seek but don't find. I prefer songs where the lovers find one another, don't you?"

The warm breath in his ear made Hong Deming shiver as his body reacted far ahead of his mind. He moved to the other side of the bench.

"Is there something wrong?" Wu Fan asked. His eyes looked directly into Hong Deming's — dark and inviting — reminding him of something he couldn't quite place.

Wu Fan reached over with one hand, and gently touched the sleeve of Hong Deming's outer robe, pulling it very slightly. "Would you like to…go somewhere else?"

Hong Deming took a deep breath, trying to gather himself together. "I– no." He breathed again. "I'll stay here. You must have other things you need to do and other guests to see to."

Wu Fan smiled and got up, perhaps even a little reluctantly. "I hope I'll see you again. Another night, perhaps we could spend more time together." He bowed, as self-contained as any lord, and moved off to speak to another man.

Mo Xiang came back over when he saw Wu Fan had left. He tapped Hong Deming with his fan. "What happened? It was going so well! You still owe me a jar of wine. I found the type you like, didn't I?"

Hong Deming pushed the wine jar over to him, acknowledging defeat.

Mo Xiang poured them both another bowl. "Now I'm interested in this. As a friend, I have to look out for you. I knew you were human like us, not a stone! Crane Moon must just make you anxious about these things. You really don't need to be. So you like beautiful young men — it's nothing to be ashamed of. If it were a problem, people like Wu Fan would be out of business. Why not do him and you a favor and take him upstairs? He doesn't go with just anyone, you know. He's the most exclusive person they have. He can pick and choose. Top-shelf." He tossed down his bowl and poured himself another. "Are you afraid of the price?"

Hong Deming felt his stomach turn. "There shouldn't be a price."

"There's always a price," snorted Mo Xiang.

"He's not…it's not real." He drank his own bowl as well and pushed it back over.

Mo Xiang laughed, not offended. "What's real in this world? Pleasure is real, so why not share it with one another?"

Hong Deming shook his head. He was a little drunk at this point and more than a little frustrated, both by his body's reaction and his inability to explain how he felt. "Anyway, it's not him that I like."

"Ah, there it is! That's why you're all high and mighty and idealistic. Well, it all makes sense now. Who does he remind you of? Someone here, or someone back at your sect? Have you confessed to this person yet?"

Hong Deming drank down the last bowl of liquor. "I need to go out. I'll get you another jar when I come back in." He walked very carefully out into the courtyard, breathing deeply to try to clear his head. The yard was dimly lit by a few lampions hung strategically in the trees to provide privacy for couples among the paths and shrubbery. He followed a path that led to a decorative pond to find the shining scales of dark fish breaking the surface. He breathed again and looked up at the sky. There was no moon, but the stars were bright.

He was still hot and flushed all over, as if the warmth of Wu Fan's breath and body were next to him. He wasn't a child, his body functioned as it should, yet he'd never had such a reaction to a person before — never experienced that rush of physical desire. He'd been coming to the brothel with the disciples for weeks. Why tonight? What was it that made him so eager for Wu Fan? Yet at the same time, it wasn't for Wu Fan, not really, because he didn't want to pursue it. It felt wrong, mistaken. Something made him send Wu Fan away when he thought he might respond to him.

And then, he remembered Wu Fan tugging gently on his robe and wondered how it might be if he just let that happen. Why would it be wrong? Why did it

147

feel wrong?

"Tainu?!"

A slender young man with long, smooth hair, gentle features, and shining dark eyes stared at him in shock. He wore a scholar's robes and carried a gourd at his waist: the mark of a physician. "Tainu, why are you here?"

Hong Deming swallowed hard. "Taine, why are *you* here?"

It had been more than a year.

He looked at this person — his eyes and lips, the shape of his body; in that time, he had grown taller, but he was still delicate, still had that quiet, fearless air about him that Hong Deming remembered so clearly. Eyes that shone and laughed, his smile at all the wonders of the world. His scent and breath in the dark.

This person.

Hong Deming's fingers twitched. He brushed his hand over his eyes, trying to get his balance.

Liu Chenguang came over to him, standing close to see him in the dim starlight. "It really is you? I never thought that *you* would–" He cut off whatever he was going to say. "Teacher Zhu brought me to Gunan, but he's busy with the court now. I'm just practicing my skills." He indicated the gourd hanging below his sash, which drew Hong Deming's eyes down to an area that brought uncomfortable thoughts into his mind immediately.

He closed his eyes. Coughing a little, Hong Deming said, "Zhu Guiren allows you to come to brothels? What kind of training is he giving you?"

Liu Chenguang laughed. "No, he has no idea. He doesn't care about these people. Actually, he'd probably be angry if he knew, but he's at the court for days at a time. It's boring just to sit around and read books. But there's often illness and injury in places like this... Anyway, I didn't think you'd be...here."

Hong Deming realized what Liu Chenguang must be thinking but didn't really know how to correct it, and felt a little defiant as well. "Of course I come here, why would you think I wouldn't come to places like this? The people from the Peaceful River sect often come here so I–"

Liu Chenguang stepped a little bit closer. His scent of incense and herbs surrounded Hong Deming — the scent that had last come to him in the dark of the caverns, with the feeling of Liu Chenguang's hair brushing his wrist. Now, he was close enough that he needed to look up into Hong Deming's eyes. Liu Chenguang's eyes were brilliant and shining, catching all the light of the stars like the fish in the dark water. His black hair fell back from his forehead as he examined Hong Deming closely, a tiny frown between his brows. "Are you all right? You look a little unwell."

Liu Chenguang's focused gaze was making him dizzy. Hong Deming's hand was suddenly possessed. Without his conscious intention, he reached out with one finger and touched that little furrow between Liu Chenguang's eyebrows.

Liu Chenguang froze, his lips slightly parted as though he was planning to say something else, but had forgotten language.

"Stop frowning," Hong Deming whispered. His fingers traced the delicate shape of Liu Chenguang's eyebrow down the side of his face, stroking under his jaw, and then Hong Deming bent down and kissed his lips.

Liu Chenguang's shock kept him standing still; his parted lips opened more fully, and Hong Deming tasted him, his tongue exploring his mouth. The hand on his throat slipped back to the nape of his neck, beneath his hair, holding him in place. Hong Deming felt his own body push helplessly to press against Liu Chenguang's. His other hand stroked through Liu Chenguang's hair down to grasp the small of his back, all the while kissing him harder, his tongue becoming greedy for Liu Chenguang's mouth, making it hard for either of them to breathe.

Suddenly Liu Chenguang gasped for air, and stepped back, breathing heavily. "Hong Deming. Hong Deming, what–"

Hong Deming suddenly woke up from his daze and stuttered, "You– you are– Liu Chenguang, I–"

Liu Chenguang was still breathing hard and unevenly, staring at him with those eyes. "It's not– I–"

"I'm sorry. I– I drank too much." Hong Deming pulled himself back, taking another step away despite his entire and complete desire to push Liu Chenguang against a nearby wall to continue to kiss him and do…other things.

"I know, I could taste it," Liu Chenguang blurted out.

Even in the darkness, Hong Deming could see him blush. Hong Deming closed his eyes in shame, and then felt Liu Chenguang moving closer again. He swallowed. "I'm sorry, taine. That shouldn't have happened."

This was all his own fault — coming to a place like this thinking it wouldn't affect him, allowing his body to be stimulated knowing he wouldn't have any release, what had he been thinking? Now, he'd crossed this line with Liu Chenguang. Had imposed himself on the person he truly valued and cared for, as though Liu Chenguang was available for his taking. If he could have sunk into the earth, he would have.

"It's all right, tainu. It's– I was– I was just surprised. I didn't…" Liu Chenguang seemed to be struggling for words.

"It's nothing. Nothing. Just me being drunk. It didn't mean anything," he said quickly. He couldn't imagine that Liu Chenguang — who was so kind and gentle with everyone, who he'd known since he was a little child — could understand the kind of desire that was still surging inside him. Liu Chenguang was so innocent, and he himself had been innocent until just a moment ago. He now knew that he wanted Liu Chenguang so badly that his entire body ached and that it wasn't because Wu Fan had been touching him; Wu Fan had made him excited because he looked slightly like Liu Chenguang. Imagining Liu Chenguang stroking his hand, warm breath whispering in his ear, taking him upstairs...There was no way to hide this from himself anymore, but he could at least spare Liu Chenguang from knowing the ugly details. He coughed awkwardly and took several more steps back.

"But I–"

Another voice cut through the courtyard — an endlessly haughty, cold voice. "Student Liu, what are you doing here?"

Liu Chenguang quickly turned away. "Teacher Zhu, I'm here visiting a patient." His voice shook very slightly.

"Who gave you permission to leave our quarters?" Zhu Guiren came into the dim light of the yard.

Hong Deming looked at him, wondering how he had ever thought this person was the most beautiful in the world. His features were perfect, but his bearing was so distant and removed. In addition, he was now in charge of Liu Chenguang's days and nights, responsible for his safety and training, and somehow Hong Deming felt that he wasn't to be trusted with something so precious.

"I did not approve you coming here. This is not a place that anyone associated with me should be seen. Who is your patient?" He looked over, and his facial expression changed to surprise.

Hong Deming saluted. "Master Zhu, I am training with the Peaceful River sect. They often come here. I was only saying hello to my taine. I'm not the patient."

Zhu Guiren nodded, dismissing him. "My greetings to the sect leader of Peaceful River. I will come to visit before the court reconvenes. I hope that your training is going well. Student Liu, we will leave first."

Liu Chenguang said, quietly, "Tainu, I'll leave now."

"Taine, I'll see you another time," he replied helplessly. What else could he say in front of Zhu Guiren's cold, angry face? There was so much else he needed to say, but couldn't. He watched them walk out of the courtyard, Zhu Guiren still berating Liu Chenguang in a low voice.

His mind was a whirlpool of images and emotions, and his body was still un-comfortably aroused; he didn't dare to go back into the brothel. After he splashed some cold water from the pond on his face, drenching his hair, he walked back to the Peaceful River compound alone in the dark.

The next morning, for the first time since coming to Peaceful River, he woke up with a hangover.

Mo Xiang peeked into his room as soon as he started moaning. "How much did you drink? Not more than usual while you were with me! Did you drink more when you got home? Why did you leave without getting me?"

Hong Deming just groaned and put his face down in the pillow.

"Stay there. The sober tea is ready, like always." Mo Xiang dashed out to the kitchen and brought back a teapot and cups. "I, of course, never need this. But I guess you do. How much did you drink, really?"

Hong Deming finished a cup, then held it out for more. "I came back and drank two more jars."

"By yourself?"

"That I remember."

Mo Xiang shook his head. "All right, talk to your elder brother now. Was it Wu Fan? Did you regret walking away? Don't worry, he liked you. I can tell. If you go back, I'm sure he'd be willing to talk with you again. And more than talk with you."

"Not...not that."

"Then, it's the person you like?"

"I saw him last night. He was there." He rubbed his eyes with both hands and held the cup out again.

Mo Xiang winced. "He's a courtesan? He was with someone else?"

Hong Deming laughed out loud. "Oh no, much worse than that. He was just passing by, and I..." The smile fell off his face. "I was drunk, and acted like a drunk person, and made a fool out of myself. He probably hates me now."

Mo Xiang waited expectantly to hear something more dramatic. "That's it? You are so easily discouraged."

Hong Deming shook his head. He didn't want to tell anyone else, ever, that he had grabbed Liu Chenguang and physically forced him to kiss him. He couldn't imagine that Liu Chenguang would ever want to speak with him again. He also couldn't forget what it felt like to touch him...like that...

151

He put his head down into his hands. "Ugh. No more."

"Well, time for cultivation anyway. Get your qin. We'll be sparring today."

"Wonderful." He sighed and reached over for his qin. Going through high-level sword forms and knocking over a few trees felt more like what he wanted to do today, but no one at the Peaceful River sect was very comfortable with him doing such things.

After the morning's cultivation practice — where Hong Deming was soundly beaten in qin battle by several Peaceful River disciples in a row since he wasn't paying attention — he went into the largest courtyard to get some aggression out with the sword. As he moved through a basic sword formation, then a more advanced one, En began to shine energetically, the qi moving in proper patterns between his body and the sword. He started adding lightness skills: leaping several feet in the air and hanging like a hummingbird for a few minutes at a time, practicing the sword form while held by qi rather than earth.

"Tainu, you have your sword now?"

He crashed onto the pavement of the courtyard and rolled several times.

"Oh, I'm sorry!" Liu Chenguang rushed over to help him get up.

Hong Deming frantically waved him away and stumbled to his feet on his own, using En to hold himself upright and try to regain some dignity. "Taine," he said helplessly. He could feel his face flushing bright red.

Liu Chenguang stood there, smiling shyly. His hair was up in a pincrown now, so he had had his adulthood crowning ceremony, but the rest flowed down his back. He didn't wear a doctor's cap — only the gourd hanging from his sash so that observers could recognize him as a cultivator rather than a true scholarly doctor. He really had grown quite a bit.

The moment this thought crossed Hong Deming's mind, he remembered exactly how tall Liu Chenguang now was in relation to his own body and blushed even more, closing his eyes and desperately trying to think of something else. "I'm sorry," he said at last. "For last night. It was...wrong of me."

"Of course," Liu Chenguang said quickly; he blushed too. "There's nothing, really, I–"

"I didn't mean it," Hong Deming said just as quickly, talking over him. "You aren't– I wouldn't ever think of you in that way. It was just the liquor..."

"Oh." Liu Chenguang continued smiling, but the hand he had reached out was drawn back. "It's all right, then. Let's...let's go back to the way we were before?"

Hong Deming nodded, relieved, and took a deep breath. "I never thanked you properly for saving me when I was in seclusion. I don't know how to thank you. When I came out, you were gone already."

"Yes, I completed my seclusion and you were still in the caverns...then Teacher Zhu came and tested my qi levels. He said I had completed my foundation, so Taiqian sent me off with him to study medicine intensively. We've traveled all over. Teacher Zhu is always running errands for the emperor. We just came a few weeks ago for the court, and he's locked up with that most days now. He brought me today because he needed to visit the sect leader anyway."

"What for?"

"I don't know. To be honest, I don't really pay attention to all that. And most of it is secret — the things he discusses with the emperor and the court officials. That's why he doesn't take me to court with him. Otherwise, he takes me everywhere."

"Really?" Hong Deming felt very unhappy with this situation.

"Yes," Liu Chenguang continued uncaringly. "He says it will help me learn to understand people better, but it doesn't because I can't really follow all the politics and I wouldn't want to if I could. It's such an ugly side of humanity. Even when he tries to explain to me, my mind just stops paying attention, and then he tries more, so I end up having to go everywhere he goes and then listen to him talk all day and night."

Hong Deming was very, very not happy.

"But I wanted to come today, so I could see you. Can you show me the sword? It's your spiritual weapon?"

"Yes," he said, and brought it over close so Liu Chenguang could see it. "Its name is En," he said, a little embarrassed now. He had imagined this many ways, but none of them had included meeting Liu Chenguang after drunkenly kissing him in a brothel the night before. "Because of you."

"Because of me?" Liu Chenguang's eyes came up to his again.

Hong Deming swallowed. "I don't know how to say thank you enough, but I'm grateful for you, always, and it's because of you that I was able to complete my cultivation. So I named the sword En."

Liu Chenguang was silent, looking at the sword. En was a slender blade, shining white and gold. It seemed to be pleased to be near Liu Chenguang, surrounding itself with a dance of light. He looked up again, his long eyes opened wide, and met Hong Deming's eyes, for once seeming unable to say anything.

"Are you Liu Chenguang?" came Mo Xiang's voice.

Hong Deming looked up to see him glancing back and forth between the two of them, frowning.

"Yes, is my teacher looking for me?"

"Master Zhu requested that you join him in his meeting with our sect leader," Mo Xiang said. "I'll bring you there, please follow me in."

Liu Chenguang nodded, smiled one last time at Hong Deming, and followed him off. Just before they turned the corner Mo Xiang looked back at Hong Deming and winked.

Hong Deming grabbed En and started the basic formation. Again.

Later that night, Mo Xiang brought a jar of wine over to his room along with two bowls. "So, that's the person."

"How do you know?" Hong Deming sighed and drank.

"First of all, it's completely obvious in the way you look at him. You're not at all subtle, my friend. Also, he looks a little like Wu Fan, so he really is the kind of person you like. I don't know why I'm the one that keeps providing the wine here. You owe me."

"I know."

"I wanted to say..." Mo Xiang drank down his bowl and looked at him seriously. "I hope you don't take this the wrong way. I'm speaking as a friend. But you know that my older brother is often at court. He's actually mentioned your friend to me before. I just didn't know that's who you were thinking of — I've never met him before. But..."

Hong Deming looked up from the bowl of liquor. "What is it?"

"Well...the court gossip is that he's...well...he and Zhu Guiren...Everyone says so. They're never apart. Zhu Guiren won't let him out of his sight for more than a few minutes. They share a room together when Zhu Guiren's at court."

Hong Deming drank quickly, then poured himself another bowl and immediately drank that.

"And you know how Zhu Guiren's very beautiful. They say that he could easily have had the emperor's favor at one time but he left the court for several years, so that's why now everyone is talking about this person Zhu Guiren keeps at his side and, and..."

"It doesn't necessarily mean they are..." Hong Deming drank two more bowls of liquor while Mo Xiang fiddled with the jar.

"I know," Mo Xiang sighed. "But you have to admit...Zhu Guiren's very powerful and influential at court, and my brother says he can be very vicious when he's crossed. You shouldn't do something that would draw his attention to you."

"Who cares about that?!" He grabbed the jar from Mo Xiang and poured the remainder of the liquor down his throat directly, since bowls were too slow.

Mo Xiang watched, eyes wide.

"Zhu Guiren– he's nothing to me. The court doesn't mean anything to me. Why should I care? If I want to do something, I will. It's all just gossip. Court gossip. You've told me before, those people always– always say bad things about others. They're always looking for the worst interpretation of things."

"I know." Mo Xiang said. "But honestly, forgive me for saying it, and with your best interests in mind, I think you would be better off just visiting with Wu Fan."

"It doesn't matter, anyway," Hong Deming said, as firmly as he could. He was both burning with jealousy and starting to feel as though the room was twirling around him; his eyes had refused to focus since the fourth bowl. "He's my taine."

Mo Xiang stared at him. "What do you mean, it doesn't matter?"

"He'll always be my taine, forever," he explained thickly. "That's all that matters. I'll always protect him. I'll take care of him. He– Liu Chenguang…"

Mo Xiang reached over and tried to hold up his face as he pitched forward onto the table. Through his buzzing ears, he heard Mo Xiang say, "I'll forget all about this conversation, all right? All right?"

Then, everything went black.

155

CHAPTER 14
ATTACK

FOR SEVERAL DAYS, Hong Deming stayed at home with the Peaceful River sect. When Mo Xiang invited him to the brothel again, he didn't go. He focused on his qin cultivation, or sometimes sat quietly at the gate of peonies, looking toward Gunan. When the air was clear, he thought he could see the roofs of the Imperial Palace.

At last, he decided he had to do something. Who knew when Zhu Guiren would take him away again? He needed to know; he couldn't just spend the rest of his life not sleeping unless he was drunk.

He asked Mo Xiang where to find the best jadeworkers and went out to visit the market with some of the money he'd earned from guarding the convoys to Gunan. Then, he went toward the Palace and told the guards at the gate that he had a message for Liu Chenguang, Zhu Guiren's apprentice. Of course, he wasn't allowed into the imperial compound; he didn't expect to be let in the gates. He waited impatiently outside, but it was less than an hour later that he saw Liu Chenguang come through the gates, looking around for a messenger.

Hong Deming swallowed and stood up. "Taine."

Liu Chenguang's face lit up. "Tainu!" He nearly ran over, completely forgetting his own dignity, his heavy silk court robes swinging around him wildly.

Hong Deming had to smile; it was so like him.

"Tainu, you're here," he said breathlessly. "Are you here to see me, or do you really have a message?"

"To see you. I brought you something. A thank you gift." He handed over a package smaller than the palm of his hand, wrapped in silk.

Curious, Liu Chenguang carefully unwrapped it and held it up: a jade circle carved with a crane with outspread wings. "It's beautiful. It's the Crane Moon, isn't it?"

"I saw you aren't wearing any sect symbols…I thought this might be a good thing for you, to help you remember us when you're away for so long. And I wanted to give you something to say thank you…"

Liu Chenguang held it up to see more closely. "I could never forget. And you don't need to say thank you to me. Not for anything. Not ever."

His words sounded so serious, not what he had been expecting at all. "Taine," Hong Deming asked, "are you all right?"

Liu Chenguang smiled, more genuinely this time, and found a silk cord in the package to attach the ornament to his sash, hanging the jade circle as a decoration beside the gourd. "It's beautiful," he said again. "I'll wear it when we go…wherever we're going next. Teacher Zhu said we'll be leaving in a day or so. Somewhere up north this time, across the Sorrowful River."

"Isn't that dangerous? Why is Zhu Guiren taking you across the border? Can't you stay here?"

"Do you want me to stay here?"

"Do you want to stay with Zhu Guiren all the time? Is that why you're going?" he asked before he registered what Liu Chenguang had actually said.

Liu Chenguang looked down and shook his head. "Have you been listening to rumors about Teacher Zhu and me? I have to hear them all the time at court. He's my teacher," he said, suddenly very fierce. "Only my teacher. He's not anything else to me but my teacher. But if I'm going to stay a part of the Crane Moon sect–"

"Why would you not?"

"–then I have to obey Taiqian, and Taiqian has assigned me to the authority of Teacher Zhu until he says I can return to Crane Moon. So, I have to obey. The agreement was the condition on which Taiqian accepted me as a disciple. I have to honor it." He looked up, eyes flashing. "Do you really think I'm following him for any other reason? I'm not the one who thinks he's the most handsome man ever to walk the earth."

Out of everything he said, Hong Deming decided that this was the most important thing he had to clear up. "I don't think he's that handsome anymore."

They stood staring at each other for a minute, and then Liu Chenguang started snickering. Hong Deming started laughing too, and suddenly, everything was all right again. Liu Chenguang's laugh made everything good.

"Taine, why should you cross the river? Can't anyone persuade him?"

"Well, there will be many things to see and learn. I don't know why we have to go on this trip, but I don't usually know, to be honest. He doesn't tell me about what the emperor wants. But Teacher Zhu is an excellent mentor. I can't complain for that reason. Here at court, he gets me access to scrolls and cultivational manuals and ancient writings in the Imperial Library I've never even heard of. On our travels, he has me practice healing all kinds of things. Whatever we come across…he's still very careful though. He monitors my qi each time. And he has never…never done any of those things that people say about him. He has done his best by me as his student, and I owe him respect for that." He sighed. "However boring it sometimes gets. Tainu, I'd rather be with you."

Hong Deming felt his heart warm. "I'd rather have you with me too."

Liu Chenguang smiled at him, his eyes again shining as they should.

He must have been staring, because Liu Chenguang asked, "What are you looking at? Is my pincrown crooked?" He reached up to his pincrown, trying to adjust it.

"Nothing," he said. "It's fine. Wait, now you're making it crooked…" He reached over too, and their hands brushed each other. He jerked back quickly.

Liu Chenguang laughed.

Suddenly, he heard the guards at the gate come to attention; someone said, "Over there, sir."

Zhu Guiren came striding toward them, his face cold as always. "Student Liu," he said, his voice melodious though his eyes were hard. "This evening, we will discuss the cultivational manual I assigned you this morning. You may leave."

"Yes, Teacher Zhu," Liu Chenguang said, and left without another word.

Zhu Guiren turned to Hong Deming. For the first time, he met Hong Deming's eyes directly, and seemed to see him. "Hmph," he said, after a moment. "You are the youngest sword disciple of the Crane Moon. Liu Chenguang is your taine."

"Yes," he said, without any honorific or address, deciding to be as rude as he could get away with.

Zhu Guiren's cold expression softened. "Three times now in just two weeks, I've found Liu Chenguang with you when, for almost a year, he's been with me at all times, never showing a special interest in anyone. He feels closer to you than to others, I think."

Hong Deming looked at him steadily, refusing to let this man see that this news warmed him all through.

"You are also the one that he risked breaking his own seclusion for, undermining his own cultivation."

Hong Deming nodded. "I will always be grateful to him. And I want to protect him. Keep him safe in return."

"You're wondering, therefore, why I'm taking him with me on all my travels for the emperor's cause," he said shrewdly. "You're thinking it would be better for me to leave him here, or somewhere else that's safe."

"Yes," he said again.

"You must understand that Liu Chenguang's cultivation is not yet as stable as it must be to support his healing power. This is partly because of his use of his qi to heal you during your secluded meditation. I must watch him very carefully to ensure that he is able to use his own qi without falling into a coma again. If it does, could you heal him?"

"No," he said, shaken. Was Liu Chenguang so injured from helping him?

"I can," Zhu Guiren said. "I have the knowledge and the skills and the medicine that can heal him even from that state. I keep him with me constantly to observe him and to be ready for emergencies. In time — perhaps a year or so — I will be certain that he is safe. I know that you want him to be safe as well. So remember that his safety, for now, lies in staying close to me."

At close range, Zhu Guiren was as perfect as he had been at a distance, but nonetheless it was obvious to Hong Deming that his warmth and openness was feigned. He was not distracted by this, but the news that Liu Chenguang was not yet healed disturbed him deeply.

"I understand," Hong Deming said at last. "I want him to be safe."

Zhu Guiren nodded, satisfied.

He didn't see Liu Chenguang again before Mo Xiang's brother informed him that Zhu Guiren had departed on the Son of Heaven's business, taking his favorite along. Mo Xiang added that several mutually-antagonistic factions at court were delighted by this, and that a few others were now weakened. Court politics made Hong Deming's head spin, but Mo Xiang was able to simplify things enough that he could follow the basics. Since the emperor had slaughtered all the imperial eunuchs of the previous dynasty, a power vacuum had arisen in the palace and in the civil administration. Various relatives, concubines, generals, counselors, nobles, princes, and governors filled it, all vying for power and imperial attention. Zhu Guiren was part of a faction advocating to stabilize the new dynasty through military conquest. This was opposed by governors of strong cities who didn't wish to become stepping stones for the dynasty and preferred their independence, as well as the enemies of the dynasty itself, who were always a threat at the border and often sent assassins.

"It doesn't help," Mo Xiang whispered, "that the Son of Heaven himself isn't a good master to work for or obey. It sometimes seems that his most loyal supporters are the ones he turns on and destroys. And he insults people in other ways too, even by assaulting their wives and lovers…"

Hong Deming didn't dare to speak, and wished he wasn't hearing this. People were executed for far, far less than this kind of conversation. "Hush," he said, "enough. If you're not worried about yourself and me, at least worry about your brother."

Mo Xiang nodded and drew back. "You're right. You're right, enough of that." He shook it off. "Anyway, my brother said that this time, Zhu Guiren has been sent north of the Sorrowful River into enemy territory. No one really knows why, or what his purpose is there. He's useless as a spy. He's too memorable when you see him, and too well-known as a servant of the emperor, so it must be some kind of diplomatic mission. Did your friend…?"

"Liu Chenguang doesn't know anything. He's got no mind for politics. He's just training as a physician with Zhu Guiren."

"Ah, I see."

"And there's nothing between them," Hong Deming added firmly. "Tell your brother to stop spreading those rumors."

Mo Xiang looked at him almost pityingly. "Hong Deming, never go into the court. Promise me. You're far too simple for this. Don't you realize it makes no difference at all whether it's true or false? If the rumor is useful to someone, it will have a life either way."

Hong Deming found that remembering the warmth of Liu Chenguang's body and the taste of his lips was impossible when he focused on the complexities of qin cultivation, and as a result, Hong Deming's qin cultivation was improving by leaps and bounds. He could now play the qin defensively to establish wards against both human and spiritual encroachments, and offensively as well, though he was still far behind the Peaceful River disciples. Day by day, he continued with his practice.

Once, he even dared to accompany Mo Xiang back to the brothel to listen to music and to look at Wu Fan, since he couldn't see Liu Chenguang. Now that he knew what he really wanted — however impossible it might be — he found that Wu Fan no longer looked as much like Liu Chenguang as he had thought, and he could even sit with him calmly and discuss music and art when Wu Fan had no clients to engage. Wu Fan's occasional forays into flirtatious or suggestive behavior were simply ignored as though they hadn't happened; Wu Fan himself was too skilled, and indeed too popular, to press him beyond this, though sometimes he looked at Hong Deming oddly.

A few weeks later, Mo Xiang invited him out again. This time, he refused. Most of the younger male disciples went with Mo Xiang, leaving the women and the older men to sleep. Hong Deming took his qin up to one of the highest points of the sect compound — a moon-viewing platform facing away from the city and the highway in the valley below — and began to play there. Not to cultivate, but merely to enjoy the music. He knew he wasn't very good yet and would rarely play where the Peaceful River disciples could hear, but he found it very pleasant and peaceful to the spirit, rather like calligraphy.

After he had played himself out, he relaxed with his back against a pillar, looking at the stars and thinking of nothing in particular, which, as usual, led to thinking of Liu Chenguang, and then to Crane Moon and going home. He knew that true mastery of qin cultivation would require a lifetime, but he wasn't that talented, and it wasn't his sect's path. At some point, the Peaceful River sect master would send him home — back to Taiqian and Shen Lu and his other martial siblings. There might even be new little disciples, and he could help teach them. Eventually, Liu Chenguang would come home as well, Zhu Guiren had promised, and then…

When he woke up, the moon had set and he was sitting with cold, cramped muscles. He stood and stretched, recognizing it as the fourth watch. Dawn would come soon. Mo Xiang and the others should be coming back. Hong Deming turned back toward the path, yawning, then frowned. He heard a noise that didn't belong at Peaceful River. He put his head to one side and heard it again: metal clashing.

Before he was consciously aware, he had called En to his hand and was leaping down the hillside toward the peony gate. The sounds grew louder; it seemed as though there were many swords, but only a few voices, screams and shouts. Qin music clashed against sword, but only the strongest qin players could contend against a skilled sword cultivator for sheer aggressive power. They would need him. This was one of the reasons, he knew, that Peaceful River had made a practice of welcoming guest cultivators from Crane Moon.

As he leapt from wall to wall, as fast as he could, he caught up with the sect master and the senior disciples running down the paths.

"Why didn't the wards give warning?" he shouted; he knew that the peony gate should have alerted those on watch.

The sect leader said, "If they followed closely on our disciples, and they didn't notice...they may have brought them into the wards as guests, unknowing." He stopped and struck his qin, one hard note that echoed. Above them, the wards flared red in a perfect dome, then faded. "I've strengthened them. No more can come in," he said, and began running again.

Hong Deming didn't have his bow and arrows, so he couldn't send warning flights down onto the mob that was caught outside the peony gate now. It seemed as though they were ordinary bandits, but the sword clash he had heard was not that of ordinary metal swords. Some of the attackers, at least, were cultivators. En began to glow golden, sending off sparks in anticipation. Despite the terrible view of the attackers already within the gate — heavily outnumbering Mo Xiang and the remaining Peaceful River disciples, who were drawn into a circle formation in the center of the first courtyard — he felt a sense of excitement. He had never truly matched with another sword cultivator in a life-and-death battle. This was what he had trained for all his life.

Running and jumping to come in from above, he used his lightness skills to send sword energy down through the packed crowd of attackers, leaving a swath of blood and body parts through the ordinary bandits. The cultivators looked up, and several leapt up to deal with him as he landed on the opposite courtyard wall.

"Hong Deming!" Mo Xiang shouted in relief from within the defenders' circle. He struck his qin, sending out energy that blocked a sword stroke. "You're here! What took you so long?"

Hong Deming laughed and parried a stroke, then turned for another. "Mo Xiang, you shouldn't spend so long in brothels, it's almost morning," he called back, and slashed down again; he had attackers on both sides, and occasionally jumping in from above or leaping up from below to strike at his feet. There didn't seem to be a lot of chivalry involved, but En was delighted with the challenge.

Soon, the sect leader and senior disciples arrived, setting up a second circle that ground the attackers between the two groups of qin attacks with Hong Deming running about as well and striking whatever particularly powerful sword cultivator he could find. There wasn't much in his mind aside from the weight of En, managing his qi and lightness: flipping, jumping, parrying, sending out the sword light, blocking. He was using his skills to the utmost against worthy opponents at last, and it was all he had hoped it would be. Every so often, he would notice that the courtyard looked rather slippery in the dark, but aside from that, he couldn't see the damage he was doing very well. He only knew that no one had yet gotten a blade on him, and given that he'd fought off at least eight attackers, he was rather pleased with himself.

"Hong Deming!" the sect leader called. "The wards are weakening. Go deal with the gate!"

He rushed down to the gate, where he saw two Peaceful River disciples, male and female, lying dead across the threshold. Beyond, the attackers had reorganized themselves: more ordinary bandits, and more cultivators. This time, one of the cultivators also used qin, strumming a melody to undo the wards — a handsome, powerfully-built older man with a sword strapped over his back. His robes were white and green.

"Jade Bamboo," Hong Deming muttered to himself, remembering his lessons as a child. The Jade Bamboo was also a righteous sect; why were they attacking Peaceful River?

A loud voice shouted, "Send out the traitor Mo Xiang!"

The Jade Bamboo cultivator came at him immediately, sending out a powerful qin strike. Hong Deming didn't block in time, not completely; qin was hard to block, since it came in such large, dispersed attacks. The qin energy caught his throat, left shoulder, and hip, and he leaned over, coughing and gasping for breath — enough time for several swords to come at him. He ducked, spun, leapt, and came down hard, his injured hip aching, but a great surge of energy from En rushed out ahead of him. It took down three swordsmen, who fell to the ground coughing blood; for the fourth, he used the actual blade, nearly cutting him in half. The attacker had been so close that the hot spurting blood soaked through his robes. Disgusting, but he had to keep cutting a path down and down.

At last, he looked up and saw that he had reached the last of the attackers on the path. The survivors were fleeing — ordinary folk on foot, the cultivators with lightness; the leader of the Jade Bamboo was among them. Hong Deming followed them with his eyes to see where they would re-enter the highway below, then saw that the highway was choked with people.

People were fleeing Gunan.

Leaping to the top of the peony gate, he looked toward the city. Fires were set in the nearest quarter, and there were attackers, tiny at a distance, grappling with defenders and watchmen on the walls.

Mo Xiang suddenly was up on the gate with him, eyes shaded to pierce the dim, smoky distance. The sun was not yet risen, but it was no longer completely dark. "Are they attacking the city?" Mo Xiang asked, shocked. "But when we left—"

"What's happening?" Hong Deming asked. "Why did they chase you here?" Without waiting for an answer, he bowed to the Peaceful River leader who was looking sadly at the dead disciples as he picked his way down the path between them. His blood still up, he said, "Sect leader, I would like to go help defend the city."

"Go, then, if you want to," the sect leader said, his voice tired. "Come back when you desire as well. You are not my disciple, and I do not exert my authority over you in this. Mo Xiang, you must stay. Your business is with defending the sect."

"Yes, Taiqian," said Mo Xiang.

Hong Deming jumped down and began running, sword in hand, toward the highway.

The gates of Gunan hadn't been prepared for an attack, so the enemy was already inside, wreaking havoc among the houses nearest the wall. Hong Deming found a few gate guards backed into a corner; he killed the people surrounding them and took them on as his backup. Few of the people attacking had armor, and none of them had military discipline. It was only because of the cultivators inexplicably supporting them that they had been able to take down the city guard.

As they ran through the streets, Hong Deming striking freely, he asked the rescued guards, "What happened? Why are they here? Who are they?"

The bewildered guards shook their heads, eyes wide. Three cultivators blocked the street ahead of them.

Hong Deming said, "Leave now, look for ordinary enemies, bring word to the palace guard."

The soldiers ran.

Hong Deming straightened and grasped En, ready but starting to feel the effects of fighting nonstop. There were other cultivational sects in Gunan, other swordmasters, even the imperial guard; why did it seem he was the only one fighting?

To get a little breathing time, he shouted, "Why are you here? Why are you attacking Gunan?"

One of the cultivators came toward him, sword flashing, and then a second;

the third held back, looking for an opening.

Hong Deming decided to take a different tack. Cutting down the first two with slices to the throat and abdomen, he sent a sword pulse toward the third, who was caught by the sword energy and dropped to his knees, spitting blood. Hong Deming leapt over, grabbed him, and jumped to the nearest rooftop.

"Why are you here?" he demanded.

The man wore the Jade Bamboo robes. He glared at Hong Deming in impotent fury. "Traitor," he managed, continuing to cough blood, and then, "Those who threaten the dynasty must be punished."

"Who was threatening the dynasty at Peaceful River? In Gunan? Isn't this threatening the dynasty, to attack the capital city?"

The man spat at him.

Hong Deming shook his head, tied him up with his own sash, and left him there for later. There were still bandits rampaging through the streets, and the cultivators were ahead of them. He went back to the slash-and-kill practice that constituted fighting against people without cultivation, trying to grasp some sense of what the goal of these people was, aside from causing havoc. The only specific areas he could see them focusing on were the cultivational sects scattered across the mansions, abbeys, and monasteries of Gunan — not only Peaceful River, but also several smaller and lesser-known sect houses located in the city itself. He saw one, the Divine Lotus sect, on fire, corpses scattered around its broken gate. Another several streets over, the Clear Mirror, was under attack as he ran by, its disciples on the walls, shooting at the cultivators attempting to leap up with their lightness skills.

Well, that would explain why there were no cultivators fighting back in the streets. They were all busy trying to defend their own sects. He spun, leapt, slashed, stabbed, and used En to send wide pulses of aggressive energy through the crowd, over and over again. There were so many, where had they all come from?

And then, he saw Shen Lu. He shouted, "Tainu! Tainu!"

Shen Lu spun around, his Crane Moon robes spattered with blood; he sent a sword pulse at Hong Deming, who ducked.

"Tainu, it's me! What's happening? Why are you here?"

Shen Lu's eyes cleared of bloodlust and recognized him. He pulled Hong Deming over into a corner, away from the fighting, and yelled in his ear, "Taine! Why are you here? What happened at Peaceful River?"

"They've been attacked. We fought them off."

Shen Lu swore. "Taine, this is hard to explain right now. The Peaceful River shouldn't have been targeted–"

"What do you mean, shouldn't have been targeted?" As he said it, he felt a crawling sense of horror on his spine; he looked wide-eyed at his tainu — now his sect leader — whose eyes ranged coldly over the street fighting.

Shen Lu picked up his sword again, then seemed to think twice. "Taine, I can't explain now. Go back to Peaceful River and wait for me."

"No, all the people– Look, they're being attacked! We have to–"

"Fine, protect the people. But stay away from fights with cultivators. The Jade Bamboo and Stone Phoenix are our allies."

"But– I– how– They're attacking all the sects in Gunan!"

"Not all of them. Taine, I'm your sect leader now. Don't argue about things you don't know about. These are my orders," he said fiercely, "and if you don't obey them, I will cast you out. Do you understand? Go back to Peaceful River. You can fight looters on the way but no cultivators." He pushed out of their corner. "Go now."

Hong Deming looked at him, his sword half-raised, eyes blank.

Shen Lu shook his head. "Taine, trust me. This is to protect you," he said, calling his own sword and heading back into the street. "Go now."

On the way back to the gate, Hong Deming killed thirty-five looters — ordinary people who were unable to resist a cultivational sword.

Hong Deming stood in the cobbled area just outside the gate of Gunan. There were only corpses here now, scattered all along the city walls on each side of the gate. The sun had risen, throwing long shadows over the twisted bodies and pools of blood on the stones, soaking into the earth.

There was a person picking among the corpses, a gourd and a jade pendant hanging from his sash. One by one, at each body, he knelt down and felt their pulse, long hair falling forward over one shoulder. Sometimes, he would do something with his fingers, touching their mouths or the wounds on their bodies; Hong Deming couldn't see what it was in the sharp, shadowed light.

Hong Deming's lips moved without making any sound.

"Tainu! What happened? you're covered in blood–" The person ran toward him, tripped over a corpse, and stumbled forward. Everything about his body was filled with anxiety, his face pale.

Hong Deming looked down, slowly. He was indeed covered in blood. Soaked in it. The blue of his outer robe was a dappled purple. "None of it's mine," he said, looking at Liu Chenguang. He flicked En mechanically to get the blood off it and thought, how strange it is that it's so clean, and I'm so filthy.

Liu Chenguang reached out to touch his arm, distressed.

Hong Deming took a step back. "No," he said, not sure what he was refusing. "Tainu–"

"Get away from him!" A sword came for Liu Chenguang's head from behind. Automatically, Hong Deming leapt to block. "Mo– Mo Xiang? Why?"

Liu Chenguang looked on, eyes wide. For the first time, Hong Deming realized that his taine carried no weapons at all. Not even a knife.

Mo Xiang's breath came hard. "Zhu Guiren did this. He brought them from the south. He said– he said that the Peaceful River are undermining the emperor. Zhu Guiren did it. You must have known!" he screamed at Liu Chenguang

Liu Chenguang looked at him, bewildered but seemingly unafraid. "No. No, that's not right. Teacher Zhu– Teacher Zhu wouldn't have…And we were just in the north, across the Sorrowful River–"

Hong Deming kept in front of him; Mo Xiang's swordsmanship was not up to his standards, but he also carried the qin, which would make it difficult to fully protect Liu Chenguang. Hong Deming's mind had woken up again with the sudden dive back into combat. He said, "Mo Xiang, you know Liu Chenguang is only studying with Zhu Guiren as a physician. You know that he doesn't take part in Zhu Guiren's work for the emperor. Whether Zhu Guiren did this or not, he wouldn't have known about it."

"How could he not know?" Mo Xiang asked hatefully. "He's his bed partner, isn't he?"

Liu Chenguang snapped, "Shut up." He pushed Hong Deming out of the way, or tried to; Hong Deming outweighed him significantly. "How dare you? That's a lie!"

"Taine, stay behind me," Hong Deming said sharply. "Mo Xiang, that's enough. Whether you believe Liu Chenguang or not, I will fight you if you attack him and you are not…" He took a deep breath. He had never actually done this before; never made the kind of boasts that set up the competitive hierarchy of the cultivational sects. "You are not qualified to match me," he said firmly.

Mo Xiang's face crumpled. "Damn you, Hong Deming." He sheathed his sword and turned away. Over his shoulder, he shouted, "Don't come back to Peaceful River!"

Hong Deming looked around again.

From behind him, Liu Chenguang reached out, carefully, for his blood-soaked sleeve. "Hong Deming," he said, "now be honest, are you hurt?"

"No, I'm fine. But I don't have anywhere to go now. Shen Lu is in the city. He told me to go back to Peaceful River..."

"Do you think that person was telling the truth, that you can't go back there?" Liu Chenguang spoke in a calm voice, guiding Hong Deming over to the side of the road as though he were blind. "Sit here, I'll clear a place." He indicated a spot under a tree with only a few corpses and began dragging them farther away.

Hong Deming leaned down to help him, then collapsed with his back against the tree, staring out over the carnage.

"You can wait here," said Liu Chenguang. He put his hand over Hong Deming's briefly, then added, "I was looking for survivors. I'm going to keep looking for people that I can save. Promise me you will stay here. Don't wander off. Promise?" He looked very worried.

Hong Deming let Liu Chenguang's hand remain for a moment, then withdrew; his hand was spattered with blood. "Sorry. I'll stay, you don't need to worry about me. Where's Zhu Guiren?"

"I don't know. We were coming back today and I saw...well, this. I couldn't keep going without trying to help, but Teacher Zhu needed to continue to the palace."

"There's attackers in the city."

"I'm sure he'll be safe," Liu Chenguang said indifferently, "Zhu Guiren is in dangerous places all the time. He has lots of ways..."

"He takes you into dangerous places?" Hong Deming frowned; this cut through his strange lethargy.

Liu Chenguang knelt next to him. "Tainu, you don't need to worry about me so much. I am also used to dangerous places. Just because I can't use a sword doesn't mean I can't keep myself safe."

Hong Deming watched him among the corpses, paying equal attention to each one whether cultivator or common person, attacker or defender of the city. After he passed, occasionally someone would sit up, or stand to walk away, but there were few. Most of the people remaining on the field had been too seriously injured to be evacuated and had bled to death before Liu Chenguang arrived. Every so often, he could see Liu Chenguang look back, hand shading his eyes, to be sure he was still sitting in the darkness between the trees, and then continue his slow, painstaking work.

When Liu Chenguang was far across the square, working down the wall on the other side of the city gate, Shen Lu found Hong Deming and sat next to him under the tree. He handed Hong Deming a flask of liquor, which he drank down without really tasting. After a while, Shen Lu said, "Taine, you stink. The first thing you need to do when we're done here is go into the city and take a bath. And burn those robes."

Hong Deming nodded. "Into the city…not back to Peaceful River?"

"No. I've managed to smooth it over so our sects will remain allies, but you can't go back there after challenging Mo Xiang. He's not willing to back down and you defeating or killing him would be disastrous right now." He handed Hong Deming a bag. "Here's your things. They won't let you keep the qin."

"That's fine. I have one at home." He watched Liu Chenguang, now a very small figure far in the distance, bending down over the bodies again and again. Shen Lu followed his gaze, then rubbed his face as though he was very tired.

"Taine, do you know why you're not the sect leader?"

"What?" Hong Deming turned to him and frowned. "Why would I be the sect leader? I'm the youngest disciple. You're the oldest. We all always knew you were going to be the sect leader."

"No," Shen Lu said, "actually, that trip when we found Liu Chenguang, Taiqian was observing you to see if you could become sect leader in the future. Didn't you ever wonder why he took the youngest disciple on a dangerous journey, not some of your seniors? Even then, he was considering you, and he kept observing over the years. And, although you are an idiot, it must be obvious to you that your cultivation is higher than mine." The last was said with some bitterness, but not too much. "I'm the eldest, of course, but the succession doesn't necessarily go that way. The strongest disciple would also be a candidate. But Taiqian decided that you were not suited."

Hong Deming waited.

"I see it too. I've seen it since you were a child. It's as though there's something missing in you. Something a person has from birth, but you don't have it…" He shook his head. "An insult means nothing to you. There's no anger in you, no desire for vengeance. Your cultivation is high and your skills are good, but you are reluctant to use them because you regret the consequences and you have no desire to use them to prove yourself or raise the sect. You have no sense of injury and necessary redress at all."

It was not true, that he had no anger. It was just that… "Taiqian saved me," he said, trying to explain. Did Shen Lu really think that in all those years of training, all the harsh discipline of the sect with no other children to share it with, he had never been angry? He had been an orphan in a city destroyed by war, and without Taiqian's whim to pick him up from the market of Zhashan, he would have been enslaved, or a beggar on the street, or dead before he was

169

six years old. How could he dare to be angry? It was only gratitude, that was all; he must always be obedient, must show himself worthy of Crane Moon, must always be the best.

"When a person like Mo Xiang attacks you, attacks your taine, you are reluctant to fight him. You should be angry, taine. You are not angry. You've probably already let it go in your heart when you should be remembering it, thinking about how to deal with this enemy in the future. Thus, too, you are unable to make decisions that would injure others. Too unwilling to destroy an enemy, and too kind to make hard choices in hard times. You are missing that from your childhood, and you've never developed it. That was the first reason." Shen Lu looked back out at Liu Chenguang. "The second reason is that person you keep staring at."

"What? Why?" At last, he could ask this question of Shen Lu — the one he could never ask Taiqian: "I've always wondered, why didn't Taiqian like Liu Chenguang? Why doesn't anyone? He is such a good person, he's...why not?"

"Why is this not obvious to you?" Shen Lu threw his hands up in exasperation. "That is not an ordinary person, Hong Deming. But you don't seem to notice. What kind of danger is that in a sect leader, that you can't even recognize something that is abnormal when it is right in front of your face?"

"He saved my life," Hong Deming said stubbornly. "He's never done anything to hurt anyone, to hurt the sect. He's always obeyed. He's never said an unkind word about any of you. What's wrong? What more do you and Taiqian want from him?"

"Taine, *think*. Do you think that an orphaned peasant child with the language of a scholar and a unique cultivation path somehow comes across a cultivational sect leader in the wilderness by accident? And do you think he really cares about whether he's a sect disciple or not? He came to us for his own purposes, Hong Deming. Taiqian agreed to take him because Zhu Guiren said his healing abilities would be an asset eventually, but he never trusted him. And nothing I've seen since is convincing me otherwise. Look at him, Hong Deming. Can you see what he's doing? How is he healing those people? And why is he doing it? These people were just attacking one another. Surely some of them were in the wrong, but he's healing everyone that can live without a care for their responsibility for this disaster."

"That's— Of course he is! How could he know? And why should he have to make that kind of decision, tainu? That's not fair, he's not an executioner—"

"I know he saved your life, but taine, how could he possibly have done it? Not that I wish you had died in seclusion, but qi deviation isn't cured by wishing."

"Tainu—"

"Taine, he spent years of his childhood in seclusion and he's not insane. Do you think that's normal either?"

"Then why?" he demanded, frustrated. "Why did you put him through that? Just because Zhu Guiren said so?"

After a moment, Shen Lu said, "Zhu Guiren gave the order, but Taiqian wouldn't have done it if he thought that Liu Chenguang was in any way a normal human being. A normal human child, even a child born and raised in a cultivational sect, would not have survived it. Taine, you have to think. Whoever this person is, he has a purpose that we don't fully understand. He has never opened his heart to us or really trusted us."

"That's not true. Tainu, that's not true at all. You never tried to get to know him. He has trusted me, and I trust him."

Yet, he wondered, too; Liu Chenguang had never shown any interest in developing a relationship with anyone else in the sect. He had accepted everything without demur, but also without showing anything of his inward feelings to anyone but Hong Deming.

Liu Chenguang had reached the last corpse and turned back down the length of the city wall toward them. He would reach them in a few moments.

Shen Lu stood up. "Taine, there's no point in continuing this conversation. Taiqian and I have consulted about the future of the sect, and it is relevant for you in particular now. You must not return to Crane Moon yet. Taiqian and I agree on this. Since you also can't stay at Peaceful River, you should take the opportunity to wander beyond the bounds."

Hong Deming didn't ask why this was; Shen Lu's voice had the ring of authority, and he knew he wouldn't be told. "For how long?"

"At least a year. Two."

"Does the sect leader have any particular assignments for this humble disciple?" he asked formally.

"There are many reports of demons coming out of the mountains with the instability and turmoil of the lands. Report to the Stone Phoenix sect house outside Bian. You should know that we are now allied formally with Jade Bamboo and Stone Phoenix sects, although what a mess that is. It'll take quite a bit to cover that you killed several Jade Bamboo cultivators..." He sighed. "Our alliance has decided to support the emperor in establishing a stable dynasty. There are plans in motion to make this happen; we're not central to them, but we have a specific role. In any case, you are likely to be targeted by survivors, because they, unlike you, will want to take vengeance for their losses. Try to develop some anger. Try to learn to see enemies as what they are."

Hong Deming just stared at him. "It's true, tainu. I couldn't be a sect leader."

"Yes, Taiqian made a wise decision there," Shen Lu said, apparently not noticing the sarcasm, which was not generally Hong Deming's style. "I'll leave first. I don't really want to talk with that person." He walked off before Liu Chenguang came close enough to recognize him.

Hong Deming remained standing until Liu Chenguang came close enough to speak. "Taine," he said, seeing the signs of exhaustion in Liu Chenguang's face, "you're pale. Are you all right?"

"I'm fine," Liu Chenguang said. "It was just a lot of work at one time, that's all. There were some that could be saved. Now that's done, it's you I'm worried about."

"There's nothing to worry about. I'm not hurt," he said. Liu Chenguang's closeness warmed him, helped heal the sickness in his heart after talking with Shen Lu. "But I can't go back to Peaceful River, and I really need a bath."

THE CRANE MOON CYCLE

CHAPTER 15
THE INN AT GUNAN

HONG DEMING AND Liu Chenguang wandered through the city, looking for an inn. Hong Deming was glad to note that the fighting had ended, and most of the surviving wounded had already been taken from the streets; those that remained were clearly very dead and were being gathered up as well. He hadn't wanted to watch Liu Chenguang check every corpse in Gunan, especially as a good number would have been his own responsibility.

The streets were still splashed with blood, and not all the fires were out yet. The looters had seemingly settled for several high-ranked brothels when the cultivation sects had proven too difficult. They would have valuable property — not the least of which was their inhabitants — and were only well guarded against over-enthusiastic patrons. Hong Deming saw that the Delicate Orchid pavilion was one of those burnt.

Liu Chenguang looked over at the yard. Through the broken gate, they could see the willow trees overhanging the pond, choked with ash. "Was there someone you cared about there?" he asked, a little catch in his voice.

"Just one person I knew," Hong Deming said, thinking of Wu Fan. "But you must have known others. You came there that night…" He looked away.

Liu Chenguang's gaze moved over the courtyard, raking over the building. "The fire was intense," he said at last. "Anyone still in there is unlikely to have survived, but I don't see many bodies. Hopefully, your friend escaped."

"He wasn't a friend, exactly, but I hope he escaped." He turned and kept walking.

Past the quarters nearest the gate, the damage became more focused. Only specific cultivational sects had been targeted.

"It's still so obvious," Hong Deming said.

"What do you mean?"

Belatedly, he thought maybe Shen Lu hadn't meant for Liu Chenguang to know this, but then, with a burst of anger, he decided that Liu Chenguang was a disciple and he damn well deserved to know. "Shen Lu told me that this was planned. It was to cover attacks on the cultivational sects that don't support the new dynasty. Our sect is allied with others in support of the Son of Heaven."

Liu Chenguang frowned. "Teacher Zhu may well be involved then, but why Peaceful River? They support the emperor, as far as I know..."

"Aren't you shocked?" he asked.

"Not shocked exactly. Traveling with Teacher Zhu has been an education in that way...The dynasty is unstable, people are not safe, and after years of this, there's a need to take action to make things better. That's what I've gleaned from what I've heard, anyway...There are so many refugees on the road, so many poor people...Did you know that in the Wan Zhao rebellion, when Zhashan was attacked, hundreds of thousands of people came and slaughtered and looted? Starving farmers turned into bandits...and we still had a dynasty, then. The Feng had a few decades left to go." Liu Chenguang lifted his robes to step over a corpse. "So much death, tainu. So much suffering. Teacher Zhu says that it's only with a stable dynasty that holds the mandate of heaven that we can avert it. That's what he says to everyone, at least in public where I can hear. So, I'm not shocked that action is being taken to strengthen the dynasty."

"But wasn't it...wrong? For the Crane Moon to ally against cultivators? To help attack a city? So many innocent people died." *So many were killed by me,* Hong Deming thought, *innocent or not.*

Liu Chenguang stopped after walking in silence, seemingly unable to answer. "Look, here's a good place."

They were well beyond the damaged quarter now. This inn was well appointed and peaceful, as though in a different world from the corpses at the gate.

"Tainu, wait here. Let me get the room and then bring you in. You'll frighten them. They won't rent to you." He smiled. "This is another education from Teacher Zhu: how to choose a good inn."

Hong Deming watched him go up the steps and decided that he hated Zhu Guiren with all his heart.

After a while, Liu Chenguang came back out, waiting until the front counter cashier was looking away to lead him upstairs. The room was pleasant, with a window of translucent paper panes filtering the afternoon sunlight, a large bed platform, and a table for tea.

"I've already sent for hot water," Liu Chenguang said. "You should bathe up here."

For a moment they stood staring at each other. The silence drew out.

Liu Chenguang cleared his throat. "I'll have them send up extra water, so you can...get really clean. Leave the dirty robes. Do you have clean ones?"

Hong Deming gratefully held up the bag Shen Lu had brought.

"I'll go, then." Liu Chenguang turned to the door.

"Will you come back?" Hong Deming asked quickly.

Liu Chenguang turned and smiled. "Of course," he said.

Hong Deming felt something warm him inside. Everything would be well, as long as Liu Chenguang would be there and would smile at him like that.

After he left, Hong Deming stripped off the bloody robes and threw them outside the door in disgust. He wiped himself off with a bathing cloth and settled into the bathing tub after getting off the worst of it. He poured water over himself till it turned cold, thinking about what to do next; he was so exhausted that nothing seemed to come to mind. When he thought of Shen Lu's calm explanation — of the Crane Moon collaborating with bandits to hide an attack on cultivators — he felt sick to his stomach. The corpses in the street and the burned houses lingered in his mind, too, as he washed the blood from his body. He did hope Wu Fan had gotten away, somewhere safe.

The image of a ruined Zhashan kept haunting him. His birth family had been killed in the Wan Zhao rebellion. At least, Taiqian had thought so...

And Liu Chenguang...how could it be that there was so much hatred for him in the sect, so much distrust? Did he sense it, did it hurt him to know? Or did he really not care at all? Out loud, as though Shen Lu could hear, he said, "Tainu, I'm not that stupid. I know he's not like other people, but why does it matter?" Why did it matter so much that Shen Lu would simply walk away without even greeting his own taine? Why did it matter so much that his own willingness to accept Liu Chenguang's oddities was proof that he was incapable of good judgment?

His body was beginning to ache all over and he felt the drain on his qi from the nonstop fighting. The water in the bath had turned pink, and he was glad that Liu Chenguang had arranged for the second tub so that he could fully rinse off before staggering toward the bed to collapse.

He was startled awake by Liu Chenguang's voice above him. "Tainu, the food's here. You should eat. It's gotten late, almost dark."

Hong Deming struggled to get out of the bed, but winced and fell back; his arm and side wouldn't bear weight, and his entire body felt bruised and battered.

"What's wrong?" Liu Chenguang came over and stopped still, staring down at him.

Hong Deming looked down at himself. He was wearing only an inner robe after the bath and it had opened slightly, exposing enormous, multi-layered bruises over his throat, collarbone, and shoulder. His entire left side was shades of dark red, blue, and purple.

Liu Chenguang knelt next to the bed, staring at the bruises, biting his lip till the blood showed. "You said you were fine," he accused. "Why didn't you tell me? It wouldn't have gotten this bad if I'd taken care of it right away. Can you even move at all?"

Truthfully, moving felt quite difficult. He tried to get up again, but the bruises had now set deeply and his muscles and tendons didn't seem to want to respond. "I'm fine," he said nonetheless. "Really. It's just from a qin attack. I–"

He broke off into inarticulate gasping because Liu Chenguang grasped him by his right shoulder so he couldn't move and leaned over to kiss the bruise on his throat. It almost felt as though Liu Chenguang was licking him, his mouth moving over his throat and below to his collarbone, kissing, pressing gently, the blood and saliva soothing his skin. Wherever Liu Chenguang's mouth went, intense pleasure followed through Hong Deming's body, heating him beyond his ability to bear.

"Ah, please," he begged. "Please, I can't–"

Liu Chenguang looked up, blood bright on his lips. He didn't look particularly aroused; he looked furious, his long eyes narrowed. "Where else? Where else are you hurt? And don't lie this time."

Hong Deming shook his head, still trying to get his breath. He was fairly confident that if Liu Chenguang did that to his hip, he couldn't be responsible for the consequences. "There's nothing. Nothing–"

"Get up then," Liu Chenguang said coldly.

He couldn't.

"Tainu!" Liu Chenguang yelled in exasperation. "Fine then."

He laid his hands on both sides of Hong Deming's face to hold him still again, bent down, and kissed his lips. Hong Deming tasted the salt of his blood as Liu Chenguang's tongue slipped effortlessly between his lips and teeth. He groaned, grasping Liu Chenguang's shoulders and then the nape of his neck, holding on tightly. Liu Chenguang's hair fell down around him, teasing at his bared throat and chest and engulfing him in his scent and warmth. Liu Chenguang's body responded to him, not struggling to get away but pressing closer. He heard him gasp as well, the two of them softly breathing and panting together. He moved his hand down Chenguang's back to his waist, bringing them closer; it seemed to him that they couldn't get close enough.

"Chenguang," he breathed, opening his eyes at last to look at him.

Liu Chenguang's eyes were partly closed, hazy and unfocused, his bitten lip swollen, but the bleeding had already stopped. "Deming," Liu Chenguang responded, and kissed him again, gently, eyes still half closed.

Hong Deming watched him, entranced by the sound of his name in his mouth and the shape of his lips, his dreaming eyes.

"Don't lie to me anymore. If you're hurt, tell me right away."

"I'll want to get hurt all the time now," he said.

Chenguang laughed and laid his head down on his breast, half-lying on him. He couldn't see himself under Liu Chenguang's hair, but the bruises felt much better.

"I hope you don't give this treatment to everyone, though."

"Just to you..."

There was a knock at the door. Both of them started and sat up — it was quite easy now, Hong Deming noticed; being kissed by Liu Chenguang was evidently a magical panacea — flushed and disarrayed, trying to quickly make themselves decent.

Liu Chenguang dashed across the room to Hong Deming's luggage and threw an outer robe at him, then went to the door. "Yes?" he asked, clearing his throat.

"Master, sorry for the disturbance, but there's someone here that–"

"Student Liu," interrupted a cold voice that Hong Deming now thoroughly detested.

"Teacher Zhu," Liu Chenguang sighed. He opened the door.

Zhu Guiren swept in, wearing court robes. His eyes landed first on Hong Deming, sitting demurely at the tea table. "You survived the unfortunate attack on Peaceful River, I see."

Hong Deming said, "Thanks to the efforts of the disciples of the sect, we did fend off the attackers successfully."

Zhu Guiren nodded, clearly dismissing him. "Student Liu, I've completed what's necessary here. We need to depart with the Crane Moon sect leader to-night. We will require their protection on the road back, after today's events. There will be attacks from the scattered disciples of the surviving targeted sects. My name has unfortunately been associated with this."

Liu Chenguang said, "Of course, I'm ready. Hong Deming was injured to-day—"

"Have you healed him?" he cut in, as though Hong Deming wasn't right there. "I told you, no more healing until the work is complete."

"I've been healing people all morning, actually," said Liu Chenguang coolly. "And I'm fine. Check if you don't think so."

Zhu Guiren declined to touch the arm he held out. "Student Liu," he said sternly, "I am still your teacher, and you must trust that I know more than you do about this. The issue is not only whether you can survive healing others, ran-domly and constantly as the opportunity presents itself, though I'm not sure you can, but how this will affect your powers in the next few months."

Hong Deming looked at Liu Chenguang, whose expression was rebellious, then back at Zhu Guiren.

Liu Chenguang shrugged. "Well, it doesn't matter. Either way, I'm fine. Hong Deming and I will be coming, of course. Just let us gather our things. I'm sure you need to change out of court dress before we leave, Teacher Zhu."

"Oh, is he coming too?" Zhu Guiren raised his eyebrows. "I was under the impression that his sect leader had given him other commands."

Liu Chenguang turned and looked at Hong Deming, speechless.

He nodded reluctantly. "I'm to seek yaoguai. I can't return to Crane Moon for a year, at least."

"A year," Liu Chenguang echoed. He looked back at Zhu Guiren. "How fortuitous."

"Within a year," Zhu Guiren said blandly, "if all goes as planned, the current unrest should be addressed adequately by the stabilizing of the dynasty. At that point, cultivators might be able to return to their sects with the re-establishment of law and order and the guarantee of safety for the common people."

Hong Deming looked back and forth between them. Certainly, he thought to his own satisfaction, no one would think these two were involved, seeing them talk together. It seemed to be pompous demands on one side and outspoken re-sentment on the other. Liu Chenguang showed Zhu Guiren none of the warmth he had when he smiled at Hong Deming, which was a lovely thing to think about, but there would be at least a year before they could be together again.

"I'm not going to Crane Moon," Liu Chenguang said. He sat down to emphasize his words. "I'll stay with Hong Deming. We'll wander together."

Zhu Guiren opened his mouth, then closed it again and looked at Hong Deming. Eventually, he said, "Student Liu, you have to complete your cultivational healing for yourself before you can go out into the world. I know how to get you through what will happen in the next year–"

"What will happen in the next year?" Hong Deming asked sharply.

"Nothing. Nothing will happen that I won't be perfectly fine doing," Liu Chenguang said, glaring at Zhu Guiren.

"One more year, Student Liu. One more year, and everything will be done. Then, you'll be able to go do...whatever it is you want to do. A year isn't so long, is it, when it's your life at stake?"

"My life is not at stake!" Liu Chenguang shouted in frustration. "I am perfectly fine! I know my powers better than you."

"Do you refuse, then, to do what I order you to do? Your sect leader placed you under my authority."

"Then let Hong Deming come back with me. Let him come back to Crane Moon with me," Liu Chenguang said stubbornly. He met Hong Deming's eyes, fierce and pleading.

"I can't, taine. I'm forbidden to come." He held Liu Chenguang's gaze, trying to communicate things he couldn't possibly say in front of Zhu Guiren.

Zhu Guiren added, "That wasn't my decision, Student Liu. You can't blame me for it, and I can't change it."

Liu Chenguang clenched his hands into fists and stared at the floor. "Will you release me, Zhu Guiren," he asked through his teeth, "and tell Taiqian that I am able to be on my own?"

"Not yet. One more year. And Liu Chenguang," Zhu Guiren added, using his full name, "you know that if I release you, you still owe obedience to your sect leader. I am only carrying out their authority through delegation now."

Liu Chenguang stared silently at the tea table.

Zhu Guiren raised his eyes to meet Hong Deming's. He said, "Student Liu, you need one more year of work with me, in an intensive environment, to stabilize your cultivation and avoid qi deviation in your healing path. You need to be in a safe and protected place where I can help you in case of emergency."

"There will be no emergencies," Liu Chenguang said.

Hong Deming spoke, trying to be polite, although he truly wanted to smash Zhu Guiren into little pieces: "Master Zhu, please leave first. I will bring my taine to the gate to meet you and the sect leader in one hour."

Zhu Guiren nodded and swept out.

Defeated, Liu Chenguang stared at him from the tea table. Hong Deming readied himself for one last attempt to say what he meant, to make things good between them after everything that had happened. The silence stretched as Liu Chenguang looked at him with sad eyes.

At last, Hong Deming said, "I wish more than anything that you could come with me, or I could come with you. But your being safe means more than that. That's the most important thing to me — for you to be safe."

Liu Chenguang finally smiled and shook his head. "Why do you think I don't want to let you go anywhere without me, after seeing what a mess you got yourself into today?" He stood and walked over to Hong Deming, reaching out to touch his hand cautiously. "Deming, before, were you drunk?"

Hong Deming smiled and took his other hand as well, lightly tracing the shape of Liu Chenguang's fingers, his delicacy and strength. "I wasn't drunk. Were you?"

"I wanted to kiss you for so long. That's all," Liu Chenguang said, and blushed a little bit. "I took advantage. You should know, I really don't normally heal people that way. By kissing them."

"But you use your blood to heal people?" Hong Deming gently stroked the dark hair back sticking to his skin, his forehead a little warm and sweaty. It made his heart beat harder. "Your hair is a mess, Chenguang."

"My blood has healing powers, yes," Liu Chenguang said, smiling up at him. "And if my hair is a mess, it's completely your fault."

"It's your cultivational path?"

Liu Chenguang hesitated slightly. "That's the best way to explain it. Does it frighten you, that I can do that?"

"No. Nothing about you could frighten me, Chenguang." Hong Deming gathered him into his arms, where he fit completely perfectly. Liu Chenguang tipped his face up and Hong Deming very softly kissed him on his eyebrows, his nose, and his lips.

"It truly doesn't bother you, that I'm not like other people?" Liu Chenguang asked through all the kissing.

"No," Hong Deming said. He thought to himself that it was a wonderful feeling, to kiss Liu Chenguang gently like this — as though they unshakably belonged to each other and could count on having all the time in the world for everything else.

Liu Chenguang seemed to have a contradictory thought; he nestled more closely, teasing his waist with his fingers, and said, "I wish that we could have a lot of time together right now, in this pleasant inn, with this very convenient bed."

Hong Deming flushed.

"However," Liu Chenguang sighed, "I suspect that Zhu Guiren is waiting downstairs because he doesn't trust you to bring me, really." He tangled his hands up in Hong Deming's hair, tugging him down to kiss him more thoroughly.

Breathing a little more quickly, Hong Deming closed his eyes, and let himself feel everything about him: his tongue, his lips, his hands, his body's weight against him, his skin warming where they touched. Liu Chenguang made a little whimpering noise that went through him with a shock of heat, and urgently he kissed back, his hands and mouth growing more demanding.

"Ah," Liu Chenguang said at last, breaking it off to get his breath. "Deming, promise me that you will come to Crane Moon as soon as you can."

"A year," he said, taking in Liu Chenguang's eyes, dark and wide, fixed on his own. "It's not so long."

"Too long." Liu Chenguang kissed him one last time.

Hong Deming brought Liu Chenguang to the gate as he had promised and gave him up to Zhu Guiren, Shen Lu, and the senior Crane Moon disciples who had accompanied him. None of them looked at Liu Chenguang with any warmth. He sat quietly on his horse, looking at the ground, dressed in his scholar's robes with his gourd and pendant. No one spoke to him or welcomed him. Zhu Guiren talked with Shen Lu near the front of the column, ignoring him.

Hong Deming walked over to them, feeling the anger that Shen Lu told him he was missing; the most precious thing in the world was being delivered into their hands and they treated him like this. "Excuse this disciple's presumption, sect leader, may he speak with the sect leader before leaving?"

Shen Lu looked surprised. "Yes, of course."

Zhu Guiren seemed to be unwilling to withdraw, ignoring the atmosphere. Hong Deming glared silently at him until at last he nodded shortly and moved away. Hong Deming then stared malevolently at his back.

"What is it?" Shen Lu asked impatiently. "We need to head out while we can take advantage of the moonlight. I want to get us well away from here."

Now that it had come to it, he didn't know how to say it except bluntly. "Tainu, please, take care of him. Don't treat him this way — like a thing that doesn't matter. He's your taine too."

"It's like that?" Shen Lu looked at him, then looked over at Liu Chenguang and shook his head. "Taine, you…Well, it's not unexpected. Taiqian was hoping that you might find someone else at Peaceful River, but it must be something fated for you."

"Can you let me come with you?" he asked, low and desperate. "Since you know how it is?"

Shen Lu shook his head. "It's better if you're away for now. For him too. He needs to focus on his cultivation, Zhu Guiren says. And what would you do anyway, if he's in seclusion, or cultivating intensively, or whatever it is that Zhu Guiren has planned for him? You would just distract him and make things more difficult." He reached out and patted his shoulder consolingly. "Since it's important to you, taine, I'll do my best to be kind. And you know he will be safe. Where could be safer than at Crane Moon? You should be grateful that Zhu Guiren is willing to bring him to us for this last year and stay with him. You know Master Zhu has much to do. He's giving up a year for it."

Hong Deming stepped back, watching Shen Lu mount his horse and ride forward, the column following. Liu Chenguang and Zhu Guiren were near the end, just before the senior disciples of the rearguard. Liu Chenguang raised his head as they passed and smiled at him — one last smile — and he smiled back.

Only one year, he thought. *Only one year. That's all.*

When he couldn't hear the hoofbeats on the road anymore, he mounted his own horse and rode in the other direction.

CHAPTER 16
REACHING THE REFUGE

TAIREI FOLLOWED ZHU Guiren blindly through the razor grass to the shore of a river. Rivers in the spirit realm were unpredictable, and many were not normal water, but spiritual energy with different effects.

Zhu Guiren put Aili down for a moment and looked at it, frowning. "The path leads across here," he said, "but I don't see how to cross."

This place was unfamiliar to Tairei as well. Whenever a phoenix was reborn, they would be moved into the spirit realm by the phoenix gate, but the fire could bring them anywhere within it. This time — probably since she'd been in a new part of the mortal world at rebirth — she had awoken in a part of the spirit world that was completely strange to her. She knew no paths, recognized few plants, and there were no landmarks she could orient toward.

The phoenix refuges were scattered around the entire spirit world, hidden from view and findable only by the phoenixes themselves. There were not many phoenixes; less than one hundred and fifty, Tainu had told her once, spending most of their cycles hidden in the mortal realm and returning to the spirit realm only when forced to by the rebirth fire. Of course, there were many more refuges than phoenixes — established everywhere for a phoenix's safety since a phoenix might appear anywhere — but still, a few hundred or even a thousand refuges scattered throughout the spirit realm didn't necessarily mean a refuge was close.

In the life in which she had met Hong Deming, she had been reborn as usual but had not been able to reach a refuge before demons found her, forcing her back into the mortal realm before she had reached adulthood. Demons were already chasing them now, and if Tainu's distraction didn't work or if they didn't find a refuge before nightfall, they would be in a very precarious position.

Zhu Guiren said, "I don't want to go up- or downstream. This must be the quickest path to cross."

Tairei knelt at the shore, reaching out cautiously to touch the water with two fingers. She closed her eyes to concentrate. "It doesn't seem to be corrosive or spiritually damaging," she said at last. "If we could fly, this would be so much easier."

"Of the three of us, I'm the only one with that option and I'm not the one in danger," he said. "Well, I don't see anything we can use as a boat. Can you swim?"

"Not very well, but I think I can make it across this one. It's not very wide…" She shaded her hand and looked across; it was really only a little over a hundred feet, perhaps, and there didn't seem to be a strong current. And damned if she was going to let Zhu Guiren carry *her*. She'd rather drown. "But can you swim while you're carrying Aili?"

Zhu Guiren sent her a look that she remembered well from their travels around the Sorrowful River valley. "Of course," he said haughtily. He considered his robes, then shrugged and took off the outer two layers, leaving him in a thin underrobe with narrow sleeves. Tossing the outer robes over to her, he said, "Carry that for me."

Tairei rolled her eyes and made it into a neater package. Out of nowhere, she found herself saying, "Did you know Hong Deming really admired you once?"

"No," he said indifferently. "Let's go." He waded into the river water and began to swim an awkward sidestroke, holding Aili under his handless arm on his chest so that her face remained above the water.

Tairei wished she were taller so she could do this. She hated that Zhu Guiren was doing for Aili what she couldn't.

On the other side, having dog-paddled over after him — luckily nothing had attacked them in the water, because she really couldn't swim — Tairei silently handed him his robes. They were soaking wet, but he carefully wrung them out and put them back on.

"You look ridiculous," she said.

"As though there's anyone I need to impress here." He looked around, a sword in his hand once more. "If we do need to fight, I'm going to need to put her down quickly," he said. "Don't get upset if she gets a few bumps."

They walked again in single file, Zhu Guiren following a twisting, spiraling path through a flat, open meadow; it must be a requirement of the wards, to navigate through a maze. After a while, he asked, "You hate me because he died?"

Tairei looked at him, marveling at his denseness. "I hate you because you lied; because you destroyed our life together; because you ruined his life and his family; because you organized the destruction of thousands of other lives and their families and all they had; and yes, of course, because he died," she said. "The more I know about you, the more there is to hate."

Zhu Guiren hefted Aili a little higher on his shoulder, frowning as though this was a very complicated thing to understand. "Did you hate me when you first met me, or only after all that happened?"

"Why would I have hated you when I just met you?" She remembered that time, the first time they were formally introduced, right after coming to Crane Moon. Taiqian had brought him to stand in front of the gathered disciples and bow to Zhu Guiren as his future teacher. Hong Deming had been off in a corner, staring wide-eyed at Zhu Guiren rather than at him even though it was the first time they'd seen each other since his arrival at the sect. It was unlikely she would forget *that*. Zhu Guiren's perfect face and elegant demeanor drew everyone's eyes; he didn't speak kindly or warmly, his voice precise and cold. Though she hadn't known that he was a demon, she had known that what he was saying was completely false. She was not some kind of rogue cultivator with a unique cultivation path. She was not human at all. Yet, it fit so well — provided such an excellent explanation of who she was that mortals could understand.

It allowed her to stay near Hong Deming.

So she acted as though she believed it, and she obeyed.

But she didn't hate him, not until almost the very end.

"I didn't hate you," Zhu Guiren was saying. He had led them beneath some tall trees with dark purple leaves, so they were effectively walking in the dark. She could barely see him walking ahead of her, his facial expressions invisible. "I actually...liked having a student. It wasn't all lies. Aren't you glad that I taught you medicine? And astronomy?" He seemed uncertain. "I tried to teach you about politics, too, so you would understand how worthless mortals are. I could see you getting entangled...I taught you things I knew would help you in the future, when we were...done."

"I found the book of the Way of Heavenly Benevolence in the imperial library," she said. "Oddly, you never introduced me to that one."

"Ah," he said, floundering a bit. "Well. Master Shao was a little too idealistic. Not a good match for you. You were already too much...that."

"Why are you even here?" she asked, frustrated enough to finally ask it, as though she could hope for any honesty from him. "Why did you come to find me in Easterly?"

"I wasn't looking for you. It was just a coincidence. But I protected you, remember? I have no idea why you had to scream at me to get away."

"Do you think protecting me from a few random yaoguai makes up for what you did to us?" she asked, enraged. "Who the hell asked for your protection? Do you– you stupid–" She cut herself off. There was no point trying to talk to him. No point at all.

He didn't respond, perhaps wanting to save his breath as the hill steepened dramatically. Tairei jumped forward to help balance Aili as Zhu Guiren clambered over a rocky part.

After she had calmed herself enough to talk like a rational person, she added, "We're already inside the outer wards that would have alerted anyone in the refuge that someone is coming. I could feel when we crossed."

"I need a rest," Zhu Guiren said. He placed Aili down on the ground, then sat next to her, panting.

Tairei sat on the other side of Aili's limp form and held her hand. After a moment, she realized that Zhu Guiren was staring at that — her hand, holding Aili's.

"What?" she asked defensively. She thought of bringing her wings out again so he couldn't look at them, but she, too, was tired; they had been going for most of the day without a break.

"I didn't hate you," Zhu Guiren said again, as though it was a very important and necessary point. "Everything I did, I tried to make it easy for you...It was only a few years of your thousands of years of life. Only a little bit. I...aren't you fine now?"

She stared at him in contempt and considered spitting in his face, but turned back to Aili in the end, stroking her hand.

"I had to do it," he continued, "because I was doing something very important. Something I needed to complete..."

"Did you hate Hong Deming?" she asked coolly. "Or any of the other people whose lives you ruined?"

"No! That's what I'm saying. That's what you don't understand. I didn't hate any of them. I didn't do things just to hurt them. They were just...just... raw material." His voice petered out as he looked at the ground. "They were just there. Helpful or annoying or inconsequential. Hong Deming was annoying, but I didn't hate him."

"Do you see–" she said, very slowly, "–can you wrap your genius brain around the fact that whether you hated him or not made no difference whatsoever with what you did to him? To me? To everyone you touched, or spoke to — people you never even knew about who were caught up in all those machinations of yours? Have you given even a moment's thought to Hong Deming in the past thousand years?"

"No. Why would I?"

Tairei gritted her teeth. "Hatred or indifference is the same. You destroyed us and didn't even notice. You didn't even care." She bent down and kissed Aili's hair. "You're not worth my breath. You're certainly not worth my forgiveness, if that's what you're looking for."

They sat in silence until at last, Zhu Guiren said, "Let's keep going." He picked up Aili again, grunting, and started upward without looking at Tairei.

Halfway up the slope, a large, winged yao came down and swooped at Aili's head. Tairei screamed in shock. Zhu Guiren put Aili down rather carefully and yelled something vicious up at the sky that she couldn't quite catch.

The winged demon came down, transforming into a smiling, golden-haired woman who called out a sword. "Why are you hoarding these delicious little treats?"

"They're mine," Zhu Guiren said, sounding bored. "Off you go now."

The woman walked toward Tairei and Aili. "A phoenix and a…whatever that is. What is it, an experiment?"

"In a sense," said Zhu Guiren. He stepped in front of them.

"Our clans are allied," the woman said. "The phoenix is fair game if you can't protect it for yourself. If I kill you, your clan won't retaliate."

"That is not a problem you'll have to consider, since you'll be dead." Zhu Guiren leapt toward her. He aimed first at her right arm, but she was very fast, dodging around him to get to Tairei.

She smiled and grabbed Tairei's hair. "I've heard that you have a long and involved way of dealing with phoenixes. I'm more straightforward."

Then she yanked Tairei's head back and viciously stabbed her in the throat.

Tairei coughed and choked on the blood and pain. She fell to all fours on top of Aili, hoping to protect her. For a moment, she blacked out from blood loss, which was to be expected with this kind of wound; she knew the demon had attacked so that she wouldn't have the energy to transform and flee, though of course she wouldn't have been able to anyway.

When she was able to see again and the wound had closed, Zhu Guiren and the demon woman were spinning and leaping around each other almost too fast to see. Qi trailed in the air like fireworks as they threw spells and talismans at each other, as well as striking with the swords. At last, Zhu Guiren managed to strike the woman's upper arm, heavily. The woman screamed and brought her wings back out, transforming into a black eagle, dripping blood from the sky as she flew away.

Zhu Guiren limped back over to them, panting and coughing. Tairei got up, covered in blood. Aili was drenched in her blood as well; she must have bled out almost completely before she healed. He was also injured — a slash to his thigh and a talisman mark on his handless arm — but he didn't ask Tairei to heal him. Instead, he bent down, silently, to pick up Aili again.

As Zhu Guiren reached for Aili's waist, her eyes opened suddenly, a bright and terrifying blue in her blood-streaked face, and a golden sword appeared in her hand.

"Zhu Guiren," she whispered, her voice hoarse and strange.

"Aili?!" yelled Tairei. "Wait, Hong Deming!"

Aili's sword stabbed upward, piercing Zhu Guiren's chest, as he was bent over her. Zhu Guiren gave a gurgling scream and fell backward; the golden sword disappeared into thin air, his blood spurting from where it had been. Aili's eyes closed again.

"Aili?!" said Tairei, running to her. Then, reluctantly, "Zhu Guiren?"

He looked at her silently, then closed his eyes. Blood ran down from his lips.

"Damn you, Zhu Guiren," she said. She was tempted, just for the flash of a heartbeat, to watch him die. It would be so easy. But even as she thought it, she was already slashing at her hand with Zhu Guiren's sword. She anointed the wound on his chest, then reluctantly placed her blood between his lips.

It didn't take long before he opened his eyes. Tairei was already back beside Aili, holding her hand. He watched them quietly for a while before he stood up and walked over. "Let's go," he said, and bent down to pick up Aili again.

They walked up the steep, forested hill, to a lawn of short moss interspersed among the hateful razor grass that fronted a stone cliff in the hillside.

Zhu Guiren spoke at last. "This is it. This is where the path ends."

Tairei let go of the last shred of hope that she could get rid of him; she had promised her sibling. "Give me your hand," she said.

He reached out, still looking away from her; she pulled him forward until she felt a sense of resistance in the air, then paused until the refuge recognized her. Tainu had been confident it would, despite the weakening of her powers. Yes, the refuge acknowledged, yes, this is a phoenix, after all.

She opened her eyes to see the gate outlined in light on the stone in front of her and began walking forward, pulling Zhu Guiren after her. "Stay close to me," she said, feeling the wards begin to activate against him.

He gasped once, in pain. She could feel his pulse racing; this must be difficult for him.

"It will be all right," she heard herself say.

He didn't respond, his fingers spasming in her hand. Then, he only said, "Ah," and fell to his knees.

The thickness of the wall wasn't so great that they should still be inside it; clearly, the wards were not going to let a demon in. Tairei swore, realizing that she couldn't let go of his hand or he would be trapped between the ward shields forever.

"Don't let go of Aili." She bit her other hand, then drew several characters in her own blood on Zhu Guiren's forehead and started chanting softly. She wasn't as good with spells as her sibling was, but she had good instincts. He had always told her that.

Zhu Guiren's breathing smoothed out, and he staggered upright again. "Quickly," he said.

They came through into a small cavern — very small for three, and soon to be four, people — smoothed in a perfect sphere around a golden-blue fire that burned in the middle without any visible source of fuel. The walls were shining and smooth, and purely black. In them, the flames of the golden fire reflected and refracted endlessly, seeming to hint at symbols and figures deep in the stone that disappeared as soon as one tried to see them more closely.

"Here we are," Tairei sighed with relief.

Zhu Guiren half-fell down, lying Aili on the floor, then collapsed either into unconsciousness or a deep sleep. Tairei checked Aili, who seemed stable, and then Zhu Guiren; he would recover, she thought. She looked at him for a moment, remembering those days traveling with him, learning from him. They had never been friends, only teacher and student, but she had learned so much from him. He had been right, after all. She had trusted him.

It only made everything worse.

Time passed differently in the refuges than in other places, Tairei knew. There was no hint of day or night or seasons. In that sense, it was somewhat like the spiritual caverns at Crane Moon, though those were crude and brutal compared to the refuges — just enforced night and deprivation of the bodily senses.

The refuges didn't deprive, but enhanced and focused, intensifying the power of the spirit realm so that cultivation would move more quickly. As Aili and Zhu Guiren were unconscious, she settled herself into some good, hard cultivation.

"Who made this?" Zhu Guiren asked, waking up suddenly.

"I don't know, they've always been here."

"How long have we been here? Where's Tainu?"

"I don't know," she said, opening her eyes and frowning at him. He looked uneasy. "Are you worried about him?"

"Why would I be worried? I'm sure the giant bird is fine," he said pettishly.

"I'm sure he is too." She closed her eyes again. "He really will be fine, but when he arrives, he'll probably be tired. Just let him rest."

Zhu Guiren tapped his fingers on the crystalline floor in an unpredictable pattern, making an echoing noise. Tairei's eyes flew open again.

"Sorry," he said, not sounding sorry at all. "What is this made of? The substance is so hard…"

"Why are you so interested? Finding ways to undermine the refuge so you can catch phoenixes later? Don't bother — they're impregnable."

"Nothing's impregnable," he muttered. "It's not very comfortable for me. There's some pain, and pressure on my body just being here, even though you took me through the wards. I can tell it's anti-demonic, but what about the soul-devourers?"

"I don't know about that." Tainu suddenly appeared next to the wall. "We've never had a mortal soul in one of these before to attract them, so it's never been a problem." He slid down the wall and tipped his head back, eyes closed. Against the black wall, his dark brown skin made him seem like a silhouette surrounded by an aura of dancing golden lights in the stone.

Zhu Guiren stared at him. "You're tired."

"You noticed," Tainu replied, his eyes still closed. "Yes." He sighed deeply and turned his head to the side to look wearily at Tairei. "Did anything happen?"

Zhu Guiren looked at the ground and started tapping his fingers again.

Tairei said, "We were attacked by a demon. And Aili woke up for a split second and stabbed Zhu Guiren with En."

"What?!" Tainu shook himself to a more upright position. "She…"

Tairei nodded. "I couldn't have been mistaken — it was En."

"I also couldn't have been mistaken," said Zhu Guiren, "she stabbed me with it. Oh, and yes, there was a demon I fought off."

Tairei noticed that he seemed more like himself now and felt oddly relieved; it had been strange to have him quiet and withdrawn.

Tainu said, "We haven't gotten to talk about this yet, but Tairei, you should know that she can use weapons. And she can use the rebirth fire as a weapon."

Zhu Guiren and Tairei both stared at him.

"But no phoenix can use a weapon," Tairei replied. "Do you have any idea how hard I tried?"

Zhu Guiren said, "I hate to point out the obvious, but this person is not a phoenix. You can't assume that what she is or does will be the same as what you do. Just because you did whatever it was you did to her doesn't make her a phoenix. She's a mortal soul with heavy demonic affinity."

Now, Tairei and Tainu both stared at Zhu Guiren.

"Demonic affinity?" asked Tairei finally.

"All mortals have it," he said impatiently, "it's why they're so fun for us. Well, most mortals, anyway. Hers is heavier than most, so in addition to the normal mortal inclinations…" He stood and walked over to where she was lying, moved his hands in a sharp gesture, then reached out as though he was grabbing something in the air. "She's bound into three separate arrays. That's a record, as far as I know. No living being I've ever seen was bound into more than one, and to be honest, I already knew that she was bound into one. There are some ghosts, for lack of a better word, that are bound into two. She has three…incredibly bad luck for her."

"What's an array?" Tairei asked. "What does it do to her?"

Absently, Zhu Guiren said, "It's difficult to explain in a few words what it is. Demons at a certain level of power can set up an array to cultivate resentment more efficiently by capturing souls in suffering. Mostly souls of the dead, but living people can be bound into arrays as well."

He looked briefly at Tainu, then away. "The effect on a mortal living being is…not good. It's more likely than not that they experience a lot of suffering, or they cause a lot of suffering, or both. It depends on how strongly she's bound and how long it's had an effect on her…how strong the array is and how strong the demon who made it was. There are a lot of variables. With three, it would be hard to determine how they might interact with one another and which ones came from which life…" He trailed off, tapping his fingers against his handless arm.

"Can you just say what it does to her?" Tairei asked, holding tightly to Aili's hand; if Aili had been awake, she likely would have winced, but Aili slept through it all.

Zhu Guiren shrugged. "Brief life, unhappy death."

Tairei looked down at Aili's face, pale and silent.

Tainu spoke at last. "Tell me why you were confident she would have at least one."

Zhu Guiren looked at him. "Isn't it obvious? Hong Deming was bound at his death by me."

"No," Tairei said fiercely. "No, he wasn't. He was bound by me."

Zhu Guiren frowned at her, then bent down to look more closely at Aili. His hand moved in the air again, his fingers grasping and pulling at invisible threads in the air. His brows knit more seriously. "Liu Chenguang, what exactly did you *do?*"

Tairei shook her head. "Isn't it possible that some people have a phoenix affinity?" she asked.

Zhu Guiren snorted, still looking at Aili and running his fingers through the air. "Who would want a phoenix affinity? Just meat that doesn't die."

Tainu and Tairei both stared at him in silence.

"Oh, come on," he said, "don't be offended. I'm treating you like family here."

"You have a family?" asked Tainu.

"Of course not. But if I did, I would certainly talk to them like this." He tugged hard at something invisible in midair. "I'd also probably try to kill them, so, you know, you two really are like family to me..."

Tainu stood up and walked back out through the wall.

Zhu Guiren's hand froze in position. "Did I say something?" he asked.

"Are you asking me that as though it's a serious question?" Tairei glared at him and settled back into a cultivation pose.

"I was joking," he said.

"It was a terrible joke and you are giving us terrible news, so it wasn't funny. It's pathetic that I have to explain that to you, Zhu Guiren. How did you survive at court all those years?"

He shrugged. "I didn't show them my true personality. Everything about me at court was a lie."

"Lucky us." When Zhu Guiren continued silently staring at the wall where Tainu had disappeared, she said, "All right, if you really want to know, you shouldn't joke with Tainu about family. Family is very important to him."

Zhu Guiren sat up, clearly surprised. "How can that be? You don't have families. You don't have parents or children, you're not born..."

"He always wanted the phoenixes to be like a family," Tairei explained, "but most of us...we're not made that way. Most of us aren't very good at relationships."

"Unlike you," said Zhu Guiren.

"Unlike me," Tairei said. "Obviously I am amazing at relationships. Please get away from me now." She looked down at Aili and closed her eyes to cultivate.

Zhu Guiren tapped his fingers on the floor of the cavern a few more times, then went out, pushing against the wards, which clearly did not like him.

He found Tainu just outside, his back against the rock of the refuge. "You shouldn't be out here without me," he said, "it's not safe for you."

"Demon, I've been walking this realm since before you were spawned," he said, looking down the slope at the trees, "don't tell me where I can and can't go."

Zhu Guiren sat down next to him. After a while, he said, "I was born, not spawned. But we don't really have families. It's all very…violent. Highly organized and very violent. So it's not…I didn't…there wasn't…" He struggled to say something complicated, his voice starting a few times and then stopping. Tainu finally turned to look at him. He managed, "I don't know how to be with people without trying to hurt them."

"I don't know how to be with people without trying to heal them," said Tainu in return.

They sat quietly for a while.

Tainu said, "Ah, I see. Clever."

"What?" Zhu Guiren rubbed his forehead where Tainu was staring. "Oh, Tairei did that."

Tainu bit his finger and leaned over toward him, writing firmly across his forehead. Zhu Guiren felt something tingle beneath the warmth of Tainu's blood. "Mine will be more effective," he said. "You should be able to come in and out now with minimal pain."

Zhu Guiren nodded, surprised.

Tainu picked a small flower in the moss. "Not everything about the spirit realm is awful," he said. "But for us, we can't really be here unless we're inside the refuges, so we never get to see it."

Zhu Guiren took the flower from his hand, and looked at it carefully. "I don't remember flowers in the spirit realm," he said. "Growing up in the clan, flowers are…not a priority. I always preferred being in the mortal world."

"Why are you staying with us, then?" Tainu asked. "The mortal world beckons. You've already lost a hand for this. You're not a phoenix, you could go through a demonic gate any time you want. Tairei and I have to stay until she has enough cultivation to generate a phoenix gate, I can't since I haven't gone through rebirth recently. Why are you here? It must be obvious that you're not welcome."

"Your way of showing me I'm not welcome is to let me come into a phoenix refuge with you," Zhu Guiren said, nettled.

"So?" Tainu probed.

"Well, it's confusing, demons would have pulled out my heart and made me eat it, you're giving me mixed messages." Tainu laughed. Zhu Guiren frowned at him. "Why are you laughing? Aren't you worried that this is all a plan of mine to catch phoenixes?"

Tainu met his eyes thoughtfully, the smile leaving his face. "No," he said simply. "I'm not worried."

"Well, you're an idiot, then." Zhu Guiren looked back down at the flower in his hand.

"You could have captured Tairei at any time before I arrived. You could take both of us now, if I didn't fly fast enough, we can't fight you. Now you have Aili as a hostage. Whatever you wanted in that line you would already have done. That's what I don't understand."

Zhu Guiren was silent, staring at the flower.

"What was the best time of your life?" Tainu asked suddenly.

Zhu Guiren said, without thinking, "When Liu Chenguang and I traveled around and I would teach him things and we would talk."

Tainu said, "What was good about it?"

The silence stretched out.

"The best time in my life," Tainu went on, when he didn't answer, "was early in my third cycle. Around eight thousand years ago, in mortal time. Tairei was probably just coming into consciousness then, she's the youngest of us...anyway, we're usually solitary, and I hadn't ever been with other beings for any long amount of time, even though I was two thousand years old by then. But there was a village...they learned who I was and what I could do, but they weren't afraid of me, and they didn't try to take advantage of me. They just...welcomed me. For myself and no other reason. We laughed and we cried and told stories and ate together and worked together and argued together and went on adventures and then told one another about them...They were my family."

Zhu Guiren said, "It was like that, a little bit, with Liu Chenguang."

Tainu nodded.

"But Liu Chenguang didn't know who I was, so it wasn't the same," Zhu Guiren said pedantically.

"So you want to do that again? With Liu Chenguang knowing who you are, this time? To have a family?"

Zhu Guiren shrugged.

"Do you think she can forgive you?" Tainu said. "Do you think any of us can? Or should?"

Zhu Guiren was quiet, and then changed the subject. "Where was the village?"

"It doesn't exist anymore; even the place where it was is covered by desert. The language we spoke is gone. Even another phoenix couldn't speak it with me, I think." Tainu's voice sounded sad.

Zhu Guiren asked, "What happened to your...family?"

"I kept them safe from harm, of course. But eventually, one by one, after they'd lived for a century or thereabouts, they came to me and asked me to stop healing them. Mortals aren't made for immortality. They couldn't bear the weight of the years, the memories. So, one by one, I stopped. And one by one, they died and left me." He looked at the flower again, in Zhu Guiren's hand, and reached out to touch it. "But they weren't afraid to go, they were ready. So that was my gift to them, that they didn't fear death."

Zhu Guiren looked at Tainu's fingers, touching the flower.

"I sometimes wonder," Tainu said, "if mortals now are more afraid of death than they used to be. More cruel. My family wasn't cruel, because they weren't afraid."

"Maybe," Zhu Guiren said. He lay the flower down gently. "Resentment builds on resentment, suffering on suffering."

Tainu said, "So that's what the array is." He said it without blame, and so Zhu Guiren answered without guilt.

Zhu Guiren said, "Yes."

CHAPTER 17
YAOGUAI

Hong Deming spent several days riding down the road away from Gunan, away from Crane Moon, and away from Liu Chenguang. The things that had happened in Gunan, the drunken kiss in the brothel, the attack on Peaceful River, the time in the inn, the feeling of Liu Chenguang's body against his, that sense of deep peace and trust that they would be together...it all began to feel like a fever dream in the quiet emptiness of the days. It was only at night, when he lay wrapped in a blanket and looked at the stars, that everything was real again, because Chenguang would also see those stars, and would think of him.

During the days, though, he had a task to do: to fight the evil beings that Shen Lu had directed him to find. He'd certainly never seen any such thing, only human beings killing each other, but he was eager to avoid killing human beings again. Once cultivators specialized in exorcising and destroying evil beings, yao-mo and yaoguai, demons and monsters, on the path to ascension to the heavens, and his childhood had been full of the ancient stories, but it seemed that being a cultivator now was about the battles and plots and resentments of human beings. He hated it, hated killing other people.

Let there be some demons. That, he could feel good about unleashing En upon.

Not knowing quite how to go about it, he decided to leave the main highway for the smaller roads and villages, traipsing down the lesser-known paths, asking if anyone was suffering from demon oppression or evil spirits or ghosts or yaoguai. In these little villages, separated from the great cities, faced with a handsome young cultivator in silk robes with a spiritual sword, the people didn't even laugh at such questions, but answered seriously. It wasn't until the fifth village that several people mentioned a local lake that had just developed a strange aura, where two children had recently drowned. Their mother, sobbing, said, "Both of them could swim. Why would they drown? Why would they even go into the water? It's not hot out, they weren't fishing…"

When he reached the shores of the lake, it was almost twilight, a good time to see if anything would happen. He sat down cross-legged, En across his lap, waiting.

In the dark, the lake was a dismal place. There were no insect or animal noises, he noticed, and the water didn't reflect the stars coming out in the sky. When the water rippled and the thing came out, there were no noises of waves lapping against the rocks, as though whatever was in the lake was no longer water at all, but some viscous, thick substance.

The creature wasn't near him, but it knew he was there. "Cultivator," it said, "are you here to kill me? How delicious."

"Do I need to kill you?" he asked it. Truthfully he was quite sure he did; the yaoguai stank of corpses and oozed resentful energy. But it seemed polite to inquire, since it hadn't attacked him first. It didn't seem as though it would be very fast as it pulled itself creeping up the shore. He stood up, En in hand.

"I will tell your fortune," the thing whispered, and crawled up the bole of a tree. The tree withered and died. "It is easy, it is written all over you." The creature opened its eyes, something like a huge salamander. Its eyes glowed hypnotic in the dark.

Suddenly, far faster than he could have imagined, the yaoguai leapt at him, its legs growing longer and clawed, its glowing eyes hidden behind the opening maw. It swiped at him, and as fast as he was in spinning away, as good as his lightness skills were, as strong as En was, nonetheless it caught him on the arm with one claw, ripping his flesh open just below the shoulder.

He yelled out loud in shock rather than pain. In all of his years of training, in the various skirmishes and battles he'd experienced, no one had ever managed to get a blade on him.

Once he got over the surprise, he was thrilled.

He leapt to the top of the tree the yaoguai had been climbing on, holding En out to get a better look by its light. It was both scaled and slimy, something like a water creature, something like a worm, except for those ridiculously long claws, half as long as its own body. It looked up at him, grinning through its three rows of teeth. "Cultivator, cultivator," it sang, "come down and play, cultivator," and then it was in the air again, fast as lightning, whipping its claws and its tail – he realized too late the tail had a sting – and spinning toward him, zipping toward wherever he himself jumped. He slashed out En with a sword pulse, and the golden light struck the scales and bounced off. The yaoguai laughed.

"You are that one," it said, "I will have a double reward for this, I will eat your delicious bones and the master will give me a gift, he has said so, he has said!"

"What master?" he asked, and jumped beneath it, rolling on the ground, to try if the sword pulse would work better on its belly. It did not, but he got a faceful of slime for his troubles. He jumped up again, spitting and retching at the foul taste.

"Hah, you are a funny one! I have eaten six cultivators so far in my travels, they taste much better than ordinary people. No one tried rolling underneath me before." The creature didn't seem to be particularly intelligent. According to what he had read in the library and learned in his training, a yaoguai such as this one was not originally a spiritual being, but a creature of the mortal realm that had failed in its cultivation, half-finished, supporting itself with blood and resentment. Its power was limited. In terms of sheer strength, he really should be able to kill it, except he had never done this before, and wasn't quite sure how.

Without anything else coming to mind, he jumped on its back and stabbed En straight down into its spine. The yaoguai screamed and scrabbled back with its claws at an impossible angle, nearly impaling him before he spun off, leaving En embedded in its scales. He now had two deep slashes, one in his arm, one in his back. "Too slow," he berated himself.

The creature screamed again and spun in circles, then rolled on the ground, forcing En in deeper. But the sword alone wouldn't kill a yaoguai.

Hong Deming breathed deeply and placed his hands into the demon-destroying seal, closing his eyes, and envisioning En. Within the creature's body, the spiritual energy he sent into the sword spiraled out, golden patterns moving into its spiritual resentment and purifying it.

When he opened his eyes, the yaoguai's body was webbed with cracks of golden light, as though it was made of fire covered over in smoke. It shrieked, louder and shriller, then dissolved.

The lake reflected the stars again.

Hong Deming sat down next on the shore in the mud and laughed endlessly at he didn't know what, then winced. En returned to his hand, and as he caught it he saw the long, bleeding slash from the yaoguai. It was slightly tinged with a hazy, dark smoke, a demonic wound polluted with resentment. He would need to cultivate to purify it, and the one in his back as well.

Liu Chenguang would be so angry at me, he thought, and smiled as he placed himself into a lotus position. "Chenguang," he said out loud, just to hear his name.

It was lonely, wandering the back paths between the little villages and isolated farmsteads. It wasn't like on the highways where he would see other people every day, or even travel with them. When he found a village that needed a monster or demon dealt with, he would often stay there for a week or so, ostensibly to recover, but really, as he eventually realized, because he so desperately wanted to hear human voices again after the silence of the forest. Truly, he was not cut out to be a hermit.

He wrote letters to Chenguang sometimes and sent them to Crane Moon via the network of messengers and casual contacts that joined the sects whenever he came across an allied cultivator in his travels. He wrote about the yaoguai, about the occasional bandit attack on a village that he needed to break up, about any beautiful thing he saw in the woods. Hong Deming wasn't a great writer, so the letters weren't very poetic, and he couldn't figure out how to say things that were romantic very well, but it was some way to try to reach out back to where Liu Chenguang was, to keep their connection, even though Liu Chenguang was going through whatever Zhu Guiren had planned for him now. To make sure Liu Chenguang knew that he hadn't forgotten, that he was still thinking of him, all the time, every day.

After several months of this, he decided to leave the mountain villages and return to Bian to report to Stone Phoenix, as Shen Lu had directed. He had a sense that he had done what he could with these small yaoguai; he had destroyed or suppressed a good number, and surely there was an endless number more, but many of them had mentioned a master in their conversations with him. The yaoguai always wanted to talk while they were fighting, perhaps because they had often been trying to cultivate into human forms when things all began for them.

On the third day down from the mountains, he came across a bandit camp.

In all his journey, during which he'd clashed with bandit groups several times, he had yet to come across a place where they lived when they weren't attacking villages or travelers. Here it was, not very different from most other poor villages — a few huts, a few fields. The differences were in the people. A few dozen young men and older men and even a few women, sitting around gossiping or eating or practicing archery; dozens of women and younger children, dressed in rags, doing the work of the day, most showing signs of being beaten or worse.

Hong Deming decided to ride up in the middle just to see what would happen.

As expected, the bandit leader immediately ordered an attack, while the people in rags threw themselves on the ground and begged for mercy and freedom. Hong Deming was quite willing to get it for them, especially after he saw a young girl of no more than nine crying, her ragged skirt stained with old blood. He didn't need qi for this, only a sword, not even lightness skill.

He dismounted to give away any unnecessary advantage and called En. "Come on then," he yelled, "if you think you're capable!"

A good number of the bandits had very elevated ideas about their capability, which he quickly disabused them of. As much as he hated unnecessary killing, he no longer had a lot of regrets over killing bandits, whatever Chenguang might say. Any suffering they had undergone to get to this point was surely balanced by the suffering they had inflicted on others.

Once those people were unconscious or dead, the remainder ran away into the forest, and for the most part, the ragged captives did as well. He would have been glad to guard them back down to the highway, but after all, he wasn't equipped to do much more for them, not even feed them. It was just as well. He flicked the blood off En and mounted up again.

"It's you," said a voice behind him.

He turned around and saw a slender young man, dressed in rags perhaps slightly cleaner than the others, long hair knotted and braided behind his head. "Wu Fan?" he asked, stunned. "Is that you?"

"It's me," he said, with that smile he had used in the brothel, gentle and caressing. "It's been a long time. Can I come with you?"

Since there was only one horse, Wu Fan had to ride behind him down the mountain, which felt awkward to Hong Deming at least. But it would have been much worse to have him riding in the front, since that would have made it obvious that Hong Deming was not as oblivious to Wu Fan as he would have liked to be. Wu Fan didn't bring this up, simply holding on to him while they rode silently, sometimes leaning against his back. Hong Deming was very aware of the warmth of his body, and the feeling of his hands, and it was very lucky that they didn't run into any other bandits on the way down the mountain.

That night, Hong Deming shot a rabbit for them to eat, and Wu Fan helped him skin and roast it. "I learned to do this in the bandit camp," he said, "it's not something they teach you at the Delicate Orchid." He smiled. "Although I'm not alive because of my cooking."

"I'm glad that you survived," Hong Deming said, awkwardly, after they had eaten. "I saw the pavilion burnt, and I wondered if you were safe…"

"It hasn't been very pleasant," Wu Fan said calmly, "but truthfully, in some ways, not much different than the Delicate Orchid. Just rougher, and less food." He must have seen Hong Deming's expression, and he said quickly, "Not you, I remember you, you were very kind to me, back then." Wu Fan reached out and touched his hand, then brought it to his lips. "Thank you," he said, simply. He brushed the back of Hong Deming's hand softly with his breath, then let go.

Hong Deming took his hand back, silently.

Wu Fan looked down, and smiled. "Well, you're not totally uninterested, anyway."

"Thanks for noticing," he said, flushing. "You don't need to thank me in that way."

Wu Fan said, "It's not just to say thank you."

Hong Deming looked away.

"Ah," Wu Fan said. "I see. You're in love with someone." When Hong Deming stayed quiet, he continued, "Just so you know, I'm very good at my job."

Hong Deming shook his head. "I deeply regret that I must refuse your kind offer," he said, trying to give him some face.

"Why? Because you think I'd be upset you're imagining someone else the whole time? Believe me, you wouldn't have the energy."

Clearly, Wu Fan had no face to lose. Hong Deming said, trying to make light of it as Wu Fan did, "Really, I don't…want to." Since his body was openly denying this claim he got up and turned away.

"All right then." Wu Fan let it go as easily as he had raised the topic.

Hong Deming, still looking out into space and trying to distract himself from various images of Wu Fan doing various interesting things, asked, "Where do you want to go now? I'd like to get you there safely."

"You're very kind." Wu Fan settled himself gracefully into a seated position. Despite the dirt and grime on his face and his tangled hair, he still managed to appear beautiful. "Well, there's not much point in me going back to my home village, my parents sold me when I was six. Since at least I can read and write,

202 J C SNOW

the best plan I've been able to come up with is to develop a relationship with a merchant, and learn the business for myself." He said this calmly and as though it was quite easy to imagine. "Perhaps I should return to Gunan, it might be easier to get started with old clients…" He looked up at Hong Deming, smiling. "Don't look so shocked, it's not as though I have other skills. Can I farm? Can I fight? Can I be a government official? I only know one way to feed myself." He shrugged. "At least if I was a woman I could go have children for someone; but for someone like me…well, even if this hadn't happened it was time to think for the future, I'm getting too old. Most clients like us younger in the brothels."

Hong Deming couldn't think of any real response to this. "Tell me where you want to go, and I'll get you there."

"Where are you going?"

"I was going to visit a cultivational sect outside of Bian," he said. "But I don't really have any specific goals, I can take you back to Gunan if that's what you want."

"So you've just been wandering around the mountains, attacking bandits?" he asked, confused. "This isn't on any road to Bian."

"Not bandits, exactly…but sometimes."

"Yaoguai?"

"Yes, some." He no longer felt embarrassed about this, the people in the mountains didn't have problems believing him.

Wu Fan also nodded. "I never saw such things in the city," he said, simply. "But I think that's because in the city, the people are the demons…in the mountains, you can see what they look like when they don't need to look like people."

Hong Deming looked at him with more respect. "That makes a lot of sense," he said.

"I've seen demons in both places," he murmured, "but the ones that live among humans, the ones you can't tell apart from people, they are much worse than the ones with teeth and claws." He closed his eyes briefly, then opened them. "That's enough of that, then," he said briskly. "Do you have a spare blanket?"

He didn't, but he gave Wu Fan his to wrap up in, and stayed awake watching the stars.

It took four more days for them to reach the Stone Phoenix sect house, but Hong Deming bypassed it to bring Wu Fan directly into the city. He said that there was an old friend of his there, a courtesan from the Delicate Orchid who had come here to establish her own house. While, as Wu Fan insisted on saying, he was probably too old to get in the business directly, perhaps he could work

202

for her in managing the house or training new talent. Hong Deming felt very strange about it all, yet Wu Fan wasn't wrong. He wasn't a eunuch, at some point he would outgrow the youthful beauty that attracted many men to brothels, and then what was he to do? A female courtesan or even an ordinary prostitute could hope to be redeemed by a doting client, or by producing a wanted child. A male courtesan, no matter how celebrated, would never have a client with that kind of devotion.

"You know your own business best," he said uncomfortably when they had found the pleasure quarters and Wu Fan's friend's pavilion, and there was nothing else to be said. "I'm sorry I can't offer you any more help."

"Hong Deming." Wu Fan stopped and turned to look full at him, his eyes serious.

"Yes?"

"You've been good to me, and I'm grateful. The only thing I could give you to thank you, you don't want, so instead...I wanted to tell you..." Wu Fan seemed to be turning over his words carefully. "This person, the person you really want, don't wait too long. I don't know why you can't be together already, but you need to settle this for yourself. My work means I've had to study a lot about these things, I've seen a lot...I know enough to tell you this, it's a burden on your heart. Even when you look at me, I see it in you."

"I don't–" He wanted to deny that he looked at Wu Fan, then realized it was pointless and looked at the ground instead.

Wu Fan ignored the interruption and continued. "If you're afraid this person doesn't want you back, you still need to know this, or you'll never be able to live without false hope. If you know they like you too, whatever obstacles there are, you need to overcome them. Go confess to them if you haven't, go be with them if you have, if you've had an argument make it up, apologize even if you're not in the wrong. Life is too short and unpredictable. You don't know when it might be too late."

Hong Deming was silent.

Wu Fan touched his hand. "This is the last time I'll offer."

"No," he said. "You're right. I should go find him."

Wu Fan nodded and turned away. "Thank you," he said, one last time, and walked up the stairs to the pavilion, gracefully, his head held high.

It hadn't been a year yet. Hong Deming rode to the Stone Phoenix sect thoughtfully, considering the gift Wu Fan had given him. Life is too short, after all. Why should they be forced to waste a year of loving one another, when years might be so few? He would go back. Even if they wouldn't let him enter Crane Moon, he would remain in one of the closest villages. Let Shen Lu say whatever he wanted about it, nothing said that wandering beyond the bounds started only one hundred miles out from the sect wards. He could wander in the gorge guarding against yaoguai there and waiting for Liu Chenguang to come out of seclusion if that was necessary.

Once he made that decision, he felt much more focused on getting the current task done: telling the Stone Phoenix disciples about the yaoguai he'd hunted in the mountains, and getting their insight as to the possible "master" of the evil spirits.

The sect leader of the Stone Phoenix recognized him as an allied cultivator, and welcomed him into the sect guest quarters. One of the senior disciples, who introduced himself as Ti Jinghua, sat down with him to offer tea, and to take a record of his yaoguai encounters in the mountains. It turned out that the Stone Phoenix specialized in yaoguai battles, and it was they who had noticed the increase in activity among all sorts of evil beings over the past several years.

Ti Jinghua wrote diligently as Hong Deming described the yaoguai he had fought, asking specific questions about each: how large? What shape? What color? Did any of these change during the battle? Where were they found? Did they flee or attack when challenged? What time of day? What damage had they done previously? What techniques were used? What had been useful, what had been ineffective? How long did the battle take? What was the result? Did the cultivator receive any injuries? And last, did the yaoguai speak, and if so, what did it say?

By the time they had completed going over the fifteen yaoguai he had fought and defeated in the past months, Hong Deming was ready to collapse in exhaustion, but Ti Jinghua was jubilant. "Excellent, excellent," he murmured, "there's a lot to learn here."

"Like what?" Hong Deming sipped his tea.

Although Ti Jinghua was a senior disciple, and had fought yaoguai himself, his air was far more that of a scholar than a fighter. Right now he was excited and eager to teach. He said, "There is a pattern. The yaoguai are moving into new areas, thus encountering new people who do not know how to be safe around them, thus leading to greater loss of life. Second, the yaoguai are becoming more aggressive. Not one of the yaoguai you fought tried to flee you, all of them attacked first and didn't try to escape even when you clearly had the upper hand."

"Is that unusual?"

"Very much so, yaoguai are cowardly more often than not. I suppose it's possible that there were yaoguai who tried to avoid you completely, which would make a different picture?"

"If so," he said, thinking back, "then in that region, those yaoguai were not attacking people at all. Every time I had a report of a yaoguai, I found it and it fought me. As you say. There were no reports where I didn't find the responsible yaoguai."

"Very diligent," he murmured. "So the pattern is definite. And thirdly, they all spoke."

"Also unusual?"

"Not necessarily, depending on the level of strength of the yaoguai. These were all of third rank strength according to the hierarchy we use in our Stone Phoenix records, but they were not weak. Such yaoguai do not always choose to speak, they can strategize whether it is worth their while. Yet every one of them spoke to you, and every one mentioned a master." He tapped his brush-end against his chin. "Thus we can assume that there is such a master, the master would be of first-rank, probably yaomo rather than yaoguai, an evil spiritual being rather than a being created through incomplete cultivation. Second-level yaoguai, and perhaps also other yao and yaomo depending on his strength, are his immediate subordinates. These mountain beings are simply along for the ride, hoping for rewards. The master wouldn't give these beings any instructions that he truly needed carried out, they're too unreliable and too remote."

Hong Deming looked at the table. "Several of them mentioned…"

"Yes, I remember," he said, "they said 'you are that one,' and that there would be an extra reward. Thus we can assume that this master desires your death, probably along with that of many others. Your death is almost certainly not his primary goal," he said analytically, "I don't mean to insult you, Hong Deming, but you can't possibly be that important to a first rank yaomo."

Hong Deming nodded. "I'm certainly not insulted," he said. "I'm going back after this to Crane Moon, what word should I bring?"

Ti Jinghua gave him some more tea and ordered the servant to bring more to eat, then left him while he consulted with the sect leader. When he returned, he looked solemn, and gave Hong Deming a written letter, sealed. "This is for your sect leader," he said, "for you, the gist of this is that there is a demon lord, a strong yaomo, moving among people. The yaomo is likely to have a human form and is unrecognizable as a yao. Given that the yaoguai recognize you and attack you, it is likely that the yaomo has had some encounter with you or with the Crane Moon sect or Peaceful River sect, as these are the only places where you

205

have been in your life. It may not be about you personally," he said, consolingly. "If the yaomo has decided that the Crane Moon or Peaceful River sects are its enemies it may have ordered yaoguai to target anyone they find; it's just that you are the only one from your sect that has reported this to us."

Hong Deming took the letter, shocked. All of these things were happening under the surface, and who knew? When had he ever met a demon? He shook his head. Ti Jinghua said, "Don't be so surprised. If all sects paid more attention we would know more about these things, they are always there. Other sects do not always consider the yao world even though as cultivators defending against it should be our first priority." He bowed and added, "Your guest room is ready for tonight, and your horse will be ready for your departure tomorrow."

Hong Deming slept well, unworried about great yao or yaoguai attacks. He now had a perfect, watertight excuse to go back to Crane Moon and report to Shen Lu.

CHAPTER 18
RETURN TO CRANE MOON

HONG DEMING RODE up the gorge past the little village at the foot of the mountain, and left his horse there to be stabled, then began his climb up the first thousand steps. His heart was beating wildly, not because of the exertion, but imagining Chenguang's face after so many months, so much earlier than he would have thought. Perhaps a little bit of worry, about Shen Lu and Taiqian's reaction, but after all he had been sent back with a message by their ally, the sect leader of the Stone Phoenix. Even though he would have ignored their orders and come anyway they didn't need to know that, everyone's face could be saved this way. It was ideal.

At the first, lowest gate, he was challenged by two of his tainu on guard, who were visibly shocked to see him. "Hong Deming? Taine?" blurted out Shen Feng, Shen Lu's biological brother, in shock. "You're not supposed to–" He exchanged glances with Xia Zhiming behind him. "Go back down, taine," he said, "back to the village, you can't come up."

"I have a message for the sect leader," he said. "From Stone Phoenix, I'm charged to give it only to the sect leader from my own hand." This was a complete fabrication, of course, but he had already decided to insist on it.

"Wait here," said Shen Feng. "I'll go get tainu."

About half an hour later, during which Hong Deming politely remained silent while Xia Zhiming ignored him, Shen Lu hurried down behind Shen Feng, his face thunderous. "Taine," he said sternly, "you were warned, how dare you disobey my commands?"

Hong Deming formally saluted. "This disciple brings a message from the honored sect leader Qin Yuan," he said, offering it with both hands.

Shen Lu took it with little grace and opened the seal, reading through it. Afterward his face was calmer. "I see," he said. "You've done well on your journey, taine, the sect leader speaks highly of your skills and diligence." He tapped the scroll against his other hand for a moment, as though thinking what to do. At last, he said, as Hong Deming had hoped, "Come on up for one night so you can discuss this with Taiqian. He will want to hear details directly from you. Afterward, you must go back down, Taiqian and I may have new commands for you because of this development."

Hong Deming bowed again and followed up the next thousand steps. When they reached the gate to the second level, the largest one which held most of the buildings, Shen Lu looked at him directly. "Liu Chenguang is in seclusion," he said abruptly. "He will be in seclusion for at least three more months, according to Zhu Guiren."

"Thank you for telling me," he said, his heart sinking; but he had known it would probably be like this. Later, he would tell Shen Lu his plan of staying in the villages close by. Or perhaps not, perhaps he would just do it without telling him. He wondered if Liu Chenguang had received any of his letters. "When did he enter seclusion?"

"Almost as soon as we arrived," Shen Lu said, continuing through the gate. Hong Deming tried to hide his shock. "Don't worry, it's not like a normal seclusion, Zhu Guiren and Taiqian check on him regularly. It's part of his cultivation path."

"If they can see him—"

"No," Shen Lu said firmly. "No one else is allowed to enter, not even me. Only Taiqian and Master Zhu." He shrugged; his resentment at being left out was so evident that Hong Deming believed him. "Master Zhu says that Taiqian is assisting with his own spiritual power, since he himself doesn't have any, to direct something that has to be done at this juncture. Or something like that, it doesn't really make sense to me, to be honest, Zhu Guiren is full of words..."

Hong Deming went to his own little cell, where he found his old bed, books, and qin, just as he had left them. It seemed like a lifetime ago, that he had left seclusion with En, and then been sent out to Peaceful River.

Later on came word from Shen Lu that Taiqian was unavailable to meet that evening, but they would breakfast together in the morning to discuss the

Stone Phoenix's report and what was to be done about it. That was even better, he thought. After a good night's sleep he'd be much more prepared to talk with them and convince them to let him stay close by. He asked the messenger, a new little disciple only seven years old, his first martial nephew, to have the kitchen send up a tray for his meal.

Liu Chenguang's cell was just down the hall, though he had rarely used it compared to the amount of time he spent in seclusion. When it seemed that no one else was around, Hong Deming stole into it — no one locked doors in the sect dormitory — and sank down on the bed. It still had Liu Chenguang's scent of herbs and incense, even though he couldn't have slept in it for months now. The room was permeated with him. He curled up on it, breathing deeply, eyes closed, imagining that Chenguang was there, lying with him.

For some reason his eyes were wet, why? He would see him soon enough.

Chenguang's books were still on the rack. He had little appreciation for poetry, there were mostly medical treatises, star charts, and some history. The book of the Master of the Pathless Way was there, of course, and a heavily marked copy of the book of the Master of Heavenly Benevolence, which probably Chenguang shouldn't have had in a Pathless sect, where had he gotten it? Surely not from Zhu Guiren.

The letters he had sent were all there, in a neat pile. Someone had opened them, had read them. He touched them briefly, then left.

At dusk, he was in his favorite place, watching the sunset spark in the waterfall mist, when a woman came up to greet him. He looked up, surprised. The female disciples at Crane Moon had a separate place, except those who were married to senior disciples. They lived together with their spouses in individual homes on the third and highest level of the sect, but even they didn't come down into this area unless for a particular reason. The servants on this side of the sect home were all male as well. Yet this woman was dressed as a sect servant, her hair pulled up into a servant's simple coil.

She prostrated herself, shaking, as though something had terrified her.

"What is it?" he asked, frowning.

"You're Deming," she said. "You sent the letters."

He frowned even more; a servant shouldn't be using his personal name like this. "*Hong* Deming," he corrected.

The woman knelt up so he could see her face. She was very beautiful, with large dark eyes and delicate features, but her face was blotchy with tears. She whispered, "Please, master. Liu Chenguang?"

A chill ran down his back, all the hair on his arms rising. "What is it?" he asked, also whispering. There was something wrong, there was…

He had known it in his heart. There was something wrong.

The servant whispered, "Go to the spiritual caverns when the sun sets."

"Tell me first," he said.

"You, you will need to take him away," she said. "If you care about him, you can't leave him here. You must take him. Please."

The sun was already set; the fire in the waterfall had turned to grey mist.

"I will meet you down at the stables," she said, "I will have a good horse ready." She turned and fled along the wall, back toward the women's quarters.

Hong Deming ran for the entrance to the caverns.

No one went to the caverns to play or to explore; there was no ward, no guard. Normally.

Now there was a ward.

Hong Deming swore and ran back to his room for his qin, feeling as though time was running out on something, though he couldn't imagine what. Liu Chenguang had been in seclusion for months already, would be for months more, Taiqian was checking on him, what could have gone wrong? With the qin in his hand, running back to the entrance, dodging to avoid the notice of other disciples who were out on their evening walks after dinner, chatting animatedly about this and that, he wondered why he was so certain that he could trust that strange servant woman. It was only because he had already known, he had known there was something, some reason he needed to return. Those tears in Liu Chenguang's bed, where had they come from? He had known.

At the ward, he set himself with the qin across his lap and closed his eyes, sensing the patterns. This couldn't be rushed, however much he wanted to; a wrong note would strengthen the ward and alert whomever had set it. When he was confident that he understood how the ward had been set, he plucked out a short, echoing melody, and broke it.

There was a noise in the cavern of multiple breaths, and something else, a sound that picked at his memory but that he couldn't identify. He followed the breaths through the dark, and felt his way along a wall, realizing that the darkness was becoming only dimness, and then becoming bright. A room, only one room, one cavern, had been lit with spiritual lights, dancing about its ceiling to illuminate three people. One of them stood by the wall, hands behind his back, observing the second person, who was using a spiritual sword to carefully cut into the arms and legs and torso of a third person, a nearly naked person. The sound he had heard, the sound without a name, was the sound of the sword cutting deeply into the flesh. The cuts went on repeatedly, over and over again, as they healed and they were cut once more, an endlessly repeated execution.

The person being cut was a young man, obviously unconscious, his frame small and thin, wearing only the light, short trousers usually hidden beneath robes. His long black hair fell unnoticed from the low couch where he lay onto the floor, where it puddled like ink. Where the sword cut, blood oozed and poured and spurted, caught into channels cut into the stone couch like the channel of the waterfall by the cliff where he had just been sitting. All the captured blood poured in a slow, thin waterfall from one corner of the couch into an open bowl, making occasionally a low burbling sound. Hong Deming stared at the blood fall for a frozen moment, unable to look again at Liu Chenguang's naked body.

Hong Deming launched himself at Taiqian, not even taking his sword out, tackling him to the ground bodily and throwing Taiqian's sword into a corner. He realized, dimly, that he was screaming.

After Taiqian was on the ground he went for Zhu Guiren, standing by the wall. For this he used his sword. Just before En stabbed him in the heart, with a clang Taiqian blocked him.

He retreated and stood in front of Liu Chenguang, gasping for air in distress, his rhythm of breath completely broken. "I will kill you," he said. "I will kill you both."

Zhu Guiren sighed and pushed Taiqian's sword away where it blocked in front of his face. "Hong Deming. This is part of his cultivation—"

"THIS IS NOT CULTIVATION!" he roared. "What are you doing to him? How could you? Taiqian!"

Taiqian looked at him with no hint of warmth. "You were told not to be here," he said. "This is why, we knew you would act this way. We didn't want to worry you. However, all of our care was evidently for nothing." Suddenly he shouted, "Useless disciple, why are you not kneeling to ask for my forgiveness? How dare you lay your hands on your sect father?"

"No," he said, his voice shaking with rage. "I will not."

Zhu Guiren, his voice smooth, said, "Now, now, as your Taiqian said, we knew this would distress you to see, thus you should never have seen it. But now that you have, we can explain. You know, I believe, that Liu Chenguang's—"

"Do not say his name," he said, low and fierce. "You are not qualified."

Zhu Guiren coughed. "Very well. This person's cultivation includes a certain

211

power in the blood. This power is actually too high for him to manage and will eventually destroy his meridians and kill him. This process of bleeding allows us to remove some of the overflowing qi. Believe me, he will heal from it. Look now, you see? The cuts are already closed."

He risked a brief glance. They were closed, that was true. But there were also scars, Many, many layers of scars.

"You are seeking death," he whispered.

"What?" Zhu Guiren asked, apparently taken completely by surprise.

"Hong Deming," said Taiqian. "Be silent."

He was silent, but didn't release En.

Zhu Guiren glanced at Taiqian, then continued. "In addition, as you know, we are working to support the new dynasty in order to bring stability back to the Divine Land. Liu Che– This person's blood may help in that it is an ingredient in the elixir of immortality, which we can then present to the Son of Heaven. Your sect leader understands. Liu Chenguang has agreed to all of this."

Hong Deming stared at Zhu Guiren, his cold and perfect face, and considered trusting him. Then he looked back at Liu Chenguang. He was so thin. Beneath his closed eyes were dark circles like black bruises. The scars covered him all over, everywhere but his face and neck; pink scars that were new, white scars that were older, red scars from tonight, still trickling and oozing blood.

"No," he said. "You tricked him, or you drugged him, or he didn't understand." He took a step backward, released En, then turned swiftly and picked Liu Chenguang up bodily. He was pathetically light, and didn't wake up. He smelled like blood and death. "I am taking him," he said. "If you try to stop me, I will kill you both right here."

Taiqian sent a sword pulse at him, and Hong Deming quickly shifted Liu Chenguang over one shoulder to have his sword hand free, blocking the strike. Forcing himself to bottle up his rage and keep his breathing smooth, he leapt out of the way, behind Taiqian, and sent a sword pulse at him in return. It missed, but shattered the stone couch. Liu Chenguang's blood poured from the bowl all over the floor in little rivers, and Zhu Guiren fell to the ground, trying to gather it up with a small crystal chalice.

He was closer to the entrance to the cavern, but he didn't dare turn his back on Taiqian, so Hong Deming gently lay Liu Chenguang down again on the rock, and then ran to meet him, slashing his sword down. Taiqian blocked and blocked again, then shouted in rage and slashed down toward Hong Deming's wrist, but Hong Deming spun, sent a sword pulse at Zhu Guiren to keep him away, and then landed behind Taiqian's back and reached out to quickly strike his acupoints, temporarily paralyzing his legs and arms.

Taiqian fell heavily to the stone, and Zhu Guiren crawled toward him, one leg dragging limp from Hong Deming's second sword pulse, making tracks through Liu Chenguang's blood. His eyes met Hong Deming's, glittering in such open malevolence that Hong Deming froze.

Taiqian shouted, his face twisted in fury, "I repudiate you. You are no longer a member of the sect. Every cultivator's hand is turned against you from this day, false son, traitorous disciple, thief of the sect's teachings."

Hong Deming's heart hurt for one moment, and then it was gone, a white scar. He said, "I don't care."

He ran out and leapt down the cliff, rock to rock, tree to tree, carrying Chenguang's body from which his soul seemed to have fled. If he hadn't felt the heartbeat through the visible ribs, he would have thought him dead.

At that thought, he almost lost his qinggong, but then recovered, and kept racing down.

The servant woman was there, outside the stables, a saddled horse with bags of provisions on a rein next to her. "Go, go," she whispered, looking all around. "When Liu Chenguang wakes up, tell him that there is a yaomo here. You must take him far away. Take him to the eastern sacred mountain."

Hong Deming nodded and mounted up, putting a robe the servant woman offered onto Chenguang's unresisting body. The servant woman brought out strong silk ribbons and tied Liu Chenguang's hands to the saddle, then wrapped his legs and tied them together beneath the horse's belly: uncomfortable had he been conscious, but a wise precaution since Hong Deming might need his arms free to fight. "Are you coming?" he asked.

"I would only slow you down, I will find my own way and meet you there," the servant woman said. "Go now."

"What is your name? How do you know–"

"There's no time. He'll know who I am when you give him the message. Go, go!" She whistled something at the horse, hard and shrill, and they were off.

In a nightmare, Hong Deming galloped down through the gorge, holding Liu Chenguang against him as much as he could to shield him from the roughness of the ride. Once out of the gorge into the wide flatlands around the Cui River, he veered off the road into the forest, riding along the riverbank in the hopes of finding a ferry to bring them across. His mind was a snowstorm of blank white and wind, thinking only of how cold Chenguang's body was, how he had lost so much blood, how he was dressed only in a single robe against the chill of the night, how they would soon be followed and when word got out every cultivator would be bound to attack them. How to reach Mount Shi without using the highways that went past Zhashan and Gunan where they would certainly be found. How there was a yaomo at Crane Moon.

He didn't dare try to swim the horse across the river, not with Chenguang like this, so he had to lose hours riding along the bank until he found a boat that some fisherman or ferryman had left unguarded. He would have to leave the horse, but there were always more horses in the world. Laying Chenguang gently on the bottom of the boat, he removed the saddle and tack from the horse and threw it in the river, and took the saddlebags of provisions on his shoulders, then slapped the horse's rump so it would run. It would, unfortunately, probably run back to the sect, but it seemed too cruel to kill it. Hopefully some peasant would find it first and take it home, muddying the trail.

On the other side of the river, he cut a hole in the bottom of the boat, then sank it.

Still dazed, he carried Chenguang into the forest of the mountains on the other side of the river, cradling him bridal style since he was still too deeply unconscious to hold on, the saddlebags over his shoulder. With his qinggong Hong Deming could move much more quickly than an ordinary person, and went quite far before the weight and his sick heart told on him. At last he had to admit defeat, at least until he could sleep and cultivate and rejuvenate his qi.

He didn't dare to make a fire, either, not when searchers would probably already be out. He dug into the packs for blankets and extra robes, and wrapped Liu Chenguang in them. Then, on second thought, he sat beneath a tree and held him, sitting up, with Chenguang's back to his chest, comforted in his arms. He placed the blankets over them both, so that as much of Chenguang's body as possible could be held and warmed. He looked down at Chenguang's pale face, drooping against him, and bent his own head down, as though he could be a shield for him against all the cold and the darkness.

A long time later, but still well before dawn, he felt Chenguang stirring against him, and his heart leapt. "Chenguang," he called gently, kissing his hair that was still clotted with blood. "Chenguang, wake up, Deming is here."

His eyes opened, bleary. "Tainu," he said, "what…" He tried to sit up, and couldn't. "What happened to me?" His eyes fixed on Hong Deming's, confused and uncertain.

"I took you from the sect," he said. "Taine, they were hurting you."

"What do you mean, you took me?" He tried to sit up again, and succeeded slightly, his eyes focusing a bit more. "Tainu, what happened, why are you here, where are we? Are we in the woods?"

"In the woods, somewhere, across the river." He hesitated. "Hiding."

"I was– I was in seclusion?" He raised a shaking hand to his own forehead. "That's the last thing I remember, going into the caverns, what happened? Why am I like this?"

Hong Deming paused for a while, trying to think how to say it. "Zhu Guiren was having Taiqian…cut you, all over your body, making you bleed," he said. "He said you agreed to it as part of your cultivation."

"I didn't agree to it," he said, frowning, "but it shouldn't matter…it shouldn't…"

Hong Deming swallowed, trying to get the picture out of his mind; he was afraid it would always be there. "They were…collecting your blood. Zhu Guiren said that they could make the elixir of immortality out of it."

"He said *what?*" Liu Chenguang's voice became sharper, more like himself. "I would never have agreed to *that*, that's just ridiculous, there's no such thing, and he knows it too, we've talked about it."

"He said you would help by bringing the mandate of heaven for the emperor."

"What?" He leaned his head against Hong Deming's chest, exhausted again. "Tainu, I don't understand, what is he talking about?" Tears suddenly leaked from beneath his closed eyes. "Tainu, why do I feel this way? My body hurts… all over…"

Hong Deming's heart ached. He tried to gather him up, as gently as possible, murmuring, "Taine…"

Liu Chenguang was crying without any sound, tears falling. "Everything is burning, my body is burning all over, tainu, I'm frightened." He ran his hand over his own forearm, feeling the raised scars, bewildered. "There are scars, how can there be scars, how can it be?"

"Shh, shhh…" Hong Deming rocked him back and forth, trying to comfort him. "It's only scars. Scars mean you're healing," he said meaninglessly, "you will feel better soon, you're away from there now." He wished he had killed them all. "You're getting warm because you are getting feverish, that's all, it's better than before, you were so cold…"

Liu Chenguang looked up at him, eyes fever-bright. "But tainu, I can't get fevers, I can't…"

Hong Deming held him, kissed his forehead, brought his hands into his chest to warm them. "I'm here, taine," he said, "sleep, tomorrow will be better."

At last Liu Chenguang settled again into normal, if somewhat fevered, sleep, his heart beating strongly, his body alive against him even if so fragile. Hong Deming kissed the top of his head, all that he could reach now that he was nestled down, curled up to rest on him. He leaned back against the tree for a few hours of sleep, until dawn.

The next morning, Liu Chenguang was noticeably better. If his cultivational powers of self-healing were still damaged, they were still certainly better than most people's; after a night sleeping in the woods, preceded by months of blood loss and torture, he awoke with the fever broken. Hong Deming still held him in his arms, unwilling to let him go, as he examined his own arms and his body silently in the dawn light.

Liu Chenguang looked up at him from his position leaning against his chest when his self-examination was complete. At last he said, his voice calm and clinical, "They must have given me something, some kind of drug or spirit-blocking spell. Even with what they were doing to me, even for as long as they did it, I shouldn't have scars like this."

Hong Deming simply nodded, not caring about the mystery of the scars. Having seen what they were doing to him, he wasn't surprised by them at all. How many nights over the past months must they have cut him, to have so many of such varying ages? He bit back his rage. "We need to keep going," he said, "but we also need to hide for a while till you can get your strength back."

"It won't take long," Liu Chenguang said, confidently, but he still couldn't quite walk on his own when they got up. Hong Deming made him ride on his back for most of the day, and he could feel that for much of it he was sleeping. That was fine, as long as he could still hold on. Sleep was the best thing for him, the thing he would most need to heal, and he was still so very light to carry. Hong Deming had seldom crossed the Cui before and he wasn't completely certain of his ground, but he thought that within the day he should reach a village partway up the mountain, one with an inn and an apothecary.

He woke up Liu Chenguang as they came to the outskirts, and he was already recovered enough to walk the rest of the way into town, so as not to make too much of a fuss. Liu Chenguang was wearing a very dark blue robe, almost black, that the servant woman had found somewhere, and with his incredibly pale skin and unbound, blood-tangled black hair he looked like a very beautiful ghost exploring the daylight world. The villagers stood up in the fields to watch them as they walked by. Liu Chenguang looked down at the ground, embarrassed.

"It's my turn this time," Hong Deming said, encouragingly. "I'm at least as good as Zhu Guiren at finding an inn."

Liu Chenguang smiled. "Tainu, if there's more than one inn in this place I would be very surprised."

"True," he admitted. "I will get us the best room in town."

It was not as fine as the inn they had visited in Gunan, of course, but there was one good room with a decent bed and table, it was clean, and they sent up hot water immediately. Liu Chenguang stripped without any consideration of shyness and got right in, eager to wash the dried blood off his skin and hair. Hong Deming watched with his eyes wide and then turned around.

"Come help me," Liu Chenguang called. "I hate this feeling, this blood on my skin, help me get it all off." He held up a bathing cloth, already washing with his other hand. "Can you ask them to send up some dried herbs for the bath, too? And more water?"

He yelled out the door at the innkeeper — they were the only guests — and returned to where Liu Chenguang was scrubbing at his skin with the cloth. "Not so hard, you'll open the wounds–" he said.

"No, that can't happen," Liu Chenguang replied, "they are closed now for good, I can feel a little bit of power coming back. Can you check?" He held out his arm, and Hong Deming checked the pulse. He wasn't an expert, but he could feel that the qi was settling back into normal patterns, and sighed with relief.

"Are you still in pain?" he asked, picking up the bathing cloth and carefully stroking Liu Chenguang's back with it, trying not to press too hard.

Liu Chenguang shivered, and laughed, turning his head back over his shoulder to smile at him. "Not like that, tainu, or we will be doing something else besides bathing soon."

Hong Deming turned bright red and dropped the cloth into the water, then had to feel around inside the tub for it, touching Liu Chenguang in all sorts of inappropriate places. Liu Chenguang finally reached down and found the cloth himself, handing it back to him. "Deming," he said, "it's all right, really. I'm not hurt any more. I don't know what they did to me, but I'll heal. Please don't be scared for me, all right? You don't need to worry that I'll break." He reached out and touched his arm briefly. "Just get the blood off of me. Can you pour water over my head? My hair feels disgusting." As he obediently rinsed out his long hair, Liu Chenguang added, "So that's what it feels like, to be sick…how awful. No wonder people are so desperate for healing."

"You've never been sick at all?"

"Never…just those times when I had the weakness of my qi and I was unconscious, but that was just like sleeping, I didn't feel anything. It's so awful to feel pain in your body when it doesn't go away."

The second batch of hot water came up, this one with herbs to give a nice scent. Liu Chenguang stood up to rinse and then went to the second tub, standing, pouring more water over his hair a few times. Hong Deming took his unspoken invitation to look openly at him and thought, despite the scars — all turning white now — how beautiful he was, every part of him. He felt his body becoming aroused and closed his eyes for a few moments to get things under control. He hadn't slept more than a few hours for two nights now, with all the exertion of taking Liu Chenguang from the sect and their flight here, and before he realized it, he had fallen asleep sitting up.

It felt like the deep night when he woke up, still sitting in the chair. At the table, he saw Liu Chenguang sitting fully dressed in that dark blue robe, now with his hair clean and the scent of herbs rather than blood. He must have gone out to the apothecary, he was preparing something at the table, chopping and grinding herbs and putting them into small paper wrappings. He looked up at him and smiled. "You're awake, tainu," he said. "The innkeeper's second daughter has a weakness of the liver, I'm making some medicine for them to give her."

Hong Deming stood up and stretched, yawning. "I needed to sleep, what about you, are you getting medicine for yourself?"

Liu Chenguang tapped a second batch of packets. "I pre-made these so we can take them on the road with us, they'll help strengthen my blood and purify it, I can't tell what drugs they gave me but these will help." He looked up expectantly. "Where are we going?"

"Mount Shi," he said, sitting down at next to him, and aimlessly picking up one of the packets. He was a little worried about how Liu Chenguang would take this, and a little curious as well. "Did you read any of my letters?"

"You wrote me letters?" Liu Chenguang's eyes warmed at him. "No, they put me into seclusion right away when I arrived. Did you bring them with you so I can read them?"

"No, there wasn't time." He thought more. "Liu Chenguang, do you know a woman who is a servant at Crane Moon?"

"No?" he replied curiously.

"I just came, it hasn't been a year but I didn't want to wait so long." Liu Chenguang's eyes warmed even more. "I had a message for Taiqian and Shen Lu, that was my good excuse to come back...I didn't know anything was wrong with you until a woman servant came to me. She knew me even though I've never seen her. She said 'You wrote the letters.' How would that servant woman know? How

218

could a servant woman even read?"

Liu Chenguang's eyes sharpened, but he didn't respond.

Hong Deming continued, "She was the one who said I needed to get you out, she sent me into the caverns to find you, and she told me to give you a message. She said you would know who she was."

Reluctantly, Liu Chenguang said, "She's most likely my relative, my older sibling. She must have come looking for me when I was in seclusion, I didn't know she was there…"

Hong Deming, shocked, said, "You have relatives?"

Liu Chenguang shook his head. "I haven't seen my sibling since before I met you, that's not important. What was the message?"

Hong Deming didn't want to let this subject go, but there truly were more urgent matters. "She said you needed to go to Mount Shi, and to tell you that there is an evil yaomo at Crane Moon. A demon."

Liu Chenguang's face became, if possible, even paler. The packet he had been holding in his hand dropped to the table. "You have to get away," he said, his voice low and shaking. "Hong Deming. If there's a yaomo–"

"It's all right, Chenguang," he reached out and held his hands in both of his, folding them together. "It's all right. I've been fighting yaoguai all this time. I know how to do it — there's nothing to be afraid of…"

"You don't understand. A demon will never give up. It will come after me to the ends of the earth, as long as it has a trace to follow." Liu Chenguang put his head down on top of their folded hands. "I need to– I need to fully recover, then I can get away and hide, I'm not able now– Hong Deming, you can't stay near me–"

"No," he said sharply. "Taine, listen, I'm not leaving you. I'll get you to Mount Shi. Will that be safe for you?"

"Safer, not completely safe…but it's so far. Deming, please." His eyes were wide and terrified. "I can't bear it if you're hurt for me."

"Could you get there on your own, taine?" he asked. "Be honest."

Liu Chenguang was still for a few moments before answering, seeming to consider his own resources. "Being honest, not now. I need a few months to fully recover before I could…on my own."

"I am not leaving you anywhere for a few months," Hong Deming said. "I am not leaving you anywhere for even a day. A few hours is all you're going to have to yourself until we get to Mount Shi."

Liu Chenguang shook his head. "Tainu, I can't…I can't defend myself." It seemed as though it took a great deal of effort for him to admit this. "I can only

219

run and hide. Do you know how it would be for me, if you were hurt or killed trying to protect me?"

"It's not a safe world," he replied. "I've been away for you for more than half a year. And I've been attacked by fifteen yaoguai–"

"Fifteen!"

"–and who knows how many bandits, I stopped counting. Before that when Peaceful River was attacked, cultivators as well attacked me. And I'm fine. And none of that was because of you. It will be all right, taine. Don't worry so much."

Liu Chenguang shook his head again. "Fifteen yaoguai? So many. What's happening?" He accepted without demur that the yaomo and yaoguai existed and were a real danger. There was no surprise in his voice.

Hong Deming looked at his face, pale in the candlelight, his dark eyes thoughtful and distant, and wondered, *Chenguang, who are you, what are you? Where did you come from, before we found you? Why does the yaomo want you, why will it keep pursuing you?*

In the end, though, he didn't ask because it didn't make a difference at all. This person was his person, always.

Instead, he said, "Liu Chenguang...I shouldn't call you taine anymore, and you shouldn't call me tainu. I left the sect. We're not martial siblings anymore."

"I'll call you tainu if I want to," he said stubbornly. "But Deming, what happened? The sect is your family. Family is important."

Hong Deming noticed that he didn't say *the sect is our family,* and felt sad for him. But that was all in the past now. "I attacked Taiqian because he was hurting you, and took you away. I disobeyed him and injured him. He repudiated me." He didn't go into the fact that as a traitor to the sect, all cultivators from the Crane Moon and their allies would challenge him on sight. If Liu Chenguang didn't already realize it, he wouldn't add to his worries. "We can't go back there, Chenguang."

Liu Chenguang knelt next to him. Hong Deming looked down at his eyes, dark and longing, and felt his heart move inside him, his hand reaching out to touch Chenguang's hair. From the bath he was wearing nothing to keep his hair back, and a long lock flowed uninterrupted down in front of his temple past his collarbone, blocking the edge of his eye a little bit. Carefully, with great care because he wanted so much to do more, Hong Deming picked it up, warm and smooth, and stroked it back behind his ear. He kept two fingers on his ear, tracing its curves, feeling the heat of Chenguang's skin, watching him shiver slightly and breathe in at his touch.

Liu Chenguang reached up and touched his cheek, then drew his fingers down to his lips. Hong Deming softly kissed Liu Chenguang's fingertips. Liu Chenguang leaned forward, his eyes half closed, to meet his lips with his own. "Deming," he said, breathing into him, "didn't you know? Since the beginning, since we met, since we were children, I've only stayed for you."

CHAPTER 19
FLIGHT

THE NEXT MORNING, Liu Chenguang couldn't get out of bed immediately, for which Hong Deming blamed himself and ran down to the innkeeper to demand an extravagant congee for breakfast and hot water for bathing. By the time the hot water arrived, Chenguang was laughing, sitting up and tossing pieces of leftover ginseng root peel at him from his medical packets. "I'll have to make you a tea to fix your anxiety and keep your vitality strong," he said, and threw another piece of ginseng. "Have them send up hot water in a teapot too."

Hong Deming blushed and said, "Are you all right? I didn't mean to hurt you."

"I told you, I'm fine, it only hurt for a bit," he said. "I'm well now. Very well." He smiled innocently, eyes sparkling. "Would you like to make sure?"

"*Chenguang*," he said, and silently recited some scripture. "Enough, eat breakfast, we need to plan."

Hong Deming used his chopsticks to draw a map of tea on the table. "Mount Shi is here," he said, "and the quickest road to it is the road east along the Sorrowful River, but that road is heavily-traveled and passes the great cities. The slower way, if we are trying to hide, would be to stay near the edges of the northern mountains and travel that way, but it would be much more difficult. I'm not even sure we could ride all the way."

Liu Chenguang looked carefully at the tea map. "I'm familiar with a lot of

222

these paths," he said, "the high ones through the mountains. There are also paths we could take around the cities."

"Do you think Zhu Guiren is a yaomo?" Hong Deming asked suddenly.

Liu Chenguang nodded slowly. "It is possible it's Taiqian," he said, "but Zhu Guiren is more likely, of the people at Crane Moon. I've never seen any sign of demonic power from him, he says he doesn't have any spiritual power at all, but if he is a strong yaomo of course he could hide it if he chooses to. And he…he never wanted me to be away from him. A yaomo would be like that if he had… me." He looked up and said, "He was very angry whenever he found me with you, and I couldn't understand it. I think he thought you might take me away." He smiled. "Which of course you have."

Eventually they decided on the plan of staying as close to the mountainous areas as possible, traveling over ridges by foot using their qinggong, slower but harder to find, they hoped. Hong Deming wanted to avoid meeting cultivators above all.

Unfortunately, however, staying in the mountains seemed to attract yaoguai instead.

Ten days later Hong Deming wiped his forehead and looked down at the latest contender, a creature that seemed to have cultivated from a poisonous vine. Its thorny tendrils still whipped around even though En had cut it into dozens of pieces, some of them growing new limbs and trying to attack one final time. He took a deep breath and put his hands in the demon-quelling seal, and sent qi into En, stabbed into the creature's largest part, for the tenth time in ten days.

Liu Chenguang came up to him from where he had been waiting off to the side. "I'm so useless," he said, frustrated. He put his hands on Hong Deming's back to transfer qi to him, but Hong Deming shook him off.

"You don't have enough," he said, leaning on En.

"Neither do you," Liu Chenguang said, his eyes sweeping over the yaoguai pieces dissolving on the ground. "Every time you have less for the final strike. I can tell."

Hong Deming sighed and reached out for him. Liu Chenguang squeezed his hand. "I have some medicines I can give you," he said, "and acupuncture tonight to stimulate the meridians. I'm getting better, soon I'll be able to help you more. Do you have any injuries?"

"Just this, a thorn got me," he said, pulling his hair aside to show a festering scratch on the back of his shoulder, leaking red and yellow fluid, and showing red threads running out into his flesh from all directions.

"It must have been very poisonous," Liu Chenguang muttered, and bit his finger to spread blood on it. But nothing happened. Liu Chenguang swore vociferously. "Still nothing, when will it come back?" He leaned forward and sucked the poison out of the wound, spitting it out on the ground vehemently. Then he reached into his sleeves for a healing powder and sprinkled it on. "Deming," he said, seriously, "we may need to go down to the highway after all. You can't keep going on like this."

"Would it be safer for me to have to fight cultivators?" he said, a little angry. "No matter what I'll still be fighting."

"It would be safer," Liu Chenguang said firmly. "These yaoguai are harder to fight than humans, even strong humans, and they take too much of your spiritual energy to disperse them. If you have a serious injury, I can't heal you right now." He took his hand again. "Deming, we're trying to hide, but I think these yaoguai have been sent, they are looking for us, we've been attacked so frequently, and we're not deep in the mountains at all to be encountering them so often by accident. I think we need to accept that hiding is useless now, and try speed instead. We need to go down."

Hong Deming kicked at the remaining dried leaves of the yaoguai. "I don't want to fight people," he said at last. "People I may know."

"I know." Liu Chenguang looked up at the sky. Gently, he said, "Deming, you can leave me. Just find a cave, set a ward for me, I'll cultivate and heal on my own."

He shook his head stubbornly. "No. I won't leave you again."

"I wouldn't be that much safer at Mount Shi. It's only a sacred place with a strong ward, that's all."

"No. Mount Shi is so far away, surely the yaomo will give up chasing you by then."

"No. He won't."

Hong Deming turned to go. "All right then. We'll go down and get horses."

Liu Chenguang stood and watched him walk down the slope, then sighed and followed him into the trees.

Days later, they were on the highway between Zhashan and Gunan, going as fast as they could. Hong Deming hadn't brought much money, so they couldn't afford to change horses regularly or ride these into the ground, as he would have liked to; they needed to let them rest sometimes at a walk rather than galloping all day. While they'd been in the mountains they'd been able to sleep on the ground, and gather food for free with Liu Chenguang's foraging skills, but now they would have to stay in inns and buy food as well. So many opportunities to be caught, so many places where they were leaving a trail to be followed. Hong Deming's skin crawled every time they passed a traveler on the road, or rode past the turnoff to a sect house.

Mo Xiang caught them at evening, just before Sanmen, on an empty stretch of road.

"Hong Deming!"

Hong Deming closed his eyes briefly. They had been so lucky, and they had come so far, but their luck had run out.

Mo Xiang stood on the road in front of them, and raised his qin. "Traitor and betrayer. Please," he said with exaggerated courtesy, "show me your skills."

Liu Chenguang stepped back out of the way. "You're next," Mo Xiang added. "Prepare yourself."

Hong Deming couldn't very well say that Liu Chenguang couldn't fight, but this made it crucial that he defeat Mo Xiang quickly, before he was able to attack Chenguang. He drew En. "Come then," he said, "I look forward to learning from you."

Mo Xiang's qin strikes came fast, doubling one upon the other, filling the entire space of the roadway. Hong Deming was tired from traveling and the residual spiritual weariness of the fights in the mountains, but his qi was almost fully restored. Sword against qin, he needed to block the qin attacks that Mo Xiang sent from all directions, before he could find an opening to attack himself. He sent a pulse of sword energy toward the qin, but Mo Xiang had already jumped aside, using his own qinggong. Hong Deming had often lost qin battles at Peaceful River, and Mo Xiang was one of the best. A sword was more powerful on attack, but the qin was very difficult to completely defend against with only a sword.

Hong Deming took a qin strike to his back and then to his shoulder, unable to block everything when three qin strikes came from three different directions; Mo Xiang's qinggong was very impressive, allowing him to strike and leap to a new position and strike again almost faster than Hong Deming's eyes could follow. Hong Deming flipped into the air and tried to gain a high position, but a powerful qin blow took down the tree he had landed on, and he had to leap again.

He held his flying crane position in midair for a moment, sending three sword pulses out, one to where Mo Xiang was, two to where he thought he might be next, and came down to lightly touch the ground and leap away. Another qin strike took him in the knee, a bad strike for him, and he had to fall to the ground and roll away, but one of his own sword pulses had taken Mo Xiang in the chest, and he was coughing blood.

Hong Deming staggered upright. He couldn't put any weight on his knee yet, but he leapt from the working leg straight upward to avoid a qin strike. It passed beneath him, and he flipped backward to land, again, on his weak leg and fall, again, and have to roll. This time, Mo Xiang went for him with a sword, and caught him on the forearm; if he had had a better angle, Hong Deming would have lost his left hand. Hong Deming's blood spattered heavily on the ground.

Out of the corner of his eye, he saw Liu Chenguang move forward, distressed. "No!" he yelled, hit his own acupoints to stop the bleeding, and rolled back up, spinning with En to send a sword pulse and then a slash: the pulse at the qin, the slash at Mo Xiang's right arm. It took him deep in the elbow, and he staggered backward.

With that wound Mo Xiang could no longer use the qin beyond single notes, and would have to switch fully to sword. This meant that he had lost, because he was far below Hong Deming in sword skill, and must have known it. Nonetheless, he refused to yield, leaping up with his qinggong and coming down, shouting out his battle cry and slashing down with his most powerful strike. Because he couldn't move quickly on the bad leg, it caught Hong Deming glancingly in the shoulder — glancing, but enough to cut deeply into the muscle above his collarbone. It was the same shoulder that had already received a qin strike. That arm was now completely useless, and although Hong Deming could fight with either hand, now one was unusable, the other still bleeding from the slash to the wrist.

Hong Deming gritted his teeth, hit the acupoints on his shoulder and chest with the bleeding hand that still could move, and spun to release a final sword pulse at Mo Xiang, using much more qi than he ever had before in a single sword strike. It threw Mo Xiang into the air and back more than ten body lengths to crash heavily against the ground, bleeding from all his orifices and vomiting blood.

Hong Deming limped over to him to see that he was still alive. Liu Chenguang also came up, pale, and lifted a bleeding hand to Hong Deming's worst visible wound, the cut into his collar and shoulder muscles. He felt that something happened; the bleeding stopped and the pain lessened, but it didn't instantly heal. Liu Chenguang clenched his fists.

"Mo Xiang," Hong Deming said, struggling not to fall over, "I've beaten you."

Mo Xiang spat blood and mucus at him. It landed on his lower robe, making a glutinous red stain.

Hong Deming stared at him. He knew he should kill him, for their safety, for Liu Chenguang's safety.

"Will he live?" he asked Liu Chenguang.

Liu Chenguang knelt down and tried to check his pulse, but Mo Xiang spat at him as well and jerked his arm out of his hands. "He may," Liu Chenguang said finally. "If someone comes to help him." He looked up at Hong Deming. "I could help him."

Hong Deming looked at Mo Xiang again, remembering. Mo Xiang looked at him bleeding and nearly unconscious, his limbs all at strange angles, eyes full of hatred.

"It's because of you," Mo Xiang suddenly said, his voice thick with blood. "Because of you. My brother is dead. Zhu Guiren had him killed. You told that piece of stained filth next to you and he told his master."

Liu Chenguang said, "Hong Deming never mentioned your brother to me. I don't even know who you are."

Mo Xiang spat at him again.

Hong Deming said at last, "Do it."

Swiftly, Liu Chenguang struck Mo Xiang's acupoints to freeze his movements, checked his pulse, struck other acupoints to stop and start bleeding, and took some medicinal powder from his sleeves, carefully sprinkling it on the visible wounds. Then he bit his finger, and touched his lips.

"I don't have enough power now to heal immediately or fully," Liu Chenguang said quietly, "but he won't die of these wounds." He stood up.

"Let's go," said Hong Deming, walking back toward the road. "Take his horse with us, we need a spare."

Neither of them spoke much for a while. It was night now, but they rode hard, past several towns on the roundabout paths, at last finding an inn near midnight in a small village.

That night, Liu Chenguang tried again to heal Hong Deming's wounds. His blood closed them fully, but it was not a full healing, there was still pain and Hong Deming didn't have a full range of movement. "I don't think my blood is healing the internal wounds," Liu Chenguang, said, his voice low and frustrated, "from the qin. I'm not able to do what I want to do yet."

Hong Deming lay quietly on the bed, aching all over, his heart as well as his body. "Mo Xiang," he said after a while. "He was my friend at Peaceful River. He must have thought...thought I told you that his brother doesn't like the emperor...but..."

Liu Chenguang sat next to him, and interlaced their fingers, looking at their hands together. "I'm sorry," he said at last. "All this has happened to you because of me. You've lost so much."

"Don't cry."

"I won't cry, why should I cry." Liu Chenguang stared fixedly at the opposite wall for a moment. "Tomorrow turn around and go back, I can go from here on my own."

"Don't be ridiculous." He was too tired to soften it. "There's no point, Chenguang, I can't turn around now and say 'I'm sorry,' no one is going to accept that apology unless maybe I bring you back with me as proof of my repentance. This is not the kind of thing where Taiqian makes me face the wall and reflect on my shortcomings."

Liu Chenguang said, "Then take me back with you. When I'm recovered I can escape on my own, I promise you I can."

"How long do you need to recover."

"Six weeks, I think?"

Hong Deming closed his eyes, exhausted beyond belief. "This is a stupid conversation. I won't do that. Come here and lie next to me." He felt Chenguang's body next to him, warming him, Chenguang's scent surrounding him, his hair brushing his arm as he lay on his side next to him, carefully extending an arm across his chest to hold him without touching the huge bruises from the qin strikes. Hong Deming brought his own hand across, heavily because of the aching pains, to touch his head briefly. "Just sleep, taine," he said, too tired to think well. "It will be all right."

He drifted off, knowing that next to him, Chenguang was watching him through the darkness.

The next morning, his bruises were better. As he had half expected through his exhausted haze from their conversation last night, Chenguang had gone before he got up, leaving a note that he was going on his own and Hong Deming should go back. Hong Deming saddled both his horse and Mo Xiang's as the spare and caught up to him before the sun was halfway to noon. After they yelled at each other a few times, they kept going, east toward Mount Shi.

Mo Xiang had spread the word. Hong Deming fought four other cultivators, two from Jade Bamboo and two from Peaceful River, in the next three days. Liu Chenguang was able to heal them, so Hong Deming hadn't yet killed a cultivator in this endeavor, but he knew it was a matter of time.

They were racing toward the sunrise, the eastern sacred mountain, and Hong Deming began to feel that perhaps they would make it. Mount Shi was visible across the horizon now. They were almost into Hai'an, and they rode late every night and rose early every morning.

Hong Deming woke up, his head aching and all his muscles feeling strangely slack. His balance felt off, and when he reached out he couldn't summon En. "Chenguang?" he called out, dazed. "Taine? Is there something wrong with me?" He blindly held out his arm for Liu Chenguang to check his pulse.

No one touched his arm or replied.

Still not fully able to focus his eyes, he felt around the bed. Except where his body had lain, the mat and blankets were cold. No one was there.

He staggered up, holding on to the wall, and began to call out loudly. "Chenguang? Where are you?"

There was no answer.

He steadied himself, trying to calm his heart, which was galloping painfully in his chest. He wouldn't have tried to leave on his own again, they had already dealt with all that. Surely Chenguang had just gone down to the baths, that was all. He would be back in a moment. Hong Deming breathed deeply, trying to regulate his body again, and at last felt that he could both see and control his movements.

Liu Chenguang was not in the room. Nothing was disarranged, and his belongings were still there, except the clothes he had been wearing at dinner, and the jade pendant.

He sat at the table, trying to remember the night before. He didn't remember getting into bed at all, actually, or falling asleep; his last memory was of a maid bringing tea and a simple meal of rice and vegetables for them to share. Liu Chenguang had especially liked the braised tofu, he remembered. For a meal at a low-rank inn, it had been quite well flavored.

He put his head in his hands. Obviously, they had been drugged. For whatever reason, they had left him alive, but Liu Chenguang was gone.

He got up again, and reached out to summon En. This time, it came to his hand.

Hong Deming walked down into the kitchen. "Who cooked our dinner last night?" he asked quietly.

He had no patience for kindness now. He went through the kitchen staff like the wind through the grass, trying to leave as little permanent damage as he could but unwilling to be too gentle. At last he determined that the food they had eaten had been likely safe when it was cooked — others had eaten the same meal with no ill-effects — but that no one could recall the maid who had brought it up to them. The maid assigned to their room had not done it, but no one could remember who it was.

Hong Deming went outside, panting for air. His head still hurt, he still felt weak, and his terror was rising, making him unable to think, unable to wait, unable to make a plan. He would just have to look for their tracks, follow them, try his best, they could only go so far with lightness skills, they would have to get horses eventually, but where could they have gone, why had they taken him, what did they need? *Why?*

He returned to their room in a panic, to grab their belongings, to bring Chenguang's things too because surely he would want them when he found him. There was a woman already there, dressed only in an inner robe. She was holding Chenguang's extra robe in her hands, looking at it curiously.

"Get away," he said, then changed his mind.

The woman was extraordinarily beautiful, her features and skin perfect, her hair unbound down to her knees, her robe very thin, showing the shape of her body beneath. She smiled at him, and moved closer, reaching out a hand.

This gave him the opportunity to put his hand on her throat and push her roughly against the wall. "Where?" he hissed. "Where did they take him?"

She laughed, unafraid. When his hand loosened slightly, she suddenly reached out and sensuously drew her fingers across his collarbone. "How pretty," she said. "I don't know where they went. My master doesn't tell me such things. Which is just as well for him, as now I can't tell you no matter what you do with me." She smiled and added, "What would you like to do with me? I will be much better for you than that one."

She suddenly kissed him, full on the lips, her tongue slipping between his teeth and delicately touching inside. Furious, he pushed her away and spat, wiping his mouth fiercely. She laughed and licked her lips. "Delicious," she said. Her face changed, harsh and angry, though no less beautiful. She grabbed his face with both hands and hissed, "Brief life, unhappy death."

The woman turned in his hands to a tiny fox, its fur soft as silk. It squirmed out of his hands and leapt out of the window. Hong Deming stared for a moment, swore and rubbed his mouth again, then ran out to find the horses.

That night, he hadn't found any traces, but had had to kill two yaoguai, cultivated crow-beings who had near-human form, who had dived at him from the sky at the same time. Their cultivation was high and he took several wounds to his arms and one to his torso, The yaoguai had nearly disemboweled him. One of the horses was dead, and more crows came to feast on it, cawing at him mockingly. He sat next to the road and put his head in his hands for a moment, despairing, but then staggered up and mounted again, riding back west. Surely they would take Chenguang west, back toward Crane Moon? It was his only guess. The panic in his heart was rising. As when he had entered the caverns to find Chenguang that night at Crane Moon, he felt that he was running out of time.

The next day, he was challenged in the road by Shen Lu.

"No," he said. "Tainu, I won't fight you."

Shen Lu sighed. "Don't call me tainu. Hong Deming, I will attack you and you can defend yourself or not. You've left us no choice in this." He raised his sword and saluted.

"Tainu—"

"You are not qualified to call me tainu, Hong Deming," Shen Lu said, and made his first strike.

Hong Deming leapt the blade and its pulse and came down, leapt up again with En in his hand. "Tainu! Shen Lu, they were torturing him, I had to take him— please, do you know where he is, where they took him—"

"Shut up." Two more sword strikes. Shen Lu was aiming for the wound in his belly from yesterday, making him move quickly to reopen it. Hong Deming winced as he felt the edges tear and the blood begin to ooze out. Another strike. He used En to parry and leapt backward. The wound was affecting his qinggong, he couldn't be as fast or agile as usual. "What made that?" Shen Lu asked, conversationally. "It's pretty ugly."

"Yaoguai," he gasped, "two of them. Shen Lu, did you know, did you know what they were doing to him?"

"I didn't. And I don't want to know now." A slash came for his ankles, Hong Deming jumped up and flipped, nearly screaming as the wound in his belly tore completely, tore wider, the muscles separating in blood. He hit his acupoints and landed, and at last had to attack, sending out a sword pulse. Shen Lu parried and continued, "Whatever he was doing, Taiqian is Taiqian. Loyalty and obedience are what you need to concern yourself with. What he orders, you obey. It doesn't matter. You've never understood this."

"Where is he now, where did they take him?" he asked desperately.

Shen Lu moved forward in a flurry of rapid sword strikes, this time aiming at the unhealed wounds of Hong Deming's shoulder and arms. Hong Deming parried, dodged, and leapt, feeling blood dripping down onto the earth beneath him. "This is a question that doesn't concern you," said Shen Lu. "That's something else that you never understood." A cut came across his chest, burning through the skin to his ribs. Hong Deming grunted and hit the acupoints.

Realizing at last that Shen Lu would indeed kill him, he finally attacked with all the strength he had left, throwing qi into En's strikes and rushing forward. Shen Lu had said it himself, Hong Deming's cultivation was higher. With a supreme effort he put the pain out of his mind and slashed a pattern that would cage Shen Lu into one specific area, forcing him to move in a predictable defensive pattern and show a weakness, with the final cut through his thigh designed to disable him.

But because his qinggong was limited, because he was wounded, because he was not able to focus properly, he hit the femoral artery instead of the tendon and muscle, a killing strike.

Shen Lu struck his own acupoints, but the wound was too deep to stop the bleeding completely.

Hong Deming knelt next to him, frantic, pressing on the wound. "I'm sorry, I'm sorry, tainu," he said, "please don't die."

Shen Lu put his own hands over Hong Deming's. "Hong Deming," he said, "don't call me tainu." He moved his hands out of the way and pressed himself. "Go to the next town and send a doctor back."

They both knew a doctor wouldn't reach him in time. Hong Deming remained next to him, helpless. "If Chenguang were here he could help you," he said. "I didn't mean, I didn't want to fight you, tai– Shen Lu."

Shen Lu's pressure on the acupoints and the wound was failing. The blood didn't spurt anymore, but oozed out, pulsing softly with his heartbeat, creating a great pool where he lay and Hong Deming knelt, crying. "Hong Deming," he said after a while, "you've killed people before, I'm not your first, don't sit there like a child weeping over a broken toy." He thought a little while, his mind wandering. "My wife is back at Peaceful River, send her the letter in my saddlebags."

I wrote it before I went out to find you, Mo Xiang brought word, you've been followed...I knew I probably couldn't win against you, taine. But I'm the sect leader, after all."

Hong Deming was silent.

"That person, I wish we never found him, I wish Taiqian never brought him back," Shen Lu said with sudden vehemence. "It's because of him, all of this, what happened to you, he ruined you, taine."

"It's not his fault," Hong Deming said. "I love him, tainu, what else could I have done?"

Shen Lu's face was nearly bloodless now, his eyes unfocused. "You're very stubborn, taine." An endless time went by. Hong Deming held his hand and waited. "They took him across, the Fei have been attacking cities north of the Sorrowful River," he said at last. "The imperial army has been fighting for two months now. Zhu Guiren says that person has an ability, he'll be able to break the Fei army with one blow. Mandate of Heaven."

"But he can't even fight," Hong Deming said. "You know it, tainu — he can't even hold a weapon—"

"I just tell you what I know. I don't need to know everything, I'm not like you. Leave it, taine," he said. "By the time you can get there he'll probably already be dead, or he will have done what Zhu Guiren says he can, and either way you'll be forgiven after that if you confess your guilt...Let it be, don't interfere anymore." Shen Lu tried to squeeze his hand, but he had no strength left. "Taine, I also did what I had to do. I don't have regrets."

He didn't speak again.

Hong Deming finally arranged Shen Lu's limbs and placed a ward shield around his body, to keep it from animals or corruption until it was found. He placed the letter to his wife on his chest, under his hands. He knew he would never be able to send it.

That day when Chenguang had tried to run away, along with the note he had left packets of medicine for Hong Deming, labeled with their use and how to take them. He rummaged through Chenguang's bag and found them, one labeled for wounds as a poultice. He looked at the wound in his belly for a while, holding Liu Chenguang's needle and thread and considering whether he could stitch it up himself. Thinking about this took him a very long time; it seemed as though it were a hard decision. He finally decided that he couldn't, and put the needle and thread down on the ground and forgot about them. Then he needed to think about whether he should stop somewhere for a doctor to do it. It also took him a long time to think about this. He sat on the ground by the horses, just out of view of Shen Lu's body by the roadside, staring at the medicine pack-et, and then at the wound, a long slash from the yaoguai's claw that at one end might have gone completely through the inner wall of his abdomen, he couldn't really tell, at least nothing was falling out. The bleeding was slow, but it wouldn't stop. He tried to hold the edges together and considered, then finally bandaged it tightly with the poultice herbs. He forgot to actually make the poultice, he just put the herbs in the bandages and tied them on. He thought that if he passed a town with a doctor, he would stop and ask for help then.

He pulled himself onto the horse, wincing, and started riding toward the Sorrowful River, looking for a way to cross into the territory of the Prince of Fei.

CHAPTER 20
THE SORROWFUL RIVER

HE WAS ABLE to find a doctor before he crossed the river. The physician looked very serious when he saw his wounds but sewed him up and gave him medicine anyway. "Your vitality is greatly weakened, and you need to reinvigorate your vital energy. Rest. Don't exert yourself," the doctor said, hopelessly, and took his silver. Hong Deming didn't feel much better, but at least the bandages were tightly done and clean now. Just past that town he found a ferry to take him across and began riding aimlessly, trying to find clues as to where the armies of the Fei and the Son of Heaven were circling about one another. He heard that there had been fighting throughout the circuit, but he always arrived late to the battles. This slowed him down, as he had to walk through the corpses left on the field, looking for Chenguang's body. The first time he had to do this he nearly lost his mind, but it soon became easier through practice.

The days grew shorter and colder, and the trees lost their leaves. Hong Deming sat dazed under one, after searching the most recent battlefield, too tired even to start a fire. He had no idea where to go next, he would follow the trail that seemed to belong to the dynasty's forces, but this was always a guess. He carefully unwound the bandages around his middle, rubbed the ointment from the doctor on the oozing red wound, and then put clean bandages on. There was a lot of weakness in that area of his body since the muscles had been cut, which would be a severe disability when next he had to fight. Nonetheless, he hoped it would be sooner rather than later. These days and weeks were growing together, and whenever he thought of Chenguang he saw that image of his naked body, cut and bleeding on the stone couch. There was no one to stop them from doing that now.

He got up to his feet, grabbed En, and began walking. It was good to give the horse a rest occasionally, it was in almost as bad a shape as he was after the endless weeks of travel and short rations. He saw a rabbit dash off through the underbrush, and remembered he would need to shoot something for the day's meal. Grabbing his bow and arrow off the saddle, he moved softly through the woods, arrow on string. At a movement, he shot and missed.

Hong Deming looked at the arrow quivering in the earth, astonished. He never missed.

Walking over, he pulled the arrow out of the ground and noticed something bright red next to it: a small red bird with golden eyes, looking up at him.

"Hello," he said, and bent down. "Are you hurt? Why aren't you flying?"

But it immediately spread its wings and took flight.

Shortly afterward, he successfully shot a rabbit, skinned and wrapped it, and went back to where he'd tethered the horse to make a fire and cook it, well away from the corpse-littered field. He ate about half of it, stowed the rest for later, and mounted up again, riding toward the way he guessed the dynastic forces had gone.

The red bird was suddenly fluttering in the air in front of him. It dashed at the horse's face, making it shy and turn back. The bird, as though surprised, flew slowly in the other direction.

Hong Deming started forward again. The red bird again blocked the horse, and flew in the other direction.

After this had happened a third time, and a fourth, Hong Deming gave up and followed the bird, down the track of the other departing army.

The bird perched on a tree ahead, its golden eyes watching him. He greeted it respectfully, wondering if it were a yao. Ti Jinghua, back at the Stone Phoenix, had said that there were yao that didn't harm humans, though he'd never met one. Remembering the tiny, silken-haired fox, he watched the bird uncertainly, but it didn't try to interfere. Some long-tailed crows flew down and chased it away.

The trail of the army was easy to follow, with occasional dead horses or men to one side or another. He could even follow it under the light of the moon. On the third day, he heard a clash of swords and screams ahead of him, behind some low hills, notable only because the landscape was generally so flat. For once, he hadn't come too late. He rode to the bottom of one of the hills, tethered the horse, and crawled up to the top to view what was happening, the wound in his belly screaming at the unaccustomed movement.

In the shallow valley below, an immense confusion of forces were fully intertwined in an orgy of mutual slaughter, killing each other in a little stream that ran red down the middle, in the marshes on either slide, throughout the small town already nearly burned to the ground, in the fields, in the stables, in the outlying farmsteads, among the copses of leafless trees that hid nothing of the events. He couldn't easily tell which side was which, or who was who. The banners were mixed together, the soldiers' uniforms were torn and bloodied, the officers were shouting and screaming as much as anyone. On a hill to one side he saw the general, as he supposed, of the dynasty, so far as the banners went; they were too far away to identify any individuals. There was a squadron of archers there as well, and some reserve forces. On a hill farther away were the generals of the Prince of Fei, waving signal flags for whomever might be able to watch and interpret them.

Everyone else was in the blood cauldron.

Near a copse of trees, tiny from the distance, there was a person without armor or weapons, his robe a dark blue, his hair flowing down his back, pressing against a tree trunk, ducking and running among the trees to avoid swords and spears. This person had a little qinggong, and sometimes leapt into the trees himself, but then had to come back down because of the arrows immediately flying toward him.

Hong Deming stood up, called En, and ran down the hillside.

These were ordinary people. There were no cultivators on either side, and En cut a bloody swathe through the first line. Anyone who stood between him and the person in the blue robe was cut down. He didn't wait to see if they were friend or foe, they were all foes, Chenguang was a rabbit and the whole world was his enemy. However, this meant that both sides began to target him equally, and there was no safe place for him. As the soldiers of both sides closed in around his back, and he was immersed in the blood cauldron, spears and arrows began to fly. He couldn't block all of them, all of the time. He felt an arrow take him in the back, not too deep, not a killing wound, not yet. He tore it out and kept running, slashing with En and sending sword energy forward, always going toward the trees.

Liu Chenguang was bleeding heavily from a wound in his arm. He hadn't noticed him yet.

"Chenguang!" he shouted with all his breath. "Chenguang, I'm here!"

He saw Chenguang look up, his face striped with blood from a wound on his forehead, and scream despairingly.

"Go back!" he shouted. "Deming, go, I'm fine!" Distracted, Chenguang took a sword slash into his leg and fell forward to one knee.

Hong Deming killed the attacker and picked Liu Chenguang up. "Chenguang," he said, and looked at his leg. It wasn't a fatal wound, but it wasn't healing, why not?

"Deming," Liu Chenguang said, his face deadly pale under the bloody stripes, his hands clutching desperately to Hong Deming's arms despite his words, "no, Deming, leave, please leave—"

An arrow came for them, and Hong Deming blocked it, but there were more, and he couldn't block them all. This one hit Hong Deming in the chest, on the right side.

Chenguang screamed and for the first time Hong Deming saw him try to use a sword. Liu Chenguang rushed forward, limping on his bleeding leg, and stood in front of him, trying to block arrows. When someone came to attack him and he slashed down, the sword disintegrated in his hands. Hong Deming leapt in front again and blocked the return sword, cutting the attacker in half. "Chenguang!" he shouted. "Get behind me and stay there!"

With shaking hands, Liu Chenguang picked up a bow and arrow from a corpse, drawing with an arrow set. When he released the arrow, the bow broke, and the arrow snapped in two. Liu Chenguang screamed again in rage and fury and turned to him, begging him, "Deming, Deming, please, please go—"

Hong Deming considered whether he had enough energy left to simply pick Chenguang up and carry him out with his qinggong, and then realized that he didn't, and he knew he didn't when he came in, and the sole purpose of being here was to die with him. Realizing this made his mind clear, and almost joyful, except that Chenguang would die too, and that he couldn't bear to see. "Stay behind me, taine," he said, his voice calm.

More arrows came. He remembered what Taiqian had said that day very long ago, about the arrows that were like clouds, the ants that could defeat a mountain. En swung again and again, blocking, sending out sword energy. Corpses piled up in front of him, blood like a thin waterfall, he remembered Chenguang's blood in the cavern, flowing from the stone couch. He retreated step by step, feeling Chenguang behind him, and then they stopped with a strong tree at their backs. Chenguang came out and stood next to him. The soldiers were still for a moment, afraid of the sword, but it would be no more than that last moment.

He felt Chenguang's eyes on him, pleading, but he didn't say anything, didn't try to take his hand, not wanting to distract him. "Chenguang," he said, one last time, "get behind–"

The cloud of arrows flew out, and he blocked some. But not all. He felt the hot pain of an arrow in his throat, several in his chest. These were killing strikes. With his last power of movement, he turned and gathered Chenguang under his arm, twisted, and fell forward on top of him to shield him.

He could see Chenguang's face beneath his, his eyes full of tears, his mouth moving, but he couldn't really hear sounds anymore. The last thing he wanted to see in this life was Chenguang's eyes, so he watched them until everything grew dark.

Liu Chenguang felt Hong Deming die, his body shuddering into stillness, his breathing rattling into nothing, the light leaving his eyes as they grew fixed and dull. Then he lay there beneath him, feeling the dead weight of Hong Deming's body grow cold because he couldn't bear to miss the one last moment when his body was warm and remembered being alive. Tears fell like blood, the blood that continued to run from the deep wounds in his arm and leg.

Once the cultivators were dead, the soldiers went to kill each other elsewhere on the battlefield, looking for other meaningless places to defend and die for. Liu Chenguang lay beneath Hong Deming until a red bird fluttered to the ground next to him. Liu Chenguang turned his head to look at the bird, in silence.

The bird transformed into a woman, the servant woman Hong Deming had met at the Crane Moon sect. She knelt next to the bodies. "I'm sorry," she said. "I thought he could rescue you."

"Then you could at least have come earlier and healed him, why weren't you here to save him?" Liu Chenguang said. Hot tears fell from his eyes again. The servant woman reached forward and began to pull out the arrows that had pierced Hong Deming's back, then gently pulled his body off of Liu Chenguang. There were arrows in his front, in the throat and chest, that had been broken in his fall onto Liu Chenguang. She pulled those out too.

Liu Chenguang slowly sat up. The servant woman said, "You're still bleeding, why are you not healing?"

He gave an angry cry that was half a scream. "If I could heal do you think I wouldn't heal him? They've been bleeding me for months. I've got nothing left."

239

The servant woman shook her head. "I've been chased by yaoguai for days, we need to go. Can you transform?"

"No I can't transform, why are you asking stupid questions, if I could transform would I be here with the person I love dead in front of me?" He reached out and pulled Deming's body against him, holding him, and rocking slowly back and forth. "He died for me, Tielende. He died for me. He died for nothing. For nothing."

"It's not nothing," the woman said. "He loved you, Eftahede."

Liu Chenguang rocked back and forth. He reached out and moved Hong Deming's robes aside to look at his wounds, touching them one by one. "He was hurt when he came already, this would have killed him eventually if I couldn't heal him," he said softly, tracing the wound in his belly. "His body must have been full of sick blood when he was fighting, he must have been in pain for so long." He traced the wound in Hong Deming's throat, and ended with his fingers on the arrow wound in his left breast. "This is the wound that killed him." He leaned down and kissed it. "Deming," he said. He bit his lip and kissed it again. "Deming…"

"Eftahede," said the servant woman, "he's dead. There's nothing you can do. He's gone now. He's not suffering anymore. There's no pain here for you to heal."

Liu Chenguang looked up. "Is there no pain here, Tielende?" He reached again to Hong Deming's fatal wound, reaching inside as though to touch his heart, and touched his own lips with Hong Deming's smeared blood, already clotting and drying.

The servant woman watched with a calm face and narrowed eyes. "What are you doing, Eftahede?"

Liu Chenguang reached out with shaking hands and picked up En. He cut a piece of fabric from his white inner robe, and then cut it again into two long narrow strips. "I don't know." Liu Chenguang took the strips of cloth and smeared them with Hong Deming's blood, then trailed them through the bleeding wound on his own leg, soaking them deep red.

"Eftahede," said the servant woman, very gently, almost pleading, "this man's soul is on the journey that all mortal souls take. Don't pull him off his path."

Liu Chenguang bit his lip, reached over and kissed Hong Deming again, anointing him with his blood, on his eyes, on the tip of his nose, his lips, the wounds in his throat and breast.

"Eftahede," the woman tried again, "he's dead, sibling. In a thousand years, will you even remember that such a person once existed?"

Liu Chenguang looked at her, and the woman lowered her head. "I will remember," he said, fiercely, very soft.

He tied one of the bloody ribbons around Hong Deming's wrist, and the other around his own. The servant woman watched, and was silent.

Liu Chenguang kissed Hong Deming one last time, then lay him down, as though he were sleeping, though he never let go of his hand. Not looking up, he said, "The yaomo will be coming soon, I think. You should go now."

"Can you not come with me?" she asked.

"No," he said. "Even if I had the strength, this is over for me, Tielende. I want it to end. I want to go with him."

Very, very gently, as though speaking to a child that can't comprehend death, the servant woman said, "Eftahede, you know you can never go with him."

"I know," he said. "But I will not walk away from where he died."

"I won't leave you alone," the servant woman said. "I will be here with you."

"It's not necessary." When the woman didn't move, Liu Chenguang said, "At least transform, go to the other end of the valley. Don't let him get two of us. It doesn't matter how close you are. I'll know you're here."

After a moment the woman nodded. Liu Chenguang said, with his eyes closed, "Take the jade decoration on my sash, keep it safe for me."

The servant woman untied the jade crane ornament. With it in her hand, she transformed into a red bird and flew away.

For an unmeasurable time, Liu Chenguang lay partly on Hong Deming's body, his head against his breast, his hair falling over his shoulders, as though they were falling asleep together, as though he could hear his heartbeat. A stray arrow came and struck Liu Chenguang in the back, but he didn't move. Blood seeped out slowly from the wound. The sounds of the battle around them didn't stop, sometimes closer, sometimes more distant, but no one paid attention to two corpses among thousands.

Suddenly there was a foot between them, kicking Liu Chenguang over onto his back. The arrow ground in the wound and pierced through his chest before breaking. He gasped a little bit; the arrow was in his lung. Dark blood was dripping from his lips.

"Still all in one piece, I see," said Zhu Guiren disapprovingly. "Ah well."

Liu Chenguang looked toward the sky, ignoring him.

Zhu Guiren squatted down next to him. Conversationally, he added, "I'd like you to know that this was not how I initially wanted to end things. You should have just died in the battle, cut to pieces here. But Taiqian's on the way to clean things up, and truthfully it's probably better that way for me. More convenient for the timing."

Silence.

"It's all right if you don't want to talk. I'm sure you don't have much energy left. It won't be long." He looked at Hong Deming's body. "I see your little friend didn't make it. I've been trying to kill him for quite a while now, but he wasn't supposed to be here today at all. My subordinate at that inn will have some explaining to do…the irony is that if he hadn't come today, I would have let him live. It's only you I need."

Liu Chenguang choked a little bit, blood dribbling out of the side of his mouth. After he spat, he said thickly, "Let me hold his hand."

Zhu Guiren raised his eyebrows. "That's a dead man, phoenix. Holding his hand won't change anything."

He turned his head to look into Zhu Guiren's eyes. After a moment, he said, "Please."

Zhu Guiren stared back, then laughed. "Fine." He picked up Hong Deming's cold hand and placed it in Liu Chenguang's. "Ugh, how disgusting."

Liu Chenguang just watched Hong Deming's face, quietly, as though hoping against hope that he would notice him holding his hand, trying to warm him, trying to store up a memory of this face against any future need. "Did you ever say anything to me that wasn't a lie?" Liu Chenguang asked.

"Many things. I told you many truths about human beings and how they are with one another," Zhu Guiren said. "You just didn't want to listen. Typical phoenix." He reached out with one finger and flicked him on the forehead. "Next time around, don't be so trusting."

Liu Chenguang heard footsteps, but didn't look away from Hong Deming. The footsteps came up behind his body, and stopped. Taiqian's face looked down coldly. He stepped over Hong Deming's body to speak to Zhu Guiren. "Zhu Guiren," he said, "what was the point of all this? You brought us here, weeks of my time, and promised that Liu Chenguang would be able to end this war decisively, with one blow. As far as I can tell, he's completely useless."

"Not quite, sect leader," Zhu Guiren replied. "There is one more step. It should have happened during the battle, but as it was interrupted, it needs to be completed now. As I have explained before, Liu Chenguang's ability to unlock his true powers, to be able to attack as strongly as he can heal, is being blocked by the weakness of his meridians compared to his inner power. The meridians have to be completely severed, then they can regrow appropriate to the power he holds."

Taiqian looked down at Liu Chenguang, lying there stained with blood, with a complicated expression. "Zhu Guiren, you've shown me that Liu Chenguang's blood can heal others, and that he can heal himself, but look at him now. It seems that the power is weakened, not strengthened."

"That's why this final step needs to be taken exactly now, before the body heals again," Zhu Guiren explained. "If you leave him in this state, without taking the final steps, his body will eventually heal itself completely, but it will still be unable to attain the full power he is capable of."

Liu Chenguang continued to watch Hong Deming's face, holding his hand, as though this conversation had nothing to do with him. On the hillside above the battle, the servant woman pressed her face further into the ground. Her body shook a little bit, but then she was still.

Zhu Guiren nodded to Taiqian. "Continue the cutting, as before," he said.

Taiqian took up his sword, a little reluctantly, but began slicing. After the first few cuts, Liu Chenguang started shivering and crying out softly, though he never looked away from Hong Deming's face. Everywhere the sword touched, Liu Chenguang's skin and flesh opened, and blood oozed out slowly, dripping into the earth. Some of it fell on Hong Deming, warm where he was cold.

As the blood fell, behind Taiqian, where he couldn't see, Zhu Guiren held his fingers in unrecognizable hand seals, shifting swiftly from one to another while softly murmuring under his breath. Liu Chenguang's voice fell silent.

"He's unconscious now," Taiqian said, at last. "I think he doesn't have much blood left."

"The last step is dismemberment and decapitation," Zhu Guiren said calmly. "In that order."

"What?!" Taiqian stepped back, his face disgusted. "I'm not an executioner, Zhu Guiren–"

"It's the only way," Zhu Guiren said, encouragingly. "And after all, he's unconscious now, isn't he? Don't wait too long. If he heals, you'll have to do it all over again."

Taiqian raised the sword, then stopped. "You do it."

"I can't," Zhu Guiren said, "it needs to be a high-level spiritual sword, you know I can't use one. My expertise comes from long study, but I don't have a spiritual weapon, I have no spiritual power of my own."

Taiqian raised the sword again, quickly, then, one-handed, slashed down. The sword was extremely sharp, and he put a great deal of qi behind it, to sever with one strike.

At the first cut, Liu Chenguang woke up briefly and screamed, his voice hoarse, his vocal cords raw with blood. But by the second cut, he was already unconscious again.

Three cuts. Four. Zhu Guiren held his hands still over the earth and chanted softly. Just before the sword swung down for the last time, at the moment Taiqian raised the sword above his head for the killing stroke, a black long-tailed crow appeared where Zhu Guiren had stood, and drove itself away to the west with a speed greater than any earthly bird.

Five cuts.

The fire poured outward, instantaneous, overwhelming, an explosion that caught up Taiqian, and the body of Hong Deming, all the corpses on the battlefield. It rolled over the valley, dynasty and rebel alike, alive and dead, incinerating them in an instant. It rolled up the hills and captured the generals, the reserves, the waiting messengers. The fire raged into the sky, no end visible to it, a pillar connecting heaven and earth.

The last bits of Hong Deming's observing soul dissolved in the flame, and the last thing his soul would remember was a small red bird turning into sparks, rushing upwards, dissolving along with him.

INTERLUDE
BETWEEN LIVES

"DOCTOR LIU! DOCTOR LIU!"

He looked up from his counter, where he was carefully compounding a prescription for a woman at risk of a miscarriage. "Yes, I'm here," he replied.

"Doctor Liu, there's news from below, grandfather wants you to come."

He completed the prescription and handed it to the child. "Bring this to Master Shen for his wife. Tell him that she is to boil it, cool it, and drink every hour today. She should remain in bed all week. That is very important. Be sure to tell him that."

"Yes, Doctor Liu. I'm going!" The young boy ran out, excited to have a mission to take him from the work in the fields.

He walked down through the stone-paved street of the village toward the headman's house. Headman Fang was standing outside, gray beard waving in the wind.

"Doctor Liu," he said, "you're here. Please come in."

They sat down together; the old man offered weak tea, the best he had. The village was isolated and poor, and in recent years trade had been bad. Nonetheless, after drinking, he said, "The heavens have blessed our village to have a divine doctor among us. But I know you will leave us soon."

Liu Chenguang drank his own tea. "What makes you say so?"

"When you came here, I was a young boy. Now my hair is gray, and you are still a young man. I remember that my father told me, when you first came, that you had been here before. His grandfather told him of the divine doctor Liu, who he remembered from his own childhood. Who cured all illnesses for us and disappeared without warning."

Liu Chenguang drank again. "Perhaps this is true, perhaps not. Who can say what happened in the lifetime of your esteemed ancestor?"

The headman continued, "You are right to say so, Doctor Liu. My ancestor's ancestor built the shrine to the divine doctor here many generations ago. My father said that it was because the divine doctor had been here then too, and all the village hoped he would return. And so you did. We are grateful. And I do not want to be greedy or disturb your peace. What you have given— You have saved our lives from all the accidents and suffering of human life, except old age and war."

"I have done my poor best."

"Doctor Liu may be concerned that perhaps the village would be unhappy that he does not age. That the foolish people would trouble him for elixirs of immortality and other things that are not appropriate for mortals. I promise you that it would not be so."

Liu Chenguang looked out from the porch where they drank at the little village: the fields around it, the laughing children chasing dragonflies. There was no sickness here, no untimely death. There was peace for the people here, at least.

He drank again.

The headman pressed on. "Doctor Liu may worry that the foolish people would tell others about him, boasting about our blessing. That he would be troubled by those coming from far away to demand what can't be given. I promise you. I promise you, this would not be so."

Liu Chenguang replied, gently, "Your grandson told me that there is news from below."

The headman sighed. "The northern barbarians are coming closer. There are many battles, many raiders. They are settled around Eifeng now, not so far. Soon, they will come here. The rumor is that they raze cities and towns to the earth to make pasture for their horses. They are unstoppable. What if they come here? Doctor Liu, divine doctor, can't you remain to protect us?"

"Headman Fang, I can't protect you. I am not a martial god. Not any kind of god. I am only a doctor. I can only heal." He said softly, then stood up and bowed formally. "Thank you for your kind words. You are correct that I must leave now."

Headman Fang tried to kneel down to prostrate himself, but Liu Chen-

246

guang reached down to lift him up.

"Don't. It's not necessary, not appropriate. I'm only a person."

"Will you come back?" he asked. "We will keep the temple for you, we will burn incense for you. We will keep your house clean–"

"It may be a long time, but I will come back. Remember not to tell anyone about me," he said, "or I won't be able to stay."

"Yes, yes," he said, delighted. "We will be discreet, divine doctor. Thank you, thank you!"

Liu Chenguang still remembered the lightness skills of the Crane Moon, and of course he could have transformed and flown, but it occurred to him to keep that aspect of things secret. He might need an escape route at some point. This journey would be better done on a horse. He obtained one from a farm near the highway and began riding, asking along the way where he could find the Mitang army. He no longer wore his hair like a cultivator — the cultivation sects had disappeared, so most people would not recognize it except as someone enacting an ancient tale — but for this journey, he decided it would be more effective. Better if word went before him. He put up his hair in the pincrown again, letting the rest flow down behind his back, and exchanged his scholar's tunic for the flowing, lightweight robes of a cultivator. Instead of a sword, which he still could not hold, he kept the gourd at his waist, along with a jade pendant figuring a crane with outspread wings. He could at least look like a proper cultivator.

First, he went to the siege of Eifeng.

He made himself highly visible, dramatically healing people near death on the battlefield — both Daxian defenders and Mitang attackers. Soon enough word reached the Mitang general, who ordered him captured. This was exactly what he had been hoping for, so he didn't try to escape.

All he would say to the general was, "I am a messenger from the spirits. I am sent to the Great Khan. Cease your warfare until I have spoken to him."

Nothing would make him say more than this.

As he had hoped, the general was superstitious enough to listen and send him to the Khan. Whether he stopped attacking Eifeng while Liu Chenguang was on the road, there was no way of knowing.

At last he stood before the Great Khan, an enormous man with a deceptively cheerful attitude. "Eh, little man, why are you here?" he asked.

Liu Chenguang bowed formally. "Great Khan, I am sent from the spirit world to offer my protection to you."

The Khan laughed out loud. "Ha, you will protect me? How?"

Liu Chenguang took a deep breath and readied himself. "Tell one of your men to cut my throat."

The Khan raised his eyebrow. "You, there. Do it."

One of the guards immediately leapt over, pulled Liu Chenguang's head back by his hair, and slashed his throat with a saber. The freezing, burning pain shot through him, and he fell to his knees, blood spurting to the floor. The room darkened before his eyes, and he felt his body slump to the ground.

Then, he woke up.

Several of the guards — big men, afraid of nothing — screamed out loud as he climbed to his feet. At least two shot at him: one arrow through the chest, one through the shoulder.

He fell to the ground again, swearing under his breath; he hadn't expected to be attacked twice, although he probably should have. Rising to his feet once more, he reached up a hand and broke off the head of the arrow piercing through his chest and jerked it out, wincing. The one that had hit his shoulder hadn't gone through completely, so that one he had to drag out, despite the barbs. "Ah," he gasped, but then it was over. And after all, it probably had a bigger effect that way, he thought.

He raised his head and bowed again to the Great Khan. The guards, pale beneath their tans, backed away, murmuring to one another.

The man in the chair leaned forward. "You can recover from any wound?"

"I can recover from any wound," Liu Chenguang said, resisting the urge to rub his throat. "However, I advise you not to behead me. I will survive that, but everyone within three miles will die immediately."

"Ha, that could be useful in its own way."

"You would not survive the attempt. The heavens forbid it."

"Good enough. You can give me this protection?"

"There are conditions," he said. "You must find a way to establish your dynasty without destroying the Daxian people and their cities. Consider, after all, the benefit to you. Farmers will provide food, tribute, taxes for you. Much better than a land where you can only ride horses and graze."

"You're not the first to say so." The Khan looked over toward another Mitang warrior — a huge man with a long beard. "Feru says the same. But the cities resist us. They must be destroyed."

"Find another way," Liu Chenguang said bluntly. "So long as you don't destroy the cities or villages, or loot the countryside, or rape the women, or massacre the people, I will protect your life. No illness or wound will hurt you."

Feru leaned over to the Khan and whispered.

"Can you give me the elixir of immortality?" he asked.

"Certainly," Liu Chenguang said. "However, for that there are additional conditions. The Elixir of Immortality is only effective if, for the next ten years before I give it to you, and then for all of eternity, you refrain from war, hunting, eating meat, and sexual relations of any kind." After a moment of reflection, he added, "Also, no alcohol. Not even fermented mare's milk."

The big man glared, then laughed out loud, slapping his thigh in amusement. "To hell with that!"

Liu Chenguang bowed, hiding his smile. "The Great Khan speaks wisely."

He was placed in a room without windows, the door locked, while the Khan considered. Liu Chenguang sat quietly in a corner, thinking. As usual at such times, he thought of Hong Deming — wishing he could talk with him again, tell him about what he was doing, about his efforts to try to stave off the suffering they had seen together. Hong Deming would have been upset that he'd been shot twice. He would have to explain why that was important. Hong Deming would try to protect him, but that wasn't always possible. He would need to understand that.

It had been such a long time.

He was used to such thoughts; in their own way, they were comforting.

As he had expected, sometime around the fourth watch the door opened and Feru entered, bending over so as not to strike his head on the lintel. Liu Chenguang remained seated.

"Your manners have declined since this afternoon," the big man noted, seating himself on the floor opposite.

"I am in a jail cell, talking to my jailor," he replied. "I choose to be courteous to the Great Khan. I don't need to be courteous to you."

Feru grinned. "We understand each other. The Great Khan is amenable to your terms. What is required?"

"I must remain close to him. I will diagnose him now and cure whatever ills he currently suffers. From this, I will know what is likely to come to him in the future as well. I guess already that he is declining from alcohol use."

"He has been told this by other physicians."

"I can keep this death from him."

Feru snorted. "For that alone, he would spare twenty cities, the old drunkard. However, he asks that you also extend this protection to his sons."

"I can't defend them when they are at war unless I am at their side." He didn't mind offering this; it would ensure that he could rein in the army from the field, rather than solely through the Great Khan's messengers. "I will not leave the central plain for any long period of time. The Great Khan, I understand, has sent his armies elsewhere as well."

Feru nodded. "The southern dynasty is resisting, although the final outcome is inevitable before the armies of the Great Khan. I will do my best to ensure that the damage is minimal. You and I are allies in this."

"It's good to have allies," he said. "I can't be everywhere, but if I receive news that this bargain has been broken — if there have been massacres or destruction by his order, or the orders of his sons, the Great Khan should know that his death approaches, and the death of his sons as well."

"You don't need to worry." Feru scratched his beard, then asked, "Why are you doing this? Are you not a patriot? Are you not angry that the Mitang people will rule the Daxian?"

"I am not a patriot," he said, "and I don't care who rules who, so long as the people are safe from harm."

"Are you truly sent from heaven? Are you a divine compassionate one?"

"What difference does it make?" he asked, smiling. "I have heard that you have compassion for the people as well. Does that make you a deity? You use the powers that you have to avert suffering, so far as you can. So do I. That's all you need to know." After a moment, he added, "Long ago, I was foolish. There are things I need to atone for."

Feru nodded as though he understood. "Very well. Come with me."

Forty years later, Liu Chenguang sat on a high cliff near a trickling waterfall. The fall came down from the cliff behind him, trickled across the ledge on which he sat, and then fell down below. As the sun descended, its rays filled the gorge and lit up the mist where the waterfall dissipated into the air. Golden-red sparks glimmered and disappeared, glimmered and disappeared.

Once, there had been a little wall at the edge of the cliff and a carved channel for the waterfall, but these things were largely worn away by time. From where he sat, he could see the remnants of stone walls above and below, some with the outline of houses and courtyards. They had long been destroyed by fire and sword. This must have happened before he returned from rebirth, even before the rise of the Ning dynasty, centuries before; it had been like this when he first came back. The fire, and whoever had attacked, had destroyed the library, the buildings, the armory. Only the spiritual caverns remained — in darkness, as they had always been, waiting for someone to enter. There was nothing left of the Crane Moon but the jade pendant he wore.

He watched the sparks glimmer and disappear as the sun set, and leaned back against the cliffside as the stars came out. Eventually, he felt the heat of his tears slowly trickling down his face; he didn't raise his hand to wipe them. Soon he was sobbing, gasping for breath. It had been so long.

This was the only place where he allowed himself to cry.

Liu Chenguang leapt down the cliff and walked the mountain paths to the village. The temple was still there; incense was still being burnt for the divine doctor.

An old man saw him walk down from the forests. "Doctor Liu," he called, "Doctor Liu, welcome back! Welcome back!"

He was gray-haired, but hale and healthy. Liu Chenguang was glad to see it. "Little Fang," he said, smiling, "I'm here."

CHAPTER 21
TAIREI AND AILI

AILI OPENED HER eyes and looked into Tairei's. "Chenguang," she heard her voice say, hoarse with disuse, as it had been after she came out of seclusion. After he had come out of seclusion. She felt a rush of warmth all through her body, as she always had whenever she saw Tairei. Now, she knew why. She stopped herself from reaching out to touch Tairei's face before the movement began.

Tairei's eyes shone. "Aili," she said.

Not Hong Deming, but Aili knew that was who she really meant.

She sat up and held her head. "That...My head hurts..."

Tairei reached out to touch her, concerned. "You've been asleep for a long time. Nightfalls and nightfalls."

"I remember everything," Aili said, her head still in her hands.

Tairei reached out again, more tentatively. "You...remember?" Her voice was hopeful.

It made Aili's heart hurt to hear how much hope she had.

"I remember," she said, and met her eyes.

She and Tairei looked at each other, neither certain how to begin.

Belatedly, Aili realized that the cavern they were in was not very large, and that Zhu Guiren and Tainu were sitting on the other side of a blue and golden fire, watching them. Zhu Guiren looked a little worried when their eyes met, which made her feel somewhat better. She had a vague memory of stabbing him with En — quite a pleasant thought, even if it had only been a dream.

"Come on," said Tainu, getting up.

Zhu Guiren settled down with his chin in his hand. "Oh no, this is going to be good. I've earned this. I'll have a scar forever."

"Now, voyeur." Tainu grabbed his ear and started pulling.

"Ow, ow, ow! I'm coming, stop it! What about the wards? You shouldn't go out like this?"

Aili could hear him complaining for quite a while — the only sound as she and Tairei looked at one another. She saw the hope slowly dim in Tairei's eyes as she looked into them, and looked, and didn't speak.

At last Tairei said, very softly, "I knew when you came back into the world. I could feel it. But you were far away. I spiraled out from where I was, systematically. It turned into a game of hot and cold. You know that game? Where if you get closer, the other person says 'getting warm'? But you were so distant that the sense was so very subtle. It took a long, long time. And then, I stood on the shore of the ocean and felt that you were on the other side. I had no way to cross the ocean, and I felt that time was running out. I knew that my time of rebirth was coming soon, and when that happened, I would need to be away from you in the spirit realm. I had already missed your childhood…you were already an adult. Because of the war, there were no ships. I couldn't…And when I found you, you didn't remember me. I was sure you would have remembered me, would have felt something…did you…not feel anything?"

Aili felt her throat constrict, but didn't respond.

Eventually, Tairei continued, "Almost as soon as I found you, you were going to leave. You were going to go back onto a battlefield, and I couldn't stop you. I was almost out of my mind with terror. I felt like this was some kind of cruel punishment. That you would die again, at the same age. That I wouldn't be able to stop it. So, I came up with this plan to protect you…To keep you alive."

"You could have explained it to me. You could have asked me." Aili realized that out of everything, that was what she was going to talk about; it wasn't what really mattered. It was helpful, though, to feel a little bit wronged, a little bit angry — helpful because her heart was lost and broken; helpful because she still loved this person, and this person did not love her.

Tairei was silent. "I'm sorry. I wasn't…I wasn't able to think that far ahead… about what it might mean to you. All I could think was that you wouldn't die."

"What did you do to me, exactly?" Aili asked eventually.

"I don't really know. Both times, I just…I did what seemed right to me at that moment. I didn't…I didn't know what would happen." she said. "When you died…"

"I saw it in my memories." She couldn't bear to hear Tairei describe it.

Tairei nodded, looking at the ground. "So you…your soul was still there? You saw everything?"

She remembered it: seeing Liu Chenguang lying under his dead body, despairing, being cut to pieces by Zhu Guiren. She clenched her fists so hard she felt the blood in her palm.

"How could you do this?" she asked, her voice rising. "How could you do this to me and not know what you were doing? What would happen to me? What am I now?"

She realized that she was actually, truly very angry after all.

"You– you lied to me! You didn't tell me what you were. I was glad to die, Liu Chenguang. Did you know it?" she asked. "I was glad to die because I thought we would go together. I thought…I came to die with you. Didn't you understand?"

"Don't *you* understand?" Tairei said, suddenly flinging back her head. Tears flew like jewels in the blue firelight with the violence of her movement. "Do you not understand that I can't die? That I can't– You were– You died for me for no reason at all. I had to watch it happen because I'm so useless. Did you think how I would feel, watching you, feeling you die?"

"Could I have had any idea you would have survived?" Aili asked, almost shouting. "That you were some kind of immortal thing? That I could have just left you there and gone on my way and met up at an inn later when you had gotten through it–"

"I tried to get away from you and keep you safe! I told you!" Tairei shouted back. "I told you to leave! You knew that I could heal myself–"

"You damn well weren't healing! You were bleeding all over! How could I have known that I was dying for nothing?"

Tairei's face turned pale beneath her tears, all the blood draining from it.

Aili felt her heart clench and turned around, unable to look at her pain. She struck the wall of the cavern with her hand and swore. Bits of fire escaped from between her fingers, running up and down the crystal walls with nothing to burn.

"All right," Aili said at last, in a low voice. "I would have stayed with you anyway. Even if I knew. I would have wanted to try to protect you from them. From the pain you were in. I would have died anyway. I knew at the time, Tairei. That's the truth. That I wouldn't survive. I knew it when I came to try to get you."

"You were in so much pain then," Tairei said. "I saw the wounds you had…"

Her voice trailed off. "I never knew what had happened to you, after they took me at the inn. I didn't even know how long it was. Zhu Guiren kept me drugged until they brought me onto the battlefield."

Aili shook her head. "Tairei, you don't want to know."

"I do."

"There were two yaoguai at once," she said, keeping it to the bare minimum. "One of them wounded me in the stomach. Then I killed my tainu. After that, I don't think I was thinking clearly."

Tairei didn't drop her gaze, but her face was even sadder than before. "Shen Lu...I'm so sorry. So sorry for everything."

"Why didn't you tell me?" Aili asked, looking past her at the black rock of the wall and the constantly-changing golden figures deep inside it.

Tairei took a deep breath. "Aili, for a thousand years, I have wished I did. Every day. But at the time...at the time, I didn't know how to say it. I was afraid that you wouldn't love me anymore if you knew. I'd never...I'd never been with people before I met you. Not really. I was like a mountain yao — living in the wilderness, only crossing paths with human beings once in a while. I didn't want you to see me the way they did. As something that needed to be avoided, or only sought out if they wanted something." She sighed. "I was afraid..."

"You were afraid of the wrong things," Aili said.

"Tell me the truth. Would you be dead now if I hadn't done this? Would you already have died?"

"Yes," Aili said. The bullets that struck Nora had struck her too. There was no doubt, she should have died for the second time without ever seeing Liu Chenguang again.

"Then I'm not sorry." Tairei came a step closer. "I am sorry if you hate me for it, but I'm not sorry that you are alive. I will never be sorry for that. If you're alive...If you're alive, then that's all that matters to me."

She was close enough that Aili could hear it when she took a deep breath, and then continued. "Would it have been better if had never come to look for you? You could have lived a good life without me. Maybe you could have...fallen in love with someone, grown old with them..."

"Stop," Aili said, desperate. There would never have been anyone else, but she couldn't say that; it wouldn't help anything.

"I can leave you alone if that's what you want," said Tairei.

Aili looked into her eyes — red-rimmed with tears, but so determined. Something like the feeling of glass over her heart, but more like ice, coldness. And yet, there was warmth too. Something almost painful that yearned to come out into the light. Something that tasted of longing and hope and fear. There was too much.

She was Hong Deming, and yet she was not. The man with a kind and gentle heart, the man whose soul was so open, the man who protected the people he loved — he had been betrayed and failed and died, suffered and failed again, and she was no longer that person. A thousand years later, her lives were only a long, shameful defeat; she was a useless coward, and the people she loved were destroyed around her.

Tairei was standing straight and rigid, her hands clenched at her sides.

Aili saw this and felt that soreness in her heart again, and at the same time that clarity and distance. "This feels familiar," she said, finally.

Tairei closed her eyes.

"Hong Deming is dead, Tairei," Aili said, very quietly. "The person you were in love with has been dead for a thousand years. I am not that person."

Tairei shivered and hung her head low.

"I remember..." Aili said. "I remember everything. I loved you. I really did love you. You were everything to me. You were the best part of my life from the day I met you. I didn't say it well then — how much I loved you. At least I can say it now."

In the firelight, she could see the glimmer of tears, falling from Tairei's chin like little sparks. She steeled herself to continue. "If I had known when I died, that you would...I didn't die so that you could feel guilty forever, or keep loving a dead person. I wanted you to live. I don't want you to torture yourself for this. It wasn't your fault. Let it go. Just...let it go. There's nothing else you need to do. Stop carrying the burden of my life and death with you. For a thousand years, Tairei...I wish..."

But she was no longer the person Tairei yearned for, and she couldn't ever be again.

Tairei nodded, jerkily, once.

Aili took a deep breath. "I am going to go out. I won't go far. I'll come back soon. You stay here."

Without waiting for an answer, she walked out past the wards that she recognized through the tingling in her skin. The sun was close to setting. About a hundred yards away, she saw Tainu sitting under a tree, still casually holding Zhu Guiren's ear.

"You two can go back now," she called, her voice steady.

The demon said, "Finally."

Tainu stood up, brushing off his legs. He looked at her, but didn't say anything before going back into the cave.

Just before he went inside the wards and became invisible to her eyes, Zhu Guiren looked back, his eyes bright and curious. "I always wondered why you did it. There was no way you could have won. You must have known you were going to die and he would die too, as far as you knew anyway. Why bother?"

Aili didn't respond; she stared up at the sky, moving toward twilight now. It was full of things that were not stars, glimmering and dashing around one another in complex patterns.

Zhu Guiren shrugged and disappeared behind the wards.

Almost immediately, he came out again. "He told me to leave," he said, sounding offended. "Liu Chenguang is crying. I don't understand. Didn't she get what she wanted?"

Aili looked at him in disgust. When he came to sit next to her, she moved away.

"Don't go too far," he said, "tonight's wave will be coming. Did you know we get attacked every night here? The spirit realm is full of entertainment. At least you'll be able to help with defense more than those useless things."

"Since I'm here now, can you stop torturing us all with your existence and just go?"

Zhu Guiren beamed. "You remember me!"

"Yes, this is why I'd like you to be dead."

"This is not an uncommon response to me," he remarked. "But I didn't reach my advanced age by being easy to kill. You used up three lives' worth of luck for that one shot. You won't get another one."

He twisted his hand and pulled a knife of ice and smoke out of nothingness. "On that topic...that is, my particular skills and what you can and can't do around me. You can lie to those phoenixes since they're stupid and innocent and unused to deception. You can possibly lie to yourself. You can't lie to me. I'm too good at it. So, stop pretending you're not Hong Deming and that you don't have...whatever feelings you have for little Chenguang."

"I am not Hong Deming. And how the hell do you know anything about my feelings?"

"I know nothing at all about your feelings. I just know lies when I hear them." He began tossing his knife and catching it in his single hand. "That little phoenix will believe you, and it will break her heart. She is the stupidest I've ever met, even among phoenixes. So trusting." He caught his knife and held it at Aili's throat; Aili already had a knife at his — a knife that glowed golden.

She whispered, "You are not qualified to speak about her."

Calmly, Zhu Guiren said, "Your speed is decent. I will admit I didn't see that coming. However, it proves my point."

Aili brought her knife closer to his throat. "Tainu is not here now, and I'm not going to heal you. Zhu Guiren, please remember that I would love to kill you."

"If you wanted it that much, I'd already be dead."

She pressed the golden knife more firmly, feeling the tautness of his skin beneath as he swallowed. "You might also remember that I don't care if I'm dead, and it's not at all clear that I can be killed. This is not an even fight for you."

A line of blood appeared under the knife. She tried to calm herself so she wouldn't cut his throat accidentally out of sheer trembling rage.

"Actually, you probably can be killed. At least here," Zhu Guiren said. "The spirit realm is the only place where a phoenix can truly die. Why do you think they're trying so hard to hide? Why do you think I'm trying to protect them? Unlike you, I don't do pointless acts of heroism. If those useless things couldn't be killed, I'd be on my merry way."

More blood trickled from under the knife. "You. Do. Not. Speak. About. Liu Chenguang."

Zhu Guiren pressed his own knife against Aili's throat in return. "Fine. I won't say anything about Liu Chenguang. I will only say things about you. These are things you need to hear, and neither of those phoenixes are able to tell you because they are—"

Aili's knife bit deeper.

"Fine. I will not mock phoenixes in your hearing."

She pulled the knife away.

"Talk. Politely."

"All right." He rubbed his throat and flicked his hand; his dagger disappeared. "I have every plan to tell Tainu about this outrage, by the way. Have you been trained in knife-fighting? In your current form, I mean."

"Training is not quite what I'd call it," she said, thinking about the bus station in Easterly.

"Do you know how to use a spiritual weapon?"

"No."

"But you just did both of those things. Because Hong Deming knew how to do one of them and you knew how to do the other, you combined them to pull a spiritual knife on me. You are not separate from Hong Deming. You are continuous: mind, soul, heart, body."

"How can our bodies be continuous?"

"I'm not going to explain the theory to you. Your little brain would explode. But the training you received as Hong Deming, the skills you developed, even the spiritual cultivation, is within the body you have now, along with everything you have learned in this life, in this body. It's not just cognitive. It's not just memories. You are the continuation of that person. Don't tell yourself otherwise. That's the lie."

She stood. "I am not Hong Deming."

Zhu Guiren looked up at her. "You are more than Hong Deming, yes. You have lived more than Hong Deming had when he was killed. But you are Hong Deming, and he is you. You are not separate beings. I don't really understand why you don't get this. You have the memories."

"No."

He rolled his eyes theatrically. "Phoenixes...all intuition and no skill. She literally has no idea what she did or why it worked. One day, I'll get the little phoenix to tell me exactly what steps she took and then I'll probably be able to analyze what happened and tell you more details. Meanwhile, don't waste my time. Your skills and abilities as Hong Deming are still with you. You've just never tried to use them properly in this body. You're a cultivator. You have the ability to create a spiritual weapon, just as I do." He held out his hand, and his sword of ice and smoke appeared in it. "It's a part of you, in a sense. It will take the form of whatever weapon you are most skilled with, or that you feel connected to in a given moment. You were a swordsman and an archer. I expect you could use either a sword or a bow."

Aili thought of En. It was true; En had been a part of her, the deepest part in some ways. She had never tried to summon anything but En, yet she had just pulled a knife on Zhu Guiren. "Why are you telling me this?"

"As I told you, first of all, to prove to you that you are lying. I don't enjoy lies done badly. They irritate me. Secondly, because we are going to be attacked tonight, and the attacks are getting worse each nightfall. I think that tomorrow, we'll also be attacked during the day, and probably more or less continuously from there on. We don't know for sure how much the refuge can take if we don't drive off some of the attacks. It will be useful to have you as backup, on the off chance that I need a break."

She looked at him. "You're lying to me now."

"Fine. Third reason. For the overly-trusting phoenix I'm not allowed to talk about."

Aili walked away. Chenguang's eyes in those last moments of Hong Deming's life wouldn't leave her; their eyes were the same — Liu Chenguang's beautiful shining eyes and Tairei's eyes just now, filled with tears, trying to be brave. How was it that she herself was so different from the person she had been? Body and soul, continuity be damned, she was not the same as Hong Deming.

"Leave me alone," she said, not sure who she was talking to.

"I'm serious," called Zhu Guiren. "Don't go too far. There are things here that are coming specifically for you–"

"Let them come." Now all the pain seemed to be pooling in her heart, like molten rock, hot and burning and full of sharp points ripping at her insides. She knelt and put her head on to the ground. "Let them come."

Sounding a little frantic, Zhu Guiren yelled, "That's not the best defensive position."

"Shut up," she whispered.

Something ripped across her back, like nothing she'd ever felt before; not like a single claw, or a sword, or an arrow, or even like a whip, though a whip was the closest memory she had to this if a whip could have teeth and intention. It tore across her back in several directions at once — ripping her skin like scissors through crumpled paper — and at the same time savaged her with a spiritual attack, a freezing coldness that hissed inward toward her heart.

She leapt up and threw a rock at it. The rock bounced off. Aili staggered and nearly lost her balance. Blood poured down her back and the coldness spread, slowing her down.

"Are you serious?" yelled Zhu Guiren. "Don't just throw rocks! Call the damn sword!" He was attacking the thing a few dozen feet away. It was huge, multi-tentacled, and covered in shifting, razor-sharp thorns — like a slug, but with legs that came and went irregularly along its length. Its eyeless head was crowned with a row of horns; its huge mouth was glowing a strange, bruised purple that made her feel sick to look at.

Zhu Guiren's sword bounced off of it just like the rock had. He tumbled out of the way of its lashing claws and shouted, "It's immune to demonic weapons. I'm just like a mosquito to it. You really need to use yours and see–"

The thing struck him in the abdomen with a razored tentacle; he spat blood and fell to the ground, unmoving, with a gaping wound in his belly. It turned its maw toward him, then back to Aili, as though Zhu Guiren was no longer of interest.

She tried to center herself and remember how this was done; she closed her eyes, reached out, and felt the hilt between her fingers.

"En," she said, and opened her eyes. Grateful. This was the right thing.

With En in hand, she ran forward, quick and even, remembering qinggong, the lightness skill. She leapt on the thing's back, still dripping her own blood everywhere she went, and sent out a sword pulse at the thing's skin. It felt like a bag full of water; she couldn't feel any structure or bones to it at all, and it made her feel a little ill to stand on it. The thing made a burbling noise and she nearly vomited. There was something so utterly *wrong* about it.

Her blood falling on it sent it into a frenzy. It reared up and turned its misshapen maw around toward her, twisting to follow her every move, the vast irregular mouth growing closer and closer to her. Aili sent a sword pulse into it, and it burbled again; along with the noise came a stench of battlefields and unburied corpses. This time, she actually did throw up. The thing was not bothered by her vomiting into its mouth.

She slashed hard, sending qi in a spiral of golden light from En into the thing's innards. A horrible, indescribable noise filled her ears. The thing flung itself from side to side in protest, but it was as though it couldn't stop itself from trying to swallow her, sword and all. Now that she was almost completely inside its mouth, its razor-like, shifting teeth tearing into her all over, she slashed again and again, cutting whatever passed for its lips and tongue into pieces. Her own blood covered it like a slick of oil, the stench overwhelming her. En's glowing, golden light shivered out from her hands, but it wasn't enough.

Ah, she thought, her skin shredded into a thousand strips, *I remember now. I don't only have a sword.*

She placed her hands together and sharply drew them apart, shouting something — she didn't know what — and then the fire was blazing in her hands.

Yes, that's right. En was gratitude. This was utter fury. *Shen Lu,* she thought, *if only you knew.*

Aili called En back, bowed her bleeding head, and placed the fire within the spiral of spiritual qi. The golden light of En now had a fiery edge of rage to it; it rampaged through the body of the creature, tearing it into pieces and incinerating it in a hill of flame. She yelled at the joy of that vicious anger, taking vengeance for every cut it had given her.

When it had burned itself into nothingness and the stink of it had dissipated, Aili dropped to the ground, covered in blood. The thing was gone, but the night was full of wailing. Collapsed next to her, Zhu Guiren was trying to cover the bloody rip in his abdomen.

Ha, see how that feels, Zhu Guiren, she thought. Nonetheless, she reached over with a shaking hand and smeared her blood onto him before passing out.

Aili woke, warm and safe, and realized that Tairei was sitting on the floor of the cavern, holding her in her arms against her chest. She looked up and saw Tairei's eyes looking down at her, her lips red with blood.

"Chenguang," she said, and struggled to sit up. Her head hurt. Everything was blurred together. Chenguang and Tairei, but they were the same person; they were not the same, because one person was her lover, and the other was not. Both of them loved the person she no longer was.

"My head," she said, and raised her hand to it.

"Does it still hurt?" Tairei asked, concerned. "You should be...you should be all right by now..."

"Did you try to heal me? Why are your lips bloody?" Aili dazedly put her finger to Tairei's lips. "You don't need to do that anymore, do you?"

Tairei blushed. "I just...I just kissed you...but you're covered with blood. It wouldn't have done any good for me to try to heal you now. Phoenixes can't heal one another."

From the other side of the fire, Zhu Guiren called, "As I keep saying, not a phoenix. Don't make assumptions."

Tairei and Aili realized at the same time that they had no privacy whatsoever and looked away from one another.

Tainu came over, sending a glare toward Zhu Guiren, who rolled his eyes.

"Tairei," he said, "cultivate. We can't leave here till you're done, and I think we're all eager to leave."

Tairei nodded and helped Aili sit up so she could settle herself into a lotus position.

"You too," Tainu said to Aili. "You used a lot of power doing whatever that was. Cultivate. You remember how now, right?"

She nodded and sat next to Tairei. Tairei looked at her beneath her lashes, then closed her eyes so they both could concentrate.

Tairei did her best to cultivate instead of letting her mind wander, but it wasn't working very well. She had been terrified watching Aili battle the soul-devourer through the golden fire which allowed them to see outside of the refuge. The beings had been exiled to the spirit realm thousands of years before and were desperate for mortal souls after so long; there would be more and more coming, drawn by Aili's soul, until she could complete her cultivation and they could leave.

When Zhu Guiren had brought Aili's body back through the wards, for a moment she forgot that Aili would be able to heal herself and fell to her knees, cradling Aili's bloody body against her. Remembering the feeling of Hong Deming's body after death — the stillness and the coldness — she bit into her own lips to do whatever she could.

As though realizing that she was on the edge of complete insanity, Tainu said sharply, "No, Tairei. Don't panic. Remember, she'll heal."

Nonetheless, she kissed Aili fiercely on her bloodstained lips, holding her tightly until her blue eyes opened in confusion. She had completely forgotten that Tainu and Zhu Guiren were watching.

Of course she knew that this body was not the body she had loved when Hong Deming was alive, but this was still her person. The body didn't matter. The kiss was as it should have been. How could Aili not understand this? The body was the way in which they loved one another, but the body wasn't the person that she loved; Hong Deming's body was dead, but the person she loved was not dead. Whether what she did back then had been wrong or right, and even if this person would never forgive her, she rejoiced that she had done it.

She regretted that she had called Deming's name when Aili kissed her back in Easterly, but Deming's name had been the one she knew; Deming's name had been her talisman all these centuries — far more than his body, which was gone forever. She knew that. Aili's name, beautiful as it was, it was new to her. She had to get used to it.

Tentatively, she said, "Aili."

"What?" Aili's voice came from beside her, sleepily.

Tairei looked over and saw that Aili had slumped to the side, lying on the cavern floor. So much for cultivating. But she needed sleep too.

She lay down next to her. They were not touching each other, but it was enough, for now.

Tainu sat in his lotus position, watching Tairei and Aili sleep, while Zhu Guiren watched Tainu's face — tired and thoughtful and a little sad.

Tainu noticed that Zhu Guiren was staring at him. He raised an eyebrow. "What?"

"Nothing." Zhu Guiren looked away.

"Is it possible to free Aili from the arrays she's bound to?" Tainu asked after a little while, tone considering.

"Maybe," Zhu Guiren said, tracing a pattern on the floor of the cavern with one finger. "I need to do some calculations."

"Calculate away."

Zhu Guiren continued to trace something no one else could see on the shining black stone; golden figures rose and fell inside it. He said, "I don't know if it's something...I think I will need..."

"Do you want me to help you?"

"Yes."

"All right, then."

Zhu Guiren looked up to meet his eyes again, but Tainu had already turned away. On the cavern floor, Tairei and Aili lay sleeping next to one another. One or the other of them had reached out, and their hands were intertwined.

CHAPTER 22
FIRST ARRAY

TAIREI WOKE UP first, since she hadn't been wounded. Zhu Guiren and Aili still slept deeply in the darkness of the cavern, but she saw Tainu was cultivating.

"Tainu," she whispered. The echoes ran around alarmingly.

"Are you all right?" he asked.

"No."

"Do you want to talk?" he asked, unfolding his long legs. "We should go outside, let them sleep."

"Is it safe?"

"We'll sit right against the rock. We can just fall backward if anything comes," he whispered.

Outside, the sun was shining.

"There are flowers," she said, "I never knew."

"What did you want to talk about?" His face was still very tired, and he rubbed his eyes.

"Last night, or whenever it was…after Aili had woken up, you started saying that I didn't understand. What don't I understand?"

"You don't understand because you are a phoenix," he said patiently. "For us, changing mortal bodies and being reborn is simple and easy. Our life and sense of who we are isn't disrupted. She is not a phoenix, as the demon keeps reminding us. I don't know how this feels to her, but it's obvious that it is not simple.

265

And what the demon said about those arrays…Her soul is bound, and that's…well…she's had a hard time."

Tairei was silent. She picked a flower and started tearing it into little pieces.

"What's done is done. You don't need to second-guess it, but she needs to find her own way through this. I don't want to see you hurt any more than you have been." He added, "I can see that she doesn't want to hurt you either, but I don't think she can give you what you're hoping for."

"I just want him back," she said. "To be together again. And now she remembers us, remembers who I am. Why is it not simple? Doesn't…does she not love me anymore? Does she blame me for dying?"

He shook his head. "Tairei, didn't you listen to what she said to you? What you told me? She has told you as bluntly as she can without being cruel. For her, I think that all she knows is that you want Hong Deming back. And you can't have Hong Deming. Not from her. Not from anyone."

"That's not what I meant," she said.

"What did you mean, then?"

Tairei tore up another flower.

He touched her hand gently. "You knew her for what, three weeks? You've been waiting a thousand years. Be patient — we're good at that. It will be what it will be, and you can't make it be something it cannot." Tainu tugged at her hair. "Get in there and cultivate, and we'll talk more. I'm going to enjoy the sunshine for a bit and think."

Time in the refuge passed without markers. Tairei settled into deep cultivation, deliberately shutting off her senses so she wouldn't be distracted by Aili's voice and not rousing unless someone shook her physically. Aili regularly went out to fight the soul-devourers, saying she had the hang of it now; she looked haggard, but Tainu let her go anyway, figuring she needed some way to get her anger out. It was obvious to him that she was very angry, even if she wasn't taking it out on Tairei.

Zhu Guiren sat opposite Tairei, back to the fire, using a stick he'd gotten from the forest and charred in the fire to scribble figures on a piece of his inner robe that he had torn off. Whenever the piece of cloth was full, he would sigh and tear off another one. At one point, he took out his sword and sliced his arm, seeming to consider the rate at which blood dripped out. He muttered to himself and wrote more figures.

"Do you want me to heal that?" Tainu asked.

"Oh, yes," he said, sticking out his arm without looking. "Thanks."

"What are you working on?" Tainu bit his lip and went over to smear the cut with his blood. "By the way, you almost hit a major artery. You need to be more careful if I'm not next to you. What if I was cultivating? You would have bled out, and I wouldn't have noticed."

"You're right. Stay there." He took his sword out and sliced again; this time he did hit an artery.

Tainu watched him, eyebrows raised, as he held the arm up and seemed to be counting until he passed out.

When he woke up, Tainu remarked, "It wasn't actually a suggestion."

"I needed to see the difference in the rate of flow," Zhu Guiren explained. "My blood is the key to undoing an array. I need to know how much I can get in a certain time frame."

Tainu laughed. "Demon, don't you know that if I'm with you it doesn't matter? I can heal you — your blood is more or less an endless supply."

"Really?" He tapped his thumb against his mouth, looking thoughtful.

"Are you chewing on your thumb?"

"Am I?" Zhu Guiren looked down at his thumb. "Yes, I am. Anyway, I'm working on the calculations I told you about. For the arrays. I'm still not sure... There are three. I think that one has a strong hold but is a weak array. That one, I'm confident I can break. The other two, I'm really not sure. They're...complicated."

"Do you need to actually break them? Can't you just cut the connection?"

"Arrays don't work that way. All in, all out. I theoretically figured out how to break arrays, but I don't know of any array that a demon has actually broken. This isn't done — usually, we just steal them from one another. They're valuable property. So...the owners of the arrays are going to show up and fight me as well."

Tainu frowned. "That's a problem, since you are both our fighter and our array-breaker."

"Will that one come with us? Aili?"

Tainu looked over at the empty place where she normally slept; she must have gone outside to kill things. "I don't know. She's not in good shape."

"As a fighter, she's not bad. Sloppy, but powerful. Better than skilled but weak," Zhu Guiren said judiciously.

"It's more her state of mind..." Tainu paused. "Actually, I wonder if it's the arrays that are affecting her? She seems to be so angry."

Zhu Guiren snorted. "Really, Tainu, do you think mortals don't get angry without demonic intervention? She's probably awash in resentment at this point. In fact, she's going to start attracting demons herself if she doesn't calm it down. Everything in range is going to see a tasty resentment snack. Aside from everything else, violent death is a source of resentment on its own, and when I was carrying her through the river, I happened to feel massive scars on her back, so she's had quite a bit of abuse in this life as well."

Tainu started. "What?"

Zhu Guiren said, "She's been heavily whipped at some point. Probably more than once, judging by the scars. Didn't you know?"

He shook his head, frowning.

"In any case, the arrays might be influencing her, yes. But they would only influence, not cause her anger. I actually think that whatever Liu Chenguang did to her is probably protective, keeping her from losing control or degenerating into deliberate cruelty, which is what the arrays would be attempting to do to her. But they could only work with what's already there."

"She would never be deliberately cruel," came Tairei's voice. "Never. Even in her first life, even at the moment of her death. So it's not because of anything I did. That's just who she is."

She unfolded from her cultivational pose and stretched. "Tainu, I'm done. Let's go."

They had to wait until Aili was done killing things. Tairei watched through the golden fire; it was a soul devourer again. It was true, Aili had gotten the hang of it. She let the thing get her in its awful maw, tearing her into bloody strips, then called En and the phoenix fire at the same time to rip it to shreds from the inside, yelling something incomprehensible the whole time. After, she fell over, a bloody mess, and looked up at the stars till she recovered, stood up, and went striding off toward the forest to look for something else to fight.

"As I said, powerful but sloppy," Zhu Guiren commented. "How can you give her all that power and not give her any guidance?"

"On what, using weapons?" asked Tainu. "We're uniquely unqualified."

This was not something anyone should do enough to get the hang of, Tairei thought. "Do you think," she asked uncertainly, "that's the only way to kill it? Or does she just...like doing it that way?"

Zhu Guiren seemed to consider this for a moment. "Nothing I've known of can kill a soul-devourer. That's why they were banished here, and not killed. It may well be that's the only way. She's using spiritual power, as an exorcist would, but also her own blood with its healing powers and the phoenix fire, both of which are probably particularly deadly to that kind of thing. It's a death-thing, and phoenixes are…life things, I guess."

"Very poetic," muttered Tainu.

"Also," Zhu Guiren continued, "speaking as someone who is very qualified with weapons, I would say that she likes doing it that way. She's certainly not showing any inclination to find a way that's less messy."

Tairei just shook her head, looking after Aili, where she had disappeared into the forest.

Around dawn, she came back up the hill, En in her hand, head down. She must have gone somewhere to bathe; her hair was damp in its single braid and the blood had been washed off of her skin, though her clothes were still essentially bloodstained rags.

"You're awake," she said to Tairei. "Are you all right?"

"I'm fine now," she said, feeling awkward. She looked up at this grim, blood-stained person with her unreadable, blue-grey eyes, remembering the wet cobblestones in Easterly. She still remembered how Aili's hair felt in her hands — marked and bent by the heavy braid, cold and wet from the water of the bay, but her ears were warm to touch. It felt farther away than her lifetime with Hong Deming.

After that, of course, Aili had kissed her — that wonderful, terrible time when she accidentally called her Deming. Was that why she was so distant now, did she think that…?

"Tairei," Tainu said, "pay attention."

Zhu Guiren cleared his throat meaningfully. "Aili is tied into three different demonic arrays," he said. "After examination, the first and weakest array is, in my opinion, near the place where she was born–"

Tainu leaned against the rock, arms folded over his chest, smiling at him.

"–in– in this life."

"What's an array? What are you talking about?" Aili asked. "Why has no one mentioned this to me before?"

"Ah, you've been busy," replied Zhu Guiren, waving his hand in the air, "killing things. And Tairei's been cultivating. We thought it would be easiest to just go over it all together so we wouldn't have to do it twice."

"We?" Aili frowned.

"Me and Tainu," he said.

Aili and Tairei both turned to look quizzically at Tainu.

"What?" Tainu asked.

"Anyway," Zhu Guiren continued, "the array is the weakest of the three and—"

"Go back to 'Aili is tied into arrays,'" Aili interrupted. "What does that mean?"

Zhu Guiren sighed dramatically. "All right, although truthfully this is more information than you need. The cultivation of demons depends on resentment—"

"What's resentment?"

"What it says — the energy mortals produce when their desires are unfulfilled. Do you want the entire list? It'll take a while." He stared at Aili.

She shook her head.

"Now," Zhu Guiren cleared his throat, "resentment occurs naturally in the mortal realm—"

Tainu snickered.

"WHAT?"

"You're funny," he said.

"This is not a funny conversation! This is very serious. Do you want this or not?"

"Want," they chorused.

"The arrays come from and shape the corruption of qi, causing the resentment of mortality to increase over time. They're built upon events of deep resentment. Unjust and violent death, usually, but sometimes other kinds of suffering. The array captures the resentment of that event, as well as the mortal souls that died, within it and essentially replays the event, thus inscribing it into those souls and providing a constant source of nourishment for demons. There are many levels of strength depending on its geographical extent, the number of souls caught into it, the strength of the demon that created it, whether a demon manipulated human beings so as to bring the array event about…" He looked at them. "Questions to this point?"

No one had questions, but Aili looked a little sick.

"Once an array has been established, living beings can be tied into it to further increase the resentment," Zhu Guiren continued. "Aili's been bound into three arrays. The first one, I believe, is connected to her birthplace in her current lifetime. Being born within the geographic node of an array, or to someone who is mortally connected to an array, is a strong binding for an individual. The nature of the array is that living beings bound in it are more likely to suffer unfairly, or to enact unjustified suffering upon others, or both. The type of suffering or violence depends on the strength of the array and how close one is to the center of it…" He trailed off.

Tainu and Tairei were both staring at Aili, whose skin had paled to complete bloodlessness. Tainu caught Zhu Guiren's eye and shook his head minutely as Tairei reached out, clearly concerned, and Aili moved away.

Zhu Guiren cleared his throat again. "It's because of this that we want to break the array. So things like that won't be…happening to Aili," he finished, awkwardly.

Still looking at Aili, Tairei said, "I agree, let's do that. What do we do now?"

"The real work will be done by me. Breaking the array requires a demon's blood and spells. Tainu will support me in case I need healing, and, if she's willing, Aili can step in to help with protection in case we're attacked during the spellcasting," Zhu Guiren said.

Aili didn't respond.

"Aili?" asked Tairei uncertainly.

As though she was just waking up, Aili said, "What?"

"Never mind." Zhu Guiren exchanged glances with Tainu. "You two can just watch. Like I said, the first one is the weakest array, even though it's a strong bond. We just have to get to the physical location of the array in the mortal world."

"Aili's birthplace?" Tairei asked. "It was near where I– where we– well, you know," she said, nodding at Tainu. "Where I last entered rebirth fire."

"That makes it easy," said Tainu, standing upright from his lazy lean against the wall of the refuge. "No point waiting. The demon is ready to get to work. Let's go."

Every phoenix could generate the rebirth fire once after entering the spirit realm for regeneration, which would return them to the location of their rebirth fire in the mortal world. In the lifetime where she had met Hong Deming, Tairei had been forced to do this before she had completed cultivation, weakening her for years afterward. Having completed cultivation now, though, it was as natural as breathing. Her wings appeared and spread wide as she moved her hands into the seal for opening the gate, and a circle of white-gold flame appeared in the air before her. "You all go first," she said.

Tainu took Zhu Guiren's hand, which evidently surprised him. "In case there's a problem taking a demon through a phoenix gate," he said, and pulled him through.

Aili looked at her silently.

"Go ahead," Tairei said. "I'm holding it open. I'll come as soon as you're through."

After Aili had disappeared, Tairei folded her wings and threw herself forward. She landed in a roll on the other side, crunching over old burned grass and new green seedlings. Aili was there, waiting for her, and reached out a hand to help her up. Tairei took her hand, looking at the coast oak, still green in the center of the little valley. Only a few black marks showed on its trunk. The late afternoon sun poured down from a cloudless sky.

"It's been months, at least," said Aili. "The grass is coming up again. It must be winter now, rainy season..." She looked around. Tairei remembered that she had burned Aili's father to death here, with the rebirth fire, and winced in case Aili was looking for the corpse. But Aili didn't say anything else.

A little bit away, Zhu Guiren and Tainu stood talking. Zhu Guiren said, "Aili, let me check something." He moved his hand carefully in front of her, focusing on an area in the center of her chest, and seemed to tug minutely on something in the air. "There it is. The central node of the array is not far. That way," he pointed, satisfied.

Aili nodded. "I was born in the house I grew up in, about a mile away in a straight line. Just follow me."

They followed her out of the valley toward the northeast in silence, single file, skirting one of the hills until they came to the little creek. Then she followed that into the valley.

She looked toward the white house on the hill. "Is it in the house?"

Zhu Guiren, seeming oblivious to the strain in her voice, tugged again on the invisible thread. "No. It's there, right by the stream. But the house would have been deeply affected, it's very close to the central node."

"Ah," said Aili. She looked around. "The cattle are gone. Let me...let me check on my mother before you...do it."

Without waiting for an answer, she started up the slope toward the white house. Tairei followed her closely.

The door was locked. Aili knocked hard; when no one answered, she broke a windowpane in the door and reached in through the glass, cutting herself a bit.

"Careful," Tairei said, but of course, the cut healed almost immediately.

Aili opened the door without looking at her and went inside. Everything in the house was dusty; it smelled of mildew.

"Mama?" Aili called.

They checked everywhere in the house, but there was no one there and no sign that anyone had been there for a long time. They ended up in the kitchen. There was mail on the table — some opened, some not. On top of the pile was a telegram. It notified the parents of Lieutenant Aili Fallon that she was missing in action and presumed dead.

"I was only gone for a few months..."

"Time in the spirit realm doesn't always coincide with time here," Tairei said. "But it hasn't been too long, I'm sure. Not...years."

Aili sat down on the table and put her head in her hands, breathing hard. "My head hurts," she said eventually.

Helplessly, Tairei put a hand on her shoulder. Aili didn't respond.

At last, Tairei said, "Let's do what we came to do. Then we can go look for your mother, all right?"

Aili got up without looking at her and went back outside.

Zhu Guiren stood at the edge of the stream where the cattle used to drink, sounding almost anxious. "Be ready. Timing will be important, and I need to do this on the first try or things will get much more difficult."

Aili and Tairei stood away from him, Tainu closer; all of them waited.

After several moments of standing still, looking down at the trampled earth with his arms folded across his chest, he said, "Damn, this is going to be complicated with only one hand. Tainu, come stand by me."

Zhu Guiren took a deep breath and held out his sword, then thrust it into the ground in front of him. He murmured something, and suddenly a cup made of ice appeared in his single hand. "Damn. Damn, none of you can hold this..."

He knelt, put it on the ground, then placed his handless forearm against the blade of the sword, slicing a deep gash that began spurting blood immediately. He held it over the cup of ice, filling it with bright red arterial blood. Filling the cup took much more than the size would suggest.

As soon as his blood reached the rim, he held his arm out to Tainu. "Fix," he demanded.

The blood in the cup began to smoke slightly.

As Tainu bit his finger, a cloud of crows descended from the trees and hills around them, beating their wings against Zhu Guiren's face and trying to overturn the cup.

"Trash," the demon muttered, and stood, grasping the sword.

"It's not done," warned Tainu.

"Oh, just keep going, I don't need two arms for this," Zhu Guiren replied. His eyes glittered. "Sorry for the inconvenience to you."

Tainu shrugged and continued to hold his arm, anointing the wound with his own blood to heal it while the crows swarmed them.

"Those crows, they're always here…" said Aili. She couldn't stop her voice from shaking.

"They're not crows. Come out, failure!" Zhu Guiren yelled from within the midst of the shrieking birds. The crows stopped beating against them and gathered a few feet away, their wings and feathers melting together into an indiscernible mass, then coalescing into a figure that looked almost human, but not quite. Its legs were shorter than its torso, its arms, still covered with dark feathers, bent like wings, and its mouth opened wider than any human mouth could.

It didn't seem to have eyes, but it turned its face toward Zhu Guiren. "Master, master, please don't," it begged. "It's all I have. I'll share it with you. I'll share it—"

"Don't call me master. Get back to your teacher and confess your shortcomings," Zhu Guiren said coldly, "or I'll destroy you permanently. Your shoddy work offends me. I don't want to share it. I want to clean up the mess."

The yaoguai screamed and threw itself on the ground. "Master, master, please!"

Zhu Guiren closed his eyes and began chanting.

The yaoguai suddenly launched itself at him, its claws elongating impossibly — longer than its entire body — while its head opened wider and wider.

Zhu Guiren continued chanting. Without opening his eyes, he pulled his standing sword from the earth and slashed down just as the claws tugged at his robe.

The creature screamed one last time and fled, trailing purple fire.

"Weak," Zhu Guiren snorted. He tossed down the sword to pick up the cup of blood, holding it at the level of his heart. The smoke immediately thickened and began to trickle out, circling around his body. It crawled across the ground as he chanted, a strange wheel with Zhu Guiren at the center. The tendrils of smoke began to curl and twist around each other, deliberately and without a discernible pattern, as though each had its own consciousness. There were beads of sweat standing out on Zhu Guiren's forehead as he swayed slightly; Tainu still held his arm and tightened his grip, keeping him upright.

"Stop! Stop! Don't come!" Aili raced past Zhu Guiren to a group of ordinary people who had suddenly appeared — women and children in loose-woven tunics, standing near a group of small houses made of reeds.

She had never noticed these little houses before. None of the people seemed to notice her.

The women took the children back inside the huts, silently. When Aili looked into one, she could see one woman rocking a child, her mouth moving as though singing a lullaby.

"You have to get out," Aili said urgently. "There's something happening here. You have to go–"

"Aili!" Tairei's voice was in her ear. "Aili, come back away from Zhu Guiren. What are you doing here?"

"They're too close. This can't be safe for them–" Aili backed out of the house, Tairei's hand on her arm.

Tairei looked up at her, a little frown between her brows; Liu Chenguang's eyes a thousand years ago. *Are you all right? You look unwell.*

Aili grabbed Tairei's hand and put it on the hut. "Can you feel it?" she demanded.

Tairei shook her head. "Aili, there's nothing there. There's no one here."

Aili looked around wildly. The women and children were coming back out of the houses now. She could see from their faces that they were screaming, some wounded and bleeding. Gunfire — she assumed it was gunfire, since she couldn't see any arrows — was tearing through the little reed houses. The women trying to run were being gunned down. The children, too.

Aili screamed as well and tried to stand between them and the gunfire, but it made no difference. She knelt down next to an injured woman and slashed at her own hand with a knife of golden flame, trying to heal her, but nothing happened. The woman died with her eyes open, her chest torn to pieces by the bullets. Two bearded men in ragged clothing walked by, their mouths agape in silent laughter.

"Aili!" She could hear Tairei shouting for her, but she was too busy — too busy trying to save these people, why couldn't she save them?

Zhu Guiren's voice, chanting, slammed through her head in a language she couldn't understand, his melodious voice terribly altered into something high and empty. The smoke curled around her feet, curled around the women and children, who lay down in it, and died. She looked around wildly for help.

In the center of the field, Zhu Guiren fell to his knees. Tainu dropped with him, still helping to hold him upright. The sound of his chanting reached a crescendo, shaking the air; he held the cup of ice high, pouring out the long, long stream of blood into the earth. As the last drop fell from the cup, the tendrils of smoke suddenly rushed back, and Zhu Guiren simultaneously slammed the cup of ice down onto the ground, smashing it.

Something rippled through the earth, through the air, through their bodies. The trees and grass whispered as though a heavy wind moved through them.

Zhu Guiren slumped over, eyes closed. Tainu held him, keeping him from falling over completely, but there was no resistance to gravity left in his body. At last, he opened his eyes and sighed. "Well, that was the easy one," he said. He grasped Tainu's arm and tried to struggle to his feet, failing the first few times.

"Do you need anything?" Tainu asked him, clearly concerned.

Zhu Guiren's head hung down as though he didn't have the strength to lift it up. "Nothing you can do," he said, but he still held on to Tainu's arm, and Tainu did not let go of his.

CHAPTER 23
SEPARATION

AILI'S EYES WERE fixed on a corner of the field near the stream; she held a whip of flame in one hand and En in the other. Tairei held the whip hand down hard.

"Aili," she said, over and over again, trying to sound calm. "It's Tairei. What's happening?"

At last, Aili's blue eyes frowned down at her. "Didn't you see them?" she asked. "The women and children? All dead...?" She wiped her mouth as though she were nauseated.

Zhu Guiren limped up slowly, Tainu supporting him. "Those were the mortal souls caught in the founding event of the array," he said after Aili explained, haltingly, what she had seen. "It's gone now. Do you feel any different?"

Aili didn't answer this. "Did the demon make them...do that?"

Zhu Guiren motioned to Tainu to help him sit down on the ground; his face was very pale. "Is it important to you to understand this for some reason?"

Aili's gaze moved to the white house and the red barn next to it. "Yes," she replied.

"No," Zhu Guiren said. "This was a weak array created by a weak demon. He just took advantage of what was already happening. He didn't encourage it to happen." He shrugged. "Lucky for us, this was not demonically initiated. It was...harder than I thought to break it." He looked down at the ground.

"Tainu," he said abruptly, "I need to rest."

They all looked at the house, then at Aili.

She said, "Fine, go on in. The door is open. I'll be out here. I need to think."

Tairei wanted to stay with her, but as she hesitated Aili met her eyes.

"You too," she said. "Just leave me here for a while."

Tairei followed Tainu and Zhu Guiren up to the house, turning around just once. Aili sat quietly by the water, her arms wrapped around her knees, watching the stream go by. She seemed well enough now, but very sad. Tairei didn't think she'd ever seen her look so sad, in this life or as Hong Deming. Surely, breaking the arrays...shouldn't it have made things better for her?

Tainu settled Zhu Guiren into one of the upstairs bedrooms to sleep, and then came back down into the kitchen. Tairei could hear him rattling around, probably trying to make some tea or finding whatever was to eat left in the pantries. They were all hungry now; she and Tainu had been cultivating heavily and hadn't eaten much in the spirit realm, and Aili and Zhu Guiren had been eating only what they'd been able to catch or forage in the forest around the refuge, much of which was not at all tasty. Probably that's part of the problem, she thought. Probably, Aili's hungry...

When dinner was ready, Tainu called her in. "Where's Aili?"

"She went into the barn," she said, sitting at the table.

He looked at her closely. "Have you been crying?"

She shrugged. Zhu Guiren came in and took a seat. He still looked pale.

Tainu had found potatoes and herbs, some unripe tomatoes growing wild, and eggs from some chickens scratching in the yard who had made nests on the back porch. "No time for bread or anything," he said. "And no rice here. Sorry, Tairei. Federatives don't usually use rice much."

"No problem," she said. "At least it's not meat. I've never seen so much meat in my life as in the restaurants in Easterly."

Not looking up, Zhu Guiren said, "Tainu, I need to talk to you. About the arrays." He didn't pick up a fork.

Tainu said, "Fine. Tairei, do you want to hear it?"

"I don't want her to," said Zhu Guiren. "It's private."

Tainu frowned, but Tairei nodded. "I'll just...take a plate out to Aili."

It was almost full night now, and there was no light. "Aili?" she called at the entrance to the barn. "Are you there?"

"Up here," came her voice from above.

"I brought food—"

Aili leapt down from the loft, using a tiny bit of qinggong to land lightly and easily next to her. "Good," she said, "I'm starving."

They sat on two hay bales near the opening to the barn so they could see the stars come out. Aili said, "It's good we did this. That those souls were freed. But it doesn't change what happened in the past." She ate some of the potatoes, then added, "Tainu's a good cook."

Cautiously, Tairei asked, "What happened in the past?"

Aili seemed to understand. "I'm wondering how much of it was my father and how much of it was the...array," she said. "If it makes a difference at all. I don't know." She ate more. "The stars are clearer now. It's as though there was a haze over this valley my whole life, as far back as I remember. Sounds were quieter. When...when there was noise, nobody seemed to hear it. Or maybe they just didn't care."

Tairei ate her potatoes, terrified of what she was going to hear.

Aili took a deep breath. "My two brothers died. Not accidents."

Tairei put her fork down.

"I couldn't protect them," Aili said. "My baby brother was crying, and my father was drunk and annoyed."

Tairei was silent, sick to her heart.

"My mother tried, but she couldn't either...There's a whip in the barn somewhere. That's what I came to look for."

Tairei could see Aili's face, turned up toward the stars.

"My second brother– He was already twelve. I don't know what he did to make my dad angry. But he was so scared that he– that he was up on the roof of the barn, and he fell. Or maybe he jumped. I wasn't here. I was at the hotel that day. I was fifteen. That was my job. I went to the hotel and helped behind the bar, cleaning and cooking and stuff like that, to make some money for us. We never had much money, and what we had my dad, would drink or gamble away. I could bring food home sometimes too, that way. That day, Mrs. Mitchell had some extra apple pie, and I brought it home for my brother. But he was dead."

After a while, Tairei said, despite knowing how completely pointless it was, "I'm so sorry, Aili."

"Did that happen because of the array? Or because my dad was just...like that?" she asked.

Tairei thought for a while, and said, "I don't think it matters. What matters is that it happened."

"That's what I think too." Aili was silent.

Tairei wanted to ask *what did your father do to you?* But she didn't dare, and in her heart, she wondered if she could bear to know it.

You survived, she thought, and you still have your kind heart, surely that means something...

But at that moment, she knew that it meant nothing at all. At least, not to Aili.

There is no good thing that has come to you from me, Tairei thought bitterly. Because of me, your first life was ruined. Because of me, you were born into this one.

Pulling up her courage, Tairei said, "Tainu told me that Nora died. I'm sorry."

"Yes." Aili's eyes remained closed. "She died."

"Are you all right?" Tairei asked eventually.

Aili laughed a little bit. "No. No, I'm not."

"Can I help you?"

"I don't think so." Aili ate some more of her potatoes. Then, suddenly said, "My head hurts."

Tairei checked her pulse. Aili's qi was unstable again; she calmed it, soothed the meridians back down, then took her hand. "Aili."

"Tairei," Aili sighed. "What do you want, Tairei?" she asked, as though she were very tired and trying very hard just to get through what needed to be done.

"I want you to be happy and well."

Aili shook her head a tiny bit. "I want that for you too."

It seemed to Tairei as though there was a glass wall between them that neither of them could break through. They sat there in silence, Aili letting Tairei hold her hand, neither moving, looking at the stars, and not at one another.

Eventually, Tairei said, "Aili, I wanted you to know...my name is Eftahede."

Aili looked at her, confused. "What?"

"Can you say it?"

"Eftahede," said Aili obediently, and then her eyes opened wider. "It feels..."

"You can feel it, can't you?" she asked. "If...if we are separated again and you want to find me, you can say my name and you'll know where I am. You'll be able to find a path to me."

"What if...you want to find me? I don't think I have a name like that." Aili frowned.

"You don't, yet," she said. "It's something that comes to you when you're ready, your name. Maybe someday you will, and maybe someday you will want to tell it to me. It's not something to be shared with anyone else, or spoken where other people can hear. You and Tainu are the only people in the world who know my name." She knew Aili couldn't really understand. But this was the only gift she had left to give her — the gift of her name.

"But…" Aili looked down. "What if you want to find me?"

"I can find you," she said. "It will just take longer. Like I told you, I have a general sense of your location from the binding. Hot and cold."

Aili nodded. "Eftahede," she said again, quietly.

"And…" Tairei said, "Aili, please don't– don't hurt yourself carelessly. I saw what you were doing with the soul-devourer. Just because you'll recover doesn't mean that your pain isn't real."

Aili gazed at her silently. Tairei had to look away.

"The same," said Aili, suddenly. "The same for you. Don't let yourself be hurt. Please."

Zhu Guiren stared at his plate of potatoes and eggs. Tainu leaned against the wall of the kitchen, waiting.

"I can't do it," Zhu Guiren said at last.

"Tell me more," said Tainu. "Were your calculations wrong somehow?"

"I underestimated how much power it takes to break an array," he said. "How much blood it takes. There's not enough blood in my body to do this."

"Even if I'm helping you?"

"I can't imagine how." He put his head in his hand. "You don't understand how…This is what I didn't tell you before. You know, I thought Hong Deming was bound by me, and Liu Chenguang said that he's not. But he is. He's both. Bound both by my array and Liu Chenguang's…whatever it was. There are a bunch of complications relating to the double binding there that I haven't worked out. Also, there's another array, although it actually may be connected to my array, I'm not sure."

Tainu sat down next to him, got a forkful of potatoes, and held it up to Zhu Guiren's mouth. "Eat," he said. "You need to eat. You're not making sense and you're exhausted."

Zhu Guiren opened his mouth and let Tainu put the forkful of potatoes into it, chewed, and swallowed. He looked at his plate some more. "Again," he said.

Tainu laughed and gave him another forkful, then another.

"You're a good cook," Zhu Guiren said, sounding surprised. "I can't cook at all."

"Late-night breakfasts in abandoned houses are my specialty," Tainu replied. "Are you better now?"

Zhu Guiren said, "Ok. Better."

"So, what's the real problem?" Tainu began eating his own dinner.

"There are two." He took a deep breath. "The first is that I'm not sure that I can break my own array. It is one of the most powerful ever made. It took me over two hundred years to set it up."

Tainu ate another forkful of potatoes. "So you started with the Fei Sukang uprising, then?"

"Around that time, yes. The fall of Zhashan, the end of the Feng dynasty… that was all me." He tossed that out casually enough. "I'm wondering if the second array on Aili is actually in Zhashan. I think Hong Deming was born there, which might mean that he is doubly bound by me. Although, Zhashan is full of arrays, not just mine…There are multiple nodes to my array because I set it up as an interlocking system over such a long period of time. The mortal souls caught in it number well over two million, spread out all over the central plain and throughout the Sorrowful River valley."

Tainu choked. "You–" he stopped, appalled.

"What?" Zhu Guiren asked defensively.

When Tainu just stared in silence, Zhu Guiren's face twisted a little bit. He pushed himself back from the table and walked outside.

Tainu finished eating his potatoes, sat there for a while, and then followed him.

Zhu Guiren was standing under the eucalyptus trees in the dark, looking out over the valley, his single hand holding his other elbow behind his back. When Tainu came up behind him, he said, "The earth is soaked with blood and hatred everywhere I've walked. Can you accept that so we can move on?"

"Continue," said Tainu.

Zhu Guiren didn't look at him. "My array is huge and powerful. I manipulated people in various ways to create the largest possible amount of resentment through cruelty and betrayal. In addition, I sealed it with the blood of a phoenix, as well as the rebirth fire and a final dose of mortal souls experiencing violent death, making the array both essentially impregnable and everlasting. The blood of a phoenix is…more powerful than my blood, of course. The normal way to seal an array is with the blood of a defenseless being." His eyes slid toward Tainu as though to see how he would take this.

Tainu didn't respond.

"Unlike the blood of any other being, the phoenix blood in connection with the rebirth fire will remain powerful and undimmed throughout time, constantly providing new life to the array. This was always going to be a challenge in trying to undo it. My plan was to begin around the edges, dismantling node by node, and at the end, the central seal would perhaps be at a manageable level of power for me to overcome with my own blood. Now here is the second problem: because it's my own array, as we begin to dismantle it, my own power will weaken. This means that my blood will have less and less effect as we come closer and closer to the central seal. Each time, I will need to use more and more blood."

Tainu remained silent.

Zhu Guiren said, "I've graphed it several times. By the time we reach the central node, my blood will not be able to overcome the sealing of the great array, no matter how much of it I use." He turned to look at Tainu directly. "I don't think it's possible."

Tainu asked, "Are you absolutely sure?"

"There are many variables. Not everything is clear yet. But, Tainu, I don't think it's possible." His gaze shifted away.

At last, Tainu said, "Do you still want to undo it?"

"I told you, I don't think I can. I don't think I can undo it."

"That wasn't what I asked," Tainu said. "Do you want to undo it?"

"Yes. I want to."

"Then I'll help you. That's all. We'll try together." He turned around. "Come finish your dinner, demon."

Zhu Guiren stood under the trees a while longer, breathing in their bitter scent.

After they had all eaten, they gathered together again, this time on the hill above the valley. No one wanted to stay in the house or near the creek anymore.

Tainu looked at all of them, gauging their energy for this. Aili looked pale, but otherwise all right; Tairei looked as though she had been crying; Zhu Guiren was looking at the ground and avoiding everyone's eyes.

Tainu sighed.

"All right," he said. "We need to decide what happens now, and how we do it. The demon and I are going to go try to break the remaining two arrays. They are in the Daxian Republic."

Tairei's head raised; Aili's dropped.

Zhu Guiren said, "Aili, when you were born as Hong Deming, was it in Zhashan?"

She nodded. "Yes. I was an orphan. Taiqian–" She shook her head. "Taiqian

283

found me and brought me back to Crane Moon as a disciple. I was only around four years old. I don't remember anything."

Tainu said, "You do remember something. You don't want to remember it. That's how it is, with children of that age. I can try to bring the memories back. It will help us pinpoint—"

Aili shook her head. "No. I've had enough memories for one day. Let me think." After a few moments of silence, she said, "Taiqian told me that my parents were probably killed in the Wan Zhao rebellion."

"That doesn't exactly narrow it down much," said Zhu Guiren.

"That's all I can give you," she said fiercely. "No more memories today."

Tairei said, "You told me once that you— Taiqian found you in what used to be the marketplace of the east quarter. That there was a beggar who was earning money with you. You were able to dodge rocks and knives…that people threw at you."

Aili closed her eyes. "That's enough," she said sharply.

Tairei looked back at the ground.

"Anyway, that was how Taiqian knew I had potential," she said. She turned her back to them.

"Aili," said Tainu.

Aili shook her head.

Tainu said, "All right, I understand. No more memories." He put his hand over his eyes. He had spent thousands of years watching human beings suffer; it never got easier and so often there was nothing he could do, but at least he could offer. At least she should know that they cared for her, as she was now, not because she had once been Hong Deming. "Aili. Is there anything— anything we can do for you? That I can do for you?"

She said, "I need this to be over. I need no more of this. I need to be away from this. All this." She waved her hand to encompass the valley, the house, the three people standing near her, herself.

Zhu Guiren glanced at Tainu and said, "She doesn't need to come. I can find it without her being physically present. It will just take longer."

Neither of them mentioned that they had been counting on Aili for protection.

Tainu nodded. "All right, we'll head to Zhashan. Tairei, will you come?"

Tairei took a deep breath. "Yes," she said. "I'll come."

The demon said, "Next question. How do we get to Daxian? Ship?"

"No," said Tairei and Tainu simultaneously. Tairei continued, "Assuming that there's still a war, which I think there is, there won't be ships we can get on as civilians."

Tainu added, "I was able to enlist because I had a documented identity here, back in the rural provinces. None of you do. They're careful with papers."

"There's a dragon gate off the coast a few miles north," Zhu Guiren said. "And I can call the dragon…Never mind."

"What?" asked Tainu.

"It'll want a sacrifice to take us through its gate. You won't like how that works out…" He tapped his arm with his fingers. "We can go through the spirit realm. If we can get in, I can easily find a demonic gate that goes to Zhashan. That area is riddled with arrays."

"Ugh, spirit realm," said Tairei.

"Don't worry. Demonic gates are all over, and they're stable. Not rare and temporary like phoenix gates," he said. "It'll be a quick trip once we're in. The closest demonic gate here in the mortal realm is about twenty miles north. We can just start walking, I guess."

Aili said, "You don't have to walk. I can make a gate for you. I can call the fire whenever I want to now. I watched Tairei do it. I think I see how."

Tainu looked at her for a moment, wondering. "All right," he said. "Try it."

Aili looked down, placed her hands together, then drew them apart with a shout. Phoenix fire — more red than gold — spun out into a sheet of flame.

"Hold my hand," Tainu said to Zhu Guiren. "I still don't know if you can go through a phoenix gate without a phoenix." To Aili, he said, "Be careful." He wanted to say more, but then shook his head and grabbed Zhu Guiren's hand, leaping forward through the flame.

When Tainu and Zhu Guiren had gone, they stood together on the hilltop, the flame of the gate in front of them between Aili's hands.

Tairei said, "Aili."

The flames flickered in silence above the earth. Aili didn't speak.

Tairei thought perhaps her eyes were glittering. Perhaps she was crying, as Tairei wanted to, but in the shadows, it was hard to tell. "Aili," she said. She found that she couldn't say anything else. "Please find me. When you can, please come, please call my name."

Aili nodded. "Go," she said, her voice calm.

Tairei threw herself through the fire.

On the other side, she fell and rolled, hoping against hope that someone would follow her.

But as soon as she was fully on the ground, the flame behind her disappeared.

Tainu was waiting for her. "It'll be all right," he said. He hugged her, letting her cry. "It'll be all right, don't worry. You did the right thing."

They had entered the spirit realm near a river, perhaps because there had been a river near where Aili had sent them through. The sun was bright and high in the emerald sky. Zhu Guiren was standing a little way away, his eyes closed, holding two fingers in the air as though testing the wind. He turned slowly in one direction. "There," he said. "Not far at all. A gate to Zhashan. No one's watching right now. It's an old one. Let's go."

On the hilltop above Fallon, the flame disappeared. There was only starlight and the sound of insects.

Aili sat, dry-eyed, at the top of the hill for a while. It had rained not so long ago; the ground was damp.

When her mind was calm, she walked slowly down toward the stream and crossed it, letting it get her wet like it had when she was a small child, feeling the water on her feet. She had always loved that stream.

She stood in the yard in front of the house. She looked at it for a long time, then at the barn and the eucalyptus trees. She looked at the place where there had been a flower garden once and wondered how long ago her mother had gotten the telegram, whether the cattle had been sold then, or before. After her father had died, her mother wouldn't have been able to manage the cattle on her own. At any rate, they were all gone now, and the horses too.

She looked upstream and down. The other houses seemed to be empty. Fallon wasn't a prosperous place; the soil wasn't good, there was only so much forage for cattle, and everyone who lived there seemed to have bad luck of some kind or another. The town had mostly been abandoned by the time she ran away at sixteen. She supposed that she should check the houses and be sure, but she found that she didn't really care. Let them run, if they were there, if they had been there all this time and never lifted a finger.

She raised her hands, and there was a whip of flame in each one. She shouted, and called down fire from heaven.

THE AUTHOR HAS SOMETHING SHE WANTS TO SAY

Thank you for reading the story of Liu Chenguang and Aili to this point. In *The Shoreless River*, their story continues – as does that of Zhu Guiren and Tainu. I hope you will continue on their journey with them to the end!

In writing this novel, I've been inspired by the work of contemporary Chinese web novelists in the danmei/BL genre. I love their work and the creative risks they take, the quick pacing and emphasis on story, the unapologetic focus on loving and complicated relationships, the playfulness around sexuality, and the frequent blending of pathos and humor. These writers publish under pseudonyms, and among my favorites are the works of MXTX (Mo Xiang Tong Xiu), Priest, Rou Bao Bu Chi Rou, and Fei Tian Ye Xiang. Many of these works are currently being published in licensed English translations and I highly recommend reading them!

I also draw heavily upon the Chinese contemporary genre of xianxia (cultivation or ascension). In xianxia, human beings, through meditation and hard work as well as luck and talent, can develop spiritual powers and even, in some cases, ascend to become deities. Spiritual beings (yao or yaomo, often translated as demons, and yaoguai, often translated as monsters) also cultivate in order to develop their powers. The yao are not demons in the western sense; like human beings, they can be good or evil, and the category of yao can include all kinds of spiritual beings, harmful and harmless, although yaoguai have more of a sinister or dangerous connotation. Xianxia builds upon wuxia, the genre of martial arts fantasy, and exaggerates the powers of wuxia martial artists into the spiritual realm, including the aspect of training in different cultivational paths that is handed down in different sects or clans. Chinese fantasy also includes xuanhuan, stories about mythological creatures and fantastic beings. While in some ways this may be considered a xuanhuan story, in other ways, it is not, as the phoenixes and demons here have many aspects that don't reflect Chinese traditions. The cultivation of resentment and the "demonic path" (mo dao) is a frequent trope in xianxia novels.

I'm grateful to an entire community of people who at various points in the writing process discussed the ideas in the books, or pointed me to learning resources, or read early drafts, or edited and commented, including Spencer Hatcher, Yilin Wang, Ali Lutz, Amy Snow, Zhui Ning Chang, and XM Moon, and of course, she without whom nothing is accomplished, my spouse, Tita Valeriano, and my child, who is very proud of my books even though they're a little above his age grade at the moment. As an indie author, community is central to being able to write and publish, and as a reader, you're part of that community too. Please consider leaving a rating or review to help other readers find a story they'll enjoy. And if you would like to keep up to date on future books and the writing process and occasionally get a free short story or novella, or stay in touch via social media, please sign up for my newsletter on my website, jcsnow.carrd.co, where I'll have all the most recent links, updates, and book progress.

Made in the USA
Las Vegas, NV
10 January 2024

84195586R00173